W9-BBP-491

THE VERIFIERS

THE VERIFIERS

JANE PEK

THORNDIKE PRESS
A part of Gale, a Cengage Company

Copyright © 2022 by Jane Pek.
Thorndike Press, a part of Gale, a Cengage Company.

ALL RIGHTS RESERVED
This is a work of fiction. Names, characters, places, and incidents either are the product of the author's imagination or are used fictitiously. Any resemblance to actual persons, living or dead, events, or locales is entirely coincidental.
Thorndike Press® Large Print Mystery.
The text of this Large Print edition is unabridged.
Other aspects of the book may vary from the original edition.
Set in 16 pt. Plantin.

**LIBRARY OF CONGRESS CIP DATA ON FILE.
CATALOGUING IN PUBLICATION FOR THIS BOOK
IS AVAILABLE FROM THE LIBRARY OF CONGRESS.**

ISBN-13: 979-8-8857-8052-0 (hardcover alk. paper)

Published in 2022 by arrangement with Vintage Anchor Publishing, an imprint of The Knopf Doubleday Publishing Group, a division of Penguin Random House LLC.

Printed in Mexico
Print Number : 1   Print Year : 2022

For my parents,
Cheo Hock Kuan and Pek Beng Choon

For my parents
Cheo Hock Kuan and Pek Beng Choon

PART ONE

PART ONE

I.

I can tell right away that Iris Lettriste isn't like the others.

Everyone else walks into Veracity wearing some residue of embarrassment. Their gazes skitter about, their sentences are potholed with *um*s and *well*s. They overexplain. They worry that we'll judge them, or they get preemptively angry because they assume we do.

Iris Lettriste. This woman sits down and tells us about the guy she wants us to verify like she's ordering her first coffee of an arduous morning and it's vital that the barista gets it right.

Not to mention: Who goes to a dating detective agency to check up on someone they were flirting with on Soulmate Messenger for all of sixteen days?

At my verifier interview, when Komla explained what Veracity did and I said, with maybe a tad too much enthusiasm, "Like a detective agency?", he looked faintly perturbed — which, I've come to realize with Komla Atsina, possibly meant he was one wrist flick away from consigning my résumé to the shred pile. That man is harder to read than *Finnegans Wake*. A detective agency might seem like an obvious parallel, he said, but he tried to dissuade clients from viewing Veracity as such. The verifiers didn't solve crimes, and they didn't intervene in the course of events beyond reporting their findings to their clients. Think of us, said Komla, as a personal investments advisory firm.

A month into the job, it's obvious to me that all our clients think of us as a detective agency.

"It's highly unusual," Komla is saying to Iris, "for clients to ask us to verify matches they haven't yet met in person."

She frowns like she thinks he's making an excuse to pass on the case. "Why?"

Iris Lettriste is rosy, compact, and purposeful. She looks like someone who makes lists for everything and derives satisfaction from checking off items one by one. According to her Soulmate profile (Flora or Fauna) she's thirty-six years old, a lawyer, into contemporary art and Japanese food. It also appears, seeing her in person now, that the photos she uploaded were all from several years ago, when she was ten pounds lighter and her skin hadn't yet had to negotiate with gravity.

"It's a waste of our time and your money," says Becks. Becks Rittel would be the Mean Girl who grew up without ever getting her comeuppance. I can't decide which aggravates me more, that I think she's hot — she looks like a Valkyrie and dresses like she runs a fashion line for overperforming female executives — or that she thoroughly intimidates me.

"Why is it a waste of your time if you're getting paid?" asks Iris.

Komla says, "We only take on cases where we feel we can have a meaningful impact." Here, given that Iris's match — whom she knows only as Charretter, his username on Soulmate — is no longer in contact with her, it would make no difference to Iris whether he was lying about anything he had written in his profile or in his chats with her.

"It might make a difference to other people."

I can sense Komla and Becks exchanging their telepathic equivalent of a *hmm interesting* look. The two of them are so in sync they could set up a trapeze act. Komla's the

11

boss, theoretically, but Becks talks shit about him all the time, both behind his back and to his face. If this were an Inspector Yuan novel, my comfort-read murder mystery series, it'd be easy: Komla would be the headline name and Becks the sidekick. But I'm pretty sure Becks would sooner self-defenestrate than be thought of as anyone's Watson.

Komla says, "Do you have any reason to believe he might be lying?"

"He disappeared once I said I didn't see the point of continuing to correspond if we weren't planning to meet in person soon."

"He could just be shy," I say. I'm thinking of my roommate, Max, and his disappointment when he finally coaxed a 96 percent compatible match into meeting up after two months of innuendo-heavy texting. On Let's Meet, Kilonova was witty, tender, as sensitive as an emotional tuning fork. Offline, Caleb turned out to be monosyllabic, allergic to eye contact, and prone to panicked disquisitions on his PhD research in organic chemistry.

Everyone looks at me like I'm a backup dancer who's started gyrating in the spotlight. "Debilitatingly shy," I add.

Komla nods. "Occam's razor. Why pursue a complicated explanation when the straightforward one is most likely to be correct? Excellent point, Claudia."

In my peripheral vision I see Becks pretzel her mouth like she knows Komla just made me sound smarter than I really am.

"It was more than that," says Iris. "He was a perfectly nice guy, especially compared to some of the winners on Soulmate. But it felt . . . How do I put it? Like he had an agenda." She stops. "I'd like to hear your opinion before I tell you mine. Assuming you decide to help me."

Again something zings between Komla and Becks. Komla says, "Even if we establish that he's lying, and about something material, what could you do?"

Iris rubs at the top joint of her ring finger. It's crooked, in a way that looks like it was sprained or fractured at some point and never healed properly. "Report his account to Soulmate."

"They'll ask to see evidence of what you're claiming."

"Then I'll provide it."

"Not if it's anything we've told you. All that remains confidential into perpetuity. You won't even be able to say that you came to us and asked us to look into this."

After a moment she says, "I'll tell them

something that will start them investigating."

"You mean, you'll make shit up," says Becks.

Iris says, as easily as if she's clarifying that she wants her latte made with 1 percent, "If that's the only way to get the truth out."

In an Inspector Yuan mystery, here is where the chapter would close, along with a spoiler from the omniscient narrator: *If they had only known how great the price of the truth would be,* or something else comparably ominous.

In my world, Komla sits back in his chair and says, "Let's talk about logistics."

Veracity will review Charretter's activity on Soulmate over the past six months, he tells Iris, and monitor it going forward. We will also check if Charretter is active on other matchmakers by searching for similar profiles. Iris will have to come into the office to be updated in person, given the sensitive nature of the data. The verification will end after six weeks unless earlier terminated by either Iris or Veracity.

"Are you sure," he says, "you want to proceed?"

"Yes," says Iris Lettriste, and her eagerness flashes up like the edge of a blade turned to the light. "When can you start?"

II.

There aren't too many things my mother and I can bond over. Braised chicken feet. Poor hand-eye coordination. And Inspector Yuan. When I was a kid she would tell me highly abridged versions of those stories until I fell asleep, usually as she stood beside the bed ironing her clothes for work the next day. Really she deployed them as cannons to blast forth key Confucian values of filial piety, hard work, filial piety, honesty, and — oh, right — filial piety. Everyone who got killed had neglected their elderly mother or cheated her of a family heirloom, and each story ended with Inspector Yuan visiting his parents with gifts and thanking them for all the sacrifices they made for him. When I started reading the books for myself, borrowing the English translations at the library, I was shocked to discover that in the author's actual conception of the Inspector Yuan universe, the man is an orphan.

If nothing else, Inspector Yuan gives me something safe to talk about with my mother. Whenever I visit her in Flushing — which is way less often than I should (filial impiety, shame) — I make sure to be reading an Inspector Yuan mystery I know she has already read, so she can spoil it for me the way she delights in doing.

My sister, Coraline, likes to say the fact that our mother even bothered with any kind of bedtime story for me proves I'm her favorite. Also the fact that I slept in my mother's room until our brother, Charles, went off to college, which is when Coraline moved into his room and I got to move into the converted closet that had been hers. (Charles and Coraline think it's oh-so-hilarious that I was living in the closet.) I tell Coraline she's just suffering from middle-child syndrome and she's crazy if she thinks my having zero privacy until the age of ten was a sign of favor.

The thing is, I suspect Coraline is right, in the *just because you're paranoid doesn't mean they aren't after you* kind of way, and what I can never say to her is *So what?* I'm still not enough for our mother. Like Coraline isn't, and Charles isn't, and all of us combined can never be. If my mother could go back to when she was twenty-six, stepping off the plane and into the gray holding pen of JFK, achy and befuddled by the thirty-hour flight from Taipei and the enormity of her isolation in this strange land where the only person she knew was her husband of two months, I am certain she would make a run for it. Through baggage claim, through the arrivals hall teeming with migrants carting along the bags and boxes into which they had stuffed all their hopes and fears and misconceptions about America, out onto the sidewalk, and into a cab she couldn't afford — away, away from the man who would otherwise avalanche their savings into his dumbass business ventures and smash things up when he was drunk (and, occasionally, her as well), who would finally disappear, leaving a note saying that he fed the dog. Away from the three children who would otherwise tyrannize her with their weakness and their need. She would hurl herself at the chance for a life where she could make things happen instead of one where things happened to her.

On Friday after work I bike from Veracity's offices in Tribeca to Flushing, where we're celebrating Charles's thirty-third birthday. It's a ninety-minute ride past waste-treatment plants and under the oceanic roar

17

of the BQE, slipstreaming behind cement mixers and tractor trailers that suck at sharing the road. While I ride I breathe in exhaust and consider Iris Lettriste.

She's my first case — I suspect because Becks thinks maintaining a spreadsheet of Charretter's online activity is too menial for her. I'll take it, though. Until now I've just been reading industry magazines like *Datebook* and the *Match,* and setting up what Becks calls *training profiles.* The latter feels like a Sisyphean Mad Libs exercise that still goes on long after I've run out of entertaining ideas. I am a *blank* who likes *blank* and is looking for *blank.* Here are three quirky/ fun/surprising things about me. If I were a type of *blank,* I would be a *blank.* On and on. Before I can work on actual cases, says Becks, I must familiarize myself with all the dating platforms Veracity provides coverage of — more than four dozen, even though so far every single client I've met has been on one of the Big Three matchmakers. She's probably just seeing if she can break me.

To me, what's interesting about Iris's case isn't whether Charretter lied or why he ghosted Iris. In matching land people do both all the time, often in quick succession. Whenever Max gets forlorn about his latest perfect match AWOL-ing, I remind him of

18

the universally acknowledged truth that a single person in possession of a superlative dating profile must not be lying about anything.

However. Why does Iris want to know, and so badly? That, in my opinion, informed by a lifetime spent in the company of Holmes, Poirot, Maigret, and Yuan, is the real mystery.

As always I'm the second-to-last person to arrive at Golden Phoenix, befitting my role as the feckless youngest child of the Lin family. Charles and his girlfriend, Jessie, and our mother are already there, sitting side by side at one of the large round tables in the middle of the room. Charles is frowning down at his phone. Jessie is trying to make small talk with my mother, who is blatantly uninterested in anything she might have to say. Also befitting their roles.

"Hi Mom," I say as I drop into a chair across from the three of them. I smile at Jessie, who looks at me the way the Spartan three hundred might have at reinforcements making it to Thermopylae in time. She and Charles have been dating for the past several months, and Charles has recently started subjecting her to Lin family events. They matched on Bubble Meets Tea, an invitation-only matchmaker for overachieving Asian Americans. My primary impression of her so far is that she's too nice for our family.

"Claudia," says my mother. "You look very sweaty."

"I feel very sweaty." I tear open one of the individually wrapped towelettes that the restaurant puts on the table in lieu of napkins, thinking to wipe my face with it. It smells vaguely like toilet cleaner, which gives me pause.

"Don't use that," says my mother. "They will charge you for it. I have tissue."

"Okay," I say. I know if I try to point out that Golden Phoenix almost certainly adheres to a once-opened-considered-sold policy, like any sane retail establishment, she'll just start explaining to me why it shouldn't since this towelette hasn't been touched and another customer can have it.

Now Charles looks up. "Don't tell me you biked here."

"Happy birthday, *Dà gē,*" I say. "You act like you don't know me at all."

He puts his phone down on the table, screen-up. "Did you come from Aurum? Please don't tell me you dress like a bicycle messenger at work."

My family thinks I'm still working at Aurum Financial, where I languished for twelve purgatorial months copyediting industry trends reports and department presentations and my boss's grammatically indifferent emails until a message from a Komla Atsina appeared in my inbox. A wish granted that I hadn't even known I had. I haven't told my family about Veracity because . . . oh, so many reasons. I don't want to create any association for my mother between the concepts *matchmaking* or *dating* or *romance* and anything I might conceivably be doing. Charles got me the job at Aurum, through one of his business school contacts, and he'll be disappointed at how blithely I've tossed it aside. They'll all think I'm silly for giving up a well-paying job in the financial industry — as Charles likes to say, double what I'm worth as an English and history double major — to hang out in a Tribeca town house (Veracity takes up the third floor, above a spa) and play dating detective. Not that I can even tell them that. We're not supposed to disclose what Veracity really does, since our efficacy as verifiers depends on our anonymity, so supposedly I work for a start-up that conducts independent research for dating platforms.

Which explanation would be less unlikely: That Aurum has instituted Excessively

Casual Friday, or that I stopped off at my apartment first to change? I live in a desolate crevice of Gowanus — Max and I decided we would take affordability and space in exchange for the company of plastic bag warehouses and car repair shops — so the latter would mean I've been pedaling around the boroughs of New York since 3:00 p.m. I'm still trying to decide when I'm saved by Coraline's arrival. She moves around the table hugging each of us in turn, effusive with apologies, glittery with glamour, wreathed in the blossomy scent of her perfume. When she gets to Charles she thrusts at him a paper bag patterned with King Charles spaniels. Of course, the only member of our family to get him anything. With all that activity it's only after she sits next to me that I realize she's alone. I take out my phone and text her under the table: *Where's the Lion?*

"Have you ordered yet?" asks Coraline.

"We were waiting for you," says my mother.

"I'm so sorry!" she says, as if her being twenty minutes late isn't standard Coraline behavior at every family get-together. "I was getting my eyelashes done and it took so much longer than it was supposed to."

Her response bloops up on my screen: *We*

had a fight. <enraged emoji>

"Can you even see through those things?" I ask. It looks like someone has attached two miniature sets of broom bristles to her eyelids. *About what?*

"It makes your eyes look really pretty," says Jessie. "Where do you go?"

Tell you later.

While Coraline holds forth on eyelash-extension vendors, Charles flags down one of the mic'd-up servers patrolling the room like a Secret Service detail. We don't even look at the menu anymore, because we've ordered the same dishes for the past two decades. Last year my family got all discombobulated when our server informed us the restaurant had stopped serving shark-fin soup because of animal cruelty concerns. The manager was called over, and my mother had a combative conversation with him in Mandarin while the neighboring tables eavesdropped and I excused myself to the bathroom.

The server finishes taking our order and refills our teeny cups of tea with a perfunctoriness that spills scalding liquid across the table. Within minutes the food starts arriving. A whole flounder, mouth agape as if wondering how it had ended up here. Wobbly squares of tofu topped with mushrooms.

A platter of *char siu,* charred and lacquered with sauce, and another of crisp-skinned Peking duck. Nothing like sitting before a glistening array of roasted meats to make me feel proud of my heritage.

As we eat Charles tells us about his impending promotion. Since graduating from business school he has been working for Precision Consulting, a Super Big Deal management consulting firm that helps companies *fuel digital transformation* and *craft innovative solutions* in order to *unlock value.* He's in its social-tech group. I've tried before to pin down how exactly he spends his fourteen-hour workdays, and it seems to revolve around Power-Point slides and scheduling multi–time zone calls. Six months ago, he says, he took over as acting lead on a project for a big client after the prior lead left the firm. The client has been impressed with his work, and his supervisor has told him he can expect to be an engage-ment manager by year-end.

"There won't be that much change to my base, but my bonus will be at least two *x* what it is now. And the bonus is what really matters. The downside," he adds, sounding quite ecstatic, "is that I'll be moving up a tax bracket."

How strange to think I used to worship

my brother. Literally: when I was seven years old, I swiped one of his debate trophies from his room and toted it around in my backpack like some sort of sacred object. Charles taught me how to swim and ride a bike and walk on my hands and, since this is New York, how to kick someone in the groin and run. He brought me to the Met for sarcophagi and water lilies, to the Natural History Museum for fossils and the Ice Age. For my birthday each year he would create a mystery for me to solve, placing clues throughout our neighborhood and conscripting Coraline and my mother into the supporting cast. (The purpose of these birthday mysteries, I later realized, being to educate as much as entertain. Codes to be cracked involved mathematical sequences. I had to review chemical compounds whenever someone was poisoned. The location of treasure required triangulation.) No other big brother was cool like that. My theory, which Coraline agrees with, is that Harvard wiped his personality and uploaded that of a WASP-wannabe clone. Now all he ever talks about are tax strategies and golf handicaps and the merits of owning versus renting.

"We get it," says Coraline. "You make a lot of money. Doesn't mean you have to be so gross about it."

Across from us Charles looks, for a moment, like the flounder on our table. I'm guessing he hasn't registered that Coraline came without Lionel or that she's been pushing the same slice of *char siu* around on her plate this whole time. I bite my tongue to keep from asking Coraline if she means *gauche,* which would further piss off both my siblings, and then say to Charles, "Congrats. Who's this client that's your number one fan?"

"You wouldn't have heard of it," he says. "But it's a major player in the matching space."

So tempted to bust out some of my newly acquired knowledge about the matching space. Is it one of the Big Three, which dominate 80 percent of the market? Or an ancillary, as the companies that provide related services are called: Your Best Self, the leading profile-enhancement service, or maybe an aftermarket provider like Eternal Flame, which provides customized date packages? "Anyone want the last piece of tofu?" I ask.

Our mother says, coming out of the Zen state she gets into when she's peeling prawns, "Charlie, you work for a matchmaker?"

"Sort of," he says. "But not, you know, like your friend Auntie Yi."

"We're not friends." Our mother sounds offended. "We just pretend because we're in the same mah-jongg group."

"These matchmakers are what the industry calls *relationship-management companies*. They use technology to help people find romantic partners. Like providing a digital platform for people to meet and using data to predict whether two people will be compatible."

"Mom is sixty-three," I say, "not six hundred."

"Sixty-two," says Coraline.

Oops. "I was rounding up."

"Your matchmaker, can you use it to help your sisters?"

My sister clacks her chopsticks down against the rim of her plate. Here we go. "What are you talking about? I have a boyfriend."

Our mother says, "But he's not here."

"He had to help out a friend."

"Friend is more important to him than family?"

"It's not *his* family."

"You don't want us to be his family? Or he doesn't want to be our family?"

"Neither! Mom, we've been dating for

27

eleven months. It's way too early to be talking about whether anyone wants to join anyone else's family."

Our mother says, and a part of me has to admire this conversational-jiujitsu master move, "But not too early to live like you're married."

"That's different."

"Why? Now he doesn't have to marry you to get what he wants."

"Maybe I don't want to marry him."

"Then you are wasting your time," says our mother. "You are not getting younger."

I say, "It's not like Charles can help us find the loves of our lives just because his company happens to have a client that's a matchmaker." Now I'm pissed at my brother for just sitting there, picking the last few flakes of meat off the bones of the doomed fish instead of blowing the whistle and calling a time-out. "That's like saying we should ask the janitor at Goldman Sachs to help us invest our money."

Charles digs out the fish's eye with his chopsticks. "Nice, Claw," he says. "Next time I want to share some good news at my birthday dinner, I'll give you both a heads-up so you can stay away."

It isn't a proper Lin family gathering until everyone is upset.

■ ■ ■ ■

In the women's restroom Coraline says, "Fucking Lion."

I watch her in the mirror as she touches up her lipstick with a blank professionalism, like a concert violinist tuning her Stradivarius, or a sharpshooter oiling her rifle. My sister is beautiful, and not of the girl-next-door, appreciate-over-time variety. Her type of beauty commandeers. People always assume she's a model, and she did do some minor-league modeling until she had a bad experience with a photographer — she's never told us the details — and said fuck it. Now she does marketing for an unpronounceable French fashion brand that makes clothes impractical for anything other than runway strutting and gala mingling. She doesn't care for the job but enjoys the generous employee discount; she keeps the occasional less outrageous outfit and resells the rest. On the side she and a friend have a YouTube makeup-tutorial series they started so they could get free samples from cosmetic companies. Clearly, of the three of us, Coraline is the hustler.

Sometimes it feels like my sister being so beautiful is the kind of gift a witch in a fairy tale would bequeath. It's hard for people to notice anything else about her, which is my theory for the quality of the men she ends up dating. (Until Lionel. Or, at least, I've thought so.) But, also, because her beauty has become the axis around which she's organized her being. She turned thirty in June, and since then she's been acting like Napoleon trying to come to grips with Waterloo. Which of course is why our mother said what she said at dinner.

"What happened?" I ask.

Coraline clicks open her compact. "I think he's cheating."

According to her, Lionel seems perpetually distracted, like he's thinking about something that he wants to keep from her. Or, maybe, someone. He's not goofy around her anymore, trying to make her laugh. "It's been like this ever since he got back from writer prison," she says. "I bet he slept with someone while he was there and it's still going on."

I like to describe my sister's romantic life to my friends as analogous to the historical record of a wealthy yet turbulent kingdom during a period of conquest and adventure: tributes continually being received, alliances forged and then sundered, border skirmishes and declarations of war a fact of life.

And — this part I've kept to myself for now, for fear of jinxing it — I've started to hope that Lionel Timbers is what subsequent scholars will cite as the reason for the Kingdom of Coraline's transition into an era of peace and relative contentment. Lionel's not one-percenter wealthy, or so successful in his career he gets profiled by *Businessweek,* or a douchebag. He has a day job in some administrative capacity at a financial firm, and otherwise he dedicates himself to being a writer and to making my sister happy. Which, by virtue of his being a gentle, considerate, well-socialized person, he has actually seemed to be succeeding at so far.

I say, "He wouldn't do that. Plus he's known all those people for years before he met you." Lionel belongs to a writing group, and every August they engage in a *creative cleanse,* where they cloister themselves in an Airbnb cabin in Upstate New York, no laptops or cell phones, so they can write by hand for eight hours a day.

"And one of the women has been in love with him that whole time," says Coraline. "If he's fucking her, that would explain why we haven't had sex in forever."

"Quantify *forever.*"

After a moment she says, "Six days."

Or, possibly, the problem is that happiness isn't my sister's natural state; suspicion and paranoia are.

A middle-aged Chinese woman bangs out of her stall. She eyes us and I hope she doesn't understand English. Coraline, unconcerned, continues talking. This morning she started to go down on him and he said no, he wasn't in the mood — "What guy is ever not in the mood for a blow job?" — which pissed her off because she doesn't even like doing it, it's —

"TMI!" I say. Next to us the woman shakes her hands briskly over the sink, spraying us, and leaves.

"Anyway, we start arguing, but then he has to leave for work before we can resolve it. I hate it when that happens." So much so that Coraline spent her commute into Manhattan texting Lionel a point-by-point analysis of why his behavior was so infuriating: body language, tone of voice, facial expressions, so on. He didn't respond until midafternoon — although she could see that he had read her messages — when he asked, *Do you still want me at your family dinner tonight?* (Coraline shows the text to me, which follows a bevy of furious emojis from her.) To which my sister, tempestuous take-no-prisoners soul that she is, declared that there would be no point now because his attitude had pre-ruined the occasion for her.

"So you asked him to stay away."

She waves her phone at me. "He made it clear he didn't want to come!"

The restroom door swings open: it's Jessie. "Hi," she says. "Charles asked me to check on you. He's paid the bill so I think they're getting ready to leave."

I feel like we've been caught by the teacher hanging out in the bathroom instead of being in class, especially since Jessie *is* a teacher, at a school for special-needs students on the Upper East Side. When Charles told us he had started seeing someone who teaches deaf fifth graders, the first thing my mother said, in a tone of alarm, was "Is *she* deaf?"

"Shit," I say. "We were supposed to treat him."

Coraline zips up her makeup case. "He can afford it."

Charles and our mother are waiting in the parking lot. The heat of the day has subsided to a clammy warmth. Over a week past Labor Day and it still feels like we're in the armpit of August. Charles is carrying Coraline's gift in one hand and two bags of takeout containers in the other. When he sees us he says, "Come on," and starts walking toward his Lexus.

"I'll call a Lyft," says Coraline.

"I'll drop you off," he says. "It'll cost at least sixty to get to Williamsburg." He looks at me. "Claudia?"

When I first started biking everywhere in New York and Charles realized he couldn't talk me out of it, he bought a trunk rack — as yet unused — for my bike. So he could be the Claudia Lin support van if I ever didn't feel like biking back from one of our Flushing outings, he told me. Thinking about that now makes me feel sad about how the evening imploded on him — and, also, because I miss my brother.

"Thanks, *Dà gē,*" I say, "but the first rule of Bike Club is never to bike somewhere you can't bike back from."

III.

In matchmaker-speak, Charretter is a proactive, high-conversion, high-consistency, medium-activity user. He makes the first move, he reaches out to at least one profile per search, he maintains approximately the same level of activity over time, and he averages between three and six contacts a week. At any one time, he's chatting on Soulmate Messenger with four or five women. The shortest chat record is less than a day, the longest almost two months.

His profile says he is thirty-five, works in advertising, grew up in the Chicago area, enjoys art museums and adventurous travel and whiskey bars. Assuming his pictures are accurate, he's pleasant looking, if ever so slightly walleyed. He writes complete, well-crafted sentences. He's looking for a woman to connect with on an intellectual, emotional, and physical level. His profile would get a Significantly Exceeds Expectations rating from all my straight female friends, who are always telling me how their standards have been worn down over time by the paucity of eligible men in New York.

Veracity has access to Charretter's activity on Soulmate via Match Insights, a vendor that consolidates customer data across matchmakers and resells it to businesses in the industry. I've tried googling Match Insights: nada. Just like Veracity itself. There's nothing on the Internet about the company, or even about Komla Atsina or Rebecca Rittel (Becks's given name). Our clients have to take a vow of silence a Freemason would balk at, with one exception: they're permitted to refer a total of three other romantically mistrustful individuals to us. These client referrals are the exclusive basis on which Veracity accepts new cases. In the verifiers' line of work, Komla likes to say, discretion is the best part of everything. It all makes me feel delightfully like I'm a heroine in a spy novel, even if I know better than to say *that* out loud.

The irony of where I currently work is, I've never tried matching myself. I fessed up during the interview when Komla asked me how my experience with dating platforms had been. This was after his opening spiel about what he called *our quest for love,* how central it was to our conception of ourselves, what a hobbled process of trial and error it had been for millennia, until now! The promise of data and technology, the matchmakers knowing us better than we knew ourselves, reaching further into the world than we could reach ourselves, securing happiness for us.

"Aha," he said. "You are a skeptic." He didn't sound surprised, even though — as my friends like to remind me — 90 percent of our single, city-dwelling, midtwenties demographic is online. Hopefully it wasn't because I was self-evidently undatable.

"I believe it works," I said. It was certainly helping to usher in an era of matrimony among my friends. One of my freshman-year roommates had just announced her engagement to a guy she met on a match-maker for pescatarian pickleball enthusiasts, possibly because there was no one else on that platform. I'd also been to two matchmaker-brokered weddings earlier this summer, one of them sponsored by Let's Meet as part of a social media campaign. "It just feels like a bit too much trouble. For me. Right now."

What I couldn't say to the man who had just lauded matchmakers as the solution to humanity's romantic woes: Matching feels sort of unromantic, no? The way e-cards do, and prenups, and gift certificates for presents, and my demographic's obsession with recording and publicizing every single meal, sunset, vacation, and unoriginal thought of their lives. Sometimes I fear I may be out of joint with my time.

Komla said, "You have no desire, then, to be matching?"

I can usually tell, in interviews, which direction the questioner is pointing: *How do you feel about working on tedious, repetitive tasks that are necessary for the success of your organization?* But with Komla it was like I was standing in a bank of fog, barely able to make out his outline next to me.

"Not particularly," I said.

"Excellent," he said.

I extract Charretter's chats with Iris from his Soulmate Messenger records and go through them thinking about what Iris said. Or rather, started to say — *like he had an agenda* — and then stopped herself. Maybe that was a ploy to tweak our interest, get us to say yes to the case. If so, it worked, and I'm definitely curious.

Halfway through my first reading, making notes in the margins as I go, I have an epiphany. This is Literary Analysis 101 all over again! Except now, in lieu of *Pride and Prejudice* or *Anna Karenina* or *Othello,* I'm teasing out meaning and intent from the arguably less inspired language of Charretter and Flora or Fauna. Looks like an English degree might have some practical use after all.

August 18

CHARRETTER: Saw you're into contemporary art. Been to anything good lately?

FLORA OR FAUNA: I should confess something.

CHARRETTER: What?

FLORA OR FAUNA: I have no idea what "good" is supposed to mean when we're talking about contemporary art. So much of it just looks like self-indulgent BS to me.

[*CL: Can't disagree there!*]

CHARRETTER: What about the artists you listed in your profile? Karsten Auer,

George Bloom, Raquel Vega? What do you like about their work?

FLORA OR FAUNA: Honestly? They felt like artists I *should* say I'm into. To signal that, you know, I'm a Serious Art Person.

CHARRETTER: Is that what you want to be?

[*CL: That's quite a Serious Response to what is (imho) a joke by Iris.*]

FLORA OR FAUNA: Ha, there are so many things I want to be. Getting a drink and having this conversation in person, for example. Are you free Friday?

August 19

CHARRETTER: Doesn't work for me, sorry. But I'd like to keep chatting if that's okay with you.

[*CL: Why doesn't he just suggest an alternative date? Shy, à la Max's Caleb? Or he wants to get to know Iris better first before committing to a meetup?*]

FLORA OR FAUNA: Of course!

CHARRETTER: You know what you were saying about art? There's a show by an artist called Norah Simmons you should check out. It's at Freshfield Galleries until the end of September. She's similar to Auer and Bloom but more accessible. If you want to get a handle on what's going on right now in the contemporary art scene, she's a good place to start.

FLORA OR FAUNA: Thanks for the rec! I feel like I've been hogging the conversation. Tell me what's going on with you. How was your day?

CHARRETTER: The usual. Work, gym. How about you?

[*CL: Immediate switch of focus back to Iris. Maybe he's just more comfortable talking about other people vs. himself. Or . . . something to hide? What if he's not really in advertising, so can't talk about it in any detail?*]

FLORA OR FAUNA: Busy doing the bidding of the evil corporate empire.

41

CHARRETTER: What kind of law do you practice?

FLORA OR FAUNA: Murders and executions.

August 20

CHARRETTER: And how's that going? Killed anyone lately?

FLORA OR FAUNA: I thought I scared you away. Have you heard that one before? Mergers and acquisitions. My sister loves to say *murders and executions.* She thinks it's hilarious.

CHARRETTER: Do you enjoy what you do?

FLORA OR FAUNA: I enjoy how well paid it is. And lording the fact that I have a successful career over my sister. Just kidding.

[*CL: Except not really . . .*]

CHARRETTER: Have you thought about other careers?

FLORA OR FAUNA: Not really. Why?

42

CHARRETTER: Just curious. You seem like you might not be 100% happy with your job.

FLORA OR FAUNA: Who is? Are you?

CHARRETTER: Not 100%, true. The suits drive me crazy. A lot of times the clients, too, especially when they don't know what the hell they want. But I run out there every day psyched about what I'm doing. Creating a brand. Designing a campaign. Making people feel the way you want them to. It doesn't matter what they think, intellectually, or what they know they should do, what's good for them, all of that. You have to grab their hearts. That's always my approach. I try to grab their hearts. And when I do, it's the biggest rush in the world.

[*CL: Okay, sounds like he probably is in advertising after all. This is the most he's said about himself in the entire chat. Am I imagining it or does his voice seem different here?*]

FLORA OR FAUNA: Sounds like falling in love.

[*CL: Bold!*]

CHARRETTER: I get the sense you don't feel the same way about what you do.

[*CL: And . . . subtext completely ignored.*]

August 24

CHARRETTER: Meant to ask, did you check out the Norah Simmons show? What did you think?

FLORA OR FAUNA: Not yet. It's on my list! Also the Whitney Biennial — I've been reading good reviews. Do you want to go this weekend?

CHARRETTER: I'm out of town, unfortunately. Let me know how it is.

FLORA OR FAUNA: Sometime next week would work as well.

CHARRETTER: Next week is going to be really busy for me. You should go ahead. I'd love to hear your thoughts on it, though. Also the Simmons. Like I

44

said, I think it will help with building an appreciation of contemporary art.

Three read-throughs later, Charretter hasn't expanded for me beyond the smiling blond flatness of his pictures. He has no interest in meeting Iris, but he seems sincerely interested in learning more about her. He hardly talks about himself — very rare — and the one time he does, he sounds almost like a different person. Also, why does he care so much about whether Iris takes him up on his art recommendation?

If this were a novel, he might simply be a poorly written character. But there are no poorly written people. Only ones you don't yet understand.

The day before Iris Lettriste is scheduled to return to Veracity for an update, Becks tells me to turn my spreadsheet into, kid you not, a PowerPoint presentation. "Pictures and colors," she says. "And a few bullet points. Our clients don't have the attention span, or the mental acuity, for much else."

After an hour I have half a slide and a newfound appreciation for Charles's Power-Point travails. I text him: *I have to put together a PowerPoint deck and I have no idea how to make a graph without drawing it out myself. Help?*

He texts back: *Call me.*

When I do he puts me on speakerphone and talks me through the process. Before he hangs up he says, "They have you doing slides at Aurum now?"

"Just this one." And I can only hope that's a true statement.

I plot out three metrics along a six-month x-axis: the numbers of searches Charretter has run, profiles he has contacted, and chat sessions he's engaged in. The lines stretch across the page like low-amplitude sound waves echoing into eternity. Is it really that hard for him to find one woman who can rise to his intellectual, emotional, and physical standards? The only break in these patterns occurred several weeks ago, when he went offline for four days.

I email the deck to Becks: no reply. Later that afternoon, however, she comes by my desk. "That draft wasn't as shitty as I expected."

"That's what I aim for," I say, "to be just a little less shitty than people expect me to be."

Becks arches an eyebrow without the rest of her face moving at all, which is impressive and scary at the same time. In an Inspector Yuan novel she would be the most

46

disdainful noble at the emperor's court, or an undercover professional assassin. She would always be a suspect but never the killer. That would be too obvious.

"Maybe you should take care of all our slide decks going forward," she says, "since you seem to have a knack for it."

She starts to turn away. I say, "What do you think about that hiatus?"

"Nothing," she says. "Taking a break for four days, that's nothing."

Maybe. But she knew immediately what I was referring to, and the number of days of Charretter's absence from Soulmate. She'd noticed it as well.

Iris Lettriste sits silently through most of our presentation. At first I think Becks is right about the limitations of our clients, and I'm disappointed. I expected more from Iris given that first meeting. But when Becks gets to the graph slide Iris leans forward in her chair, slowly, as if an abrupt movement might undo her, and asks, "Isn't that unusual?"

"Isn't what?" says Becks.

"It's so consistent. His activity. Almost like he has a quota to fill or something."

Komla, sitting next to me, says, "It's easy for people to get into a routine."

"And that." Iris points to where the three lines plunge to the ground of the x-axis and then soar back up to their prior heights. "What happened there?"

"He took a break," says Becks. "That's typical."

"But in the context of the rest of his behavior," says Iris. She's staring at the graph as if its lines are some kind of code only she can decipher. Like the martial arts manual in *Inspector Yuan and the Temple of Sorrow,* maybe, where the illustrations of the Tiger's Claw sequence are in fact characters spelling out the location of the stolen Buddha figurines. I indulge in that possibility for a few seconds before I remember: *I'm* the one who created this slide.

Iris is saying that the graph shows Charretter to have been chatting with three profiles right before he went offline, on the tenth of August, and with four profiles when he logs back into Soulmate four days later. She turns her chair away from the screen, another careful motion, and toward Komla. "Are any of those profiles the same?"

"They're all different," I say.

Once again everyone else looks around, like they're surprised there's this fourth thinking, talking being in the room. I say, "When Charretter logs into Soulmate on

48

the fourteenth of August, he runs a new search. The usual parameters: women between the ages of twenty-four and thirty-six who live in Manhattan. He messages four new profiles based on those search results."

Iris says, to me this time, "And you can look at his chat history with those profiles, right?"

Komla says, "How would that be relevant to your verification?"

"He might have said something to one of them that made her think he wasn't what he seemed to be. When she asked him about it he disappeared on her."

"But then why also disappear on the two other women he was talking to at that time?" says Becks.

Iris says, "Isn't that your job to find out?"

Becks stares at Iris like she's calculating how many seconds it would take for her to vault across the table and snap her neck. She opens her mouth — I'm simultaneously thinking, *Oh shit* and also *How exciting* — and then Komla says, "We are all aligned in wanting to help you find out the truth." He's using his client-whisperer voice: calm, sympathetic, unimpeachably reasonable. "Asking the right questions can clarify what we should be looking for."

After a moment Iris says, "That makes

sense. I didn't mean to . . ." She pauses. "I'm sorry. I've been dealing with a migraine since last night, and it's literally-as-in-figuratively killing me. Not that that's an excuse." She closes her eyes. "I'd appreciate whatever help you can give."

"Do you want some water?" I ask. "We could also dim the lights, if that would help." My mother was prone to migraines, and the three of us were Pavlov-trained accordingly. Water and painkillers on the bedside table, the house shrouded, and, above all, to keep from angering her, which, especially when she was in pain, could result from us doing anything or nothing at all. Charles turned it into a game. "It's time for us to be ghosts," he would say, and we would practice moving so quietly it felt like we didn't even displace the air. Then one time our mother overheard him whispering it to us and slapped him so hard her wedding ring — she wore it for years after our father fled, I suspect as a reminder of his worthlessness and a way to sustain her rage and contempt for him — gouged open his cheek. "What ghost?" she said. "You want me dead?" But I know she regretted it, because the next day, when her migraine had subsided, she cooked all his favorite dishes for dinner.

Iris opens her eyes and smiles at me. "I'm fine. Thanks."

After a moment Komla says, "We'll review the chat records for any indications that he might have lied to those profiles."

Becks, still standing next to the projector screen, doesn't say anything, but I can practically see the air around her warp with disapproval. When it comes to Iris Lettriste, Becks and Komla might not be that in sync after all.

"To the extent we find anything," says Komla, "we can discuss it at our next session."

"What about my chat with him?" asks Iris. "Did you notice anything there?"

I try to make eye contact with Becks, because I emailed her that chat record ages ago, with a note that some things did seem a tad odd and did she want to talk about it? True to form, she never responded. Did she even look at it? She must have. That record, along with Charretter's profile and historical activity, are the key pieces of information we have about the target.

Komla says, "I don't believe we did."

Becks is staring straight ahead of her like I'm Medusa in disguise. Fine. "He wanted you to go to that art show," I say, and as I do I realize. "Not to go *with* you, but for

51

you to go and then . . . tell him what you thought of it." But why would anyone want that? Could he be some sort of recluse or agoraphobic, living vicariously through the women he meets online?

Iris looks from Komla to me and back again. "That's part of it. Yes. Information. It felt like what he wanted was information."

Information about Iris Lettriste's tastes in art? If she intended that as a hint, it whizzed about ten feet over my head.

Becks glances at me for just long enough to make it clear she's going to assign me to the Veracity equivalent of toilet-cleaning duty for speaking out of turn the way I did. Then she's saying to Iris, "Isn't that why people talk to each other? To get information."

Iris continues to gaze at Komla like he's her third and final roll of the dice.

"Say you're right," he says. "Why is that of such concern to you?"

She rubs at her crooked finger. "Isn't it? For you?"

He smiles at her as if he were hoping for this exact, mystifying response. "Many things concern me. Do you want to set a date now for our next meeting?"

"There's one more thing," she says.

She wants to start a second verification.

At the start of the summer, before Charretter, she matched with a man with whom she went on a few dates before he dropped out of touch. He resurfaced after Labor Day, apologizing for his absence: last-minute travel, work deadlines. "He could be telling the truth," she says. "He's in private equity. Those guys work crazy hours." She says this with a strange lilt in her voice, as if she wants us to assure her that's correct.

Komla pauses, and I can tell he and Becks are having one of their telepathic tête-à-têtes. Iris's ask has surprised them both. "You would like us to conduct both verifications simultaneously?"

"Let me guess," she says. "It's highly unusual for your clients to ask for more than one verification at a time."

Becks says, "We'd have to bill this as a new matter. You're looking at twice the original fee. At least."

Iris takes a breath, and then she says, "That's not an issue."

Komla says, "Do you have a name for this target?"

"Jude," she says. "Jude Kalman. His Soulmate handle is Captain Bubbles." She smiles as she says *Captain Bubbles*, and for that moment Iris Lettriste is just like every other client I've seen.

IV.

After Iris leaves, Komla and Becks sequester themselves in Komla's office. I can't see them through the frosted glass, and Komla's room is soundproofed too well for me to hear anything except the occasional jagged edge of Becks's voice. When Becks finally comes out of the room, she stalks over to my desk. "I'll deal with Charretter from now on," she says. "You take care of Jude Kalman."

I was braced for her to excoriate me, but this sounds like an upgrade — not in Becks's tone, admittedly, but certainly in substance. "Really?" I say. "I mean, sure!" Finally, a case with an IRL identity. I'm going to verify the hell out of this Jude Kalman.

"You'll need Finders Keepers," says Becks. "Email Squirrel with the subject line *Mary Poppins* and he'll push it out to your phone."

I replay that statement in my head to see

if it makes any more sense the second time around. "I'm sorry, did you say Squirrel?" I've never heard Komla or Becks mention this person.

Becks flicks her hair back with a *for fuck's sake* torque of her neck, in a way that shouldn't work for anyone not starring in a shampoo commercial. "Yes."

"Who is he?"

"Our IT guy."

"We have one?"

"Only when he feels like it," says Becks, and walks away before I can ask her what Finders Keepers is supposed to be.

Luckily Squirrel is feeling like it when I email him, because within a few minutes I get a response from Account Setup: *Restart your device after 22:00 EST.* No sign-off. People at Veracity really go out of their way to avoid any impression of user-friendliness. Still, having learned at Aurum the importance of sucking up to IT — mainly from the examples of coworkers who dissed tech support and then found themselves passed over for laptop upgrades or waiting days for software update issues to be resolved — I send a second email to Squirrel: *Thanks so much for all your help! Hope we have the chance to work together again soon!*

Then I check out Captain Bubbles's

Soulmate profile and activity. Thirty-six years old, finance guy, marathoner. Jaunty eyebrows and a jaw worthy of a superhero. He's originally from Philadelphia and has been in New York for the past ten years. Ideal first date: drinks at Virgil's (I google it — one of those crypt-like bars in the West Village) and a film at the IFC. His dating MO seems to be feast or famine: he binge-views profiles, then goes for weeks without logging in. He's picky, contacting only a small percentage of the profiles he views but then transitioning pretty quickly from Soulmate Messenger to text and, presumably, in-person meetups. According to Iris, Jude Kalman first messaged her in early June, they met up within a week (at his suggestion), and he stopped responding to her texts in late July. They saw each other once or twice a week, exclusively on weeknights, which led Iris to assume, she told us, that he was dating other people as well.

Based on Soulmate activity, though, it looks like Iris might have been the only person Jude Kalman was seeing. He did run searches now and then but never actually contacted anyone. Keeping an eye on the market, I suppose. Or else whoever he was seeing on weekends was someone he had met before Iris. I check his activity between late July and Labor Day, when he dropped out of touch with Iris. He did not log in once. Post–Labor Day to the present, there have been a few occasions when he spent hours clicking through profiles, but he has messaged only two women from those searches and neither has written back.

I spin myself around in my chair and a theory begins to wind itself together. Jude Kalman toggles between Weekend Lady and Iris Lettriste for a while before deciding to focus on Weekend Lady. Things don't go well there, so back to Iris. It's rather calculated, but then again, the whole point of using a matchmaker is to calculate your way to your ideal match. Would Iris mind if she knew? I would, because I'd want that meteorite-collision effect you get in fiction when two characters fall for each other, the rest of the world vaporized, the prospect of backup plans or people unthinkable. Iris strikes me as the outcome-driven type, though, and not someone to harbor illusions about the men she meets.

Moreover, it doesn't seem like Jude Kalman is lying about anything. The website of Apex Partners, a private equity fund, lists him as a principal in the tech group. He's in the race results for this past spring's Rome Marathon. His high school has a

Philly-area address. He's told Iris he lives on the Upper West Side, went to Northwestern University for college, worked at Credit Suisse before Apex. Check, check, and check: his name shows up as the homeowner of a two-bed, two-bath unit in a luxury condo building on Columbus Avenue and Seventy-Fourth Street, he's quoted in an article in the *Daily Northwestern* exploring the possibility of coed dorms (he's for it), he's mentioned in Credit Suisse press releases as a member of various teams that worked on corporate transactions involving shocking sums of money.

I put all this in an email to Becks. I can't deny that I feel a tad let down. Surely Jude Kalman could have given me the satisfaction of uncovering at least one lie. But then I think of the way Iris told us about this guy, her emphasis on how they had been dating *only* for a short time and were *just* getting to know each other. The constant guardrailing of her own expectations. She's afraid he won't be legit, because she wants him to be. It will be nice to be able to tell her he checks out.

The next morning Finders Keepers has been installed on my phone. It looks like a poor man's version of Google Maps, and I have no idea how it's supposed to help with anything. Becks is out of the office on an observation for another case, so I wait for Komla to wander out of his room and then pretend to bump into him in the pantry. He beams at me when I walk in with my mug in one hand and my phone in the other. "Another tea drinker," he says. "Excellent."

Total Sherlock Holmes moment. "How can you tell?"

"Our supply of tea has been diminishing at an unprecedented rate since you joined."

I start to apologize, but he waves at the cabinet where the tea is kept, half a dozen tins of fragrant loose leaf, and says, "Have as much as you want. I'm glad someone else is enjoying it. Becks thinks tea is for the weak."

He tells me that he developed his appreciation of tea during his time in England, as a student at Cambridge University. To him, he says, it encapsulates the grandeur and the tyranny of the British Empire. The East India Company, the Opium Wars, plantations across India and Africa, silver bullion up the wazoo. "One almost has to admire a nation willing to commit such horrific acts for a nonalcoholic, bitter-tasting beverage."

"There *is* something very cozy about it," I say.

He smiles. "So how are you finding it with us so far?"

"It's a lot of fun." Being paid to investigate romantic mysteries like some latter-day love child of Jane Austen and Sherlock Holmes? Not to mention the tea, the nonexistence of a dress code, and that no one cares what time I roll in and out as long as I keep on top of my assignments. I can't say I'm thrilled about working for Becks, but I'll get used to it over time, the way the pugilist in *Inspector Yuan and the Curse of the Gray Widow* built up his resistance by continually exposing himself to poisonous snakes and spiders. I add, "And I think I'm making headway on verifying Jude Kalman."

I share my theory about the guy's disappearance and reappearance. Komla nods. "What about our client?" he asks. "Iris Lettriste. What do you think of her?"

I consider; I want to impress him with some *ta-da!* insight. "I think the real question is why she wants to find out about Charretter."

He regards me with his thoughtful, heavy-lidded gaze. "We don't concern ourselves with our clients' motivations."

I feel a bit like a puppy being bopped —

gently but firmly — on the nose with a rolled-up newspaper: *Stay away from the trash can.* "But," I say, because that is some mighty sweet-smelling trash, "we can help them more if we know what they're after."

"We help by providing them with the facts to make an informed decision. To be any more involved wouldn't be beneficial. For us or for them." His face eases and he's smiley, sanguine Komla once again. "Also, you'll find that most of the time people have no idea what they're after."

He picks up his mug: chat over. I abandon any plan of a graceful segue and say, "Becks asked me to install this app on my phone. I was wondering if you could show me how it's supposed to work . . ."

"Ah, yes. Finders Keepers. I'd be happy to."

He talks me through setting up what he calls *a watch* for Jude Kalman on Finders Keepers, by adding his phone number and specifying a few parameters, such as what I want the icon to look like, whether any alerts should be set for particular locations, and whether historical data should be retained. At which point I realize that Finders Keepers is an app that can track a person's movements through their cell phone.

"We can follow anyone with this, as long as we have their number?" It's pretty cool from a sleuthing perspective, but that can't possibly be kosher.

He smiles at me as if I said that thought aloud. "And their consent."

I look back down at the screen, which is a map view of Midtown East with a little blue dot pulsing away at 375 Park Avenue, the office address of Apex Partners. When did Jude Kalman give us consent to do anything with him?

Komla explains that when people sign up with a dating platform, they give their consent for the platform to, among other things, access their current location via GPS. That consent extends to allowing the matchmaker to share such information with third parties, such as Match Insights; and Match Insights can in turn grant its clients, such as Veracity, consent to access that information. "Most companies are interested in location data because it helps to improve the accuracy of compatibility and taste prediction algorithms," says Komla. "Our focus is different, of course, so we developed Finders Keepers to optimize the data for our purposes."

"Did you write this app?" I ask. "As well?"

When I asked Komla, at my interview, the

why me? question, he told me he had reached out to me based on my high score in *Murder Most Foul,* an online game I'd recently completed. I've never been big on computer games — I can't sit still for extended periods for anything except a book — but I had checked out *Murder Most Foul* after three separate friends texted and essentially said, with varying degrees of snark, that this game was what the inside of my brain must be like. The player solves murders adapted from classic literary mysteries: the king dead in his Scottish castle, the abbot dead in his monastery library, the traveler dead on the overnight train, the botanist dead on the Yorkshire moor. I blitzed through the game on a thunderstormy Sunday and then texted everyone back to brag. According to Komla, he had wanted to try a change from the typical job recruitment process, and so created *Murder Most Foul* as a diagnostic test to identify individuals with traits well suited to verifying. (That *really* got my hopes up, until Komla started explaining what Veracity did and it became clear that verifier work wouldn't involve any deaths under mysterious circumstances.)

"I had some help," he says.

As we walk out of the pantry together he

asks me not to discuss Finders Keepers, or location tracking in general, with anyone. "It's happening all the time, of course, apps collecting information on what you look at on the Internet, what you spend on, where you go, how long you stay there. But people don't like to think about it." He stops in the doorway of his office and adds, smiling, "So we'll all just continue on with the illusion until something big enough blows up."

V.

Jude Kalman's workday routine: two loops in Central Park at 6:15 a.m., back to the apartment for fifteen-ish minutes, out again for a stop-start walk around the neighborhood that concludes at the bagel shop on his block, back to the apartment, then into the office by nine thirty. He eats his lunches at four- or five-dollar-sign restaurants in Midtown. Dinners as well. He gets home between ten and eleven at night, and shortly after he does he comes out again for a second walk that duplicates the route of the morning.

I'm logging his movements on yet another spreadsheet. I've been following him on Finders Keepers all week now, and in that time there's been only one deviation. On Wednesday night, he went to Lincoln Square Cinemas for a 7:00 p.m. showing, followed by a tasting-menu-only restaurant in Hell's Kitchen, and then crosstown and up to a residential address on the Upper East Side. A midweek date with Iris, I'm guessing; I've emailed her to confirm this. He left that address at around three in the morning to return to his apartment and was out running around Central Park a few hours later.

I can't make up my mind about Finders Keepers. It's fun being able to trace the patterns of other people's lives like this, especially someone whose circumstances are so different from my humble own — the Four Seasons restaurant *again,* Jude? — but at the same time it leaves me feeling sort of sleazy. (Maybe I wouldn't make such an ideal spy heroine after all.) I tell myself I'm just making sure Jude Kalman isn't lying to Iris; also, as Komla said, he consented. I suppose it's all part of the deal we've struck with the tech companies. We've asked them for map apps to tell us where to go and ride-hailing apps to get us there, banking apps to pay our bills, meal-delivery apps to feed us, content-streaming apps to entertain us. Dating apps to find us love? In exchange we open up our lives to them so they can learn how to make even more money from us. It's either Rousseau's social contract rejiggered for the twenty-first century or Faust's doomed attempt to get one over the devil.

On Friday afternoon Jude Kalman's dot floats out of 375 Park Avenue just before five o'clock. I can practically see it morphing into a TGIF sign. I watch it moving uptown on my phone. How will our eligible bachelor celebrate the start of the weekend?

Chilling at home, it looks like. Over an hour later he still hasn't emerged, not even for his customary neighborhood stroll that I've decided is him walking his dog, although his profile says — and he's told Iris — he has no pets. That's the one potential lie I've been able to suss out, except there'd be no reason for him to lie about something like that, so maybe he's just looking after a friend's dog for the time being. I must keep reminding myself that this is real life, not an Inspector Yuan novel, and the least exciting explanation I can think of is the most likely to be correct. Occam's razor, as Komla said.

I email Becks to update her. Her office is ten feet from my desk, but the door is always closed and this way I don't have to deal with the inevitability of her censure. Two minutes later she bangs out of her room and tells me, "Go up there tomorrow morning. Early."

"Where?"

Becks does her exasperated hair flick. "The target's overpriced condo building."

So many things I want to ask. Does Becks not realize tomorrow is Saturday and I have plans to play Ultimate Frisbee in Prospect Park? What part of my update has led her to think an observation might be warranted? Is she really going to turn me loose when I haven't figured out how to arm or disarm the office security system?

"The only reason I'm assigning you to this," she says, "is because it should be impossible to fuck up." All I am to do is wait for Jude to leave the building in the company of another person, watch how they behave, take some pictures.

"You think . . . he has someone staying over?"

"Maybe."

"How long should I wait?"

This must be the first time Becks has smiled at me. "Until you see them."

Saturday morning, eight o'clock, Upper West Side. Hour of the dog owner, plastic bag in hand, waiting for his pet to finish evacuating in the middle of the sidewalk; the early runner en route to Central Park, self-satisfied in perspiration-wicking, breathable-mesh fabrics; the new parent, pushing along his designer stroller, residually zombified.

As it turns out, the hour of Jude Kalman.

I'm chugging hot chocolate in the Starbucks across the street when he comes out of his building. I rode up here from Gowanus almost an hour ago, and it was both awful, as you might expect biking sixteen chilly miles before dawn on no breakfast and too little sleep to be, and glorious. The cut of the wind against my face, the way the sky lightened like someone was gradually drawing a veil back from the surface of the world, and, best of all, the immense quiet of this city, as if everyone had been vaporized off the streets and I was the only person left in New York — me, and all the sinewy spandex cyclists passing me on the West Side bike path like I was moving backward.

The embarrassing thing, which Becks never has to know, is that I would totally have missed seeing Jude Kalman if I hadn't set Finders Keepers to alert me when the target changes location. Even when I look up and see him — see *them* — I don't believe it at first. I think the app must have glitched, or maybe Jude Kalman walked out right behind this couple and I missed him because I was distracted by how adorable the couple's chocolate Labrador retriever is, all sad-eyed and soft-snouted, tongue unrolling like a bright pink ribbon. I toggle over to the profile pictures of Jude Kalman that I've saved on my phone. The guy I'm looking at has an unfortunate case of bed-head, and his face is puffier than I'd have expected from the photos, but. Same coloring, same save-the-world jaw. In Inspector Yuan's universe there would be an evil twin running around somewhere. Here it's just one asshole, trying to have two lives.

They — Jude Kalman and the woman with him — stand on the sidewalk outside the building. I'd guess they're conferring on the vital New York weekend question: where to brunch later. So this is Weekend Lady. Who isn't Weekend Lady after all but almost certainly the man's wife. They are one of those couples who match, like dolls cast from the same mold. Height, dark hair, sharp features. She's holding the leash; he's in charge of the stroller. From where I am all I can see of the kid sitting in it is a pair of tiny legs trying to do the cancan. How old do children get before they age out of strollers? I feel like I see five-year-olds being perambulated around in Tribeca all the time. How long has Jude Kalman been Captain Bubbles?

Jude Kalman and the woman kiss, the reflexive *see you later* gesture of the long-term couple. He wheels the stroller around bring it in yesterday," she says. "How to be done today? We tell her Tuesday."

Perfect. "They just told me to come pick it up," I say. "Maybe they forgot?"

The woman shakes her head. "Only ready on Tuesday."

"Would you mind printing me a copy of the receipt? That way I can show them the date they brought it in." I add, one put-upon member of the service class to another, "Otherwise I'll get in trouble."

One good thing about being a petite, soft-spoken Asian female is that nobody ever thinks you'll do anything sketchy. I never get selected for randomized screening at the airport. I'm invisible to policemen and security guards. I have run red lights on my bike with an NYPD SUV idling right behind me at the intersection and never been ticketed, unlike just about everyone else I know who rides in the city. During my wayward high school years my friend Helena and I tried shoplifting a few times, and what happened was that she was eventually caught and, being a pretty Caucasian girl, let off with a warning, and I was told I had to be a positive influence on her.

The green slip is out of the receipt printer even before I finish talking. Before the woman hands it to me she flattens it on the counter and points at the date. "Look — Friday."

I nod. What I'm looking at is *CASALES/ Lucia* across the top of the paper, with Jude Kalman's address right below that. Not a picture, but it shows that a woman is sharing Jude Kalman's residence, and now we have a name. Maybe I can handle this gig after all.

As I leave the shop, I think, *Dirty laundry,* and I wish I had someone to share that pun with.

VI.

"Congratulations," says Becks.

She hands my phone, with its useless set of photographs, back to me. "You've proven me wrong. What I told you to do can be fucked up after all."

"I also have this?" I mean to say that in a cool *in your face* manner, but I just sound like a student guessing at an answer on a test.

She stares at the dry-cleaning receipt. "How did you get that?"

I explain. Instead of praising me for, I don't know, my initiative and problem-solving skills, or even just acknowledging the utility of the evidence I've gathered, she says, "Jesus Christ."

"It shows that she's living there, and —"

"I can read. What part of my instructions on the scope of your assignment did you not comprehend?"

"I knew we would need proof," I say, "and

the pictures I was able to take, I wasn't sure if they would be sufficient —"

"So you decided to play Sherlock fucking Holmes."

Becks takes the piece of paper and folds it in half and then in half again. She looks at me like she's surprised to see me still sitting here. *I'm* surprised I'm still sitting here and haven't puddled into abject disgrace.

"You can leave now," she says. "I'll figure out how to deal with this."

When Iris comes in, Becks says, "Let's start with Jude Kalman." She tells Iris that, as a first step, we ran our standard public-domain diligence process and found no indications that the target was lying. "We were able to verify a substantial majority of the facts that he included in his profile and that he had told you."

Iris considers this. "But not all the facts?"

"That wouldn't be possible relying only on publicly available sources," says Komla.

"So then, didn't you do any further, I don't know, research?"

"I was getting to that." Becks doesn't bother to smooth out the edge of irritation in her voice. I hope she goes easy on Iris Lettriste when we come to the big reveal. Who am I kidding?

In addition to public sources, Becks is saying, the verifiers have been tracking the target's matchmaker activity, similar to the work being done for Charretter. "Nothing noteworthy there, either." During the period that Jude Kalman dropped out of touch with Iris, he was dormant online. Since contacting Iris again, he hasn't reached out to anyone new. "Of course, he might have gotten back in touch with other prior matches. That's not something we can see if he did so off the matchmaker platform."

"Of course," says Iris.

"The final thing we did," says Becks, "was conduct an in-person observation."

"We spoke about this at our last meeting," says Komla. "It's part of the second stage of our verification process, where we monitor the target's whereabouts to see how closely they fit with what the person is saying."

Becks says, "Claudia will report on her findings."

I look at her: *Seriously?* She stares back at me with a gaze that could drill through ice, as if we discussed all this beforehand and why am I not getting on with it? So *this* was what she was figuring out — how to time shoving me onto the road right before a bus rolls by. Goddammit.

Iris is watching me. I can sense her willing me to say that this bit, like everything else, checks out.

I describe waiting outside Jude Kalman's building, seeing him walk out with a woman. "That was at eight a.m. last Saturday," I say, "and he was in his apartment from around six p.m. the day before."

"So he's seeing someone else as well," says Iris. "Not unexpected."

"Yes," I say, "but it seemed . . . more involved." I tell her about the stroller he was pushing, the dog the woman was walking. "It looked like . . ." I stop. There's no need for me to tell Iris what that looked like.

Iris squints at me the way you would when you're walking up to someone you haven't met in a while and you can't square your memory of them with this specimen before you. It's the expression I would probably have if I ever saw my father again, right before I sprint up to him and kick him in the balls.

"We can assume he's married," says Becks. "We see no point in continuing this verification. Any questions?"

Here it comes: Iris will ask for the supporting evidence that any self-respecting detective agency would provide, and I will

excuse myself from the room because of a sudden stomachache.

"The dog," she says. "What breed was it?"

Becks tilts her chin at me. I say, "Um, a chocolate Lab."

"Good choice for a family," says Iris. "Especially with small children." She exhales. "That fucker. I knew he was hiding something."

And right then I have the strangest impression, like seeing a shadow pass behind the curtained window of a room that should be empty, that Iris Lettriste is . . . reassured. Which makes me wonder: What did she fear the truth about Jude Kalman would be?

After a moment Komla says, "If you have no further questions about Jude Kalman's verification, would it make sense to move on to talk about Charretter?"

"Yes. Please."

I slouch back into my chair. Relief.

Becks is saying that the verifiers have reviewed Charretter's three active Soulmate Messenger chats at the time of his hiatus from the matchmaker and concluded that they contain nothing of relevance. "In terms of ongoing matchmaker activity —"

"Wait." Iris glances at Komla like a player waiting for a referee to call foul. "He didn't try any of the same tricks he did with me?

Wanting to keep talking but avoiding meeting up, making suggestions about things they liked? Or wanted?"

"Like I said," says Becks. "Nothing relevant."

"Can I see those records?"

"Of course not."

Komla says, "We can't share any third-party records. For the security and privacy of those individuals."

"You could redact them."

"I'm afraid our policies contain a blanket prohibition on this issue."

Iris Lettriste folds her hands together on the table. "You keep telling me this is what is going on," she says. "With Charretter, with Jude. But you haven't shown me a single thing that backs up anything you're saying."

"In other words," says Komla, "you don't know why you should believe us. It's a fair concern. We have been wondering the same on our end."

He says this so genially that the meaning of his words accost me like the timer-delayed flash of a camera. Did he just accuse our client of lying to us?

"The purpose of this agency," says Iris. "Is it really to find out the truth?"

"What else would it be?" says Komla.

"I don't know. You seem quite reluctant to find out about what Charretter is doing."

"What he's doing is chatting with women online, getting to know them better. The way people are supposed to do on dating platforms when they look for potential romantic partners."

"Except there's something wrong about it. Surely you see it." Iris swings around to look at me. "*You* do. You basically said it the other day."

"Um," I say, "I did?"

Iris's cheeks are swatched red, and there's a recklessness in the way she's acting — not to mention that I have no idea what she's going on about — that makes me feel a touch nervous for her.

"And Jude Kalman!" She says this to all of us. "I would be a fucking idiot if I ended things with him because you crossed your heart and told me you saw him with another woman. If any of that was true — baby, dog, whatever — wouldn't you at least have taken a picture to show me?"

Now I see: she was hoarding this point all along. Time for Becks to put the bus in reverse and finish the job of making me one with the asphalt.

Becks sighs like she's trapped with an especially tedious conversation partner at a

dinner party. She slides a creased green piece of paper halfway across the table, keeping her fingers on it. It takes me a second to recognize it, and another to register that Lucia's last name and phone number have been blacked out.

"The address for delivery is the same address listed as being owned by Jude Kalman," says Becks.

Iris is staring at the receipt as if trying to memorize this sampling of the Kalman-Casales wardrobe. "What about Charretter?"

As Becks retracts the paper she says, "All we have for him are the chat records and, like we said, those are off-limits."

"But you don't know what to look out for."

Komla leans forward. "We would if you tell us."

Iris looks up at him. She's rubbing at her finger like she can erase the swelling this way, straighten it out again.

"This is what we can do," says Komla the client whisperer. "If you give us more specifics. We'll take another look, and if we find anything relating to those points, we'll excerpt that section of the chat and show it to you."

Becks makes a sound exactly, I swear, like

a cat choking on a hair ball. I probably shouldn't enjoy it as much as I do. It occurs to me that, for all his lecturing in the pantry, Komla wants to know as much as I do what Iris Lettriste is after.

"Can I ask you something?" says Iris.

"Please," says Komla.

"How accurate do you think Soulmate's compatibility algorithm is?"

"Aha." Komla actually sounds pleased, as opposed to baffled, by this swerve into online-dating theory. "For a particular match? It depends on the accuracy and the completeness of the data available for the algorithm to work with. If both criteria are met, I see no reason why the algorithm wouldn't be able to predict whether any two people are compatible with each other."

Iris raises her eyebrows. "You have a lot of faith in the matchmakers."

"On the contrary. I'm highly skeptical of their ability to ensure either accurate or complete data. That's why Veracity exists, after all."

"You're right." Iris says this suddenly, and at first I think she's agreeing with Komla's assessment of the matchmakers' shortcomings. But then she says, "I haven't been fully honest with you."

He chuckles. "Our clients very seldom are."

"I'm still . . . figuring things out," she says. "What they might mean. But I can explain more at our next meeting. If you'll continue helping me with Charretter. Does that work for you?"

"It does," he says, and it sounds like a promise.

As Iris picks up her bag, she says, "If you're closing the verification for Jude now, does that mean the payment for that is due?"

"Not if you don't want it to be," he says. "We can just include it in the final bill."

"Actually, would it be possible if . . . That verification was so short, and it doesn't sound like it involved that much work."

"There was an in-person observation," says Becks, "with follow-up."

"Yes, of course. It's just . . . paying for two full verifications, it feels a bit much."

Komla and Becks stand up; I follow. I have my phone out like I'm checking something, so I don't have to look at Iris. I'm remembering the way my mother was right after my father left, how she kept asking our landlord if he could lower our rent. The man lived on the first floor of our building with his two bulldogs, and she brought us with her whenever she went downstairs to knock on his door so he would have to see what she was dealing with, this woman with anxious eyes and messy hair, three children and no husband.

I hear Komla say, "We talked about the cost before we started the second verification." So much gentler than our landlord was. All I remember is the indomitable swell of his belly — I was six, I thought maybe he was pregnant — and how his apartment, what I could see of it, felt like a lair. The darkness, the white flickering of the TV, the stink of dog and feet.

"I know, but . . ."

Komla does not say anything. I peek at him. His smile is patience with no expiration date. Gentler, and so much harsher, too. Our landlord gave in, in the end. That Christmas, Charles and Coraline and I baked him cookies. They tasted terrible.

"Fine," says Iris Lettriste.

I sprint for the bathroom once the meeting is over: serves me right for quaffing three cups of tea just before Iris showed up. When I come out Iris is standing against the opposite wall, waiting. She looks up from her phone at the sound of the door opening and we make eye contact like two secret agents on a hectic train platform. I step aside and hold the door for her.

She doesn't move. "I meant to ask, after our last meeting," she says. "You sounded like you're familiar with migraines?"

I explain about my mother. "In her case it was just the burden of bringing us up. My siblings and me. Once we went away, so did the migraines." It sounds like a joke, but it's true, or at least my mother believes it is.

Iris smiles. "I was going to recommend a new medication I've started taking. It's really helped. With work, getting my life together, everything. I'm glad you don't need it, though."

I say, "It must be hard having to read through legal agreements when you're having a migraine." Not that I'd have the slightest idea, but I imagine contracts as word mazes, the reader increasingly lost as they wander through one run-on sentence after another.

She pauses. "Yes."

I'm about to excuse myself — my arm is starting to ache from holding the door open — when she says, "Did you guess that he was married? Before you saw, I mean."

I think of Becks telling me to stake out Jude Kalman's building, her certainty. "I didn't."

"What was she like, his wife?"

I let the bathroom door swing shut. "Hmm," I say. "Tall."

Iris nods like I've offered a brilliant insight. "It seems so obvious now," she says. The no-weekends policy. How they always went back to her place but he would never stay the night. "Of course I had explanations for everything."

"I'm sorry about how this turned out," I say.

"Me too," she says. "For him as well. I think it's worse for him."

I wonder if Iris is saying that to comfort herself — but I do get what she means. Jude Kalman is the one tightroping through both of his lives knowing how far above the ground he is. "That's generous of you."

"Between deceiving and being deceived, I prefer the second option."

This is a strange conversation Iris and I are having, like we were just wading out from the shore and now the floor has dropped away beneath our feet, leaving us suspended in the ghost-blue light of deep water. It feels apt, though. Who else could Iris Lettriste talk to about this? Maybe that's part of why people come to us instead of DIY-ing their dating investigations. It's less lonely, and it's probably easier to hear from us that your promising match is already unavailable than to see his wife, her commanding height and wealth of hair, for yourself.

"I really wonder why he's doing this," says Iris. "I almost want to ask."

I can sense her removing Jude Kalman from one box in her mind and placing him in another. No longer a possibility for herself but still interesting as a phenomenon to be explained. Which is the way she is, I realize, with Charretter.

"Not that I would," she adds. "I know. Your policies. You guys seem to have a million of those. Do you really follow all of them?"

"The ones we can remember," I say.

"In the beginning I worried it wasn't real," she says. "Then I worried that it was. At least, now, I don't need to worry at all."

Becks tells me to draft a summary case memo for the Captain Bubbles verification, which really means copying and pasting from the precedent she sends me; the only edits I need to make are to the dates.

This case was opened on September 20, 20—, and closed on September 27, 20—. On September 20 Veracity met with

Client, who commissioned a simultaneous public-domain diligence review and standard time frame observation. On September 27 Veracity met with Client to discuss the findings of the observation. Client agreed with Veracity's recommendation.

It reminds me of the useless, jargonified reports I used to spend my days reading at Aurum, except worse, because here there are things that actually matter and we've elided them all: who Iris Lettriste and Jude Kalman are, what Iris wanted, what Jude did. We don't even name the two of them in any of our documentation; the only hint to their identities is in the case record number, 048-011-il-jk-p.

I send my draft to Becks, count to twenty, and then knock on the door of her office. "Yes," I hear, a sound like a warning: *Are you sure you want to open this door?*

No, but I do anyway. "Do you have a couple of minutes?"

Becks looks up from whichever of her two computer screens she's been scowling at, hands splayed like she's about to zombie-attack her keyboard. "What is it."

I step inside and close the door behind me. The air is fragrant with the scent she always wears, a smoky sort of sweetness, and it's distracting. I look to see what book is currently on her desk: the new Amelia Earhart biography. The previous time I was in here it was *The Golden Bowl,* and before that a book about privately run prisons. The range and voracity of her reading habits surprise me; also, that she would prefer paper. I'm still trying to come up with a not-dumb way to start a conversation about books. (*I like to read, too* — I don't think so.)

"What we found out about Jude Kalman," I say. "Do we ever . . . should we tell . . ."

"No," says Becks.

"I meant his wife . . . ?"

She flicks her hair back. "I know what you meant."

My thoughts feel like a bagful of Scrabble tiles, all letters, no words. If we saw someone getting his wallet stolen we would tell him, wouldn't we? But that's a crime and what Jude Kalman is doing, wretched as it may be, isn't. But Lucia Casales should know — if I were her I would want to — and there's their child as well —

"It's none of our business," says Becks, "how people choose to fuck up their lives."

For our next meeting, Iris Lettriste is late. Ten minutes after the time she's supposed to show, Komla calls her. She doesn't pick up. We give it another twenty minutes, Becks kvetching like she's the Queen of England and the notion of having to wait for anyone or anything is treasonous. Finally Komla decides to cancel the meeting. He will let Iris know, he says, and reschedule with her.

Three days later Becks stops by my desk to tell me that Iris hasn't responded to Komla's emails, and she's still not picking up her phone, so Komla has decided to close the case. I'm to write up another summary memo for Charretter.

After all the hullabaloo over those chat records, Iris Lettriste is flaking on us? Talk about anticlimactic. Unless . . . "Do you think something happened to her?" When people don't show up for appointments in Inspector Yuan's universe, they tend to have joined an itinerant opera troupe, or disavowed the material world and entered a monastery, or been kidnapped or imprisoned or murdered. In Iris's case, all I can think of is a mega-migraine, but then she would have let us know, surely.

Becks's mouth twists. "She decided she didn't want to spend her money after all."

That would do it. "Has she paid us anything?"

Just the 20 percent deposit. Komla has

already emailed her the invoice and will follow up with a copy in the mail, but Becks thinks this is one we'll have to write off. "It's not like we're going to take her to court, and she knows it. Still," she adds, in a way that makes clear she thinks the trade-off is worth it, "at least now we're rid of her."

The next time we hear from Iris Lettriste, the leaves are just starting to mulch brown into the ground and the person we all believed to be Iris has been dead for almost two weeks.

PART TWO

I.

Komla gathers us in his office to tell us. "I received an email," he says, "from someone who says she is Iris Lettriste."

He speaks in his usual deliberate manner, settled in his armchair with his knees wide and his hands loose, but I can tell he's bothered, and anything that can bother Komla Atsina so much that I notice must be a shit show.

"She said," Komla continues, "that our client was in fact her sister, Sarah Reaves."

"Can she prove it?" says Becks. She's leaning against the window ledge with her arms and ankles crossed, all angular grace and skeptical lines.

"She's coming in today to do that."

I glance out of the windows, which in old-school New York style just reflect back the row of windows across the narrow street and, above that, a hard slate strip of sky. It's a gusty day. Biking over the bridge I felt like a gigantic palm was pushing me back, and I found myself thinking about how in Greek myths or Chinese legends this would have been a warning from the gods: *You really shouldn't go to work today.*

I look back at Komla. Each time he shifts I can almost see the unease rise up around him, like a cloud of flies momentarily disturbed by motion before settling down again. He couldn't possibly mean . . . could he?

"You said *was.* As in . . . ?"

"Yes," says Komla.

"Fuck," says Becks.

There are so many kinds of silence that can inhabit a room. This one feels ancient, like it's always been here, woven gray into the carpet, lacquered into the walnut of the desk and the shelves, waiting for us to notice.

Then Komla is speaking again. Apparently the woman we knew as Iris killed herself ten days ago, right before she was supposed to meet with us. An overdose of her medication. Her body was found in her apartment a few days later.

Becks says again, "Fuck."

"It always surprises me," says Komla, "how surprising death is, when it's the one thing that's inevitable."

96

Which sounds like something Inspector Yuan would say as he rises to his feet after examining the strangled body of the crown prince's favorite concubine. So many ways to die, or be killed. I'm suddenly dizzy, like I've been yanked from my body to observe myself sitting here on the third floor of a Tribeca town house, talking with two strangers about a third stranger who lied to us and is now dead: How did I end up here?

Komla says, "She wants to know what services we were providing to her sister."

"And?" Becks says it like a challenge.

"Our obligation of confidentiality is perpetual."

If I heard that Coraline or Charles had . . . "But," I say, and I feel a quivery sort of sympathy for this woman. Her sister. Maybe her only sister, her only sibling. "If it would help her understand why."

Becks says, "It would help her understand nothing."

Komla says, to me, "What makes you think our interactions with her might have had anything to do with her decision to kill herself?"

"For fuck's sake, don't encourage her."

Komla continues to watch me. His eyes are tired, as if he's been squinting at small print all day. He's one of those people whose age is impossible to guesstimate. His features look like they have had time to settle into his face, and yet his skin is enviably glossy; his manner vacillates between the steadiness of middle age and the open delight of a geeky, precocious preteen. This is the first time, though, that I find myself thinking he seems old.

"Jude Kalman?" I say.

"If people went around killing themselves because their matches were lying," says Becks, "we would be running a fucking morgue."

"But not all matches lie about the fact that they're married," I say. "Or have a kid." Not-Iris asking me what Jude Kalman's wife was like. Saying that at least now she no longer needed to worry.

Becks pushes herself upright and steps away from the ledge. "You don't know shit," she says. "Don't try to pretend you do."

This is the thing (one of several) I'm hypersensitive about: people trampling on me because I'm a petite, soft-spoken Asian female and they assume I'll just make like a carpet. And so, even though it's Becks and I think she might literally destroy me, I say, "Don't talk to me like that."

Immediately I wish I had come up with something more original.

Becks stares at me. When she speaks, though, I can tell she's really saying this to Komla: "We should never have taken the fucking case." And then she's exiting like the opera diva at the end of act 3. I jump to catch the door before it can slam shut behind her.

I turn to Komla. Incredibly, he's still sitting in the exact same position as at the start of the meeting. His fingers dent into the arms of the chair like he is about to pull himself upright, but he doesn't move. He says, "She's right."

"Is there anything I can . . . ?" I say.

He smiles at me, a dim, minor-key smile that feels borrowed from someone else. "I don't think so, no," he says. "Thank you."

On my lunch break I walk the couple of blocks west to the Hudson River and sit down on a bench facing the water. The heavy sky and the choppy murk of the waves feel like a manifestation of my mood. Now I see why Georges Simenon always describes Inspector Maigret trudging through hailstorms or biblical rains in whatever Podunk French town that's the site of the latest murder. The right weather can do a lot for atmospherics.

I eat my sandwich and then I call my

mother. She picks up on the sixth ring. "What's wrong?"

"What?" I say. "Nothing." I can hear the clacking of mahjongg tiles in the background. She must be at the community center.

"Then why did you call?"

"Just saying hi."

"Okay. Hi." She sounds suspicious. "I'm playing mah-jongg. I can't talk."

What I say next surprises me: "Mom, I love you."

There is a pause. "Are you sure nothing is wrong?"

"Positive," I say. "Okay, I'll talk to you later."

"Oh, Claudia — Mei Ling was telling me about her son. He's twenty-seven and works at a bank. He owns his apartment in Forest Hills. Mei Ling says he takes very good care of her. He visits her every day."

Nothing like the unworthy Claudia Lin. "Sounds like an upstanding young man."

"He's looking for a girlfriend. I will send his picture to you."

"Bye, Mom," I say.

Iris Lettriste — the actual Iris Lettriste — is taller and thinner than her sister, with shoulders that hunch up as she speaks. They have the same coloring, medium-brown hair and eyes a shade lighter, but on this woman it looks faded, like she's a painting in need of restoration.

She spreads out her evidence across the table. Passports and driver's licenses. Employee ID (Iris). University ID (Sarah). Library card (Sarah).

Komla asks, "Did she use your name like this with anyone or anything else?"

"Not that I know of." She says this dryly, in a way that reminds me of Charles, sometimes, when he's dealing with Coraline or me.

"The different family names. Is that because of marriage?"

Iris's shoulders rise another notch. She shakes her head. *Lettriste* is their father's name; *Reaves,* their mother's. Their parents divorced when Iris and Sarah were in high school. "Our father was one of those people," says Iris, "who are the center of every world they're in. It could be a bit . . . overwhelming." He was an eminent law professor who passed away a few years ago; Iris references some theory of contract law he came up with like it's a pillar of our civilization. "For whatever reason, I was his favorite, from the time we were children. It really affected Sarah." When she turned thirty, Sarah legally changed her last name to *Reaves*. "I think it was symbolic: she wasn't going to try to please our father anymore. If you ask me, she should have done it much sooner."

I can sympathize; I'm not crazy myself about having to hoist around my absentee father's name. It's too bad my mother's last name is *Kok,* which has a nonideal homophone in English.

Iris says, "What did Sarah hire you to do?"

Komla says, "I'm afraid we can't disclose that without our client's permission."

"You know she can't give her permission." This Iris has the voice of a librarian, quiet, unhurried, steeped in the codes of order and knowledge. "She's dead."

"Forgive me for asking this, but did you bring any proof?"

Iris opens a folder and takes out a piece of paper. I'm sitting closest to her; she slides it toward me. It's a photocopy of the death certificate. As I hand it to Komla I see *Sarah Emily Reaves. 11/01/19— – 10/05/20—. Drug Intoxication: Strobinex (synthetic virodhamine).*

Komla looks at it and then passes it to Becks. "Thank you," he says. "I hope you understand us asking this, given the circumstances."

Iris's head shifts. I can't tell if it means yes or no or nothing at all. She says, "Is your company . . . Are you some sort of matchmaker?"

Komla says, his tone one of mild puzzlement, "Why would you think that?"

She explains that the majority of the emails in the account her sister had used to contact Veracity were from matchmakers: confirmations that she had set up a profile with them and subsequent update messages. "Your emails with her were the only ones I saw from another human being."

"Which matchmakers were these?" asks Komla.

Becks says, "That's not relevant."

Damn, this is the first time I've seen either of them contradict the other in front of a client. And so rudely, too, although I suppose that's just the way Becks engages with the world. I'm hoping Komla will put her in her place, but he chuckles and says to Iris, "Becks is right, as usual. I have a tendency to digress."

Iris says, "So are you, then? A matchmaker?"

"I am sorry for your loss." He sounds so sincere that my chest aches with a vicarious sorrow. "But as I said, we can't tell you anything."

After a moment she says, "I saw your invoice. Your services are expensive."

"That depends," says Komla. And in Sarah's case, yes. Veracity charges on a sliding scale, based on the client's financial situation. Sarah would have weighed in at the higher end of our rates, given the Big Law job and Manhattan zip code.

"What if I paid it on her behalf?" says Iris. "Twice that amount. Three times."

She says this so easily. I remember Sarah's hesitation when Becks said that verifying Jude Kalman would double her fees and how she tried to ask, at the end of the last meeting, if we could write off the cost of that verification.

I lean forward so I can see the name of the firm on Iris Lettriste's employee ID card. I google *Murkstone Banderby LLP* on my phone, under the table: a corporate law firm, offices in Midtown East, a slew of Fortune 500 companies as clients. Sarah Reaves held herself out to be a lawyer, to us and on Soulmate. I glance at the driver's licenses. Sarah was thirty-four years old, two years younger than the age on her profile. Iris Lettriste is the one who's thirty-six. What if Sarah's entire persona online was borrowed from her sister?

"Thank you for the offer," says Komla,

"but we only accept payments from clients, and we're not taking on clients right now."

I ask, "What was Sarah's job?"

I'm expecting Becks to smack me down as well, but she doesn't say anything. After a moment Iris Lettriste says, "Well, that depends on how generously you define *job.*" There it is again, that *how hard can it be to get your shit together* exasperation, and again I'm thinking of my brother. How pissy he got, for instance, after he learned I had missed the application deadlines for half the schools on my list, which was really the list he had drawn up for me. When I subsequently texted him — he was at Harvard Business School then — to say that I had decided on tiny, zero-name-recognition Margrave College in a nook of Vermont with a high heifer-to-human ratio, he called me to chastise me about wasting my potential, what my procrastination had cost me. The big sibling's burden; I suspect Iris Lettriste would have understood.

But what Charles didn't know was that I'd let those deadlines slide on purpose. After seeing what happened to him, I sure as hell wasn't going to let myself be trimmed into the Ivy League model-minority mold. There must have been reasons for Sarah's decisions that Iris didn't know about as well. I feel like I can see, maybe, the outlines of . . . *something,* the way after your eyes adjust to the darkness it changes from an absence to a backdrop. Two sisters and the silences between them.

Becks says, "She said she was a lawyer."

Iris's lips tilt at the corners in a way that could be mistaken for a smile. "*I'm* a lawyer."

I say, a tad more assertively after my deductive feat, "And if you were generous? About Sarah's job?"

After a moment Iris says, "She'd probably have said that she was a journalist. She hadn't written anything in a while, though."

Iris tells us that Sarah suffered from migraines all her life, which could be debilitating and could last for days at a time. Her condition made it difficult to maintain full-time employment. After college, she worked for Bloomberg as a finance reporter for a few years before switching to freelance work. She developed a bit of a niche, writing about lifestyle aspects of technological innovations. Topics like the implications of wearables on personal health and the commoditization of romance in the age of online dating. Two years ago she started a journalism graduate program at Columbia.

This time I worry that even Iris can see

the current crackling back and forth between Komla and Becks, and for once I feel like I'm in on what they're thinking. What if Sarah Reaves's true purpose in hiring Veracity was to write some sort of exposé? *Your Date May Be Spying on You: A Look Inside New York's Dating Detective Agency.* If so, a fake identity would make sense. Despite myself I'm excited. This plot is thickening faster than a cooling bowl of tonkatsu ramen, as Inspector Yuan would say in one of the series's many sloppily translated cultural references.

"Sarah was a good writer." Iris says this like it discomfits her to concede that much. "When she got around to writing."

"Was she working on anything at the time of her death?" asks Komla.

"I doubt it. She had lots of ideas, but following through with them . . . that was one of her weaknesses."

"What about her health issues? Was there any possibility of a tumor?"

Iris shakes her head. The MRI scans always came out clean, and none of the neurologists Sarah consulted could identify the cause of the attacks. "It was highly frustrating, as you might imagine. She tried everything." Diet, meditation, acupuncture. And medication. "She's been on something or another since she was fourteen. I mean, she was."

"Strobinex," says Komla, looking down at the death certificate. "That was her latest prescription?"

"It must have been. I didn't know the details."

The photocopy comes back around the table. As Iris slips it into her folder she says, "I'm just trying to understand why Sarah would do this."

"Of course," says Komla. "But that's not something we can help with."

Iris picks up one of the ID cards scattered across the table and then another. I have the sense of watching something vanish — the fact of this person, Sarah Reaves — not just from my life but from existence itself.

There is still one more card left — Sarah's driver's license — when Iris says, "You really don't think so?" The way she tips her head to the side makes me think of a bird, one of those small, hoppy, watchful kinds. She's stubborn, that's obvious. Like her sister was. The thought feels like someone whispering in my ear, more breath than sound: *Surely Sarah Reaves wouldn't have killed herself.* "Because she didn't conceal her identity from anyone else."

"I don't believe you know that," says

Komla, in the same impeccably pleasant tone he has used throughout this session. "I don't believe you knew your sister well at all and what she might or might not have done. You're trying to find out now, because you wish you had done things differently while she was alive. But it's too late. Not all mistakes can be fixed."

II.

I try to go back to diligencing my current target — Jessica Vuong (Strawberry Choux), a banker turned pastry chef and CrossFit enthusiast — but all I can think about is Iris Lettriste's visit. It's as if a film projector has lit up in my mind and it's stuck on that scene of Komla indicting Iris for her failures as a sister. With such benign courtesy. A line keeps scrolling across my mental screen like a subtitle in a silent movie: *That one may smile, and smile, and be a villain.* Not that what Komla did makes him a villain; he was just trying to stop Iris from asking her questions. But in such a cruel way, and with an aptitude that kind of freaks me out. For the first time since I started at Veracity I feel lost, the way I continually did when I was at Aurum Financial, and not just because that office was a cubicle maze.

Komla and Becks both shut themselves up in their respective offices right after Iris left, and they're incommunicado for the rest of the day. Not a single snippy email from Becks — how unsettling. I give up on Jessica Vuong and sit at my desk reading *The Third Man* until the clock on my screen blinks 6:00 p.m. and I can legitimately head out.

I'm surprised by how dark it is, already, when I step out onto the street. That's the one thing about fall I could do without, how the days shrink. I zip up my hoodie and walk to the NO PARKING sign at which I've taken to parking my bike.

"Claudia."

I turn and Iris Lettriste is walking toward me from the corner of Greenwich and Harrison Streets. Has she been waiting there since she left our office over an hour ago? The click of her heels across the sidewalk is brisk but deliberate, and in her long black coat and beige scarf — wool and cashmere, I bet — she looks every discreet, tailored inch the corporate professional. Much more so, I can see now, than Sarah Reaves ever did.

"Do you have a few minutes?"

I know what I should do. Say I'm sorry but I'm in a hurry, and in any case if she has further queries she should speak to Komla. Hop on my bike, pedal away. Iris

Lettriste doesn't seem like the sort to chase me down the block, and even if she does she won't catch me.

"What is it?" I say.

"Komla Atsina was right," says Iris.

I almost say that doesn't mean he should have said what he did. "Okay."

Iris tells me that she and Sarah weren't close, and she's aware that what she's doing now, trying to find an explanation for her sister's suicide, is for herself, so she can feel marginally better about all of this. "But," she says, "it's only because I loved her."

"I understand."

"Do you have a sister?"

"Yes," I say.

She tilts her head at me in that intent, birdlike manner. "Can you help me?"

Why is she so sure that whatever her sister was doing with us was relevant to her death? And then I get it.

"Is there some other connection between Veracity and Sarah?" I ask.

Iris's eyebrows lift like they have little helium balloons attached to them. She reaches into her bag and takes out what I've started thinking of as the Sarah Reaves File. What she passes to me is a notepad sheet of hotel stationery: THE PLAZA. Fancy. It's a list of four items, out of which I recognize three:

Compatibility?!
Precision
Veracity
Romantick

Iris tells me she noticed this tucked between the pages of a book Sarah left on the coffee table. "I meant to show this to all of you when we met," she says, "but after Komla's little speech I just wanted to leave."

"What book was it?" That's the first question Inspector Yuan would ask. I've read at least three of his mysteries where a book is found in close proximity to the corpse, and it's invariably a key if somewhat contrived clue: the author's name is a homonym of the murderer's name, the murderer left it behind by accident or by design, that sort of thing.

Iris can't remember the title, only that it was short — a single word — and it was about, of all things, the Vietnam War.

"Was it the kind of book Sarah would read?"

"I don't know. Why not? She read all kinds of books."

I'm about to say that we shouldn't discount the relevance of any details we find at a crime scene, and then I catch myself. This isn't one of my murder mystery novels.

Iris gestures at the paper in my hand. "Are you familiar with the other names on the list? Are they also in the matching industry?"

I pass the sheet back to her. Pretty sneaky, this Iris. "You don't know that Veracity is in the matching industry."

She lip-smiles at me. "Neither admit nor deny. That's a very lawyerly approach."

I don't say anything. I haven't heard of a matchmaker, or any other type of dating-related company, called Compatibility, probably because it's too generic of a name. But Iris *is* right that the other items on Sarah's list are connected to matching, each in its own different way. Precision provides consulting services in, as Charles would put it, the *matching space.* We, Veracity, help users to screen their matches. And then there's the Romantick.

I learned about the Romantick, an anti-matching group, as part of the background reading Becks assigned to me when I joined Veracity. I was curious to see what its positions might be, especially given my own reservations about online dating — plus, I mean, it uses the Middle English form of the word *romantic.* Too bad it seems to be a

114

bunch of disgruntled loons who, I suspect, just couldn't get lucky online. According to the Romantick website, online dating will destroy us all by irreparably degrading interpersonal relationships and ultimately ceding control over humanity to the instruments of eugenics (also known as the matchmakers' compatibility algorithms). The group's efforts are focused on lobbying Congress to outlaw matchmakers and populating its blog with semi-grammatical rants.

The vast majority of the American public — Iris Lettriste included, it seems — has no idea the Romantick exists. Google *romantick* or *the romantick,* as I did when I was trying to find out more about the group, and the first several pages of hits relate to a Regency vampire romance series and an emo-pop band from Glasgow. You would never hear about it unless you were in the industry. Or, maybe, researching a story about that industry.

Iris is saying that she's also wondering how Sarah got hold of this stationery. "The girl who lives in the Plaza hotel," she says. "Are you familiar with the Eloise books? Sarah loved them."

I shake my head: not the kind of title a Chinese kid growing up in Jackson Heights has on her bedtime list. "Maybe she splurged and spent a night there."

"She couldn't have afforded it."

Again the problem of money. Lawyer at a top New York law firm versus out-of-work journalist with out-of-control medical bills. I wonder how much Iris was helping out her sister. "Then maybe she was with someone else and he paid."

"I did think of that." Iris pauses. "Except my sister didn't go for the type of men who would take her to the Plaza. If anything, she would have viewed that as a negative."

"Who did she go for?"

Public-interest types, according to Iris, and the odd artist or academic. "As long as they didn't make too much money or work for a corporation. Because then, of course, they would be selling out."

Really. I'll have to check out Sarah Reaves's historical profile activity; now I'm curious to see who else she was talking to or searching for. Based on what Iris has said, Sarah should have dissed both Charretter and Captain Bubbles. Iris could be wrong about her sister's tastes, or this could be more evidence that Sarah wasn't online to find a match.

The evening light is a violet dimness around us. Iris says, in her quiet librarian voice, "I would like to pay you. Like I said earlier, what my sister should have paid. Or more, if you think that's appropriate. I know this is an imposition."

"No," I say, without knowing exactly what I'm trying to demur.

"I just want to know what you knew about my sister. Why she came to you, what she was looking for. You're the only one who can help."

Talk about the hard sell. But she's right. There are three people who work at Veracity — three and a half, if you count our disembodied IT guy (who never responded to my thank-you email — whatever). Only one of whom, at this point, is willing to entertain her.

I say, "Can I think about it?"

I think about it throughout happy hour in the East Village with my high school friends Maddie and Julia. When we walk out of the bar, the shift from its noisy, enclosed warmth to the cool darkness outside nudges me out of my reverie long enough to remember something I wanted to ask Maddie. "Did you and Rex end up adopting a rescue dog after all?" I say. "If so I volunteer myself as dog-sitter whenever you guys want to have a date night."

Julia punches me on the arm, hard — Julia

doesn't do anything half-assed. "Ow!" I say. "You promised you'd stop trying out your BJJ moves on me."

"We broke up," says Maddie.

"If that was BJJ you'd be on the ground," says Julia. "And I spent the last thirty minutes comforting Maddie while you sat there lost in Claudia fantasy land as usual."

I turn to Maddie. "I'm so sorry."

"Is something on your mind?" she says. "You've been so quiet tonight."

Maddie doesn't really look it, with her sturdy build and stoic features, but she treads at the high watermark of grace and emotional astuteness. I attribute it to a superior upbringing; I still remember the first time I had dinner at her house in eighth grade, my wonder at the way the Wheeler family comported itself, everyone engaging in friendly and thoughtful discourse, children helping parents to clean up, no raised voices or overturned table or abrupt exits.

"Weird day at work," I say. "No excuse." I hug her, squeezing as tight as I can.

Julia asks, "Did you find out some big secret about the matchmakers?"

By now most of my friends know the sanitized version of my job change. I've told them I'm doing matchmaker research for a start-up, as per Komla's instructions, and

I've taken to regaling them with boss-from-hell stories about Becks, whom I refer to as the Blonde Assassin. They generally think it's hilarious that I'm working in the matching industry — as Julia put it, *It's like a vegan getting into the dairy business.* Doesn't put them above asking for intel, though.

"It's really a big Sorting Hat," I say, "that matches people up based on which Hogwarts house they belong to." That's in fact the premise of two boutique matchmakers I've come across.

They head on to dinner; I beg off, citing my geriatric bedtime habits, and pedal home to get my Sarah Reaves googling on.

It turns out representations of Sarah, poised and polished, remain across the Internet. A professional website provides a concise bio (originally from the Midwest, master's in journalism from Columbia), a headshot far more up to date than the one she used for dating, and a list of publications. A Twitter account with ninety-seven followers, mainly used to retweet quotes from socialist politicians and feminist stand-up comics. A LinkedIn profile in which she describes herself as a freelance writer and editor *exploring questions around the digitization of life.* It feels like some kind of macabre mirror trick, reflections dazzling off one another so convincingly I forget, once or twice, that no person lies behind them anymore.

I look at the articles she's included on her website. Most of them were for progressive news and culture sites. The latest one appeared in *Nth Degree* earlier this year, a rundown of ten under-the-radar health care start-ups with the potential to transform patients' lives. Among them: a depression diagnosis and support app, an app that monitors your medication schedule for you, a drug-delivery service that drops off your prescriptions at your door.

Next I read her piece on online dating that Iris had mentioned to us during our meeting. It was published a few years ago, and its datedness — pun intended — shows. It's an account of Sarah's thirty-day dating odyssey on three platforms, two of which I've never heard of: E-uphoria, Other Fish, and Matched. (I check in with Google — both Other Fish and Matched have folded.)

I've reached day seventeen when I hear Max bang in through the front door. Sarah Reaves has decided to venture beyond her romance sweet spot of criminal justice attorneys and social reform activists. *For me one of the biggest draws of online dating,* she writes, *is the opportunity to meet people you never would have otherwise, and perhaps being surprised — by them, and by yourself.* It's an intriguing way to think about matching, as a journey of self-discovery, even if today's algorithms largely preclude that by defining your sweet spot as precisely as possible and then pairing you up with people who fit within it. Although I guess one way to get around that would be, as Sarah did, to pretend to be someone you're not.

I register that Max is standing in my doorway, his smile wide enough to span the Atlantic and both his coat and shoes still on. Before I can remind him, yet again, of our no-shoes-inside policy, he grabs on to the sides of the doorframe and says, "I went on the most amazing date tonight. What are you doing right now?"

I glance back at my laptop screen. "Um —"

"Have you had dinner? We got a bite to eat, but I'm still hungry."

"More or less." When I'm in the apartment alone I default to yogurt and granola. It's probably an early symptom of terminal spinsterhood.

"Don't you want dessert?"

What I really want to do is finish reading about Sarah Reaves's online-dating adventures. But I can tell Max needs to debrief, and I can never say no to that boy. I push my chair back. "Where do you want to go?"

Really it's a trick question, because Groucho's is the only eating establishment within a four-block radius of our apartment. It's a twenty-four-hour diner on a stretch of busted streetlights and empty lots, which makes me suspicious that it's a front for some sort of illegality. It also features eight varieties of pancakes on the menu, so whatever shenanigans the guys who own Groucho's may be up to, I hope they never get caught.

We score our usual booth in the back, which has duct-taped seats and a table decorated with more graffiti than the walls of a public restroom. As we wait for our food Max tells me about the boy he's calling Greenpoint for now: yoga teacher, killer dimples, sweet and smart, an even bigger comic-book geek than Max is.

Max has a naming hierarchy for his matches. They start out as the neighborhoods they live in, then acquire more specific nicknames. I can tell when he's really into someone because he'll start referring to them by their actual name. For instance, Caleb the awkward chemist was originally *Morningside Heights*, unknowingly endured being called *Mister Bacteria* for a bit, and then finally received his due as *Caleb.* I still feel vicariously wistful about what happened — or didn't happen — with Caleb. He and Max are friends now. I hang out with them sometimes, and it's endearing, if a tad annoying, how funny they find each other's jokes. If only Caleb hadn't been so shy, and Max too impatient to deal with that. But I guess that's the story of every mismatch: perfect but for the insurmountable *fill in the blank.* And, luckily for Max, this city is teeming with beautiful boys, all beaconing out their romantic availability via smartphone.

"I want to text him," he says. "It's too soon. Right?"

"Wife of Bath," I say. One of the truest pronouncements on courtship I've ever encountered is contained in *The Canterbury Tales,* in the Wife of Bath's prologue: *Forbede us thyng, and that desiren we; / Preesse on us faste, and thanne wol we fle.* "You have to play hard to get."

"You must be the only millennial in the world to rely on romantic advice from the Middle Ages."

"And see how well that's worked out for me." My own romantic record is a hopscotch of hookups in college that I would, with the best of intentions but short-lived enthusiasm, try to develop into something more significant. I liked those girls well enough, but I never *longed* for any of them. And, these days, I might as well be a poster child for celibacy. Soon after I graduated and moved back to New York, I endured a visit with my mother where she wouldn't stop going on about how I should find a nice boy (unspecified but understood: Chinese). Since then, whenever I've tried to imagine myself on a date, I see my mother's shadow there, like the smudge at the edge of a photograph when someone has left a finger on the viewfinder.

"Like I've said," says Max. "Any time you decide to join the rest of us in the twenty-first century, I'll create a profile for you that will make every cute girl in New York desperate to date you. Even the so-called straight ones."

"But will anything in it even be true?"

"All of it! It's just about presenting the best possible version of you. Also, getting the algorithm on your side."

"How?"

"You look at the people you'd like to date and what they're looking for in the people *they'd* like to date. Then you edit your own profile accordingly so you come up higher in their matching rankings."

It occurs to me, not for the first time since starting at Veracity, that daters like Max are one of the reasons we have clients.

Our server sashays up to us. She thunks my order down in front of Max and his in front of me. "Let me know if there's anything else you need, okay?" she says, and then leaves before I can ask for either cutlery or a water refill.

Max and I swap our plates. Against my healthier judgment I ordered the pumpkin pancakes, which comes with an Appalachia of whipped cream. I'm a sucker for seasonal foods, even though I know that, in our Whole Foods era, seasonality is a trick of self-imposed scarcity played by restaurants on their customers.

As he picks up his burger, Max says, "Greenpoint gave me a new idea for a Brief Encounter."

"Who?" I ask. Max is an artist. Rather, I call him an artist and he calls himself a recovering art major. *Brief Encounters* was his senior thesis, a series of fictional portraits that paired literary characters from separate works. At my request, he did one of Hercule Poirot and Inspector Yuan Lei.

"Gulliver and Crusoe."

Adventurers and castaways. "That's a

good one," I say. "Are you going to paint it?"

The thing is, Max's art was the big reason he decided to join me in New York after Margrave, so he could burst onto the scene like a triumphantly overstuffed piñata. Instead he's barely painted in the two years since. He works at a children's watch company layering the likenesses of popular animated characters onto straps and faces. He's on the Batman-and-frenemies line. He despises what he does but claims he has to stay for health insurance reasons.

Max shrugs and wedges what remains of his burger into his mouth. I am continually impressed and aghast by how quickly guys eat. When he's able to speak again he says, "I like it, too. I think it's another sign that we're compatible."

All this talk about compatibility. The four words on Sarah's list are lilting through my head like some sort of annoying children's rhyme: *Compatibility, Precision, Veracity, Romantick.* I wonder about the way a portion of each word was underlined. Was Sarah just doodling, or is that significant? I wonder about *Compatibility.* Was Sarah referring to an entity or to a concept? And what's up with the punctuation marks?!

Max takes two sets of silverware from the

neighboring table and scoots back into the booth to sit next to me. We spend the rest of the meal sharing the pancakes and doing the *New York Times* crossword puzzle on my phone. It's a Thursday so we cheat, quite a bit. When the server brings the bill, she says, "I love seeing the two of you come in. You're such a happy couple."

After we get home I read the rest of Sarah Reaves's matchmaking article in bed. From day eighteen on, Sarah tries dating the types of men she would previously have scorned on principle. Oscar, private banker. Bert, mergers and acquisitions lawyer. Grover, Big Pharma VP. Elmo, consultant at — wait for it — Precision Consulting. (Sarah notes that all names have been changed.) She gets into a throwdown over universal health care with Grover, but otherwise the dates go better than she expected. The men are reasonably intelligent and not overtly condescending, and each asks her at least three questions about herself. A couple of them even have hobbies! Elmo loves reading about Greek history, Bert plays the drums. Also, she concedes, Michelin-starred restaurants and rooftop lounges are a pleasant change from dive bars and ramen shops.

When I'm done I set my laptop on the

floor and turn off the lights, and spend what feels like the next hundred years staring up into the witching dark. It's not Sarah I keep seeing; I'm grateful for that, at least. It's her sister, Real Iris. How she smoothed out the copy of the death certificate before she put it back in her folder. That tilt of her head as she watched us across the conference room table. Standing there in the orange shadow of the streetlight. She's just trying to under-stand why Sarah would have done this, run offstage in the middle of a scene without even looking around, leaving all this space behind. If I have a theory, I can't not share it with her.

Fuck. I guess this means I've decided to help her after all.

III.

"No," says Iris.

"No?" I say, meaning: *You can't know that when I'm only two sentences in!*

"Sarah wasn't working on a story."

We're in a coffee shop in Midtown East, a place with antiseptic lighting and tables in such tight rows that whenever anyone on either side of us stands up there's a low-level earthquake effect. Even though it's Sunday, Iris asked if we could meet someplace close to her office, where she's been all weekend in a series of meetings.

I watch her sip at her drink. She presses both palms around her mug like she's trying to suction warmth from it. I say, "But I think that would explain the list. Everything on it relates in some way to the matching industry."

I tell her what I know about its items: Precision Consulting, Veracity LLC, the Romantick. "The one that I'm not sure about is Compatibility, but —"

"I'm sorry. What you just said, about Veracity. It's some sort of detective agency? For dating?"

I wish Komla could hear this. "It's more of a personal investments advisory firm model." What am I thinking? Komla must never hear about this. "Um, I should have said this earlier, but what I'm telling you —"

"I understand," she says. "You have nothing to worry about. I'm not going to tell anyone about any of this." She pauses. "Who did Sarah ask Veracity to . . . confirm?"

I tell her about Charretter and Jude Kalman without identifying them. I note that Sarah never even met Charretter in person and that, based on their profiles, both Charretter and Jude Kalman don't seem like the type of men Sarah would be interested in dating. According to Iris.

Iris's gaze flicks to her phone, which she's placed screen-up on the table in front of her. Since we sat down it's been lighting up every few seconds with email notifications. She says, "Sarah was prepared to spend a lot of money on your services. She must have cared about those relationships."

Back to money and what Sarah Reaves

could or couldn't afford. In a murder mystery the victim would have oodles of money and everyone else would stand to gain from her untimely demise. But here the dead person was broke, the person still alive the one who's rich. In the midst of all my Sarah googling I took a few minutes to search for Iris Lettriste as well and learned that she made partner at Murkstone Banderby last fall. She must be earning more than a million a year, even if she has no time to spend any of it.

"I wouldn't call them *relationships,*" I say. "Like I said, she never actually met one of them. And the other . . ." He was married; he had a child. His life was already a castle and he would never have let Sarah Reaves behind those walls. I think of Sarah talking about deceiving and being deceived. "She wasn't seeing him for more than a couple of months, at most. We confirmed that using our . . . proprietary techniques." Coming from me, Komla's magic words sound like what they are: utter BS.

"A lot can happen in a few months," says Iris.

"Sure," I say, "but I think Sarah was focused on something else." I remember Komla asking Sarah what she thought we had missed in our review of Charretter's chat records, and her saying that she would tell us more. Next time. "I think she wanted to verify these men as part of a story she was trying to write." Charretter, at least; I must admit I'm not so sure about Jude Kalman, but I feel compelled to talk up my theory in the face of Iris's relentless skepticism. "That would explain why she lied to us about her identity — she didn't want us finding out she was a journalist. You said it'd been a while since she had been able to write anything. That could have been on her mind, how she needed this story to be a success to get her back on track, and then either she thought she wasn't up to it or the story turned out not to be as big as she'd hoped, and —"

"I told you," says Iris. "That's not it. Sarah wasn't trying to write anything. She was done with that."

"But —"

"And. She dropped out of her journalism program over the summer."

What? "Her website says . . ."

"I know." Iris's tone is dry. Sarah was scheduled to graduate in the spring, but she never submitted her thesis. She obtained an extension until the end of the summer but then decided to withdraw altogether instead.

"She was so close."

"I'm not sure," says Iris. "I don't know how much work she actually did on her thesis."

"Maybe . . . that was why?" It seems plausible. Sarah Reaves's failure to complete the program could have come to feel insurmountable, or like a gloomy indie-film preview of what the rest of her life would be like.

Iris shakes her head. "She was already considering a career change. Which might be a good thing. Might have been, I mean. Sarah kind of fell into journalism. I don't know how much she really enjoyed it."

There goes the thwarted journalist theory. But then: Why *did* Sarah Reaves kill herself?

"So," says Iris. "Were they lying?"

I blink at her. "Who?"

"The men my sister asked you to look into."

"One of them was," I say. "The other, we don't know."

"What was he lying about?"

I know I shouldn't get into the details, but Iris obviously has her own theory and I'm curious to hear it. "He was already married."

Iris shifts forward in her seat. "How did Sarah react?"

"She was disappointed," I say. "The way

133

anyone would be."

After a moment Iris says, "Actually, I think Sarah would have been more affected than most."

She tells me that Sarah's last relationship was with a married man, and it ended badly. Sarah convinced herself — foolishly, in Iris's opinion — that the man would divorce his wife. She was distraught when he finally made it clear he had no intention of leaving his family.

I remember the peculiar expression on Sarah Reaves's face, right after she said that thing about a chocolate Lab being a good dog for a family with small children. "Did that man have children?"

He did, although Iris didn't know the specifics — and, from the way she speaks, I suspect didn't care to know. "It must have really upset her to find out that this was happening all over again."

"This was different, though," I say. "She was just getting to know the guy."

Iris is smiling at me in a polite *you can say what you like but I know I'm right* way. Suddenly I can see how Iris Lettriste would have annoyed the hell out of her younger sister. I say, "He wasn't even the kind of person she would have dated, according to you." And in that case, why would Sarah have pretended to be someone else?

"It doesn't sound like he was," says Iris. "But I think that was part of it. I think Sarah . . ." For a moment her face looks like a piece of cloth that was crumpled and then flattened out again. "I think she might have gotten tired of being herself."

Out on the sidewalk, Iris says, "I've started the book."

"Which . . . oh."

"It's called *Dispatches*." The author, she tells me, is Michael Herr, a war correspondent.

I nod along. I know all this already — I read the book at Margrave, part of a class on the Cold War. After I finished it I walked around in a jittery fugue for days. It's not like I believe in ghosts, but that's what the book made me think of. All those people who died in the jungles and caves and tunnels of Vietnam, the villages and camps and Humvees and choppers, unable to ever leave that drenched, devastated landscape, crammed together for eternity. The awful pun occurs to me, that Sarah was dispatched. Except that's not quite right, not if she killed herself.

"What do you think?" I ask.

"It's all about death," says Iris.

135

When she reaches into her bag I think for a moment that's what she's bringing out, Sarah's book. "I'd like to give you this," she says. "For your help."

I look at the bulky manila envelope. What is this, a street-corner drug sale? "It's fine."

"You came all the way here."

"It was an excuse for a bike ride."

"You biked here?" Iris says this like I snowshoed across the Yukon. "Aren't you concerned about the cars?"

"I'm used to them by now," I say. And the thing is, I actually really enjoy cycling on the streets. I like the judgments you have to make and how little time you have to make them, cutting between cars and hopping on and off sidewalks to get past traffic clogs. I never feel like I'm more fully in New York than when I'm coasting along on my bike inhaling the meaty aroma from the halal food carts, nodding to the reggaeton playing through a car's open windows, admiring the nonchalant grace of a girl pulling her hair up into a ponytail as she walks, trying to guess what a storefront called the Ugliest Duckling would sell — and then having to swerve to avoid the idiot who steps out onto the road in the middle of the block while wearing headphones and texting.

She likes to cycle as well, says Iris, but

navigating Manhattan traffic would be too much for her. Instead she does loops in Central Park, and if she wakes up early enough on the weekends she'll cycle to the Palisades and back. "Bike paths the whole way."

"Are you one of those spandex cyclists?" I can totally see her crouched over the handlebars of a thousand-dollar racing bike, decked out in a bullet-shaped helmet and reflective sunglasses and Lycra. It seems like her kind of physical activity: expensive, grueling, quantifiable. Solitary. I wonder if she has any dating profiles up. Presumably not, which was why her sister felt confident borrowing her identity. Is she currently dating someone, then? I doubt it; she has the closed, contained air of an inveterate singleton. She must look at me and think the same thing.

This time her smile discloses a glimmer of teeth. "I've been known to wear spandex while on a bicycle, yes." She shakes the envelope at me. "Take it. Please. I'll feel better about troubling you."

It's freakily heavy: How much has she stuffed inside? I'll give it to my mother, say that I got a bonus at Aurum.

Iris tells me she's planning to finish packing up Sarah's apartment this weekend; the landlord is eager to put the unit back on the market. "And then . . . and then maybe it'll be easier to stop thinking about her. It's not going to do anyone any good, anyway." She's silent for a moment. Then she says, "Please forget about this. We never spoke."

I have a momentary sense of unease, like I'm being asked to step onto a potentially leaky raft. But all I say is "Memory deleted."

On my way downtown I decide I'll stop by Veracity so I can log in to Match Insights and take another look at what Sarah Reaves was doing online before she died. Now that someone else has said it out loud, it's clear to me that Sarah didn't keel over because Jude Kalman hurt her feelings. She was upset, true, but what she said about no longer having to worry — it wasn't because she was planning to abdicate her life. She just meant she was done with the douche-bag. Iris may want to believe that's what happened because it fits into her narrative of her sister as fuckup, but, as Inspector Yuan likes to say, believing something for its convenience is at best negligence and at worst culpability.

I search for Sarah Reaves using her handle Flora or Fauna, and Match Insights informs me that no such profile exists. At first I

138

think the database is down — but no, I'm able to access other people's profiles. I try searching using what key terms I can remember Sarah including in her profile — as we now know, half of them fake — and spend too long clicking through other women's profiles. Who'd have thought there were so many thirty-six-year-old female lawyers in Manhattan looking for men?

I go to the Soulmate website thinking maybe I can find her profile this way. Soulmate makes me log in (I use my shell account), take a survey, and agree to three different sets of disclosures before I can navigate to the search page. This might be the closest I'll ever come to understanding how people who have gotten used to private jets feel when they are forced to fly commercial.

For my trouble I get a no results response and am redirected to a page of other people's thumbnail profile pictures, women Soulmate thinks would be good matches for me based on what I've told the matchmaker about myself, which is that I'm a forty-five-year-old white male who enjoys woodworking and playing the harmonica. Compatibility ratings blink above these pictures, each one in the ninetieth or higher percentile.

I close the browser. Sarah Reaves must have deleted her Soulmate profile before she killed herself. Iris would say this shows how disheartened Sarah was by what she learned about Jude Kalman. But Iris never talked to Sarah about Jude; I did.

The new theory springs up before me like my subconscious is one of those three-dimensional pop-up cards I've finally figured out how to open. Maybe Sarah did ask Jude Kalman why, like she said she wanted to. Maybe the confrontation escalated and she said she would tell his wife, and then he —

I suddenly notice how grayishly dim the office is, beyond the glow of my computer screen — I didn't bother turning on the lights — and how still the air feels, like that beat in a horror movie right before the first monster explodes forth. I tell myself that all the murder mysteries I've read have addled my brain. Sarah Reaves died alone in her apartment of a drug overdose. No way Jude Kalman could have set that up. In *Inspector Yuan and the Charlatan's Cure,* the killer did hypnotize the phony healer into ingesting his own powders in toxic quantities. But we're not in a fantasy theme-park version of Ming Dynasty Beijing; we're in New York, circa early twenty-first century.

Where we have a dead person who was faking her identity, who got involved with a man she found out was married, who had a prior bad experience with another married man, and who left behind a cryptic list that, let's not forget, was written on the stationery of a luxury hotel she could not have afforded.

I open Match Insights and search for Captain Bubbles. Nothing. I search on the Soulmate website: nothing either. When did I last look at Jude Kalman's profile? The day I last saw Sarah Reaves, almost four weeks ago. Between then and now both their profiles were deleted, and Sarah Reaves died. A coincidence. Unless, as Inspector Yuan is constantly telling Constable Zhang, there are no coincidences.

My phone buzzes and I jump. It's Coraline. *We need another 15 mins, sorry! Are you there already?*

Shit, I'm supposed to be meeting her — and Lionel — in Williamsburg right now. I wait until I'm running into the stairwell to type *On my way* so it will technically be true.

IV.

I spot them standing outside the entrance to Smorgasburg as I roll by on Kent Avenue, looking out for bike parking — always a challenge in Hipsterville. Lionel is on his phone. Coraline, who's wearing a sun hat even though the sky is quilted white and gray, is gazing across the street at a group of girls in prairie dresses, no doubt appraising the aesthetic merits of their outfits. I grab an unoccupied sign pole two blocks north, lock my bike, and walk back. Maybe it's my current frazzled state of mind, but as I approach them I swear I can feel the air thinning like I'm about to enter a malignant biosphere.

Coraline hugs me and then wrinkles her nose. "Why are you always so sweaty?"

Racing here from Manhattan will do that. Maybe they're just pissed because I'm so late? "Sorry," I say. "I hope you haven't been waiting too long."

Behind Coraline, Lionel hasn't glanced up from his phone. "Hey Lion," I say.

Now he blinks at me. He pushes his bangs to one side, a classic Lionel gesture. "Hey, Claudia," he says. "How's it going?"

Lionel looks and talks like a blond surfer dude, which is ironic because he can't swim. When Coraline first met him he was also sporting a man bun, but then she made a comment — which she swears wasn't aimed at him — that she thought men generally looked better with short hair, and by their next date he had chopped it off. After she told him that our parents came from Taiwan, he started reading up on Chinese history and politics. He brings her breakfast in bed and massages her feet. That's the way it is with them: Lionel adores my sister.

Except everyone around Jude Kalman must think he adores his wife, his entire eminently Instagrammable family unit.

And he might have wanted to make sure it stays that way.

That thought feels both less frightening and less believable in natural light, amid the smells of frying butter and charred meat, surrounded by a crowd of people all eager to get their brunch on. "Looking forward to some overpriced finger food," I say.

We head into the open-air food market

143

that sets up in Williamsburg on weekends. Coraline and Lionel, who live a few blocks away, are Smorgasburg veterans. As we do an initial reconnaissance of all the stalls, Coraline keeps up a Food Network patter about what's good ("the arepas" — "those Peking duck buns, whenever you see an old Chinese woman slicing up entire roasted ducks on the spot you know it's going to be amazing" — "and oh my god, the dough-nuts") and what's not ("anything that's vegan, obviously" — "the ramen burger sounds like a good idea but so disappoint-ing"). Lionel stays half a step behind us. Google Maps and the Smorgasburg website both say the market is located in East River State Park, but really it's in a holding pen of concrete and wire fencing. The water is right there, but you can't see it through the mob of hipsters, tourists, and hipster tour-ists, all of whom I despise with the snob-bery of a native New Yorker.

Eventually we end up back at the Jamaican food stall where we began. "I think I'm go-ing to start out with some dumplings," I say. "What about you guys?"

Coraline says to Lionel, "Want to share something, babe?"

"Sure."

After a moment she says, "Like?"

He shrugs. "Whatever you want."

"The pupusas? You like those, right?"

"Sure," he says again.

"Are you just saying that?"

I say to both of them, "I'll meet you back here."

When I return, Lionel is standing by himself right where I left him. I hold out my paper tray of dumplings. "Edamame, bulgogi, jerk chicken. I got carried away."

Lionel takes one with his fingers. "Thanks."

We gaze off in separate directions. I feel like he might be masticating extra slowly so he doesn't have to make conversation. "How's the writing going?" I say. Lionel writes the kind of story you read in the *New Yorker,* where nothing happens but the characters are all thrumming with anguish. His biggest ambition is to make it into that magazine's next "20 Under 40" fiction issue. (He's thirty-two.)

He pushes his hair aside and says, "It's okay."

I prod a dumpling with my fork. Such reticence to an invitation to discuss his writing: unprecedented. He must have received another rejection, from a literary magazine or a fellowship. The writer's life, going by Lionel's example, is a hamster wheel of submission and rejection. He's told me he has an email folder labeled *Dreamcrushers,* where he archives all the rejection notes he has ever received.

He says, "How about you? What have you been up to?"

Where to even begin. "The usual," I say. "Work. Hanging out." Dear god, my life must sound surpassingly dull. I add — not that this will do anything to mitigate that impression — "Rereading *Pride and Prejudice* for the twentieth time." It feels like an apt novel to accompany me into my new job, and as I enjoy Elizabeth's and Darcy's feinting and parrying, I've found myself wondering what Jane Austen would have made of our era's matchmakers. She'd probably have appreciated the efficiency; she was certainly clear-eyed about marriage as an arrangement for economic security in her time. But I also think she would have been a tad disappointed. All her heroines are romantics, after all.

"You know," says Lionel, with the first show of liveliness I've seen so far, "I could never get into that book."

Not too surprising; Lionel is a devotee of the terse, elliptical, emotionally constipated, quote-unquote *masculine* style of writing. He's carried around the same copy of Hemingway's collected short stories since he was fifteen and decided he wanted to be a writer, from small-town Michigan to Chicago to New York, which he moved to for his fiction MFA. I'm revving up to convince him of Elizabeth Bennet's many charms when Coraline rejoins us. She flourishes a pancake stack of pupusas at us, crater-charred and glimmery with oil. The Lins have a tendency to get carried away when it comes to food. "I couldn't decide," she says, "so I ordered one of everything."

We head out of the market and into the park proper. We sit down on the ground close to the water, and Coraline passes her plate to Lionel. He begins to eat with the air of someone assigned to a task. I offer her my dumplings. She takes a bite and then deposits the remainder of the dumpling on Lionel's plate. "Not as good as Grandpa's," she says.

Charles and Coraline were brought up by my mother's parents in Taiwan until he was eleven and she was eight, and now and then they will reference that period of their lives. To hear them tell it, it was Eden with beef noodle soup and lychee jelly desserts. Our grandparents lived on a farm on the east coast of Taiwan. It probably felt like some barbaric form of punishment to go from open skies and loving indulgence to Jackson Heights and our parents' perpetually frayed tempers, which was all *I* ever knew.

On another occasion I might have expressed my skepticism about Coraline's ability to recall the taste of dumplings she ate more than two decades ago, but this time I just say, "I think they're delicious," and pop another one into my mouth.

Across the river the skyline of Manhattan plots a volatile graph of glass and steel. I imagine Jude Kalman knocking around in one of those towers, shouting at the speakerphone and high-fiving his coworkers and doing whatever else it is that popular culture tells me finance bros do. Thinking himself untouchable. It occurs to me that he's the kind of character Lionel might write about, an upper-middle-class white man who's outwardly blessed and privately unhappy. What would Lionel think of the proposition that someone in Jude Kalman's circumstances would commit murder to maintain the pristine facade of his life?

"Hey, Lionel," I say, "I have an idea for a short story. Can I run it by you?"

A pause, and then he says, "Sure."

Coraline says, "Can we not talk about writing? It's all Lionel does. He comes home from work and sits in front of his computer until we go to bed."

Lionel says to me, with his *aw shucks* smile, "I put on a good show. Really I'm wasting away my life on the Internet."

"Then why do you keep saying you're busy when I want to spend time together?"

He blinks like a startled rabbit. "We spend time together. We're spending time together right now."

"Because I dragged you out. You didn't want to come."

"I just said that we go to Smorgasburg all the time."

"Claudia doesn't."

I call that *the hostage move.* It's one of my mother's favorite tricks, and it annoys the hell out of me, especially when in this case I didn't even ask to meet at Smorgasburg. But Lin loyalty dictates that I back up my sister. "I wanted to check it out before they close for the season," I say.

Lionel says, kind of mumbly, "I never said I didn't want to come."

Everyone looks down at the ground and I get a pained, cringey feeling, like I'm watching an increasingly stuttery comedian bomb his jokes. (Max dated an improv comedian for a couple of months. He — Max — ended it because he said watching the guy's shows was too stressful.) Then Lionel says,

149

"I'm going to get something to drink. Anyone want anything?"

After he walks away Coraline says, "I don't know why he said that. He's always working on one of his precious short stories."

"Has he gotten another rejection?"

She shrugs. "You know he doesn't really tell me about this stuff."

Because she broadcasts her boredom whenever Lionel and I talk about books or writing. In a strange way, that's what I've found so hopeful about my sister's relationship with Lionel: the apparent irrationality of it. Love as an engine that can power you off the edge of a cliff and across a chasm of dissimilarity to land, exhausted but exhilarated, on the other side. Now, though, watching my sister watch the water like she knows there's a sea monster beneath and she's readying herself for battle, I'm thinking maybe that's just some silly romantic ideal I have, poetic in theory and masochistic in practice.

"You should ask him," I say.

"I do."

"But like you actually care about what he says."

"I do! I want him to become a famous writer."

150

I chew on that, together with my last dumpling. Not so tasty now that it's cold and the skin has acquired a semi-leathery texture. For a moment I reflect on the ephemerality of things: dumplings, relationships, life. The matchmakers are always touting their success rates, but how the hell do you measure success in their world? A relationship that lasts longer than x amount of time? Marriage? Marriage sans divorce? No longer being on a matchmaker? To have loved someone, once. Success or failure?

"Can you help me find out if he's cheating?"

For an instant I think Coraline knows, through some feat of sibling intuition, about Veracity. I turn to look at her. "What? How?" I know exactly how. Add his phone number to Finders Keepers and see how his movements line up with what he's telling Coraline about where he's going. Check the Match Insights database for any active dating profiles. Conduct an in-person observation.

"Follow him around for a few weeks. Or something. You're the one who reads all the detective novels."

I say, "You really think . . . ?"

"I can't tell anymore." She glances back at the river. "Maybe I should just go back

151

on my medication."

In her midtwenties, after a taxing breakup that involved a suicide attempt (by the guy) and a restraining order (against his wife), Coraline tried seeing a therapist for a while. He diagnosed her with anxiety attributable to a seismically unstable childhood. No shit. I could have told her that for free, although I guess I couldn't also have prescribed a catalogue's worth of antidepressants to help her chill out about it.

Coraline is saying that she hated the side effects, how taking those pills made her feel swaddled in dullness, incapable of caring about anything ever again. "I was like that bean that was buried under a thousand blankets. Isn't that a fairy tale?"

"The princess and the pea." Should I note that the point of that story was how *overly* sensitive the royal brat was? My mind slides away to Sarah Reaves for a moment; perhaps depression was among the side effects of her medication. It could be as simple as that.

"Will you?" says my sister. "Please?"

I crumple up my empty dumpling tray. The thing is, Coraline has always treated male infidelity like I would milk going bad: sniff to confirm, toss, pick up a new bottle. She's too pragmatic to linger, or even to get angry. Or maybe she's just never cared enough.

"Don't you trust him?" I say.

"I don't trust anyone. Except you and Charles."

I think of those future historians of the Kingdom of Coraline, sighing at how close the realm was to ushering in an age of prosperity until its official policy of paranoia destroyed it from within. "I'll do it," I say. "So you'll see that nothing's wrong."

She leans into me for a moment. "Thanks, Claw."

We agree on a plan. I'll surveil Lionel for two weeks; Coraline will text me each day to let me know his schedule. I ask for his number — I say that if I catch him somewhere he shouldn't be, I can call him and ask if he knows where Coraline is and monitor for any signs of guilt or nervousness. (Which, for a fake reason, is actually not a bad idea.)

As I'm saving the number — and adding it to Finders Keepers — I say, "When he first contacted you on Partnered Up, what made you respond?"

My sister's smile is like the patchy light overhead. "I got him mixed up with someone else." She realized this twenty minutes into their date, when it became clear that he *worked in the financial sector* the way you could say a hen worked in the agrarian sector, at which point she told him she had confused him with a man who had started his own hedge fund at the age of thirty-two.

That's one thing beauty is good for: it lets you get away with all kinds of shit. "You couldn't just have let him think he scored a date on his own merit?"

"He was relieved! He said he couldn't stop wondering why I said yes." They hadn't been matched at all by the algorithm. He had simply been bewitched — his words through her words — by her profile and messaged her, not expecting a reply.

This is the kind of story that gets the pot of cheese fondue at my very core all gooey. The serendipity of it, the unlooked-for gift that makes you feel all the more fortunate. "What was it about him?"

"I don't know. He was sweet. He wasn't arrogant. He was really cute, in this scruffy kind of way. Except for the hair."

I see Lionel ambling back across the grass, looking like he wouldn't mind taking his time to get here. He's carrying two drinks, even though neither Coraline nor I asked for anything, and I'm guessing the cup of pulpy red liquid is watermelon juice, Coraline's favorite. "Well," I say, "you don't have to worry about the hair anymore."

V.

When I tell Becks that Sarah Reaves's Soulmate profile has been deleted, she says, "Why the fuck were you searching for her profile?"

Pretty much the reaction I'd anticipated. "I wanted to look at it one more time after what Iris Lettriste told us," I say, "to see if any of it was real."

She sighs. Not her usual grand *I am surrounded by dullards* exhale, something more like the soft, slow leak of a bicycle tire. After a moment she says, "We only access a profile when there's an open case. Risk management policy."

Should I have known this? She probably said it during my orientation. I archive that thought in the deal-with-later folder of my mind and say, "Do you think that's weird? That Sarah's profile is gone?"

"She no longer needed it."

"But why go to the trouble of deleting it?"

Becks shrugs. "I knew someone who took out the trash before he killed himself."

Yeah, yeah: sometimes there is no why. But as Inspector Yuan would say, the only question that matters in a murder is *why*. Not that this is a murder. I hope. "Also, guess which other Soulmate profile has been deleted?"

"Clearly I'm not keeping you busy enough," says Becks, "if you have time to ask me these pointless questions."

"Jude Kalman's."

Her face is a porcelain void; I can't deduce anything from it except disapproval. I say anyway, because I need to say this to someone, the urgent way Midas's barber did when he learned his king had donkey ears, and Becks is marginally better than a hole in the ground: "What if Sarah Reaves told Jude Kalman that she knew he was married?"

Becks doesn't say anything, so I keep going.

"And what if she threatened to tell his wife?"

Now she says, like a teacher confronted with a spectacularly inept student, "She didn't know who Jude Kalman's wife was."

"She knew her first name." Thanks to me. "Maybe she was able to figure out the last name as well. Or she could have bluffed. And he could have —"

"So he's able to stage a murder that fools the NYPD, but we catch him cheating one week into our verification."

"The police miss things all the time," I say. They may be the ones to lock up the villain, but only after the brilliant amateur sleuth tells them who it is.

"Do you think killing someone is like turning off the lights?"

"It happens."

"In those fucking mystery novels you like to read. Last I checked, we aren't in one."

"How do you know I like to read murder mysteries?"

She looks at me like this is the dumbest question I've ever asked. "It's written all over you."

I can't help it. "Pun intended?"

"This," says Becks, at a volume that makes me suspect she wants Komla to hear her from within his office, "is what happens when we hire someone because a fucking computer game tells us to." She starts to turn away, then swings back around. "Drop it," she says. "Sarah Reaves is dead. The best thing we can do is forget we ever met her."

I put Jude Kalman back on Finders Keepers. Of course I'm not going to drop it. Inspector Yuan is always telling Constable Zhang that a detective's intuition is the torch that illuminates the darkness, and what mine is showing me is that Sarah Reaves's death is not as simple as it seems.

Every murder mystery contains an illusion that the detective must dispel in order to solve the crime. In *Inspector Yuan and the Blood Pearl,* for example, the inspector was flummoxed by the murder of the pearl diver until he realized the girl hadn't died during the Festival of the Water Dragon, as it seemed at first, but in fact two days earlier. An illusion of timing. In Sarah Reaves's case the illusion would be the cause of death, a self-administered overdose of her daily medication while she's hanging out alone in her apartment. Could Sarah have been tricked into ingesting more of the drug than she thought she was?

I do some reading up on Strobinex. It's the first drug developed by a pharmaceutical start-up called Custom, which has hundreds of millions in venture capital funding and the ambitious goal of conquering pain. It's been on the market since the spring, and so far reception has been favorable. The Custom website lists out the usual litany of potential side effects, which includes depression, but on Migraine Warrior, the largest online forum for migraine sufferers, everyone sounds quite chipper about the drug. Unlike most other migraine medications, Strobinex is meant to be taken daily and on an ongoing basis. Patients report that within the first few weeks the pain associated with their migraines has improved, and those who have been on the drug for three months or longer even say that their incidence of migraines goes down altogether. The only complaint is cost: a month's supply is a few thousand dollars, and the drug isn't currently covered by insurance. Iris Lettriste must have been paying at least part of that bill. It's big of her, especially when she didn't even get along with her sister.

I know Becks thinks I'm Catherine Morland in *Northanger Abbey,* hyperventilating over my own imagination. But. What if I'm Jane Eyre and there *is* a crazy person banging around in the attic? I want to be the one who finds them.

VI.

On the last day of October, Jude Kalman leaves his office at 4:00 p.m. He's almost reached his apartment when I realize two things. One, trick-or-treating must start early when you have a costumed bundle of cuteness to ferry around. Two, here is a compare-and-contrast opportunity to observe him with his family. Before Sarah's death; after Sarah's death. If Jude did in fact get rid of Sarah Reaves — a part of me can't believe I'm thinking that, and at the same time it feels right, like a picture being straightened — he will have changed. There's no way he can kiss his wife or carry his child, less than one month later, without the horror of that fact between them, tainting everything. In all the Inspector Yuan books I've read there's been only one villain ever who continued on after her crime exactly as she had before, and that was because she was under the delusion that she

160

was Guānyīn, the goddess of mercy.

I have to finish a diligence review for Becks by the end of today, but she's currently out on a case, and I figure it will make no difference if I send it to her two hours later than I otherwise would have.

The entire week has been a display of virtuoso fall weather, and I ride up the West Side bike path under what feels like a freshly painted sky, the light clear and calm and golden, the asphalt ahead of me speckled with tiny leaves. (Also the occasional lump of dead rat.) Jude is still in his building when I reach Columbus Avenue and Seventy-Fourth Street. His block is avid with light-sabers and swirly capes, glitter and spandex and face paint, furry onesies. I stand outside the Starbucks where I held my stakeout and watch all the high-functioning dual-parent family units perambulate by. There's a lot of exclaiming by the adults over how adorable one another's children are, and even more frenzied prancing about by those children, who have probably maxed out their sugar intake for the year. Tolstoy's maxim that happy families are all alike appears to have some merit as far as their kids' Halloween costumes go. They favor the superheroes and princesses, and monsters as well, of the cuddly variety.

161

I always wonder if parents with bratty kids get a kick out of being able to dress them up as beasts once a year.

So does it mean anything that Jude Kalman's kid falls into the none-of-the-above category? This time I notice them right away when they come out. Jude has on a full-body seltzer bottle costume topped off with what looks like a yachting cap. His wife is at once more abstract and more explicable. She's rigged up a cardboard frame that goes from above her head to midthigh and out past her sides, and she's dressed in white paint-splattered clothes. A Jackson Pollock painting is my guess. She's also carrying their kid, who's wearing a fire-engine-red onesie and a green beanie with a leaf jaunting up to one side. The dog is a unicorn, with a cardboard horn and a rainbow whisk tail. He appears resigned to the indignity.

I cross the street a few feet north of them. There is some fussing over whether the painting's frame is properly attached and the unicorn's horn is askew, and then I see Jude take out his phone. I start walking in their direction, dodging a shrieking ice-cream cone. I reach them when they have just finished taking their selfie. Jude is frowning at the screen of his phone. "Do

162

you want me to help you take a picture?" I ask.

He grins up at me. It's jolting, the familiarity of his smile. "That would be great," he says. Not at all suspicious. Not even surprised, as if his is an existence in which strangers regularly offer to clear obstacles for him. Someone like that — what would happen if he saw himself crashing toward an obstacle larger and more dangerous than anything he had previously encountered in his charmed life?

As he's passing me his phone the dog decides to get in on the action as well and begins a vigorous olfactory assessment of my leg. I scratch him behind the ears and hope that his animal instinct can't sniff out my subterfuge.

"Miro." Jude tugs at the leash. "Be polite."

Miro gives my hand a sandpapery lick, and as always when I'm in the presence of an affectionate canine, I think about how awesome it would be to own a dog and also how the responsibility would crush me. "It's fine," I say. "I love dogs."

Jude's phone is the just-released, needlessly high-powered iPhone model. It feels heavier in my hands than it should, maybe from the cumulative weight of all the secrets sealed within its shell. Inspector Yuan would have some undetectable way of switching phones on Jude Kalman, walking away with the family's well-wishes and the key to the mystery tucked in one billowy sleeve. But then, the inspector has access to the best counterfeiter in the Ming Dynasty, who over the course of the series has forged jewels, paintings, amulets, swords, and, once, a set of Russian-doll-style Buddhas, all in the name of justice; and, also, the inspector doesn't have to deal with smartphone security codes.

I take a picture. Quite a few, actually, because I'm repeatedly thwarted by either the squirminess of the child or Miro's distractibility. When I pass the phone back to Jude I notice the sticker across the kid's mound of a tummy that says mcintosh. "Oh, I see," I say. "The apple of your eye."

That grin again, like I'm confirming the awesomeness of his existence. He says to his wife, "I told you people would get it."

Lucia Casales's head tilt is equal parts skepticism and elegance. "She's the only one so far."

"I'm not sure about you, though," I say to Jude. "Are you part of a recycling campaign?"

His wife laughs, a back-of-throat, cat-purr kind of sound — and Jude looks at her like a boy who's finally drawn the attention of a girl he has an epic, hopeless crush on. I can practically see the delight sparkling out of his pores. I'm so taken aback I only tune in again to what he's saying when I hear, like my mind is a teleprompter he's reading from, "Captain Bubbles."

"What?" I say, meaning: This *is what your adulterous Soulmate profile name is about?* and *Why are you cheating on your wife when you're obviously crazy about her?*

Lucia says, "My husband is obsessed with carbonated beverages." Her voice, the faint foreign cadence of it, sounds like it was smelted in some place where all the women are effortlessly glamorous and carry forth in low, husky tones.

"College nickname," says Jude. "What about you? Are you in costume?"

I look down at myself. I'm in my usual aspiring-bum ensemble: hoodie, T-shirt, jeans, sneakers. "Sure," I say. "Undercover detective."

Did his face twitch, or was that just an energetic blink?

"Very much undercover," I say.

Lucia says to Jude, "We should start heading over." She smiles at me, gracious, appreciative. "Thank you for taking the pictures."

165

"Of course," I say. "Your family is lovely."

"Here, I'll carry her for a bit." Jude holds out his arms and the kid tips herself into them like a ball rolling downslope. He snuggles her up against his shoulder. "You're an apple," he tells her. "The apple of all our eyes."

My throat cinches: displays of father-daughter affection tend to undo me. If I ever went to a therapist, I know what they would say about that.

As they're walking away, Jude looks over his shoulder at me. "Good luck solving your mysteries!"

Later that week, Jude Kalman changes up his evening-dog-walk route. Over the course of an hour he winds east and north through Central Park, eventually exiting on the other side. He makes it as far as Second Avenue before he turns around and heads west again on Eighty-Ninth Street.

I see all this on Finders Keepers the next morning; the app can record up to twelve hours of activity. Not only that, but it can also tell you the previous times a subject was at a particular location, and when I check I find out that Jude was in this area — Eighty-Ninth Street between Second and Third Avenues — once before, during the period that I was monitoring him for Sarah Reaves. My Captain Bubbles activity spreadsheet shows that the occasion was his date night with Sarah. Our client records confirm that Sarah provided her address as 220 East Eighty-Ninth Street, #3A.

I replay that section of the recording. Jude goes past Sarah's building once, reaches Second Avenue, comes back. The second time, he stops in the middle of Sarah's street. He's there for almost ten minutes before he continues on his way.

I rewind again. Why would Jude Kalman be visiting the site of Sarah's death . . . and why now? My skin is prickling like an invisible acupuncturist is hard at work, needling foreboding up and down my meridians. I watch the dot hovering in place on my screen, wishing I'd learned more from Operation Photographer than the uninspired backstory behind Captain Bubbles. Then I realize: I did. Jude's face set alight when Lucia laughed. This is a man who would have done everything he could, everything, to keep his wife from knowing about Sarah Reaves.

VII.

Max entreats me to be his plus-one to a Halloween party that Caleb and his room-mates are throwing in Morningside Heights, three continents away from Gowanus. I agree on the condition that he won't abandon me for a hookup opportunity. For my costume I pull up my usual ponytail into a topknot, ink a goatee on my chin, cinch the dragon-patterned dressing gown I bought a few Halloweens ago around my waist, and call it a day. When I go into the living room Max is fitting a cardboard packing box around his torso. It's been painted silver, like his face and hands, and he's wearing what looks like a gray leotard. Two of the box flaps have been cut into the shapes of birds, which both have Xs for eyes.

"What the hell are you supposed to be?" I say.

"Killing two birds with one stone!" he says. I have to admit that's pretty clever. He doesn't need to ask me who I'm going as.

The city seems set on extending Halloween festivities into the weekend: the subway is riotous with sexy nurses, characters from the latest hit Netflix series *Fall of Troy,* send-ups of political figures, and the usual miscellany of ghouls. I have plenty of time to regret giving in to Max, since it takes us two hours to get up to 119th Street, where Caleb's apartment is. The R isn't going uptown from our station, the 4/5 is running on the 2/3 line, and the 1 is operating in theory but is a ghost train in practice. We also get stink-eyed by other passengers, including a disturbingly realistic-seeming orc, because of how much space Max takes up and how pokey the corners of his costume are.

Caleb lives in grad-student housing a few blocks from the Columbia campus. From the outside his building looks like any other apartment block, but when we enter there's a vestigial dorm-like feeling about it. Bulletin boards festooned with notices of campus events and offers to buy or sell used household items, the clinical fluorescence of the hallway lights. It makes me at once nostalgic for Margrave and glad to be done with that overeager, floundery part of my life. At least by now I've learned to flounder a tad more discreetly.

We're let into the apartment by a guy wearing a crown and carrying a length of rubber hose attached to a nozzle. When we ask he tells us he's a noble gas, which gives me some idea of what this party is going to be like. We sidle into the living room. The vibe is crowded-but-tame. The prime source of excitement is a board game that half a dozen people dressed like extras from *Star Wars* are clustered around.

Caleb is standing across the room, and once I see him I understand why Max was so insistent about my company tonight. He notices us and waves. Max murmurs, as we head over, "That's not why I wanted you to come."

"Hi guys," says Caleb. "Thanks for coming!" He seems different from the last time I saw him, a couple of months ago. I'm not sure if it's the three balloons he has taped to his chest in an upside-down triangle, the beard he's now cultivating, or the guy nestling against him like a koala on its favorite eucalyptus trunk.

Max says, so brightly we could all go spelunking into the depths of his id, "Thanks for inviting us!"

"This is Sebastian," says Caleb. "Sebastian — Max, Claudia."

"Hi," says Sebastian. He has springy dark hair and sleepy eyes, and he's wearing a bedsheet-toga. Lazy costume, but it shows off his calves and biceps to excellent effect. He says to Max, "Did you make that entire costume yourself?" He speaks in this drawly, deadpan manner that makes it hard to tell whether he's impressed or amused.

"Sure did," says Max. "I even chopped down the tree and pulped it into paper."

Caleb says, "Max is a very talented artist."

"That's awesome," says Sebastian. "What kind of art?"

Max says, "I cut and paste images of Batman on watch straps."

"Well," says Sebastian, "at least Batman's hot."

Max says, "Sounds like we have different tastes."

Seeing as I'm the one person in this quartet who's neither contributing to nor affected by all the sexual tension frizzing around us, I might as well try to diffuse the situation. "Caleb," I say, "I'm so intrigued by your costume. Balloon seller?"

"Man," he says, "that's the fifth time I've gotten that. I'm a proton." The balloons are the quarks that make up the particle, he explains. It's a group costume; his two roommates are a neutron and an electron, respectively. "It looks better when we're together because then everyone can tell that we're an atom."

"I'm sure," I say.

"Can you tell what Sebastian is?" asks Caleb.

Beside me Max is silent. I take another look at Sebastian's getup and realize that the wreath on his head comprises limp romaine leaves and the odd crouton cube. "You're a Caesar salad!" I feel vaguely like I'm betraying Max with my enthusiasm, but I do appreciate a well-thought-out pun.

Caleb and Sebastian have no idea who I am, unsurprisingly. Finally I enlighten them — greatest fictional detective ever, et cetera — and they turn to Max. "Something with birds," says Sebastian. He seems to be one of those people who enjoys stating the unhelpful obvious, although that could also be because he's almost definitely high.

Caleb smiles. "Are you killing two birds with one stone?"

The way he says it, as if nothing could be more delightful — and what I think of is Jude Kalman, gazing upon his wife. Romance. What a royal mess.

Luckily more new party arrivals come up to say hi to Caleb and Sebastian, and the costume-guessing game circles onward. I nail the Freudian slip and, pleased with myself, am about to go off to find a drink when Caleb says, waving to some person behind me, "Claudia, there's someone I want you to meet."

The girl features cat ears poking up from the top of her blond head, whiskers penciled across her high cheekbones, and Cleopatra-dramatic eye makeup. She's also wearing a box that extends from just above the knees to just below the shoulders. Who'd have thought the humble cardboard box would be tonight's accessory of choice. "Hey," she says, looking at Max. "Great minds!"

Caleb moves to hug her but is stymied by the box. He drops his arms. "You get the idea." He introduces her to Max and me. Her name is Rina, she works in urban planning for the mayor's office, and her big new project is a revamp of the city's bike lane infrastructure. He says to me, "She's looking for bike commuters to get their thoughts on how things could be improved. I told her she had to talk to you."

"Oh boy," says Max. "Claudia has plenty of opinions about that."

"Which do you hate more, cars or pedestrians?" asks Caleb.

"That's a hard one," I say. "Cars are evil

but pedestrians are idiots. Present company excepted."

Rina and I have been talking for maybe ten minutes — we lose the boys once we get into the pros and cons of buffered versus protected bicycle lanes — when she says, "You're not Crackle Pop, are you?"

I pause to consider whether this girl could belong to a secret society and is trying, through an apparently nonsensical question, to determine whether I do as well, like in *Inspector Yuan and the Constellation of Kings,* where the members of the outlawed Sun Moon Sect identify each other by asking the question of why the moon mourns for the sun. "I'm not sure I get the question," I say, "but *Crackle Pop* would be a good name for a breakfast cereal."

"Or a street drug," she says. One of her front teeth is chipped and it gives her smile a raffish air.

Neither, it turns out. Crackle Pop is a profile Rina was recently matched with on Soulmate. I look like her from her pictures, according to Rina — which, coming from a non-Asian, should probably be discounted — she lives in Brooklyn, and she cycles everywhere. "I was just wondering," she says. "Is it bad matching etiquette to ask?"

I have to pause again. She dates girls? And

was *that* why Caleb wanted her to talk to me? "I wouldn't know about matching etiquette," I say, "so I guess you get a free pass." Technically I do know, more than your average online dater; I had to read the Datetiquette Principles as part of my Veracity orientation, a set of *don't be a jerk* guidelines that most of the matchmakers have adopted and actively exhort their users to follow. But to wildly paraphrase Jane Goodall, there's a difference between reading about the chimps and living like one.

"You're not online at all?" says Rina.

"No," I say. "I just live vicariously through my roommate."

She watches me for a moment. Her eyes are a light hazel flecked with green. Now *I* feel like the chimp, being observed for some curious condition that keeps it isolated instead of playing with the others. "I started a few months ago," she says. "I'm not sure I like it."

"Why?"

"All the choice." Not only the apparent inexhaustible quantity of potential matches lined up for her perusal each time she opens the Soulmate app, but also her ability to break them down into the traits she wants and evaluate them that way. "It feels a bit like build-your-own-partner."

"Well," I say, "I'm a big fan of the build-your-own-pancakes option at my local diner."

"You don't think it dehumanizes people?"

Whoa, this got really heavy really fast. "Not so much the people. Maybe the pancakes, but I don't think they mind."

She smiles her chipped smile at me. "Okay, *dehumanizes* is extreme. Perhaps." But she's noticed how she's started evaluating the profiles of her potential matches, sorting them into priority lists based on age, location, interests. "The other day I saw a girl's profile that said her favorite movie was *The Fast and the Furious III,* and I thought to myself, *That's too bad, she seemed promising otherwise.* And then I thought, *Did I just think* promising otherwise, *like I'm looking at an apartment listing or something?*"

"Oh," I said. "I thought what you were going to say was that you shouldn't have ruled her out because she likes one movie that you don't like."

"No," says Rina. "It was her favorite movie *of all time,* in caps and with multiple exclamation points. I couldn't . . . get past that."

We smile at each other. I must admit it's refreshing to meet someone with articulate, intelligent doubts about matching. At the same time, given the amount of time Rina's been online, it seems a bit early to be so disappointed.

She says, "So when you build your own pancake, what goes in it?"

That tangents us into a discussion of buttermilk versus ricotta, fluffy versus chewy, toppings versus fillings, and where to find the best pancakes in New York. Rina stakes all nine of her cat lives on a breakfast-only restaurant in Harlem called the Fitz. "When I lived up there I went every weekend," she says. "I was on a mission to get through their entire menu."

There's a slight hitch in the rhythm of her statement, as if, maybe, she had been about to say *when* we *lived up there.* Now I get it. The Very Recently Single and Unhappy About It. Not any kind of situation I'd want to insert myself into; I'd be like the chapter in a novel that the author clearly wrote because their editor told them it needed some sort of transition between Exciting Event A and Exciting Event B.

"Did you?" I ask.

"I made it halfway through the eggs," she says. "You know, we should go sometime."

"That sounds great," I hear myself say. How to turn down someone who leaps so boldly onto railway tracks knowing she might be in the path of an oncoming Rejection Express? If I were ever to ask anyone out, I'd hedge the question so comprehensively the other person wouldn't even know what she was or wasn't agreeing to.

Rina asks for my number and says she'll text me. "That sounds great," I say again, like a record that's not only broken but also insincere. "Wow, I'm really thirsty. I'm going to get some water. Do you want anything?"

"I'm good," says Rina. "Thanks."

The way she says it makes me suspect she can tell I'm really just trying to get away. Goddammit. I wonder if that means she won't follow up. Then I wonder if I'm wondering because I want her to, or not to, or both.

The kitchen looks like the house elves went on strike a century ago. To my surprise Caleb is the only one in here, lounging against the counter and scrolling on his phone. He appears to be enjoying this respite from his host duties, so too bad I'm going to have to disrupt him: this is the opportunity I've been watching for all evening.

"Looks like your party is a success," I say.

He glances up, the corners of his mouth pressing into a reflexive smile. "You think so?" he says. "I'm not sure if people are mixing enough."

"The covalent bonds are a bit cliquey," I say. I saw a group of three people who had tied themselves together; I didn't figure it out from their T-shirts that said H, H, and O, I had to ask. "But I guess they can't help it."

His smile widens and settles, like a cat that has entered a room and now decided it will stay. "Did you have a nice chat with Rina?"

"Sure," I say. "We talked about matching. And pancakes."

"Both fascinating topics."

I say, "Did she recently get out of a relationship? A serious one?"

He raises his eyebrows at me. "What did she say?"

"Nothing in particular. Her take on matching just made it sound like maybe she hadn't dated around in a while."

"Or ever," says Caleb. He tells me that Rina started dating her best friend in tenth grade, and they just broke up at the end of the summer. "Isn't that crazy? Can you imagine being with the same person from the age of fifteen?"

What I imagine is Rina like one of those giant sequoia trees whose heartwood has been hollowed out. There must be so much of that other girl bound up in the person she has become. "What happened?"

"I'm not supposed to talk about it," he says, and then commences to do so. Apparently Rina's girlfriend felt like she was missing out by never having dated — "read: slept with," says Caleb — anyone else. Rina, on the other hand, is not enjoying being single at all. "She's such a lesbian. She can't wait to move in with someone and get back to cooking elaborate dinners and watching nature documentaries."

"Don't stereotype."

"What do you think," says Caleb, "about going out with her for a bit?"

"What?" I say. "You want me to be her rebound?"

"More like a starter date." Rina isn't having much luck on Soulmate, he says. "She's in that stage where she's trying to plug everyone she meets into the role of her ex, which scares away all the normal people and attracts all the dysfunctional ones. Worst of both worlds."

"Are you just asking me because you don't know any other lesbians?"

"That and you're an awesome person."

"We might not be compatible at all."

"Doesn't matter," says Caleb. "In fact, it's probably better if you're not." His opinion is that it's detrimental for Rina to be matched up according to a compatibility algorithm, because it just encourages her to treat each new person she meets as a potential life partner. "What she needs right now is to have fun doing things with someone without counting down the days to when they'll get married."

"And what if I fall desperately in love with her and she ends up breaking my heart?"

"You won't."

"Why do you sound so sure?"

He pauses. "Don't take this the wrong way."

"My favorite six words to hear right before someone tells me what they think of me."

"It's not necessarily a bad thing. I just get the sense you wouldn't let it happen to you."

I frown up at him. Is he implying that I'm emotionally stunted? But a couple of guys in Viking helmets tromp in right then to retrieve the vodka they previously stashed in the freezer, effectively ending our tête-à-tête. Caleb says, "I better get back out there. I told Sebastian I was just going to clean up for a few minutes in the kitchen."

I follow him back into the festive roar of the living room, feeling like his personal bodyguard the way I'm scanning for anyone who might get too close before I have the chance to ask my question. "Hey, Caleb," I say, "I've been thinking about how to kill someone using drugs."

Right then that phenomenon occurs where a hitherto noisy room goes crypt-like, everyone either running out of things to say or pausing to take a breath at the exact same moment. Which means, since I was projecting to make myself heard through the clamor, that my incriminating statement resounds through the room like the first hint of woes to come at an Agatha Christie bridge night.

There's a possibly nervous flitter of laughter. Someone says, "Get them addicted to heroin."

"Poison darts!"

I say, glancing about without actually making eye contact with anyone, "This is all purely theoretical."

"Can I take the Fifth?" says Caleb.

Luckily two board gamers start getting rowdy over whether a spell was properly cast, thus saving the universe — or not — and the collective attention shifts. I slump back against the wall. "Now we all know who the prime suspect will be if someone turns up dead tonight," I say.

Caleb looks down at me. "Are you switching from reading murder mysteries to writing them?"

That, come to think of it, would be an excellent excuse for making inappropriate queries. "I have a potential premise for one." I lay out Sarah Reaves's situation. A woman dead in her home from an overdose of Strobinex, no signs of anyone else present or of any kind of force. "I was thinking . . . could someone have swapped pill bottles on her? She takes what she thinks is her usual pill, but it turns out to be a lethal dose." As I talk this out I feel like I'm starting to see a picture form out of the gigantic smudge of whys and what-ifs that's been my mind ever since Finders Keepers showed me Jude Kalman's dot floating up and down the block where Sarah Reaves lived. "And then, after she dies, the murderer goes back into her place and switches the pill bottles again?" This must be why Inspector Yuan is constantly musing his theories aloud to Constable Zhang despite the ever-reliable constable's habit of plodding to all the wrong conclusions. Maybe I should find a sidekick.

"Oh yeah!" says Caleb. "That's clever."

Buoyed by the positive reinforcement, I say, "The victim dies on a Sunday. That means the murderer would have to go in on Saturday to swap the medication, since it's a daily pill. Although . . . Sar— she, the victim I mean, could have been in the whole day on Saturday, and if so I'm pretty sure she wouldn't have let the murderer in. They know each other, but they had a falling-out."

"Have her die during the week," says Caleb, "so the murderer can break into her apartment while she's at work."

"I can't. Anyway, she doesn't have a nine-to-five kind of job." I explain my victim's propensity for migraines and how that has dictated the trajectory of her life, and the promise of Strobinex, after so many previous failed remedies, to finally free her. "That's why killing her with this drug . . ." I grimace. In fiction it would be satisfyingly ironic; in life it feels especially awful. "The thing that's supposed to save her destroys her."

After a moment he says, "You've really thought out this character."

"Assuming the murderer was able to get in on Saturday, then after the victim dies he has a couple of days to go in again to remove any evidence. The body is only discovered midweek." Iris Lettriste told me that a neighbor alerted the police after she didn't see Sarah for three days and tried knocking on her door to check if she was all right. Good for that woman. I can't imagine any of my neighbors caring, or even noticing, if they never sighted me again.

"How will the detective be able to prove any of this?" asks Caleb.

How indeed. "Maybe there's a security camera in the victim's building that catches the murderer coming in and out right before and after the death, or the neighbors see him at the right times?" This theory would require a lot of carefully timed swanning in and out of Sarah's apartment — and it wouldn't explain why Jude Kalman was there again a few evenings ago, weeks after he had gotten away with the crime. "I'm still putting it together," I say. "I wanted to ask you, since you deal with chemical compounds all the time . . . how would *you* kill someone with Strobinex?"

He considers, an encouragingly ruminative set to his face. Then he tells me he would get the person to drink half a gallon of grapefruit juice in the thirty minutes before they take a dose. It's been shown that grapefruit juice can interfere with how a body metabolizes a wide range of medications, including Strobinex, increasing absorption into the bloodstream above safe levels. "Depending on the individual, but if this is for a novel you can just make the victim someone who's susceptible."

So much for hoping Caleb could be the Physician Huang to my Inspector Yuan, identifying an infinite range of poisons from the color of the deceased's toenails or the swelling of their earlobes. "Grapefruit juice," I say. "I'll add that to my list of potential MOs."

"Your idea with the pill bottles is better. But you know what would create more dramatic tension?" What if, says Caleb, the killer overlooked something incriminating during his cleanup of the apartment and only realized afterward? "You can set it up so the reader knows there's this big clue out there and they're rooting for the detective to find it before the killer can get rid of it."

"Oh my god," I say. "Maybe that's why!" I almost take out my phone right then to check if Jude Kalman is anywhere near Sarah Reaves's address, even though I've set a fire-alarm alert to warn me once he gets within a half-mile radius. Except: What kind of clue could Jude Kalman have conceivably forgotten about? He was clearly careful about segregating his interactions with Sarah from the rest of his life. Apart from their dating profiles — now both deleted — there's nothing to show that these two people were ever acquainted.

The light of my intuition flares and I see Iris Lettriste holding out a piece of paper to me, the quiet puzzlement on her face at the mystery of who her sister was. Maybe the relevance of Sarah's list isn't what it says but what it's written on: the stationery of the fancy hotel Jude Kalman brought Sarah to, establishing a connection between them that would be unprovable otherwise. In any case, Jude Kalman has already been thwarted — Iris has that paper, and she would have cleared out the rest of Sarah's apartment by now. But he wouldn't know that.

"Caleb," I say, "you're a verified genius."

He's smiling as if he'd like to pat me on the head. I ask, "What?"

"It's cute how you talk about this like it really happened and you're trying to solve it, when you're the one making it all up. You could have anything happen."

"I could," I say. "But only one thing did."

As I fully expected, Max abandons me at some point during the night because Greenpoint texts to invite him to a midnight meditation on someone's Bushwick rooftop. After I guilt him about it he offers to take the train with me back to Gowanus first, but I say I think I'll stay on for a bit. Typically he would notice something was up — my stamina at parties is worse than that of a chain-smoker on a StairMaster — but this time he just says, "Wish me luck!" and jets. I get another beer and shoehorn myself into a group conversation about who will get killed off next in *Fall of Troy*. I've never watched the show, but having studied the *Iliad* it's easy enough to guess what happens in it.

Since talking to Caleb about Rina, I've become distressingly aware of her presence in the room, like she's pinging forth these faint signals I can't help but register. Right now, for instance: by the bookshelves, talking to a Super Mario who has misplaced his mustache. Her gaze is intent on his face in a way that makes me suspect she knows I'm looking at her, which in turn implies she might have been looking at me. Better look away before our lines of sight cross and we have to acknowledge each other.

The thing is, it *has* been a while.

But I'm also thinking of something wise that Maddie said to me. Actually, the girl is constantly saying wise things to me, but for once I was paying attention. She asked if I'd considered that I kept getting myself into these hookup situations because they were safer. I said I had no idea what she meant.

She said, "It's funny, because you're such a romantic, but you always start out with a hookup. Does that make any potential relationship that might come out of that feel, I don't know, nonideal? For you?"

I said, "It almost sounds like you're saying I sabotage my own chances at a relationship."

"*Sabotage* might be a bit strong," she said. There's a burst of merriment in the vestibule, the Viking helmets announcing that they're off to pillage somewhere else. Now even those dudes are leaving. I move toward the door. Rina has my number. If she wants to get in touch with me she can. I have no idea what I'd do, but at least I don't have to decide tonight.

VIII.

As I close Rina's front door behind me I'm thinking about Jude Kalman's excuses, what he might have said to Sarah Reaves to explain why he couldn't spend the night. He had to get back to the office, maybe, or he was a fussy sleeper and needed the familiarity of his own bed, or he had to pick up something from his apartment. All still better than what I'm doing, which is leaving without saying anything at all.

It's dark outside, and there's a fuzziness to things, as if the world hasn't yet decided what it wants this day to look like. I walk to the nearest street corner: I'm at Ninety-Ninth and Amsterdam. When I look behind me I don't recognize any of the buildings, their gray-and-brown facades, the lidded eyes of their windows. I couldn't tell you which one Rina brought me into or how many flights we climbed, or anything about the twilight zone of her apartment except that her room lay at the end of it. The lights stayed off, which I suspect suited us both.

I push my hands into the pockets of my hoodie as deep as they will go and head south on Amsterdam like I'm embarking on some epic walk of shame. The voice I think of as the Should Have starts up in my mind. Should have headed right out of the party instead of stopping to say an extended goodbye to Caleb, knowing Rina was within earshot. Should have pretended I couldn't hear her through my music when she called to me as I stood on the sidewalk outside, checking my route on Google Maps, aghast at how long it would take me to get home by subway. When I turned around I saw that she had upgraded her outerwear from cardboard to lumber jacket, and the way the light flooded through the open door made her glow like a golden cipher. Should have made up an excuse when she asked me to walk with her for a bit, and definitely when she asked if I wanted to come up. I've always wondered if everyone else suffers from a Should Have voice as well, and if theirs is equally obnoxious.

At some point I stop in at a twenty-four-hour CVS for a pack of gum because my mouth feels like a small creature crawled inside to die. I wander through the aisles, disoriented by the store's intense artificial brightness and how its music sounds like one endless, and endlessly saccharine, pop song. When I step back out the sky has taken on a pale, hopeful tint, and the fog of last night's poor decision-making begins to lift. Today, like tomorrow, is another day. I'll go home, take a shower, download a new Inspector Yuan novel. I pull up Google Maps to see where the nearest subway is, and that's when I realize I'm less than a block away from the Central Park exit that Jude Kalman takes on his early-morning runs.

It's a safari in here, cyclists and runners and walkers and shufflers in their dark fleeces and bright spandex patterns and college sweatshirts, all revolving around the exercise watering hole of Central Park. I see Jude Kalman when he swerves off the big park loop onto the walking path and starts dashing in my direction like he's the last character still alive in a zombie film. His usual route, at his usual Saturday morning time, except something feels different. I register what it is only when he staggers to a stop where the path meets Terrace Drive, heaving like he's about to throw up. He's by himself, no stroller.

I'm farther along on Terrace Drive, a few feet from the Seventy-Second Street exit. I chose this spot because of how well trafficked it is: plenty of eyewitnesses, just in case.

Jude Kalman walks right by. He's scrolling on his phone, probably checking his run stats. I almost let him go. Because it's insane, whichever way I look at it. Accosting a stranger, accosting a murderer, accosting a stranger who might be a murderer. I'm thinking all that and I'm also remembering Sarah Reaves the last and only time we spoke right before she left our office, saying she no longer needed to worry about Jude Kalman.

"Hey, Jude?"

The way he turns, I can tell he gets that a lot. I almost apologize — the Beatles reference didn't occur to me until after I said it. He furrows at me like he knows he's met me before and feels bad that he can't remember my name.

"Nice job swapping Sarah Reaves's Strobinex medication. Too bad you forgot something."

Now he just looks confused. "I'm sorry?"

There goes the surprise-the-villain-into-confession approach, employed with such success in *Inspector Yuan and the Hundred*

193

Cranes. "I mean, Iris Lettriste."

This time something cracks apart in his face. "How — Did she —" He stops like his thoughts are crashing one after another into a highway pileup. "You're that girl. At Halloween."

"And you're Captain Bubbles."

"What the fuck is this?"

He walks toward me, shouldering into a woman passing between us without even noticing. "Were you spying on me?" One stride closer. I smell him, suddenly, an acrid odor of sweat and anger. "My family?"

Now he's looking at me like I'm not a person at all but a locked door he can't wait to splinter through and — oh shit. Have I miscalculated? If he grabs me, a dozen people might see him do it, but he can still fuck me up pretty badly before they stop him.

"If you don't give me some personal space," I say, "I'm going to start screaming."

He continues to stare at me. I tell myself not to move, not to look away — nothing to let him even guess that my heart is pounding so hard I can feel my entire body shaking around it. He won't. Surely he won't. But what if he does —

He shifts half a step back. The roaring in

194

my ears softens, barely. This is what I'm counting on. Men like Jude Kalman have too much to lose not to play by the rules of civilization. Unless they're confident they can get away with it.

"I just want to have a conversation," I say. "When did you last see Iris Lettriste?"

"Who the fuck *are* you?"

"A friend of Iris. I —"

"What does she want now?"

He says that almost like he's . . . afraid? Suddenly another reason Sarah Reaves might have decided to tell Jude Kalman what she knew comes to me.

"Nothing," I say. "She's dead."

His shock blazes up his face like floodlights in a stadium, no dark corners. "What?" he says, and then, "But I just . . ."

He didn't know. I feel like a wind has just gusted by and snuffed out the candle flame of my intuition.

"You're fucking with me. Both of you."

Except he *was* outside Sarah's apartment just days ago. And I'd bet my bicycle Sarah went to see him at some point between her third visit to Veracity and her death, which would make him one of the last people to see her alive. Possibly the last. "I wish I were," I say.

I tell him enough to convince him I know

what I'm talking about. How he and Sarah Reaves met, how he stopped contacting her and then picked up again around two months ago. "Then she found out you were already married," I say. "She asked to speak to you, and . . ."

"I gave her what she wanted." He laughs, a tight, mock-amused sound. "Not like she left me a choice, did she."

So tempted to bring up the fact that Captain Bubbles made plenty of ill-advised choices, but I should stay on point. I say, to confirm my suspicion, "How much did she ask for?"

After a moment he says, "A hundred k." That laugh again. "That's how much she thought my marriage was worth to me."

Sarah Reaves as blackmailer. That idea of her bothers me. Maybe she figured it was her due. Jude Kalman was using her, and so she would use him right back. "Why did you do it?" I ask. Inspector Yuan calls these types of questions *tuning forks,* which I'm not sure they had back in the Ming Dynasty: the criminal's response, weighted by his awareness of the accusation inherent in that query, hums at an ever-so-slightly different pitch from everyone else's.

He glances down. He says, a confession, albeit not the one I'm looking for: "Because it is worth more."

And . . . I believe him. Jude Kalman's solution to getting rid of Sarah Reaves would never be to kill her. It would be to pay her until she went away.

"I meant," I say, "why did you cheat in the first place?"

He takes another step back like I shook a can of Mace at him. "That's none of your business."

I think of how he looked at Lucia Casales, the evening of Halloween. Still unable to believe how he had lucked out. People cheat for all kinds of reasons, and, maybe, it means different things. "She really is dead," I say. "Iris Lettriste. So you have nothing to worry about."

He doesn't say anything. I add, "I'm not going to tell your wife. I just want to find out what happened to Iris."

I start walking away. Inspector Yuan is always saying that the detective decides when the conversation with a suspect ends, some alpha dog sort of thing. Then I realize I'm heading in the wrong direction, farther into the park instead of back out onto Central Park West. Crap. It will look like amateur hour if I backtrack in front of Jude, though, so I guess I'll keep going.

Behind me he says, "Wait."

When I turn around he drags his hand down his face like he's trying to wipe something away. "I'm sorry about Iris," he says. "I liked her. She was . . ." He pauses, and I wait to hear what word he will use to describe the person Sarah Reaves was to him. But then he says, "Did she . . . It wasn't suicide, was it?"

Interesting that he would bring up that possibility first instead of an accident, say, or an illness. "What makes you ask that?"

"I got the feeling she was in over her head," he says. "Something at work. And the type of person Iris was — not that I knew her for that long, obviously, but . . . she didn't seem like someone who would let go when that happened."

I think of our final meeting with Sarah, the snap of her energy, her frustration with us for not giving her what she wanted from Charretter. (And what *did* she want?) Saying that she was still figuring out what things might mean. "Did she talk to you about it?"

"She couldn't. Client confidentiality. She just said I would read about it in the news when she was done."

For several confused seconds I think he's referring to the confidentiality restrictions Veracity placed on Sarah as a client. Then I remember that, as far as Jude is concerned, we're talking about Iris Lettriste the corporate lawyer. Whose clients would be —

"My guess is some kind of M & A with the big matchmakers."

The matching industry. Sarah's list. I'd forgotten about that amid the revelation that Jude Kalman is innocent after all. I'm starting to think it might not be entirely realistic how these fictional detectives are able to hold all their potential lines of inquiries in their heads, chess grand master–style. "Why?" I ask.

Iris was always talking about the matchmakers, says Jude. As part of his work at Apex Partners he researched potential investments in tech companies, including the dating platforms, and she would ask him for his views on each of the Big Three, their business models and data-monetization strategies, the challenges they faced with algorithm accuracy and user trustworthiness. Once, he made the joke that he feared she was dating him only for his expertise on the subject; he remembers her response because it was so strange. "She said, *What about you, is that why you met me, because of what I know about the matchmakers?* Like she was kidding, but I could tell that, on some level, she wasn't." He had no idea what she was referring to until sometime later, when it occurred to him that Iris's law firm was an adviser to a number of companies in the matching industry — including Let's Meet, a Big Three matchmaker. "Maybe she was paranoid that I was trying to get inside information about some megadeal she was working on. There've been rumors about a Let's Meet sale process for a while now." He shrugs. "Who knows. But she would've been under a lot of pressure. Too much, maybe."

Could *that* have been the story Sarah was chasing: corporate acquisitions and matchmaker expansion? It doesn't seem to fit with the other articles she'd written. And it wouldn't explain Charretter. Or all the items on her list. Or, for that matter, her dropping out of Columbia and telling her sister she was done with journalism.

"Maybe," I say. "She had a lot going on." One last thing to check on. I'm too impatient to bother with a conversational transition, so I just say, "It was nice of you to bring her to the Plaza hotel. Did you . . ."

I pause. Jude is furrowing at me again. He says, slowly, "I didn't bring her there." I can see him wondering if this is some kind of setup. "Or to any other hotel."

"She said you did." Could there be *another*

guy skulking around?

"The last time I saw her," he says, like he's just been reminded of this now. They were getting up from their table, counter-parties in a completed negotiation, and Iris laughed suddenly and said this situation made her think of a quote by Oscar Wilde: the first time was misfortune, the second time carelessness.

Sarah took a few liberties with that line, but I can guess what she was getting at. The original married man, the one Iris told me about; the breakup that, according to Iris, devastated her.

"If there was someone else in her life . . . that's who you should be talking to."

"Maybe," I say again. Partly because I have no idea how I would find the guy, and partly because I'm still not buying it, this lovelorn, hapless version of Sarah Reaves.

"He was a misfortune. I was just careless-ness."

From the way he says that I can't make out if he's relieved or disappointed. Possibly both.

Jude says that Iris asked him the same question I did: Why? He told her it didn't matter, but afterward he found himself wishing he had said more, shown her that he did have his reasons. "It wouldn't fucking stop. My mind. Explaining myself over and over again, a hundred different ways." Finally, he says, he set himself an ultimatum. "I would walk by her place. If the lights were on I got to call her and ask if she could talk. If they weren't I had to drop this, never think about it again."

"Did you really do all that?" I ask. "Go to Iris's place and . . . ?"

"I did." He speaks like he's relating something that happened in a dream or to someone else. "Except I didn't call, because I realized, what I said the first time, that was right. It didn't matter anymore."

So that's what the extended dog walk was about. Miro, at least, would have been happy. Except —

"Look." Jude's voice is abrupt — he's out of the dream, back in his currently crappy reality. "I'm not . . . I love my wife."

I refocus on him.

"And my daughter. Both of them. Very much." He sounds defeated, as if this love is the burden he has to bear as the loser of a war, and it makes me think again about why he's here, in the park, by himself. I had assumed Lucia was on babysitting duty, but maybe it's more complicated than that.

"Do you believe me?" he asks.

And in this moment I can feel that I have

the vicarious power, as if I'm channeling the ghost of Sarah Reaves, to grant Jude Kalman a small sort of solace.

But, god help my petty, judgmental self, I don't want to do it.

I shrug. "Does it matter?"

He blinks like I've thrown a Frisbee at his face and he's barely dodged. Then he says, "It does if it'll make you get the fuck away from us. Or do I need to pay you off as well? What's *your* going rate?" He looks me up and down, a man exercising his God-given right to evaluate and rank women. "Pretty low, I'd imagine."

I say, "Are you also imagining that there's still an *us* to get the fuck away from?"

His face clenches up like a fist. And this time I can't help it, I do flinch, because for an instant what I see is my father's face, and I hear him and my mother screaming at each other like their rage will break apart the world, and I know, I know what that means. Something hits me in the backs of my knees. Park bench. He's backed me against it. I've backed myself against it. I'm trapped, like I was when I was five years old, balled into myself in a corner of the kitchen next to the trash can, watching while the inevitable happens, except this time it will be happening to me.

"I'm glad she's dead," says Jude Kalman. "And why don't you go fuck yourself, you stupid fucking cunt."

He walks away and I pretend not to notice everyone side-staring at us, wondering if they've just witnessed a spectacularly unamicable breakup or the filming of a scene from a new, ethnically diverse TV show.

My hands are shaking when I take out my phone to stop the recording. Inspector Yuan would not approve.

I end up walking through the park anyway, hoping to benefit from some of nature's much-vaunted calming effects. I tell myself I'm jittery from adrenaline, not fear. Plus rage that Jude Kalman got in the last insult.

For the first mile or so all I can think about is how I should have preemptively kicked him in the balls. Gradually that becomes tedious, and I'm forced to reckon with the takeaways from the confrontation. If Jude was telling the truth — and I do think he was — then Sarah Reaves did commit suicide after all. I stray off path so I can stomp through a crackly pile of leaves. I should be glad: no one's stealthing around out there, poisoning people with their own medications. Just me with my useless intuition.

I take out my phone, since even a thwarted detective should cross-check their sources, and text Iris Lettriste: *I've been checking a few more things, just to get a fuller picture. Did Sarah receive a big deposit in her bank account right around the time she died?*

Up ahead the raggedy canopies of the trees frame the end of the path, which opens up into the plaza at Columbus Circle. And that's when I finally pinpoint what's been snagging at the edges of my mind like some phantom branch. Surely Sarah Reaves wouldn't have bothered blackmailing Jude Kalman if she intended to kill herself in a matter of days. You'd only care about money if you thought you'd be around to spend it.

I text Iris again. *Also, do you know the name of the man you said Sarah was seeing?*

The question whizzes off into the electronic ether and I immediately wish I could snatch it back. Because if the prospect of murder continues to drift around us like BO on the subway, and the cause of it isn't Jude, then it has to be someone else in Sarah's life. An ex-lover who wanted to keep the relationship a secret — that's one possibility. There's another, though.

As I walk toward the blocky marble monument that marks the park entrance, I review some key principles of the murder mystery.

One: the suspect who hogs all the attention in the first third of the book fizzles like a damp firecracker right after they disclose some crucial piece of information, which, the observant reader can see, was the purpose of that character all along.

Two: the closer someone was to the victim, the likelier it is that person killed them. In the world of the murder mystery, your best chances of survival are to eschew all meaningful human relationships. Husbands and wives. Parents and children. Brothers and sisters.

Iris said many things about her sister. That Iris wasn't aware of what medication she was taking, even though it seems likely given Sarah's financial situation (also according to Iris) that Iris was paying for the Strobinex prescription. That Sarah had quit journalism, even though her coming to Veracity and her conversations with Jude — and the list, that damn list — all point to her investigating *something* about the matching industry. That Sarah was so traumatized by a previous affair with a married man she killed herself when she found out she had, once again, landed herself in a similar situation.

My phone buzzes: new text. It's from an unknown number.

Stop looking into this. Please.

It feels like someone lobbed a stone with a note tied around it through my window, smithereening glass everywhere. I reflexively glance around. All I see are the pedicab vendors hanging out at the edge of the plaza, hassling tourists as they pass.

A second buzz. *It's not going to do anyone any good. Including you.*

IX

I can tell that the events of the past few days have been excessively exciting because I find myself almost looking forward to the routine of my visit with my mother on Sunday. Almost. When I first came back to New York I set myself a biweekly visitation schedule, but I've since fallen shamefully behind. I should just change it to a once-a-month ordeal. I text the Three Cs, my sibling chat group, to let them know I'll be paying my respects and ask if they want to join. Coraline already has plans — she doesn't clarify if they're with Lionel or apart from him — but Charles says he'll stop by after he's done with work.

My mother lives in Flushing now, in a one-bedroom co-op that Charles helped her buy. To get there I have to bike through the chaos of downtown Flushing, and as usual I find myself wondering if this is what it would be like to live in China. Crowded into invisibility, and safety, by people who look like me, hearing nothing but the jangly sounds of a half dozen Chinese dialects, at-my-fingertips access to *you tiao* and *xiao long bao* and egg tarts. The idea freaks me out a bit.

My mother and I spend the afternoon watching the latest TV remake of her favorite *wuxia* saga, *Tales of the Falcon Adventurers,* which is just fine by me despite the absence of subtitles and, I'm embarrassed to admit, my difficulty in telling the assorted characters apart. My mother intermittently takes it upon herself to play translator, although she tends to focus on the most obvious aspects of what's happening on-screen: "He's sad because his teacher is dying in front of him." This is my ideal way to hang out with her, both of us immersed in an imaginary world where we don't have to interact except to commiserate over the fates of people who don't really exist.

Charles joins us a couple of hours and several bloodstained betrayals later. When he comes in our mother asks without preamble, as she always does, "Have you eaten?" It's half past four, so it's unclear what meal she's referring to.

He says he's full, he had a late lunch at the office. Our mother wants to finish the episode we're watching, so he clears a space for his laptop at the dining table, which is swathed with bills and take-out menus and offers for our mother to part with her money in ways she would find ludicrous, like Met Opera subscriptions and World Wildlife Fund memberships. The way soldiers can go to sleep anywhere, my brother can work under any conditions, including sitting right in front of an LCD martial arts extravaganza.

The episode ends with the hero pledging upon the souls of his ancestors to avenge his brother's murder. My mother has to explain this to me, and as she does I find myself thinking again of Sarah Reaves. And, now, Iris Lettriste. She still hasn't responded to either of my questions, about whether Sarah received a bank deposit or who Sarah was seeing. However, the anonymous texts I received — right after I asked her those questions — are an echo of what she said the last time we met: *It's not going to do anyone any good, anyway.* Iris wanted me to be aware of who was threatening me without being able to accuse her of it. She's even sneakier than I thought. But not, it appears, an astute judge of character — there's no way I'm letting this go *now.* Also, I hate being told what to do.

I've been thinking over what Jude Kalman said about Iris's firm doing work for the matchmakers and the idea of inside information. Sarah Reaves wouldn't actually have been privy to any of that — but Iris would have. What if Sarah discovered that Murkstone Banderby LLP was helping a matchmaker client set up some sketchy corporate scheme and decided she would blow it wide open? That would explain why Iris was so eager to red-herring me away from any notion of Sarah investigating a story. And what if Sarah's story would have implicated Iris herself?

My mother shuts off the TV and slippers into the kitchen. I turn around on the couch. "Hey, Charles," I say, "do you think it says something about traditional Chinese culture and values that all the *wuxia* stories are so into revenge?"

My brother squints up at me. "What?"

I'd been distracted by the show when he first came in, but now that I'm looking directly at him, wow. "Never mind. When's the last time you slept? You're starting to look like a jaundiced panda."

He sighs. "It's this f— this project that I'm running." My brother still tries not to swear around me; I think a part of him genuinely fears he will set a bad example otherwise. He tells me that it turns out the guy who was in charge before him upped and left things in a mess. "The client keeps asking me why there are all these discrepancies in the data and all I can say is that I'm looking into it. They must think I'm totally incompetent."

"I'm sorry," I say. Charles's fate in life is to be the conscientious member of a group assignment who is reprimanded by the teacher for their peers' sloppy work. "What's it about? Your project?"

My shiny new theory depends on confirming that Sarah was onto something newsworthy after all, and that brings me back to her list: a baffling list scribbled by a victim is the mystery genre's equivalent of Chekhov's firearm. If I'm right that the Precision reference is to Precision Consulting, it must be because of the work that Precision is doing for the matching industry. Like, for instance, my brother's project.

"It's . . ." He pauses. "It's highly confidential."

I can tell he wants to talk about this, probably because it's what he spends eighty hours of his week on. "I can keep a secret," I say, followed by, "Who am I going to tell?"

"I guess that's true," he says, a bit too promptly for my liking. "And I won't give you the name of the client." He takes a breath: mansplainer alert. "One of the biggest problems for the matchmakers is the lying limitation," he says. "The risk that a user isn't being honest about himself."

I tamp down on the impulse to tell him that I'm familiar with the lying limitation, thank you very much. It's the reason Veracity exists. As Komla has explained it — and, come to think about it, as he said to Sarah Reaves at our last meeting with her — matching only fully succeeds if the dating platforms have access to accurate, complete information about the people on them. Problem is, people lie. All the time, especially on the Internet, and extra especially where anything with the potential for romance is concerned. This means dating algorithms are predicting compatibility on the basis of faulty data and exposing users to potential deception by their matches. Enter the verifiers. Komla has said before, though, that he sees agencies like Veracity as offering only a stopgap solution. If a target is in fact lying, it's too late by the time the client comes to us. Ideally, the matchmakers would devise a process to identify that lie at the time it is made or even dissuade a person from lying at all. I'm guessing I'll have my job for the foreseeable future.

Today's dating platforms are a superior value proposition to traditional methods of finding a partner, says Charles, looking at me over the raised cover of his laptop, because they have the ability to determine, in advance, how compatible any two people are. "Provided they have the correct data."

"Claudia, let your brother finish his work."

Our mother has come back out from the kitchen and is stacking the papers on the table into piles of uniform height, when she should just be recycling the lot. I do hope she's not turning into a hoarder.

"It's fine, Mom," says Charles. "I can pick this up later."

"Are you sure? You're always telling us you have so much work."

"I do," he says, "but I should take a break anyway."

"Poor Charlie," she says. "Is it because your boss knows you have nothing to do except work?"

The thing is, Coraline and I tease him about that all the time, but it's different when our mother says it, like she's hooking it into some tender part of him and tugging to see if anything will come out. I said to Coraline once that maybe it was because English wasn't our mother's first language. *That has nothing to do with it,* she said. *Mom*

214

just loves to put people down.

My brother adjusts his glasses. "Actually, I have plans this evening. I'm taking Jessie out for dinner."

"You're not having dinner here?" asks our mother. "I cooked for you."

Wham! That's our mother landing the guilt stick on his head. I can already tell he's not getting up from that blow, at least not without help.

He tries anyway. "I didn't say I was staying for dinner."

She glances at the clock on the wall. "You were only going to stay for one hour?"

I *should* help him. But I would really rather not have a one-on-one dinner with my mother, plus I want to continue the matchmaker conversation with Charles. I say, "You could ask Jessie to join us for dinner."

He slants me a *you're useless* look. "You know she's not going to come all the way out to Flushing."

"She doesn't want to eat with us?" says our mother.

A few more minutes of this and Charles texts Jessie to ask if he can see her later tonight instead. Our mother, pleased at having gotten her way, streams an album of Chinese love songs on her iPad and sings to herself as she heats up the dishes she prepared earlier: pork and chive dumplings, braised pork ribs, sauteed green beans with minced pork. The pig should be the Chinese national animal. Every time I let my mother know that I'm coming over, she asks me what I want her to cook. A few years ago, Coraline told me that our mother has never asked her or Charles that question; since then, I've always requested my siblings' favorite dishes. Guilt is the currency that our family traffics in.

We've just started eating when our mother says to me, "I sent you Darren's picture. You never replied."

Who the hell is Darren? Oh, right. Crap. "I didn't realize I was supposed to reply."

"Mei Ling's son is looking for a girl-friend," our mother tells Charles. "I thought I could introduce him to Claudia."

"Hmm," says my brother.

Our mother turns back to me. "He's free on weeknights. Not Wednesdays, but all the other weeknights."

"What happens on Wednesdays?"

Ballroom dance practice, it turns out, which Darren engages in competitively. He even won a prize recently. "I don't remember the name of the dance," says our mother. "It's an animal."

"Foxtrot?" I say. Charles is smirking at me from across the table. It would be so satisfying to smack him in the eye with a dumpling.

"I think so."

"If he's so into ballroom dancing, he isn't going to be interested in me," I say. "I'm the most uncoordinated person alive."

"Mei Ling said that's fine. Darren already has a dance partner."

"You told your friend I was the most uncoordinated person alive?"

"I said when you were little you were always falling down."

Charles says, "Not so little. Do you remember the time she ran into the sliding glass door because she was so excited to get out to the garden to play with the dog?"

For god's sake. My family loves to chortle over that incident. "Anyway," I say. "Darren looks nice" — the way a sitcom suburban dad does, chubby (despite the foxtrotting) and amiable — "but I don't feel like dating anyone right now."

Our mother raises her bowl and chopsticks a bite of rice into her mouth. Maybe she's finally tired of this farce. I take another pork rib, start to try to eat it with my chopsticks, and then switch to my hands.

Our mother sets down her bowl. "Charlie," she says, "why do you think Claudia has never had a boyfriend?"

My brother frowns at the green beans. "I don't know," he says. "She likes her independence."

"She's not ugly," says our mother. "Not beautiful like Cora, of course. Not someone you look at but also not someone you don't want to look at."

Charles and I keep right on chowing like we're at the Fourth of July hot dog–eating competition.

"And she's not stupid. Not smart like you, not smart enough for Harvard. But she can find a job. No, you had to find her a job. But if she was really stupid, they would fire her."

I think of deep-sea fish hovering upon the ocean floor. I think of Greek statues gleaming in the enclosed courtyard of the Met. I think of all the silent, sightless, untouchable things in the world, because I know what will get to my mother most is if I do nothing.

"So there's nothing wrong with her, except that she is ordinary. So many people are ordinary. Like me. I'm a very ordinary person. But our Claudia, she thinks she is so special. Maybe that's the problem. Maybe she thinks she deserves to be with a special

218

person, when really she is lucky if someone wants to be with her."

Fuck it's hard, though.

Charles says, "It's because she can tell you're keeping something from her."

We're sitting in his car, parked on the street outside my mother's apartment building. After dinner I accepted his offer of a lift, surprising us both. I guess I felt too worn down by my mother to undertake the fifteen-mile ride back to Gowanus. We spent way too long trying to figure out how to work the trunk rack. I could tell Charles was embarrassed. I wish he wouldn't buy into all the gendered crap; as the literal man of the house, he feels like he has to be good at these types of things. Really our mother and Coraline are the ones with the DIY knack. (We all agree I'm hopeless at anything mechanical).

"That doesn't mean she can say that kind of fucked-up shit," I say.

"It doesn't," he says. "She shouldn't."

"I appreciate you keeping that opinion to yourself while Mom was body-slamming my self-esteem."

After a moment he says, "Maybe you should just tell her."

"She's like Mrs. Bennet, the way she

wants to marry us all off," I say, "except she doesn't even have the excuse of being a silly woman."

"What are you talking about?"

"Never mind."

"Claw."

"What?"

"You're not ordinary."

"I know, I know," I say. "We are all unique snowflakes. Don't you think that's a weird metaphor to use to tell someone they're special given how quickly snowflakes melt? It's like, you may be different from everyone else, but it doesn't matter because in zero time you'll be gone."

My brother laughs. "Not in that way," he says. "You're such an original person. I feel like I could ask you about anything and you'd have something smart and interesting to say."

The warm melty sensation in my stomach is like a sense memory of how I used to feel when my brother praised me. I buckle my seat belt and say, "Should we get going? You're going to be, like, four hours late to meet Jessie."

Charles starts up the car and whatever song was last playing resumes, mournful and melodious and —

"When the hell did you start listening to

Symposium?" I say.

"That's right," says Charles, "you like them too, don't you? Jessie made me a playlist."

Like would be a not wholly accurate way to describe how I feel about Symposium, a four-member pop group from Athens, Georgia — rather aptly, given that their songs are brilliant riffs on Greek myths, which some unenlightened people such as Max think is gimmicky but is in fact fucking genius. "She listens to Symposium?"

"What, you thought you're the only person cool enough to know about obscure indie bands?"

"No," I say, which is accurate enough. What I thought was that *Jessie* wouldn't be cool enough to know about obscure indie bands. "She just . . . she comes across like someone who'd be more into classical music, that kind of thing."

"Because she played the oboe in high school?"

"I didn't know that," I say. "She just seems like . . . that kind of Asian. You know."

"You'd be surprised."

Something about the way he says that makes me twist around to look at him. "Are you really into her?"

He flicks on the turn signal even though

we're the only car on the street and checks his blind spot. He completes the turn and then says, "I think so."

"That's great!"

He doesn't say anything.

"You . . . don't think so?"

The car behind us honks: the light is green. We glide forward, and the dark fingers of the trees on both sides of the street reach within the glowing circumferences of our headlights and fall away again. This area of Queens might as well be suburbia, and all the houses have their Halloween decorations up: jack-o'-lanterns leering on front lawns, cobwebs and mummy bandages draped across porches, vampire bats hanging from branches. It amazes me how much effort some people put into this.

"She wasn't upset at all about the change of plans," says Charles. When he offered to meet her at her place after he was done with dinner, she said they should just reschedule, it wasn't worth it for him to travel all the way to the Upper East Side so late at night. "It's always like that. She never wants me to go to any trouble for her."

He says this like he's confessing to some grievous character flaw, and it makes me feel, bizarrely, all protective, wanting to push him out of the way of a rejection KO.

I say, "That's your issue? Most guys would be thrilled."

"She should want me to . . ." He stops. Who would have thought that pale, demure Jessie Shen would be leading my brother into the underexplored marshlands of his emotions? Finally he says, "It makes me feel like she doesn't need me."

"She knows how busy you are," I say. "She's trying to be considerate." I hope.

"Maybe," he says. He tells me he wants to bring Jessie on vacation, to some luxury resort in Mexico that his colleague recommended. "Someplace warm; she hates the cold. I just need to get work under control first."

"Hey," I say, like I just remembered, "you never finished telling me about what you're doing for the matchmakers."

"Since when did you get so interested in that stuff?"

I should just let my family know about my job switch — one less subterfuge to keep track of. "Matching has become so big," I say. "I bet there's a ton of job opportunities. At the matchmakers, or ancillaries."

"For you?" There's an indulgent, incredulous stretch to Charles's voice. "What would you do? Proofread people's profiles?"

So much for smart and interesting. *This* is

what my brother, in his current incarnation as a condescending ass, really thinks of me. I'm almost more pissed at myself; by now I should know better than to fall for the bait and switch. "You don't think I can cut it because I didn't grindstone my way into an Ivy League?"

We merge onto the highway, an endless river of red and white lights. Charles signals his way into the middle lane and then says, "I didn't mean it that way. It's just . . . you don't know anything about the space. You're not even on any of the platforms." He pauses. "Ah, are you?"

I came out to Charles and Coraline my junior year at Margrave, via the Three Cs, something I intermittently regret. (The coming out, not the doing it by text.) Coraline will randomly interrogate me as to why I'm not dating anyone; Charles never asks.

I say, "I've looked at them."

"Okay, so, that's good. Next you should get a sense of the industry as a whole. It's a lot bigger than just the matchmakers. I can send you some industry reports if you want."

I let him meander on, apologizing without actually saying sorry the way my family likes to do. Before long he's offering to ask around for me, to see if any companies might be hiring.

"You'll find me another job?" I say, still grumpy. "No thanks. I can do that myself."

"I'm not saying you can't," he says. "But it'll be much easier if I help you. That's what a big brother is for."

"Nepotism?"

"Rich people do it all the time." Half the people he knew at Harvard, he tells me, got their summer banking internships because their fathers played golf or went to college or hosted July Fourth barbecues with the men who ran those banks.

"You didn't have any of that and you interned at Goldman Sachs." That was the very last summer the three of us spent shoving around together in the Jackson Heights apartment. The summer after Coraline graduated from high school and before Charles graduated from college; also the summer that my feverish, inexplicable feelings for our neighbors' granddaughter, visiting from Ecuador, first made me consider whether I might be gay. Charles slept in the living room, having long ceded his bedroom to Coraline by then, and woke up at five thirty each morning to commute down to Goldman Sachs's offices in Battery Park. Coraline and I would go meet him after work. It awed me how grown-up he was.

He would bring us to these restaurants along the Hudson where we could sit outside and stare at all the yachts bobbing in the harbor, the white bristle of masts and ropes and sails, the sparkle of water beyond. The bank gave him a work phone for the summer and he would check it every few minutes like he was waiting for his new mission from the CIA — a precursor, I see now, of things to come.

The Goldman Sachs building is on West and Vesey Streets, a few blocks south of Veracity, and so these days I actually walk by every once in a while. Whenever I do, I look at that vast, bright lobby on the other side of the glass, the gleam of the automated security gates, all the suited minions revolving in and out through the doors, and I think, *Suckers.*

"I used to think that made me better than the other kids," says my brother. "And then I realized they all felt sorry for me because I had no fucking idea how things worked."

I glance at him. His gaze is steady through the windshield, his hands at two o'clock and ten o'clock on the wheel. He says, as if this is what we've been talking about this whole time, "The matchmakers have access to two kinds of data: what a subscriber says about himself, and how he's actually behaving on their platform." Currently, the algorithms use the information a subscriber provides — what is known as step one data — to build an initial frame of reference for compatible matches. As the subscriber spends more time online, the algorithms refine this frame of reference based on additional data points, like the subscriber's searches and which of his suggested matches he chooses to contact — step two data. Charles's client is looking to improve its collection and analysis of step two data and has hired Precision to help.

I say, "What if the subscriber is being deceptive in the way they act as well?" Like Sarah Reaves, like Jude Kalman. A 94 percent match based on the lies they both told. It occurs to me that I never thought to check on Sarah's compatibility rating with Charretter. I'll do so on Monday. Although Sarah's profile has been deleted, I should be able to get that information through Charretter's history.

"They have to keep it up, though. Step two data is all about patterns of behavior over time. And if someone acts a certain way for long enough . . . I mean, then they *have* become that person."

I stare out of my window, at the shuttered shops that we are now driving past, the floating half globes of light that mark the entrance of a subway station, the dark loneliness of the occasional pedestrian. All these questions. What Iris Lettriste doesn't want me to find out about her sister. Who Sarah's misfortune is, the man she dated before Jude Kalman, and whether he was involved in Sarah's death. What Sarah was investigating. What I should do about any of it.

I say, "Does Precision do a lot of consulting for matchmakers?"

"It's been ramping up in the past few years," says Charles. Apparently companies in the matching industry are a cagey bunch, shy about attention because of the tremendous amounts of personal data they amass, skeptical of external consultants. Precision was only able to enter this lucrative market because of a partner who cultivated one of the managing directors of a dating platform the way you would a hothouse bloom that must be nourished on champagne, sashimi, and the occasional cruise to the Caribbean. Eventually the managing director deigned to hire Precision for a project. As Precision continued to build expertise, matchmakers as well as ancillaries began to recruit its executives for in-house roles. That was why Charles's unreliable predecessor left Precision, in fact, for a better deal at a match-maker. Precision alums, in turn, have been more than happy to engage their former firm for consulting and advisory services.

"You see?" my brother says as he pulls up outside my apartment building. "It really is all about relationships."

X.

I can't check Sarah's compatibility with Charretter after all. His profile, as with Sarah's and Jude's, has been deleted. What the hell? Either I'm the world's unluckiest detective or some malignant cyber-presence is wiping away everything Sarah Reaves came into contact with.

I decide to make my own list — analogue, to better invoke Sarah. I excavate an ancient Groucho's receipt from one of my hoodie pockets and write on the back of it: *#1. Make list of Sarah Reaves leads to track down.* I cross that out and immediately feel as if I've achieved something. I can see why people like doing this.

#2. Monitor Iris Lettriste's movements on Finders Keepers. I add Iris's number to the app, and her dot pops up on my screen at her office address.

#3. Set up Google Alert for news on Murkstone Banderby.

"What are you still doing here?"

I glance at the clock on my computer and realize I have less than ten minutes to get to the spin class in Chelsea that Becks signed me up for so I could confirm our client's suspicion that his lady friend has a crush on the (female) instructor. "I thought that since I was cycling over I could skip the warm-up portion of the class?" I say.

"The millennial work ethic," says Becks. "No wonder America is in decline."

I briefly consider pointing out that while, spiritually, she might identify with some prior, hardier, superior generation, as someone in her midthirties — assuming she hasn't cracked the antiaging code — she deserves that label as much as I do. "Maybe that's why we're happier," I say as I head for the door.

Later that morning, I hobble into the pantry to stage a run-in with Komla. Who'd have thought stationary cycling would be so intense? You don't even go anywhere. Komla and I chat for a few minutes about a recent *Datebook* article on the growing trend of gene-compatibility matchmakers, and then he says, "Did you come in here to ask me something?"

"How did you know?"

"You made a fresh cup of tea less than fifteen minutes ago, and it usually takes you at least an hour to drink it."

Huh. Who's watching whom here? "I do have a question, actually," I say. "Have you heard of a company in the matching industry called Compatibility?"

The black hedges of his eyebrows tilt up slightly. "Why do you ask?"

That sounds more like a yes than a no. I give him the answer I've prepped. My brother is a consultant who's working on a project for a matchmaker, and I overheard him bring up that company on a call; I was surprised I hadn't heard of it before.

"I didn't realize you and your brother are in the same field," says Komla.

"Sort of," I say. "He's in the social-tech group at his firm. But he doesn't know about my work at Veracity."

"Of course not. I'm sure your behavior is consistent with our policies."

"I try my best."

"Compatibility," he says. "Terrible choice of name for a dating platform. Because of how generic it is, I mean. Although, to be fair, that was during the Dark Ages, so most other platforms hadn't even started to consider the possibility of determining compatibility."

"But Compatibility — this platform — did?"

"It tried to," he says. "It was one of the first to systematically obtain and analyze data from its users so it could make meaningful recommendations for matches."

A first-gen matchmaker, then. Why would Sarah Reaves have been interested in it? "Is it still around?" I ask. "It's not on our matchmaker list."

Komla tells me it was bought out a while ago, by one of the Big Three. "Which was just as well," he says. "Its business idea was too ambitious, and executing it required too much time and capital. It wouldn't have survived long on its own."

"What idea was that?"

"A way, potentially, of verifying" — he smiles in acknowledgment of his use of the term — "the information a user provided on his profile."

"Why didn't it work?"

The eyebrow tilt again. "What makes you say that?"

"The fact that we're here, I guess," I say.

He chuckles. "Aha. Indeed. There would be no need for Veracity if Compatibility had succeeded. Why didn't it work?" His gaze shifts past me, abstracted. "If I had to guess," he says, "the founders of Compatibility underestimated how inconsistent humans can be." He looks back at me. "Including each other. They were a couple. They tested their process with their relationship, and . . . let's just say they learned a lot."

He speaks of these people the way I might talk about the March sisters or the Narnia kids, characters whose stories I followed for so long and at such an impressionable age that I feel as if I know them in some tender, nostalgic way. And maybe he does, or did, at least. Both he and Becks are tantalizingly vague about their pre-Veracity days, but Komla has said before that he's been in the matching business for as long as there have been matchmakers.

"Which consulting firm is your brother at?" says Komla.

I tell him, he asks a few questions about Charles, and somehow we end up talking about my family. "It must be nice," says Komla, "to have them so close."

"Well," I say, "it can be a double-edged sword. Um . . ." It feels both inappropriate to pose personal questions to your boss and impolite not to reciprocate when someone asks you about yourself. "How about you?"

Komla tells me that his family is in Accra, which, thanks to a fortuitous crossword clue

I solved just last week, I'm aware is the capital of Ghana. He visits a few times a year but hasn't lived there since he was eighteen. "I used to think about returning," he says, "but I was kept away for too long. Now each time I go back I see all the ways I no longer belong."

"Kept away by your work?" I say, thinking to turn the conversation back toward Compatibility, what Komla might have known or whom.

He chuckles. "It didn't feel like work at the time."

Back at my desk I run assorted Google searches for a first-generation matchmaker called Compatibility. All I get are links to extant matchmakers, each claiming to be more prescient than all the others in identifying the love of my life for me. I close the browser tab. At our final meeting, Sarah asked Komla what he thought of Soulmate's compatibility algorithm. And now we have capital-C Compatibility, one of the original dating platforms to marshal data to try to predict compatibility. Could this be what Sarah's story was about, the dating algorithms that underpin the entire rationale of matching? *Precision:* they work with the matchmakers to improve the accuracy of the algorithms. *Veracity:* we spotlight the instances where the algorithms fail, as in the case of Charretter. *Romantick:* unfortunately, I can't think of what they would contribute beyond a rabid denunciation of the entire enterprise. And none of this shows a connection to Murkstone Banderby, or to Iris.

I draw a box around #4. *Figure out what Compatibility refers to:* still to be confirmed. It ends up looking a bit like a coffin.

After an hour of being put on hold by various administrative departments, I find out what the deal really is with Sarah Reaves and the Columbia Journalism School. Sort of.

I end up being transferred to Graduate Student Resources, where I explain, yet again, that I am fact-checking Sarah Reaves's résumé for a potential employment opportunity and would like to confirm her master's degree in journalism from Columbia.

An elephantine sigh. "That's Alumni Records. Hold o—"

"Wait!" I say, panicky at the thought of being banished back into the purgatory of Columbia's filler music. "I already talked to them. They said there was no record of a degree, but it also didn't look like she

236

dropped out, so —"

"Then it's Student Records, not —"

"I also talked to them and they sent me here. Something about a special circumstance?"

The woman says, like she's doing me an unprecedented favor, "What's the name?" Some clacking and clicking, and then: "Hmm."

I wait. "Hello?"

"Leave of absence."

I say, in my best voice of mild consternation, "She didn't mention that to us in the interview. When did the leave start?"

May 1, so less than a month before the end of the spring semester, when Sarah should have graduated, and continuing until the end of this year.

"Did she give a reason?"

"No," says the woman, dropping the word like a stone on my toes. "Anything else?"

I thank her profusely, hang up, and cross out #5. *Check if Sarah really dropped out of Columbia.*

More evidence that Sarah hadn't renounced her journalistic career after all. Not only that, perhaps she had taken the leave of absence precisely so she could devote her time to whatever story she was investigating. On my imaginary suspects scoreboard

237

the numbers are really clicking up for Iris Lettriste. Except, without knowing what this story was and how Iris was involved, there's nothing I can call her out on.

So on to the last item: *#6. Talk to the Romantick about Sarah.* I open up the Romantick website, feeling a tad abashed, like I'm walking into a Flat Earth Society meeting. I can't find an email address or any kind of *Contact Us* form. How do they expect to grow their cult like this? Finally I resort to posting a comment on their latest blog entry, which is about an upcoming protest they're organizing outside Soulmate's headquarters in San Francisco. I say that I'm writing on behalf of someone who was investigating the matchmakers' compatibility algorithms, who went by either Sarah Reaves or Iris Lettriste, and ask if whoever spoke to her from the Romantick could get in touch with me. I don't want to provide my real email address, for fear of my inbox being spammed into oblivion, so tell them to email hapjackflappiness@gmail.com, an account that Max set up for me in college as part of some now-forgotten prank. Hopefully they'll still take me seriously.

I fold my list into a pellet small enough to swallow and drop it in my pocket. Now we enter the middle stage of the murder mystery. The low-hanging fruit has been plucked and sampled and discarded for being either under- or overripe. Enough brush has been cleared for the detective to see . . . well, at this point, more brush. But that's fine, because hidden in there is the mistake that the villain has made, the definitive answer to every whodunnit.

Every villain makes such a fatal mistake. The detective just has to find it.

XI.

Charles sends me a multipage email with the subject line *Matching industry background materials/suggestions for job search* and half a dozen attachments, reports about the industry with titles that all start with *Trends in . . . , Outlook for . . . ,* and *Future of . . .* I don't want to think about how he composed this how-to guide, in between being berated by his client and in lieu of spending time with Jessie, to help me land a job that I'm not interested in. I reply to express my epic gratitude and resolve not to make fun of him for the next month. Two weeks at minimum.

I scroll through the reports to see if I might learn anything new about the compatibility algorithms, the lying limitation, or capital-C Compatibility. Nope. Bar graphs showing the steady rise in the number of dating platform users over time. Pie charts breaking down the different ways in which people find their romantic partners. Bullet-point lists of the challenges facing the industry: government scrutiny and regulation, data privacy concerns, continued algorithm accuracy, cybersecurity. I read a case study purporting to illustrate all of the above, where Russian-backed bots created accounts with Let's Meet, were promptly matched up with real users, and began proselytizing that *Sesame Street* espoused communist principles. This caused some huffing in Congress about malignant foreign influences, but it doesn't look like any regulatory action was taken against Let's Meet.

I get to the last file in the batch. It's a review of diversity and inclusion in the industry, and I almost skip it; from my experience at Aurum Financial, any institutional discussion of such issues tends to be fluff, and not even quality down-jacket fluff but cheap synthetic crap. Good thing my guilt over the unnecessary work I made my brother do prods me into opening it up, because that's how I learn about Lucinda Clay.

The report consists of a series of interviews with industry leaders from minority groups, and the one with Lucinda Clay, senior vice president of innovation at Soulmate, is the most interesting by far. For one, she sounds like a badass. When asked about the early stages of her career, she talks about how she would walk in to a meeting and be thoroughly ignored by everyone else: "I was young — young*er,* anyway — African American, a woman. Of course people thought I was someone's assistant, assuming they saw me at all. Then I would introduce myself, and you could see all this recalibrating going on in the other person's mind. You've thrown them off. They feel bad about the assumption they made, or they're doubling down on their prejudices and thinking you must be here to fulfill the diversity quota. Either way, you can play them. I miss that time, actually. Not that it doesn't still happen, but . . . less so."

For another, she discusses the issues around the collection of data by tech companies in a frank, intelligent way. "Honestly," she says, "I think it's a Luddite approach to say companies shouldn't do it because there's a theoretical possibility they might misuse it. The practical reality is that the best way to make something better is to obtain more information about what it's like now and why, in order to figure out what we want that thing to be and how to get there." In the context of matching, one problem — as exemplified by the lying limitation — is that the matchmakers can't simply rely on what subscribers are telling them. "If you asked *me* what I'm really like and what I'm looking for in a mate, half the things I tell you will be wrong. We don't know ourselves that well, and our judgment is too often clouded by emotion or biases, by confusing who we would like to be with who we are. The matchmakers have the ability to collect data from multiple sources and synthesize all that to reach a deeper, truer understanding of their subscribers. Their algorithms can help us to make better choices about our relationships. In fact, it's my hope that, someday, they can help us make better choices about everything."

And, saving the best for last, when I get to her bio, I read:

Lucinda Clay joined Soulmate Inc. nine years ago as the founding head of Soulmate's strategic research division, Compatibility. Prior to Soulmate, she founded and ran a number of start-ups in the matching space. Lucinda strongly believes in the importance of mentoring and support for minority entrepreneurs. She sits on the boards of the Women Entrepreneurs Society and the Association for

Diversity in Tech. Lucinda holds a BS in psychology and economics from Harvard University as well as an MS in behavioral science from the University of Cambridge, where she was a Marshall scholar. In her free time, she enjoys cooking, playing with her Jack Russell terrier, and reading locked-room mysteries.

I wonder who her favorite mystery authors are. More to the point: Compatibility? Could this be a reference to the matchmaker Komla told me about, and if so, was Lucinda Clay one of its cofounders? It could simply be a coincidence of name. But Komla did say Compatibility was acquired by a larger matchmaker, and the timeline would fit.

I google Lucinda Clay, but I can't find any confirmation that she worked at a company called Compatibility. Instead I get the *Who We Are* page for Soulmate as well as a number of tech start-ups that she's an adviser to: SafeID, which utilizes AI and big data to monitor the risk of identity theft; Friend, which provides a personalized chatbot for lonesome people. I go through another page of hits. A conference last month where she was on a panel titled "The Implications of Predictive Technology for

Consumers' Default Preferences." An up-coming fashion-slash-charity gala; she and two other minority women who have combined professional achievement with contributions to the community will be honored. Another interview, as a distinguished Harvard alumnus; I learn, at least, that her favorite mystery author is Josephine Tey.

I look at the pictures that accompany her bios and some inaction shots of her at corporate events. She's a diminutive woman who wears her hair in braids and favors shades of green and blue for her wardrobe. She smiles with her eyes rather than her mouth. There's often an amused cast to her features, as if she finds all this posing for headshots and mingling with the matching industry's upper echelon quite silly but she'll go along if that's what she has to do in order to get what she really wants. To find us all romantic happiness, in spite of ourselves. I wish her luck in that endeavor.

For days after that damn spin class I can't climb stairs without aching. Becks is unduly amused. "Don't you cycle everywhere?"

"That's different," I say. "I make sure never to push myself."

I labor on with as much dignity as I can. At Veracity we're heading into what Komla and Becks call the winter high season. People get lonely thinking about the holidays, then they make New Year's resolutions, then they panic about not having anyone to spend Valentine's Day with. I follow a target through a supermarket to ascertain if he personally prepares the lavish meals he's been laying out for our client at his apartment. All the guy picks up are frozen waffles, tortilla chips, and a six-pack, and when he gets back to his building there's a van waiting by the curb with the logo CHEFLY printed along the sides. (I google it later — a start-up that sends Culinary Institute of America graduates to people's premises to cook special-occasion meals for them.)

For another observation, I gate-crash a party in Red Hook, in a converted warehouse loft with floor-to-ceiling views of the water and the Statue of Liberty close enough to make eye contact with. I wasn't meaning to, but it was just too easy: I followed a bunch of guests into the building, the door of the apartment was propped open, there were enough people inside to capsize the *Titanic.* In the course of the evening I do get a few questions about how I know the hosts. I say, "Oh, I play Ultimate Frisbee with Chad," and wave vaguely into the heaving center of the room, where my target is canoodling with the ex-fiancé she swore she had excised from her life like an overgrown toenail.

Both times I take pictures — that's something I'll never overlook again. And both times as I do, Sarah Reaves waves at me from the tent she has pitched for herself in the backwoods of my mind. *Come on,* I imagine her saying, *I'm counting on you to figure this out.*

Another text from an unknown number! I get all excited to see what Iris Lettriste's next move will be — and then I realize, oh shit, it's Rina.

She tells me I left what she calls my *snake robe* at her place, and I should let her know the best way for her to pass it back to me. I can hear the resolute whack of the ball being arced into my court. When I think about that night now it's as if someone dunked me in a sensory deprivation pool and shut off my higher brain function. All I remember is the taste of her mouth and that marvelous softness of skin against skin, salt and heat and density.

It's not that I don't find her cute. She has a very charming smile and clever Halloween costume ideas. When I asked what was up with that cardboard box, she told me she was Schrödinger's cat, one iteration of it. She got a friend to dress up like her and they flipped a coin to see who would get to live. But I could also sense how lonely she was that night, like she was standing on her tippy-toes to keep her chin above water, and I don't want her to reach for me just because I happened to be there.

(Which — I know, I know — is why people use matchmakers. So they don't end up with whoever happens to be standing around.)

Twenty-four hours pass. I can feel the socially acceptable window for replying to a text squeaking shut. I delete the message so I won't have to see it there each time I open the app.

A client calls, semi-hysterical about how either she's suffering from early-onset dementia or the woman she's dating — our target — is trying to gaslight her. "It said in Ella's profile that she taught English in Cambodia for two years before she moved to New York. I swear I saw that. I remember it specifically because I visited Angkor Wat last year. But when I brought it up she had no idea what I was talking about. She wasn't mad or defensive or anything, just . . .

confused. And then we looked at the profile together and it really wasn't in there! But I'm *so* sure —"

I interject to say that we'll look into it, mainly because I'm afraid that if she doesn't stop talking she will pass out from asphyxiation. After she hangs up, I do a term search through the target's Let's Meet profile and find no reference to either Cambodia or teaching English. I check my earlier verification notes: nothing.

When I report this to Becks, she says, "Did you check the target's cached profile?" like she knows better than to assume I would have done this even though a trained gerbil could have.

I have to wait a few moments for my heart rate to slow back down before I say, "I didn't know Match Insights keeps cached versions of people's profiles."

It doesn't. But Veracity does, for our clients and targets, for the duration of a case and, crucially, a one-month tail period after. "Assuming Squirrel has been keeping on top of his backup schedule." Becks pauses. "Were you actually sleeping with your eyes open during the orientation?"

I walk-run back to my desk and email Squirrel to ask, with fawning politeness, if he wouldn't mind sending me the most recent cached profiles he has for the handles Ella Train and Flora or Fauna.

It's almost the end of the day when he responds, and by then I've convinced myself it was a dumb idea anyway. I click on his email. No text, just two attachments.

I open up Sarah's profile. Her face smiles at me in forgiving soft focus, younger, un-made-up, eyes a little wide as if the photographer surprised her. Barely recognizable as the woman I met, deliberately so. I gaze back at her: What were you up to, Sarah? Then I scroll to the date and time stamp that indicates when this profile was last accessed.

The Tuesday following Sarah's death. Which means Sarah Reaves's profile was deleted *after* she died, by someone who didn't want people to know she was on Soulmate. Iris Lettriste? Mister Misfortune, the married ex? Some other nemesis altogether?

I sit back in my chair. Instead of the usual booster shot of adrenaline I get whenever one of my hunches is confirmed, I feel like I'm breaking out in hives from frustration. Here's yet more evidence that Sarah's death is not what it seems — but it's all useless! I'm no closer to understanding the who or the how or the why. It's been five days since

I started watching Iris on Finders Keepers, monitoring for any news of work that Murkstone Banderby is doing for the matchmakers, and waiting to hear from the Romantick. Nada. The silence from the Romantick is especially galling: Even the kooks are ignoring me? And all the while Sarah's death, and what she was looking into, recedes deeper into the unnavigable country of the past. I need to come up with some other way of cracking open this mystery.

XII.

At least verifying Lionel is providing some short-term gratification. There are no profiles for him in the Match Insights database, and based on Finders Keepers he's not lying to Coraline about what he's up to. His locations are limited: home, work, the bar in Prospect Heights where his writing group meets, a bookstore in his neighborhood. There's a random destination in SoHo that initially piques my curiosity, but it turns out to be the offices of a literary magazine called *Zinc Cabin.* From the chatter on aspiring-author forums, it sounds like a career trampoline with enough spring to bounce you up to the eye level of the pooh-bahs at the *Paris Review* and the *Atlantic* and, yup, the *New Yorker.*

I start to text Coraline to ask if Lionel has had any writing luck, but then I remember the way the topic of writing went down at Smorgasburg. Instead I tell her that, as fully expected, I've seen nothing so far to indicate he's cheating. In response she calls me and I have to spend an hour listening to how she and Lionel are arguing all the time now. Most recently, he asked if she could refrain from talking to him when she saw that he was at his desk, trying to write. "In this accusing tone," says my sister, "like *I'm* the reason he hasn't won the fucking Pulitzer yet, and so I said, *Are you saying that your boring short stories are more important than me?*"

She stops — Coraline excels at the dramatic pause. "What did he say?" I ask.

"He took his laptop and went into the bathroom."

"His writing means a lot to him."

"I know, but why can't he find meaning in something more fun? Whenever he asked me to read his stories it felt like he was giving me homework."

I open my mouth to suggest that she try reading more contemporary fiction, maybe avail herself of Lionel's *New Yorker* subscription. Except. That's not my sister.

After I hang up I wonder if this is an instance of a matchmaker algorithm falling short, matching two people who, over time, reveal themselves not to be that compatible after all. Or even of the lying limitation in effect: maybe Lionel, or Coraline, hadn't been entirely truthful about what they were like or the type of person they were looking for.

Then I recall what Coraline said about only going on a date with Lionel because of a mistake. The algorithm was right. Somehow that's worse.

I decide to cap things off by observing one of Lionel's writing group sessions in person. I sit at the end of the bar, across the room from the table that they're all squeezed around. There are five of them, including Lionel, ex-classmates from their MFA program. They hew to the Brooklyn-creative aesthetic: chunky glasses, tote bags, facial hair for the guys. The lighting is murky, which is ideal for my purposes, but I have no idea how they can read anything on the pages they're holding.

When they leave, Lionel walks with one of the women to the subway station on Fulton Street. I follow half a block behind. I can't hear what they're saying, but it's clear they're chattering away. Lionel seems transformed from the slouchy specimen he was at Smorgasburg. The woman is laughing, a lot, and in a way that makes me remember, suddenly, what Coraline said at Golden Phoenix. *And one of the women has been in love with him that whole time.* The scene makes me think of the Auden poem that should be the mantra of every unfortunate soul being battered about by the slings and arrows of outrageous love: *If equal affection cannot be, / Let the more loving one be me.* Maybe Lionel has grown tired of being the more loving one; maybe he wants to be the one more loved for a change.

The two of them enter the station. I turn around and start walking back to where I parked my bike. Fulton Street feels dirty and garish, overflowing garbage cans and neon signs, storefronts stacked together like crowded teeth. Suddenly I'm afraid for my sister's happiness. Should I tell her about this? I still don't think Lionel is unfaithful, but even if he isn't, there are any number of ways for things to fall apart. Jude Kalman, for example: things didn't fall apart for him and his wife because he started cheating; things already had, and Captain Bubbles was his massively misguided way of trying to deal with it. Now that time has scabbed over the scratches inflicted on my ego by our skirmish, I find myself just feeling sorry for the guy. So desperate for someone to whom he could justify himself that he would even consider seeking out Sarah Reaves, after —

Claudia. You embarrassing excuse for a detective!

The woman walking in my direction swerves away across the sidewalk like she's following the invisible skid marks of a car. Did I say that aloud?

I take out my phone, find the audio recording I made of my Central Park interview with Jude, and skip through it until I get to the bit I want. Jude's voice is low and dreamy in my ear, muffled by all the outdoor noise around us but still audible.

"If the lights were on I got to call her and ask if she could talk. If they weren't I had to drop this, never think about it again."

"Did you really do all that? Go to Iris's place and . . . ?"

(Ugh: it's always disheartening to hear how my voice must sound to other people.)

"I did. Except I didn't call, because I realized, what I said the first time, that was right. It didn't —"

I hit STOP. *Except I didn't call.* Even though, by the rules he had set himself — *if the lights were on* — he could have.

Iris was supposed to have emptied out the place more than a week before. So either a new tenant moved in during that time . . . or.

Back to my phone. Real estate records,

I've learned from my work at Veracity, are often a helpful source for cross-checking various aspects of a target's story, and by now I'm relatively adept at sieving out a person's residential history from all the information available through city government websites and broker listing portals and apps vying to disrupt the housing market. Or, in this case, the history of an apartment.

Sarah's unit is owned by one of those ubiquitous corporate landlord LLCs. It's not currently on the rental market, nor has it been since before the date of Sarah's death. One more thing Iris Lettriste lied about.

What was Caleb's mystery-novel writing advice? Have the killer leave behind an incriminating piece of evidence during their initial cleanup of the crime for the detective to pick up on later. But what if the incriminating evidence wasn't anything the killer forgot about? What if it was something they themselves were trying to find? Something that relates not to the *how* of Sarah's murder but to the deeper, underlying question: the *why*. Such as, perhaps, Sarah's draft of a story that would reveal something appropriately dastardly about the matchmakers and their law firm and maybe even Iris herself.

I toggle to Finders Keepers. Iris is in her office, as per always. Of course she wouldn't have been able to pack up Sarah's apartment in the time frame that she said she would. She's at work fourteen to eighteen hours a day; she leaves only to go back to her own home, a fancy condominium in Gramercy she bought a few years ago, and some nights she doesn't even manage that. She must have paid the landlord an extra month or two of rent, so that she could take her time, in meticulous, detail-oriented, corporate-lawyer fashion, to search through Sarah's apartment. She was there the night Jude went by. She won't be done until she's confirmed what exactly her sister knew and made sure she's destroyed it all.

Unless I get to it first.

XIII.

Fifty very sweaty minutes later, I'm standing across the street from the building where Sarah Reaves used to live. It's a beautiful prewar brownstone with a forest-green awning and stone trim and wrought-iron balconies. Actually, all the buildings on her block look like that; I could be in a scene from an Edith Wharton novel. I peep in through a lit first-floor window. Burnished pots and pans hanging along the wall, stained walnut cabinets, acres of marble counter space. I bet somewhere inside there's a custom-made dining table built out of reclaimed telephone poles and it costs more than a year of my rent. Everything is quiet, as if this street were hermetically sealed away from the interminable traffic roar of Third Avenue. I grew up less than ten miles from this spot, and if you had brought me here as a kid I would have asked you what country this was.

259

It's only now, suffused in the discreet, undeniable wealth of my surroundings, that I think to ask: How the hell could Sarah have afforded to live here? Iris must have been helping her out with the rent. On top of subsidizing her Strobinex prescription and potentially her Columbia studies as well? Unless Sarah's benefactor was Mister Misfortune. From what Jude said, Sarah was thinking of that man right until the end; it's possible he remained in her life in some residual form. Whoever it was, that person would know, obviously, that Sarah was on Strobinex.

I hit doorbells at random until someone buzzes me in, probably mistaking me for their food delivery. The inside of the building is old but well maintained. Sarah's apartment is — technically was — unit 3A. There are four apartments to a floor: 3A forms a right angle with 3B and faces 3D across the landing. On the wall above me, a security camera. Excellent.

3B's door is decorated with stickers of bats and ghosts and pumpkins, and also a magnificently abstract frenzy of a crayon drawing that could be the work of a very young child or any number of artists in the Bushwick galleries Max drags me to. The doors of 3C and 3D are both bare. A pair of women's rain boots sit slouched outside 3D; they look like something Coraline might wear. I channel Inspector Yuan, stroke my chin, and then ring the bell for 3B.

A woman opens the door. "Can I help you?" she asks, her tone calibrated to polite doubt. She's in her late thirties and has the plump, rosy look of an Alpine milkmaid, albeit a harried one. I can hear the high-pitched glee of a children's cartoon through the doorway.

"I hope this isn't a bad time," I say. "I was wondering if I could talk to you about Sarah Reaves."

Her face puckers like I pressed a suction cup to her skin and pulled it away, and I know that she's the one who noticed Sarah was no longer around. "I'm sorry," she says, "who are you?"

"I'm a friend of Sarah's," I say. "I was."

She blinks at me. I focus on beaming forth my petite, soft-spoken Asian femaleness, someone who could not possibly be a threat in any way. "Why would you want to talk to us?" she says.

I explain that I've been trying to understand what happened, why Sarah would take her own life like that, and I heard that Sarah's neighbors were the ones who found her, so to speak. "I talked to her sister as well," I add, "but she doesn't really want to say much about it."

A man calls from inside the apartment: "Mel, who is it?"

She glances over her shoulder, then back at me, and I can feel that something has changed. The mention of Iris. "I'm not sure how much we can tell you," she says. "We're in the middle of dinner." And then, like she's resigned herself to this outcome, "Do you want to come in?"

According to my mother it's a sign of good manners to refuse an offer twice before you accept, but who has time for that? "Thanks!" I say.

The woman, Melanie, introduces me to her husband, Doug, and their son, Brandon. *Middle of dinner* turns out to mean Brandon goggling at the iPad propped up on the table before him while his parents, one crouched on either side, take turns trying to sneak spoonfuls of mush into his mouth. "This is the only way he will eat," says Melanie, sounding vaguely apologetic.

"Gotta do what you gotta do," I say, although I'm judging them for letting their child glaze into a screen zombie.

"That's what I always say," says Doug, right as Brandon flings up his fat little arm in excitement at something in his cartoon and whacks the spoon out of his father's hand.

Melanie confirms she was the neighbor who called the police, and I indulge in a flush of detective pride. I'd figured that the Good Samaritan would be someone who, like Sarah herself, was around during the day, and the mother of a young child seemed like a promising option. "I should say I didn't know her too well," she says. "It's just that we were on the same schedule and after a while we started talking." Most mornings, Sarah would be heading out for her yoga class right as Melanie was bringing Brandon to his enrichment activity of the day. Sarah's yoga studio lay in the same direction as Brandon's music school and kids' gymnasium, and they often walked the three or four blocks together.

Across the table from me, Brandon is making mewing noises at the screen. Poor kid can't even talk properly and he's busier than a CEO.

I ask if Melanie noticed any changes in Sarah in the last months before her death. She tells me that, if anything, Sarah seemed happier. "The new medication she was taking for her migraines was really helping." Melanie stops, possibly remembering that this awesome new drug was what Sarah overdosed on. "Plus she was dating again, and it was going well."

"She told you that? About dating?"

"A few times. She said it was really working out for her."

I say, "Her sister told me she killed herself because she was still upset over a breakup."

Melanie glances at her husband, who is crouched on his knees with a roll of paper towels and a spray bottle of one of those useless all-natural cleaners; the spoon that Brandon smacked away had spattered a wide arc of mush across the floor. "Well," she says, "her sister would know better. Sarah never talked about specific relationships with me."

So much for finding out more about Mister Misfortune from Melanie. "Have you met her, Sarah's sister? Iris?"

Only after Sarah died: Iris introduced herself and thanked Melanie for her help. Since then, Iris has been coming over on the weekends to pack up the apartment and both Melanie and Doug have spoken to her. "She's nice," says Melanie.

Doug heaves himself to his feet. "She's competent."

I wasn't sure how Melanie would feel about discussing the day Sarah's death was discovered, but she talks like she's been making the rounds with this story at dinner parties. I can't blame her: I would certainly listen. Unfortunately her observations tend to focus on her own deeply traumatized emotional state and a generalized impression of noisy, urgent activity that sounds like the find-the-body scene in every police procedural I've seen.

"To think," says Melanie, "I almost didn't call." The way she says that makes me suspect she and her husband might have disagreed on whether she should. "I was afraid I was just overreacting and the police and ambulance and everyone would show up and everything would be fine. Although of course that would still have been a better outcome than . . . what actually happened."

A neat lead-in to my next question, about timing, because it seems excessively neighborly for Melanie to have started worrying about Sarah after only a few days, especially if they weren't close. "Overreacting to what?"

"Well," she says, "some of Sarah's migraines could be pretty bad. I thought she might have fallen or injured herself somehow. Especially after I tried knocking a couple of times."

Plausible, except that she was also just telling me how well Strobinex was working for Sarah. I wait. She glances at her husband again. "And about a week before that we heard her arguing with someone."

Aha. "In her apartment?"

Melanie says, with that same apologetic tilt in her voice as when she told me about Brandon's need for entertainment during mealtime, "The walls are thin."

"They were fucking loud," says Doug. "Sarah was, anyway."

Melanie says she and Doug couldn't make out what the argument was about, but Sarah sounded extremely upset. "At one point I think she even said something like, *Wouldn't it be better for you if I just killed myself?*"

"She was hysterical," says Doug. "And her sister was totally calm. It was bizarre."

My heart donkey-kicks the wall of my chest. "Sarah was arguing with her sister?"

"We think," says Melanie.

"It's the same woman," her husband says to her. "No doubt about it." He tells me that he recognized Iris's voice the first time he spoke to her.

"Did you tell the police?" I ask.

"I told them what we overheard," says Melanie. "At the time I didn't know that was Iris, though. I hadn't met her yet."

Doug says, "Wouldn't have made a difference to them anyway. A suicide is a suicide."

Melanie says to me, "They were in and out so quickly. I guess it was obvious, what happened."

Doug says, "Our super told me the cops looked at the security footage, and the only person who knocked on Sarah's door in the last three days before she died was a takeout delivery guy."

So much for that. I wonder what Iris and Sarah were arguing about. If my theory about Sarah's story — the matchmakers, Murkstone Banderby, some corporate caper — is correct, maybe Iris asked Sarah to stop investigating and Sarah said hell no. Given Sarah's readiness to co-opt her sister's identity for her own purposes, I doubt she would have held back because such a story would implicate Iris. In fact, that might have incentivized her. What if Iris then goaded Sarah into her suicide declaration, knowing her neighbors would overhear and present that to the police as evidence of suicide? Or saw an opportunity to commit the crime after Sarah made that statement? And, of course, Iris would be too smart to let herself be caught on the security camera. Anyone who could disguise a murder as convincingly as our killer has would be.

I thank Melanie and Doug, wave farewell in Brandon's direction — his mother tries to make him say goodbye, but he spontaneously combusts when she puts his cartoon on pause — and head back down the stairs.

I have to say I always considered it a cop-out (pun semi-intended) in the Inspector Yuan novels how everyone chatters away at the inspector whenever he and Constable Zhang come around inquiring about the latest mysterious death. It's a lazy way to get important bits of information to the detective and the reader: have someone tell them about the turbulent relationship the victim had with his youngest son, or about the overheard muttering between the couple by the lake on how best to drown someone. But now I'm thinking maybe people really do just want to talk about death. How close it got to them, and how, this time, it moseyed on by.

On the second-floor landing I take off my shoes and then tiptoe back up. I noticed when Melanie opened the door that its latch was the slanted type you can lever open if you manage to get a credit card in between the edge of the door and the strike plate. Most people would bolt that kind of door as well. If it's an apartment that you don't live in and are just clearing out, though, maybe you don't think to take the extra step.

I haven't done this in years — my Bad Influence Friend, Helena, and I used to break into her neighbors' apartments and move stuff around to mess with their minds (god, we could be such mini-assholes) — and now I can't seem to slide the card in far enough. I start to worry that Melanie or Doug will hear something and come out, which just makes my efforts more inept. I pull out the card, take a breath, remind myself that toddler feeding is a highly immersive activity, reinsert my card into the gap between the door edge and the frame, close my eyes. Bend and wiggle, as Helena used to say. Bend and wiggle. I feel something give and the door clicks open.

Sarah Reaves's apartment gives off the vibe of a small studio, five hundred square feet max, browbeaten into posing as a one-bedroom. I guess that's prime Manhattan for you. At least there's a row of windows overlooking the street, even if the blinds are scuffed and grayish like they used to be white a very long time ago. The walls are bare, but I can see, in the patchiness of the paint, the shapes of what used to hang upon them. Sarah must have been living here for a while. That, and the fact that Iris seems to have left all the furniture in place for now — Ikea classics mixed in with thrift store finds — makes me feel like Sarah Reaves is a scent that hasn't been fully aired out of a room.

I do an initial reconnaissance of the space, except all I'm seeing are the various places in the apartment where Sarah could have died. An overdose of Strobinex kills you by inhibiting your body's heat-production capabilities, in effect inducing hypothermia. And thanks to my clicking down an Internet rabbit hole while researching this, I've learned a few fun facts about what victims in the final stages of hypothermia do. Terminal burrowing, for one: crawling into small enclosed spaces. Like here, between the back of the couch and the radiator, maybe. Or somewhere in the bedroom — apparently people like to get under beds and in or behind wardrobes. Sarah might have been naked, too, or close to it. Another weird behavior, the brain like an embattled general who loses it as his siege walls continue to crumble, is paradoxical undressing, which is exactly what it sounds like.

Back in the living room I give myself a full-body shake, demon-exorcism style. Okay. I'll do what I came here to do and then get the hell out.

Unfortunately it looks like Iris has already been through most of the apartment. All the shelves and cabinets and counters are empty, and taped-up cardboard boxes have been stacked neatly by the front door. Crap, I might already be too late. There's still the bedroom, but from what I saw when I peeked through the doorway, all Iris was doing in there was sorting through Sarah's clothes.

I go in anyway so I can say I checked it out. The room is just large enough to fit a double bed and a bedside table and a wardrobe in the corner. The bedsheets have been stripped and clothes laid out across the mattress, sorted by type: coats and jackets, sweaters and cardigans, pants, dresses, skirts. Enough articles of clothing here to outfit a troupe of runaway nuns, and there are more in the wardrobe, along with a mosh pit of shoes. Sarah Reaves wore the same ensemble to all three of our meetings: dark pantsuit, cream blouse, black heels. Her interview getup, probably. It looks like her true fashion style, like her tastes in furniture, tended toward bright colors, thrift shops, and affordable mass-market brands.

I glance across the piles of clothes and I see — really? yes, really! — the silver matte rectangle of a laptop on the bedside table, next to a vintage banker's lamp. I didn't recognize it at first because it's partially obscured by something — a picture frame, looks like — lying flat on top of it. For an instant I feel as psyched as the day of my twelfth birthday, when I decoded the cipher in the missing chemist's notebook to learn the identity of her kidnappers.

But no, it's not going to be that easy. If Iris was searching for something that Sarah had written or her notes for the story, Sarah's laptop would be ground zero. Iris would already have removed all the relevant information that was on it. Unless Sarah concealed things too well.

I take a picture so I can be sure to put things back exactly the way they are, and then I pick up the photograph. It's of the Lettriste-Reaves family unit, back when its members looked delighted to be standing shoulder to shoulder in front of an uninspiring rock formation. Iris and Sarah bookend their parents. Iris is beside their mother, a fair, broad-hipped woman. Sarah leans into their father, who's one of those otherwise-thin men with a belly. I stare at their small, splotchy faces for a few minutes, willing a grand revelation to rise up at me like one of those 3-D images coalescing from a picture of dots. All that happens is that I feel my chest crumple. They're such soft, sun-dappled teenagers, the two girls in this picture, so clueless the way we all are about what kind of crap the world is going to dump on us.

I perch myself on the edge of the bed and power up the laptop. No password required, which conforms with the average home computer user's laziness but, admittedly, not the notion that this is a receptacle for secrets someone would kill to keep.

I take care of the most obvious possibility first: I search for any files that could be related to articles Sarah was working on about the matching industry. The closest I get is a subfolder titled *Stories — Relationships* with a number of Word documents in it. I open them up one by one. They each contain one or two questions of the brainstorming-session category. *DNA compatibility — would that affect free will? Implications of renting/ sharing economy — polyamory? communal? more transactional? all of the above?*

And: *Dangers of matchmakers' algorithms — emperor has no clothes? or self-fulfilling prophecy? or we lose something important in having all the work done for us?*

The file was created in May and last modified in July, before Sarah came to see us. Before, even, she met Charretter.

Here I pause. It's not unexpected that

273

there would be nothing more substantial; Iris would have deleted it. What's unexpected, though, is that Iris didn't delete *this* as well but left it coded into the laptop's hard drive, a marker of Journalist Sarah's interest in the topic.

I open up the web browser's history and scroll into the past. What was Sarah looking at in the few weeks before she died?

People's matching profiles. Mostly on Soulmate but also on a few smaller platforms like SwipeYes and Kismet. I try clicking on a couple of the links but am told I've been logged out due to inactivity.

Thesaurus.com. Words such as *privacy* (synonyms: *solitude, secrecy, concealment, confidentiality*), *predict* (synonyms: *anticipate, envision, forecast, conclude*), *taste* (synonyms: *inclination, preference, appetite, desire*), *avatar* (synonyms: *archetype, apotheosis, personification, symbol*).

Entries from the Romantick blog. One year ago: Soulmate covering up a massive data breach affecting more than a million subscribers; mainstream media and authorities bribed to look the other way. Seven months ago: A-List, one of the most elitist invitation-only matchmakers, selling customer data to Russian and Chinese secret services for blackmail purposes. Three months ago: Big Three matchmakers populating their own platforms with fake profiles to inflate subscriber counts. Seven weeks ago: federal government secretly funding matchmakers to conduct sociological experiments.

Menus on Caviar: a disposition toward Thai and sushi.

Serenity Yoga's weekly schedule.

The log-in page of a website called Dispatch.

Gmail: two accounts, with the usernames ilettriste and sarah.e.reaves. Emails to ilettriste have subject lines such as *Hello* or *Your Profile* — correspondence with her matches, I'm guessing. I try clicking on those as well but get the same logged-out message. Emails to sarah.e.reaves are largely about upcoming yoga workshops and bill payments.

I scroll further back, to early September, before Sarah Reaves came to Veracity for her intake session. Google search terms such as *Veracity LLC, Veracity matching, Veracity detective agency, Komla Atsina.* Looks like Sarah was trying to learn more about Veracity, and no doubt striking out.

Now I move forward in time, to the period between Sarah Reaves's death and the present. Upper East Side real estate sale and rental listings. Recipes of the one-pot or one-pan variety. TV show reviews. The National Institute of Mental Health's suicide prevention page. Housing Works's listing of its locations in Manhattan. The occasional piece from the *Wall Street Journal*'s business and finance section.

I shut down the laptop. Nothing in Sarah's browsing history about Murkstone Banderby or the matchmakers, Romantick conspiracy theories aside. Nothing suspicious in Iris's browsing history for someone left to deal with the material and emotional aftermath of a family member's suicide. A few musings on a potential topic for an article, consistent with Iris's view that Sarah had plenty of story ideas that she failed to follow through on.

I turn off the bedroom lights and go back out into the living room. Occam's razor. No explosive investigation into the matchmakers, no carefully planned sororicide.

But the fact remains: Iris Lettriste lied and lied again. Why?

And right then, like I called aloud to her and she's answering, I hear, muffled but unmistakable: "— take a look and let me know what you think."

My surroundings zoom back into focus

around me like I've crash-landed onto the scene. More noises, vibrating in from the other side of the front door. A different voice, all smooth deep notes, and the metallic jangle of keys.

Oh, shit.

The lock clicks. Okay. What would Inspector Yuan do?

XIV.

In *Inspector Yuan and the Jade Dragon,* the inspector — who's not above the odd covert maneuver — sneaks into a suspect's house in search of stolen jewelry. Instead he finds, in the man's study, a half-written political tract calling for the overthrow of the current emperor. He becomes so absorbed in reading it that he fails to notice the owner's untimely return until the guy is practically walking into the room. (Constable Zhang, whose assigned task is to keep the suspect away from the house for the two candles' length required for Inspector Yuan to complete his investigation, has disappointed yet again.) In the second before the suspect enters, Inspector Yuan somersaults up to the ceiling rafters and flattens himself upon them — the inspector is a master of *qinggong.*

I, on the other hand, am not, so I yield to gravity in lieu of defying it: I flatten myself on the floor under Sarah Reaves's bed. I really, really hope this wasn't where she crawled to die. Probably not, given how it's dusty enough down here to sabotage a Roomba. Once I think that I start worrying I'll sneeze, and once I think *that* my sinuses start itching like they're being teased by a phantom feather. I try to focus on listening to what Iris Lettriste and whoever she's with — a man, from the pitch of his voice — are doing in the living room. Is she concerned about the lights being on? It doesn't seem like it; I can't hear their conversation, but their voices are all soft curves, no edges. She probably figures she forgot on her last visit.

"This is the bathroom," she says, close enough now for the sound-fog of her voice to clarify into meaning. After a moment she adds, "It's small," the acknowledgment of an unfortunate fact.

"Old building," says the man.

I turn my left cheek to the floor so I'm facing the doorway. The way their legs are silhouetted against the light outside and cut off from the knee up, I feel like I'm looking at a single ungainly four-legged creature. There's a click and the room brightens, and the quadruped is replaced with two sets of professionally attired human legs.

"Bedroom," says Iris. "Also small."

"But a large window," says the man. "That could make a difference." His voice makes me think of brass plate, burnished but insincere. It's clear that he's here in some professional capacity.

"Do you really think so?"

"It's important to some people."

I watch the pair of leather loafers move across my vision, to the far corner of the room. After a moment the heels follow.

Iris: "The window doesn't close properly. I'll have to get that fixed."

The man: "Nice view."

"It is. Especially in the spring, with all the flowers in the trees . . ." Iris pauses and I know, like there's a wire strung between us and it's pulled taut, that she's thinking of her sister. In what way, though?

As they leave the room Iris says, "Do you think we can put this on the market next week? I'll need to have the proceeds in hand before I close on the new place."

"I'll see if I can get our photographer in this weekend," says the man. "How aggressive do you want to be on the opening price? Things are getting better for sellers, but it's still a buyer's market." I can't make out Iris's reply.

The front door thumps closed. I flop out

across the floorboards, beached on the shore of my relief like the world's dustiest whale. I'll give it another five minutes, just in case one of them forgot something and they need to come back in. I've learned from multiple Inspector Yuan mysteries that whenever you're hiding from someone and you think they have left, they'll walk back into the room, or cave, or forest clearing, right as you squiggle yourself out from your secret spot.

The man sounded like a real estate broker, and they were talking about selling. Which means: Iris owns this unit? I suppose she could easily have structured her ownership through a company. That would explain how Sarah was able to live here, if her sister let her stay rent-free or at a discount.

And as the owner, Iris would have her own set of keys. She could have gone into her sister's home at any time. Maybe she didn't show up on the security camera in the three days before Sarah died because she had done all her tampering in advance. *That* would explain why — and here's yet another lie — she pretended to me that Sarah had been renting her place from a third party.

The darkness presses in like someone wrapped a fist around me and squeezed. *See,* it seems to be saying, even though I can't see anything at all, not even my hand starfished on the floor right in front of me, *how easy it would be to vanish.*

Has it been five minutes? What the hell.

As I'm doing my best sucky impression of an army crawl out from under the bed my foot hits something. I hear it scrape-skid across the floor. When I turn on the light I see that it's a phone. My heart, already metronoming at presto from the exertion, kicks it up to prestissimo. Sarah Reaves's phone? Holy shit, this could be huge!

The phone is an older iPhone model, and it's seen its share of action. The screen is cracked, the case scuffed up. It doesn't turn on; it must have drained out of battery weeks ago. I heft it in my hand. I'm guessing Sarah dropped it and somehow knocked it under the bed, and that it happened pretty soon before she died because otherwise she would have searched for it and found it.

I stand next to Sarah's bed, next to her piles and piles of clothes, and I imagine a line before me. Really I've been sidling toward it all this while, ever since I started looking into Sarah's death, hoping I'll find the answers before I get right up to it, and now here I am. I can still step back. Push the phone back under the bed for Iris to find when she moves out the furniture.

Delete Iris and Jude from Finders Keepers. Recycle the receipt on which I've written my list. Not magnify this offense of breaking and entering into burglary. Never find out the truth about Sarah Reaves.

I slide the phone into my pocket. Or I can step across.

When I try to let myself out, I discover that the dead bolt has been drawn. Iris double-locked the front door on her way out. So she was suspicious about the lights being on after all — but not shocked. And if I don't want her to figure out that someone without a key has been inside the apartment in between her visits, I'll need to find another exit route.

I retreat back into the bedroom, to the window that Iris and Smooth Voice were admiring the view from. I look out at veiled squares of light, like minimalist canvases hung against a vast wall of black, and empty trees. The feathery patterns of the tree branches make me think of diagrams of the heart in biology textbooks, all those complex networks of arteries devoted to keeping us alive. I can feel the draft coming in from the bottom of the window. Why not? I shove the windowpane up as high as it will go, which is high enough for me, at five feet four and a hundredish pounds, to scooch out onto the fire escape. I look down. The world through the iron slats beneath my feet is sliced up into gray and black wafers, abstract and vertigo inducing. I look back up and tell myself I will not discover now that I have a fear of heights.

I close the window. It seems to slide shut all the way, but there's a hairline gap between its bottom edge and the sill. This could also be why the security footage didn't pick up anyone.

The only tricky bit comes when I need to figure out how to get myself from the bottom of the fire escape onto the ground. Finally I climb over the railing, reminding myself that I'm one floor up from the ground, and so even if I mess up, which I'm not going to, I won't die. I let myself hang from the floor slats monkey-bars style and drop.

It's only when I straighten up that I see there's someone a few feet away staring at me. Should I run? He walks closer, an old man with fluffy white hair and a matching poodle. "Are you all right?" he says. "What on earth were you doing up there?"

Thank god for the petite, soft-spoken Asian female superpower. "Oh," I say, "it's part of this . . . workout routine."

His face pinches and I wait for him to tell

me I'm obviously lying. He says, "You shouldn't be doing anything that reckless."

"It's really good for the core," I assure him, which is what Coraline is always saying about the latest bizarre workout she's become obsessed with.

He shakes his head. "You young people," he says as he walks away. "You all think you'll live forever."

XV.

In the morning both Sarah's phone and I are all charged up. On my part it's some extravaganza of anxiety — did I really break into Sarah's apartment, hide from her sister, and steal her phone? — exhilaration — I *did* really break into Sarah's apartment, hide from her sister, and steal her phone! — the kind of exhaustion that fuzzes up all your senses, and anticipation. This could be it. The mystery of Sarah Reaves solved.

Of course it isn't, and would never have been except in the bestest-case scenario where Sarah didn't believe in phone passwords and was the recipient of messages from her would-be killer detailing how they were planning to kill her and why. As with most things in life, I get some kind of could-be-worse situation. The phone is locked, but app notifications show up on the lock screen. I scroll for a few minutes without seeing any bloodied daggers, as Inspector

Yuan would say, but there are several hundred more to get through, and I can already tell I'll have to go slow to make sure I don't miss anything relevant amid the flotsam of Facebook and Instagram and Twitter updates. (One of the side effects of this hyper state, apparently, is that I start mixing my metaphors like a psychotic bartender.)

Soon after I get to Veracity, Becks goes into Komla's office for one of their everyone-but-Claudia catch-ups. I open up Finders Keepers on my monitor screen for cover and resume reviewing Sarah's phone notifications under my desk.

Among the final messages that Sarah received are three texts, in the week or so after she died, from a number she had saved as *When Will I Delete This?,* checking in after Sarah missed their scheduled meeting. From the contact name alone I would guess that this is Mister Misfortune. The tone of the messages makes me certain of it. The first one: *I've been waiting here for an hour. If you're not planning to come, could you let me know?* The second one, a day later: *I'm sorry if I sounded snippy, it was just that I had to move some things around to make that time slot work. I hope* — (The text preview ends, and I feel like someone snatched the final incriminating page of a letter out of my hands.) Several days later: *I respect your silence. I'm truly sorry things ended like they did.* If only he knew the truth of that statement.

Unless . . . he did?

I read through the texts again. Assuming everything they say is true, Sarah arranged to meet Mister Misfortune two days after her death. It doesn't sound like they were in regular touch. Why would she suddenly reach out to him? Obvious answer: to ask for money, as she did with Jude Kalman. Maybe she hinted as much when she first contacted him, and he decided to take preemptive steps. That would be a clever touch, texting her *after* he killed her to create the impression he had no idea what was going on.

Mister Misfortune remains a contender after all. I take down his number and keep scrolling. Other items of interest:

A calendar notification that appears to correspond to the meeting with Mister Misfortune, and multiple calendar notifications of yoga classes that Sarah booked for the two weeks following her death. Incremental evidence that Sarah was continuing to plan her life past the date of her apparent suicide.

A notification from Moolah, a financial

tracker app, that Sarah received a deposit of $100,000. Jude Kalman wasn't lying after all.

Notifications from assorted matchmakers, including Soulmate, of new matches within Sarah's zip code.

A notification from Dispatch that St. Elmo has uploaded a file. According to Google, Dispatch is a cloud-based document storage and sharing service guaranteeing anonymity and end-to-end encryption. Aha! My matching-industry investigation theory is revived: if Sarah was indeed working on such a story, she must have stored it on the Dispatch server.

A notification from A Dose a Day offering Sarah a discount if she changes her mind about unsubscribing. That name is familiar. I start to google it — but maybe it would be more efficient to start a spreadsheet first, to log all these items and any notes for follow-up. Damn, look at how well Becks has trained me.

"I didn't realize we hired you to play games on your phone."

I glance up. The devil herself is walking toward me. I slide Sarah's phone into the pocket of my hoodie. "Sorry."

I'm expecting her to select another weapon from her arsenal of snark and flagellate me with it, but she just says, "Can you do an observation in thirty minutes?"

Any other time I'd be psyched — observations are the closest I get to classic detective work, and it's always great to get away from the desk — but right now I just want to be left alone to cogitate on Sarah Reaves. "Sure."

It sounds straightforward: the target has told our client that he's an economist at a research consultancy, but according to Finders Keepers he's hanging out in an Equinox gym in Chelsea during working hours. Becks wants me to provide a quick eyeball confirmation. I look through his profile pictures and then download two of the close-ups onto my phone.

As I'm leaving Becks says, in her usual disapproving tone, "Are you really going to wear your ridiculous animal hat instead of a potentially life-saving helmet?"

I turn around. It takes me a moment to realize I'm feeling touched. This must be her abrasive way of exhibiting concern. "It's warmer."

"I hope you realize we have employer liability for your poor decisions."

"I'll do my best not to land on my head if I fall," I say.

Outside I unlock my bike and pedal the

wrong way down Harrison Street toward the Hudson River bike path. The light turns yellow and I accelerate to make it across the intersection. I'm thwarted by a T-plate SUV pulling away from the curb with tanklike insouciance — and right into my path, forcing me to brake. Goddammit. I stink-eye the driver as I swerve around him. Of course, he doesn't see me.

I coast up to the crossing and practice my track stand. I like to imagine it engenders admiration in passersby, but probably no one even notices. The air is cold and bright. Sarah's phone swings in my pocket with my movements and I'm impatient to get back to it, to continue unpacking its secrets.

The light changes again. I push down on the pedal, still standing, leaning my weight forward.

The world flips over. I slam against something hard and for a moment my bones are luminous with pain. I try to breathe. Can't: no air in lungs. Try again. My brain is frizzing like I've dialed in to a staticky radio channel. Then it clears, and I'm able to tell that I'm on the ground. Okay. My bike is toppled sideways on top of me. Okay. I sit up and find myself scrambling away from it like it's an animal that might bite.

Someone behind me says, "Are you all

right?" A woman helps me up, peers into my face. "How do you feel?"

"I'm fine." I bend to pick up my bike, willing my hands to stop trembling. Whoa, light-headed. "I'm not sure. What happened?"

"Your pedal just came out from under you." She points and now I see it on the cobblestones behind me, still with its crank arm attached, looking like some sort of amputated machine limb. The woman says to the boy with her, "Dex, can you go pick that up for this lady? Watch out for cars."

"We're going to be late, Mom," he says, but he does it anyway. He hands the severed pedal to his mother and she hands it to me. I'm starting to register other facts. My palms stinging through my gloves, some achy action going on in the region of my hip, the leash the woman is holding and the shaggy, patient mutt at the end of it. Of course: she's a professional carer of small, vulnerable creatures.

"That must have been a jolt," says the woman. "Walk it off. Nothing injured, right?"

The warm, easy solicitude of her manner envelopes me like it could bubble me away from the rest of the world, keep me safe. "No," I say, and I don't realize until I speak how tight my throat is, and the pressure behind my eyes. I'll be damned if I start blubbering in front of a stranger because she was kind. "Thanks. I'll, um, see you around."

As I wheel my bike back to its usual sign pole the last of the shock burns away. Which means I now notice more things are hurting than I originally thought, like my left wrist, which pulses alarmingly every time I bend it, and also that I start to think, in a vaguely more lucid manner, about how this could have happened to me.

Because I brought my bike for a tune-up two weekends ago. If there was any looseness with the crankset, the mechanic would have fixed it. And I cycled five miles from Gowanus this morning, no problem. *And* I bought this bike less than two years ago, when I moved back to New York.

I think of Iris Lettriste walking up to me as I stood right here, about to unlock my bike. Iris telling me she's a cyclist as well. Someone who would be familiar with bicycles and what parts could be tampered with that would avoid detection. If it had been the brakes, for instance, I would have noticed right away. But the pedals. That wouldn't have been an issue until I put enough weight on them.

I think of the messages that buzzed in after I texted Iris my questions about Sarah, telling me to stop looking into this, that it wouldn't do anyone any good, including me.

I think of Iris coming into Sarah's apartment last night to find the lights on and locking the door when she left.

I glance along the now-empty street. If that SUV hadn't happened to slow me down, if I had been sprinting to catch the light like I meant to, I could have fallen that much harder. I press my hand against the top of my head, squishing the bobble of my knit hat. Without a fucking helmet.

Then I'm running back into the building and up the stairs. I need to tell Komla and Becks about this. All of this. I'm not Sherlock Holmes, who can topple off a waterfall and reappear three years later in consummate disguise, or Inspector Yuan, who has been practically resurrected a handful of times by now through some dubious process of acupuncture and *qigong* transfer. Crashing off my bike is more suffering than I want.

Becks comes out of her room right as I dash into the office, brandishing the pedal — which I realize only now I'm still holding — like an inept bicycle thief. "Why aren't you at the observation site?" she says. "And what the fuck is *that*?"

"I —" I say, and then have to pause for air. My heart is banging itself giddy inside my chest. "I have something to tell you and Komla." Many things, more like. "About Sarah Reaves."

We take our usual positions. Komla sits in the armchair that's tilted to face the door of his office. I'm in the other armchair, with Komla's potentially carnivorous potted plant drooping its fronds above my head. Becks leans against the window ledge, the third point in our loose triangle. And I tell them. About Iris Lettriste approaching me, Sarah Reaves's list and how it looked like she came to Veracity in connection with a story she was writing, Iris's insistence that her sister killed herself because of what she found out about Jude Kalman, the disappearance of both Sarah's and Jude's profiles.

Becks makes her cat–hair ball sound.

"Wait," I say. "It gets a bit more involved."

Waylaying Jude in Central Park and finding out that Sarah was blackmailing him. Being threatened by someone who sounded like Iris. Learning that Iris lied about Sarah withdrawing from her journalism program. Talking to Sarah's neighbors about the argument Sarah had with Iris right before she died, and then (deep breath here) checking out Sarah's apartment. Iris coming in with her broker. Sarah's phone under the bed. The phone notifications. Sarah arranging to meet Mister Misfortune, receiving the money from Jude Kalman, keeping an account with a service that sounds like Google Docs for the paranoid. And now: my bicycle sabotaged.

I stop. Both because I'm done and because . . . *I* did all this? Really? In a way, the bike incident is even flattering. Iris Lettriste wouldn't have felt the need to warn me off unless she thinks I pose a threat.

Flattering, and potentially flattening. Priorities, Claudia.

"Why?" says Komla. His tone is as opaque as his expression, which has not changed throughout my increasingly frantic monologue.

"I thought . . ." I say, and as I do it comes to me, the realization that must have been percolating up through my subconscious since last night's visit to Sarah's apartment. So far, I've seen numerous examples of Sarah's interest in matching-related topics. In Murkstone Banderby? None at all. Sarah's story angle wasn't *Elite Law Firm Helps Matchmakers Do Sketchy Things,* and Iris was impelled by something more personal than her career. Figures. The evil-corporation conspiracy always felt to me like a deus ex machina solution in fiction, rescuing the author from whatever painstakingly convoluted plot they were otherwise at a loss to resolve.

I start again: "I think . . . it was some sort of sibling rivalry?" The family photograph, facedown on the bedside table. "Which reached a tipping point." Except what could Sarah have had that Iris wanted?

"I meant for you. Why you took it upon yourself to investigate."

Oh. I open my mouth and then close it again. Why, indeed? It's not a question that ever gets asked in a murder mystery. The function of the detective is to solve the crime. "I wanted to find out what really happened." It doesn't feel appropriate to voice the rest of my thought: that I wanted, I *want,* to be the one to find out what really happened. To scrape away the shiny surface of the world that no one else even thought to question.

Becks says, "I want to build a time machine. Guess what?"

"Sarah came to us," I say.

Now I see a crack in Komla's face, maybe, a hairline one. "I know."

"She wanted our help," I say. "We can't

just leave this. Especially when we have all this evidence that shows she didn't kill herself."

Becks says, "But no evidence that shows how anyone else could have killed her."

Trust her to spot the chink in my argument and rapier right through. "Yet," I say, adding — surely this must pique their interest — "even if you don't agree about Iris, there's Sarah's story about the matching industry. Who knows what she was onto?"

"Also zero proof of any such story. Your mythical list aside."

I want to point out that the list itself can't be mythical if I saw it, by definition, but I should learn to let these kinds of things go. "She must have saved everything on Dispatch. And it looks like she had a collaborator — or a source." I look from Becks to Komla. He's the one I need to convince. "And that's the whole point of Veracity, isn't it? To establish the truth." Does that sound too pompous?

He shifts, almost like a statue discovering it has been animated. "You're right," he says. "Sarah's phone . . . do you have it with you?"

"Yes!" I say, and pass it over before he can change his mind.

He presses the HOME button and the

screen lights up. He scrolls for a few seconds, and then he stands and walks across the room to his desk. I glance at Becks. She's watching Komla as well. For once I'm not getting any telepathic vibes between them. It's as if one of them — both? — has cranked up the psychic drawbridge.

"So," I say, "what should we do now?" Go to the police? They would listen to Komla; everyone would listen to Komla. Although maybe first we should follow up on the other leads that Sarah's phone has given us: Mister Misfortune, St. Elmo. I'm feeling suddenly buoyant, even with the scraped palms and achy hip and rapidly swelling wrist. I should have done this long ago.

Komla slides open a desk drawer and places Sarah's phone inside. He closes the drawer and looks back up at me. "What you should do," he says, "is leave. You're fired."

■ ■ ■ ■

PART THREE

■ ■ ■ ■

I.

Thanksgiving has never been big on the Lins' calendar of holidays. Growing up, Chinese New Year was always *the* festive event of the year for us. I'd like to say it was because we were so tuned in to our cultural heritage, but really it was the *hongbao*s and our mother letting us stay home from school the whole week the way people do in China. While our father was still around we would gamble as well, heart-fluttery hours of poker and blackjack, because apparently that's how the Chinese get a start to their year. That was one thing he knew how to do with us. No doubt because he had a gambling addiction.

Thanksgiving is a distant third, after Christmas, and possibly fourth if you take into account the Mid-Autumn Festival, which at least features mooncakes and lanterns. Really we get together because of societal pressure: this is what an American family does. So we order takeout from Golden Phoenix and we eat it at our mother's place, usually while rewatching one of the six Jet Li *Once Upon a Time in China* movies.

This year, things feel especially unfestive. It rains all day, the kind of steady, soaking rain that gives the city the air of a crumbling cardboard diorama. My wrist still hurts too much to cycle, so I take the subway, which is slick with grime and smells like an oversize wet dog. Everyone is late getting to our mother's apartment, even Charles. Coraline won't stop complaining about the effects of the humidity on her hair. Charles says he's too tired to drive back out to Golden Phoenix to pick up food and can't we order pizza? Our mother is pissed with us for showing up late, but instead of calling us out on it she makes passive-aggressive remarks about how if she had known what time we would *really* be here she wouldn't have canceled her regular pedicure, declined a mah-jongg invite, et cetera.

Usually all this is my cue to be the goofy, upbeat one and bench-press the group mood from toxic to tepid, but this time, I can't. The best I can do is slouch in a corner rereading *The Bostonians* on my phone so I won't start telling various members of my family to just shut up already. Henry James is about the only author I can bear right now. I could do with some eloquent introspection and regret, and he's safely ensconced in the pre-Internet age. Also, his female protagonists' subpar decision-making skills are really resonating with me.

One week now since I walked out of Veracity. Actually, adding an insult to all my physical injuries, Becks walked me out, like they thought I might filch one of their precious wireless mice otherwise. The way Komla put it, you'd think I'd slashed and burned my path through entire protected rain forests of Veracity's policies. Usage of company property. Disclosure of confidential information. Contact with persons of interest. All of which would have warranted immediate dismissal, even if I hadn't also committed *crime* crimes like breaking and entering and theft. "The police," he said then, with a small sigh, as if talking about relatives he disliked but felt an obligation to keep in touch with, and I saw my already somewhat dim future flicker like the power had gone out altogether for a moment. But, he continued, he appreciated that my motivations had been well-intentioned, if misguided. He would offer me a deal. I would forget everything about Veracity, and in return Veracity would forget me.

I understood this was where I was supposed to say, *Thank you* and *What is this place and why am I here?* and *Goodbye.* I opened my mouth to do all that, but what I said was "What about Sarah Reaves? If she didn't kill herself —"

"You never knew her," said Komla, gently chiding, as if I wasn't paying attention. "You have never known any of us."

I have a couple months before I run out of money. I can't ask my family for help. I'd have to belatedly explain about quitting Aurum, they'd all take turns castigating me for my dumb life choices, and while Charles would Venmo me whatever I needed, he would be insufferable about it for the foreseeable future. Max would buoy me up for as long as he could, but he earns less than a Third World cobbler himself. So I should be stalking the jobs forums, except everything else sounds so dull now, so . . . expected.

I keep thinking about standing in Sarah's apartment, holding her phone in my hand, asking myself what I should do next. The line between what was real and what was fantasy. That fucking mystery. It made me believe there was something to be solved

306

and I was the only one who could solve it. I let myself think that I was the protagonist in some grand adventure, that I could be in any way special. And for that I forfeited what I did have that was real: I forfeited Veracity.

My mother. She sure knows how to call it.

Halfway through *Once Upon a Time in China II* Coraline disappears. At first I figure she's in the bathroom remedying some makeup defect visible only to her, but when she still hasn't returned by the time of the White Lotus Sect showdown, I start to wonder. I look around. Our mother in the La-Z-Boy, legs up, scrolling on her iPad. Next to me on the couch, Charles asleep with his mouth canted open. I'm guessing work hasn't let up for him since the last time we spoke. The bleached lighting of my mother's living room really brings out the grayish tint of his skin.

I get up and step into the hallway. The door to my mother's bedroom is shut, and when I crouch against it I can hear the sound of my sister's voice, hushed but with that shrillness that indicates she's particularly annoyed. Good god. Is she arguing with Lionel long-distance while he's back in

Michigan for the holiday?

I straighten. Coraline hasn't asked anything further of me with respect to Lionel. We met for lunch a few weeks ago, at her instigation, and I braced myself, but she didn't bring up his name once. When I asked why she'd wanted to meet, she said we should spend more time together and she knew I would never reach out so she had. My sister likes to say such things when we're both aware that we have nothing in common beyond genetic material and dysfunctional Lin family dynamics. In the art of inflicting guilt, she's our mother's most adept disciple.

But maybe Coraline stopped talking about Lionel because I didn't ask. And maybe — as in probably, definitely, why the hell didn't I? — I should have. I never mentioned to my sister, in the end, what I saw on Fulton Street. Lionel and the woman from his writing group, their ease with each other, the shifting of Lionel's orbit, perhaps, beyond my sister's once-formidable gravitational pull. I wish it was because I considered all the variables and made an informed decision, but, really, I just forgot amid all my Sarah Reaves–related antics. What if I had said something — could that have made a difference?

The door swings open and Coraline shrieks like she's the sorority girl in a horror movie realizing she's the first to be literally axed. "Jesus!" she says. "What are you doing?"

From the living room our mother calls, "Did you see the mouse?"

My sister and I look at each other. "*The* mouse?" she says. "There's a mouse in this fucking apartment?"

Our mother hasn't actually sighted one, but she's heard scrabbling behind the stove, and snacks she's left out overnight tend to acquire oddly crimped edges. She points us to potential evidence on the kitchen counter: a plate of the cashew nut cookies she likes to buy from the Chinese bakery down the street.

"Mom!" I say. "*We* could have eaten that."

"You need to stop leaving food out," says Coraline, "and throw all this shit away." She gestures at the dining table, its swamp of papers. "There could be an entire nest of them in there and you'd have no idea."

"I don't mind if there's a mouse," says our mother. "It will keep me company."

Which, for her, is just a practice jab, and the three of us learned long ago: if it doesn't hurt too much, let her have her fun. But now Coraline says, as if this is her first foray ever into the Lin family UFC ring, "What, because we don't?"

Our mother leans back in the La-Z-Boy and blinks like she's surprised by my sister's reaction. "I haven't seen you since Charlie's birthday."

"Since when do you want to see me?"

"What do you mean?" says our mother. "You're my daughter. Of course I want to see you."

Don't say it, I think right as Coraline says, "Is that why you dropped me off in Taiwan right after I was born? You wanted to see me so much you couldn't wait to get rid of me?"

"Claudia came to visit me last month. She asked Charles to come, too."

Fuck. I can practically see my sister swelling like some Incredible Hulk of grievance and resentment, except instead of green she's turning red, a rosy hue — it's Coraline, after all — that lights her up like Aphrodite in a Renaissance painting. "I," she says, imbuing that sound with all the magnificence of a wrathful goddess, "have done so much more for you than Claudia ever has. When you had that lung infection, I went with you to every single fucking doctor's appointment. I stayed with you overnight at the hospital! Claudia came to

310

see you *once,* for thirty fucking minutes."
More examples: when our mother moved into the Flushing apartment, Coraline spent her weekend helping her unpack, while I was on an impromptu road trip to Montreal with some Ultimate Frisbee friends; every year for the reunion dinner on Chinese New Year's Eve, Coraline will buy groceries and prepare the dishes with our mother, and I'll show up to eat and comment on how tacky the decorations look. More.

And what shocks me isn't so much that Coraline remembers all these incidents. She has an encyclopedic memory for certain details, like the provenance of every single item of clothing she owns, which, given that she could start her own clothing rental company, borders on savant-like. It's how all this has become a cosmic ledger of credits on her side, deficits on mine, the judgment clear for all to see. I'm feeling a queasiness in my stomach, halfway between food poisoning and period cramps, and it's because I understand now that a submolecular part of my sister might hate me, might always have, from the moment she and Charles walked into the apartment in Jackson Heights and saw, propped up by the TV, the photograph of our mother holding me at my one-month celebration — a photograph I personally have never seen and so half suspect Coraline of making up — and me scampering about butt-naked (again allegedly) in the living room.

"Well?" says Coraline.

"What?" says our mother.

"Aren't you going to say anything?"

Our mother considers. "You swear so much now. It's very unpleasant. Is it because of all this fighting with your boyfriend?"

I edge around the coffee table and kick Charles in the shin. He splutters to the surface of consciousness. "What?" he croaks.

"You know what?" says Coraline. "Fuck this family." She marches to the door, jams her feet into her boots, and leaves.

"What?" Charles says again. "We're not watching the movie?"

"Why did you do that?" I say to our mother.

"Do what?"

"Say all those mean things to Coraline."

She looks at me like she's trying, but not especially hard, to see who's on the other side of a pane of fogged glass. "She's right, you know," she says. "You never do anything for me."

"I —" I say. "I'm going to ask her to come back."

I catch up with Coraline just as she

reaches the elevator bank. For once I'm glad that the hallways in this building are so damn long. "Cor, wait," I say. "Don't be like this."

She marches across the bank and smacks both DOWN buttons. "Don't tell me what I can and can't be like."

"Sorry," I say. "I just meant don't let Mom get to you."

"That's easy for you to say."

"Come on. She does it to me, too."

Coraline rolls her eyes with such force I fear she'll dislodge them from their sockets altogether. "It's different. She loves you."

I say, which is all I will ever say to that accusation, "She loves us all." It's like the foundational myth of some scraggly little tribe cowering before a volcano. The world will end otherwise.

My mind warps suddenly to another family, another pair of sisters, and finally I understand what I've been missing about the photograph I saw in Sarah's apartment. Iris told us that their father chose her, brought her into the ambit of his favor, and left Sarah shut outside. The picture shows the opposite, literally. Sarah with their father and Iris apart. It could be a coincidence, how they happened to line themselves up when the photo was being taken. But I'm nothing if not familiar with the casual cues of favoritism, and the way Sarah was leaning into her father? She was the golden one and she knew it.

And if that's true, maybe the entire narrative was the other way around as well. Iris was the one who spent her life seeking approval from their father (law school, partnership, a worthy successor to his legal career), who begrudged Sarah her privileged position. Enough to kill her, though, and years after all the passions of childhood and adolescence should have played themselves out? (I realize I've taken a step back from Coraline.) Even Regan and Goneril only went after Cordelia the way they did because a kingdom was at stake.

I tell myself to stop. I will *not* get sucked back into the black hole of Sarah Reaves's death. What happened to her has nothing to do with me. It never did.

Coraline is saying she's tired of us, all of us. "Our mother is a manipulative bitch, our brother is a self-satisfied automation —"

"I think you mean *automaton.* Sorry, sorry. Continue."

"And *you* —" She stops.

"You can keep going," I say. "You're clearly on a roll."

314

She sighs. The doors of the elevator in front of us slide open. The young Asian man inside looks up from his phone only as the doors begin to close. I watch his face go slack with wonder as he beholds Coraline's visage right before it's sealed away from him forever.

"You don't deserve it. The way she loves you."

Her contempt shoves me in the chest like a playground bully. I guess I didn't actually think she *would* keep going. "It's not my fault," I say.

"Our fucking family," says Coraline. I'm not sure if she can't be bothered to respond to me or has just stopped listening. "That's why."

"Why what?" I can't seem to stop hearing my mother's voice beneath my own, like a faint discordant chiming: *You never do anything for me.*

"Lionel. He doesn't want any part of this shit. I don't blame him. I wouldn't if I had a choice."

I blink. "Did he say that to you?"

A few months back, says my sister, Lionel asked her why she and Charles had been brought up in Taiwan when our parents were already in New York by then. None of her previous boyfriends had ever noticed or, if they had, asked. So she told Lionel the truth. Our father hadn't given a fuck, our mother had been depressed and unstable after giving birth to Charles, our grandparents had had to take him away when he was six months old and they didn't wait that long when Coraline was born. The first time Coraline saw our mother was when she came home from school one day and there was a stranger in the kitchen with our grandmother. "I remember being really excited because I had gotten some stupid sticker on a test or something, and I ran around the house trying to find Grandma, and when I got to the kitchen this woman was standing there glaring at me like everything was my fault."

I say, as I've said any number of times over the years at this point in the story, "She was out of it. It's like two days straight of travel, getting there from New York."

"They never came to see us," says Coraline. "Or did anything to show that they knew we were there."

"If Mom didn't care, she wouldn't have brought you and Charles back."

"She felt bad after Grandpa's heart attack. Although I guess not enough to move back to Taiwan to be closer to them."

I don't say anything. I hate thinking about

our mother back then, because when I do, it feels like that scene in an Indiana Jones movie where you trip a wire and all the walls start sliding in on you. A useless husband. A city of concrete and filth. A baby who wouldn't quit screaming unless she was being carried. (Apparently I was a brat from the get-go.) And eight thousand miles away, in the same house she grew up in and couldn't wait to leave, two other children she knew nothing of and her stoically aging parents, waiting for her to abandon this foolishness of America, to return to them and fall at their feet the way a good Chinese child would, repenting all the ways she had disappointed them. Coraline and Charles might have adored our grandparents, but from things our mother has said to me, they don't sound like the most progressive, or forgiving, sort. Of course she couldn't go back to Taiwan. Although what did she become in New York, with her dreams and her degree in sociology? A cleaner of offices, a seller of women's shoes, a server of inauthentic Sichuan food.

Coraline is staring at me in that furious, twitchy way she has, waiting for me to raise my shield over our mother's reputation so she can continue to bash her mace against it. I say, "So you told Lionel all this and he freaked out? He needs to finish reading *Pride and Prejudice.*"

"What has that got to do with anything?"

"Mister Darcy," I say, and then I stop. Darcy decided he wanted Elizabeth Bennet enough to hold his nose around her family and everyone reacted like he'd donated a kidney. But we're in twenty-first-century America now, and the standard to aspire to is no longer the oh-so-generous toleration of one's social inferiors. Fuck Lionel Timbers if he really thinks his middle-class European-mutt family is better than ours in any way. "Forget it."

"Lionel used to listen," says Coraline. "To all that stuff. He wanted to." He was sympathetic, he was outraged on her behalf, he asked all about what it had been like for Coraline and how she felt about her parents now. "I never thought it could happen, but I ran out of complaints about Mom. I told him everything." Then Lionel left for his week channeling Thoreau with his writing group, and when he returned his attitude had changed. "Any time I said anything about our family he shut it down. Like he was done with it."

I have to say, this sounds like a classic case of Coraline hyper-sensitivity. The princess and the pea, in fact. "What happened to

318

your theory about the writing retreat, and that woman in his writing group . . . ?"

"Oh, right," says Coraline. "Isabel. I saw her again at one of Lionel's writing things and she's much plainer than I remembered. Plus she's one of those women who overcompensates with makeup, which just makes it more obvious that, you know, there's nothing there. Lionel would never be into someone like that."

I'm always a tad appalled at how candid Coraline's aesthetic judgments are. I guess if you live in a fortress you can fire off mortars at everyone else. "There's more to a person than how they look."

"Yeah, but Lionel has standards."

I hesitate, thinking of watching Lionel and Isabel on Fulton Street that night. Then it occurs to me. "You went to one of his writer events!"

She shrugs. "He used to ask me to go with him all the time and I never did. I felt bad."

My heart aches for my sister, for her reliance on the past imperfective, and how she's trying and it might not be enough. "How was it?"

"The cocktails were tasty." She pauses. "I don't think he wanted me there."

"Why wouldn't he? I'm sure he's happy that you're showing an interest."

She shrugs again. "I don't know. It felt like he didn't want me talking to his friends."

I say, "Whatever might be going on between you guys, I don't think it has anything to do with our family."

"So . . ." says my sister. "I wasn't snooping."

Oh boy. "If I were you," I say, "I wouldn't start off a confession that way. *The lady doth protest too much* and all that."

"I'm not protesting. It's the truth." According to Coraline, last week she picked up Lionel's phone thinking it was hers and saw two text messages from a name she didn't recognize, a Jennifer Lane. The first message read: *This family is so compellingly fucked up.* The second message, three minutes later: *Is her mother really that much of a villain, though?*

I'm not buying Coraline's purported inability to distinguish between phones, given that hers is clad in a Totoro case. But that doesn't change what she read. For a moment my insides feel like they're being fed through a shredder, and I'm however many degrees of closeness removed from this asshole and his opinions about our family. "Did you google this Jennifer Lane?"

"There are hundreds of them on the

Internet. All stupid bitches probably."

"It might not be referring to . . . us."

"So my boyfriend is texting about some other woman's fucked-up family with a third woman. Is that supposed to be better?"

"Or," I say, my desire to exculpate Lionel pinballing about in my mind, seeking a target to hit, "or they're not talking about anyone. Maybe it's a story he's writing. You know how writers always talk about their characters like they're real."

"According to him he hasn't been writing. Remember?"

I'm about to remind her that she herself refuted that statement when Lionel made it at Smorgasburg — and then those two facts snap together like newly magnetized opposite poles. I ask, "Has Lionel said anything to you about *Zinc Cabin*?"

"What's that? A home-improvement show?"

Of course he wouldn't have, not if I'm right. I ask when he's due back in New York. "Give me a week," I say, "and I think I can figure this out."

I'm expecting some kind of *thank god,* or maybe *thank you,* response, but Coraline squints past me and then says, "Forget it."

"What? You wanted me to find out what

was going on."

She continues to stare over my shoulder like she's watching someone approach. I glance around, just to check. This hallway makes me think of a conveyer belt, wide and interminable, except carpeted in a shade of beige that preserves every single stain ever inflicted upon it like fossils in amber. Someone is cooking — someone is always cooking, fogging the air with the odors of wok-fried garlic and fish sauce and sesame oil, occasionally to the extent of setting off the hallway smoke detector. Coraline and I like to joke that she could never bring Lionel here because his olfactory system wasn't hardy enough. *Liked* to. We stopped joking about Lionel a while ago.

The other day, says Coraline, she thought of this sweet thing Lionel did for her, shortly after they started living together. She had left her phone at home, and during his lunch break Lionel went back into Williamsburg to retrieve it and then up to Columbus Circle to give it to her. Except he didn't tell her what he was doing, and she was all pissy from phone separation anxiety and the underwhelming results of her latest marketing campaign, so when she heard he was at the reception she told him to stop being so needy and go the hell away. "I felt so bad afterward," she says, "but he didn't mind." He bought her a cone from a hipster ice-cream cart on Central Park West, and they walked through the park pretending they were tourists.

"I said to him," says my sister, "that I'd been all fizzy with happiness ever since we met. Like a can of soda that's been shaken too much and if you try to open it, it will explode. He said that was a wonderful image and he would have to use it in one of his stories." She remembers how he laughed when he spoke, the light speckling across his face as they walked beneath the summering trees. She should have seen, right then, she says to the invisible audience behind me. The danger. No one was meant to be so happy.

II.

How I spend the week following my debacle of a Thanksgiving: staking out Charlene's, the Prospect Heights bar where Lionel's writing group meets. On Wednesday evening they show up. My original plan is to confront Lionel in front of his friends, but as I'm trailing them out of the bar at the end of their session, I hear them talking about a book launch they'll be attending the next day. A debut novelist who graduated from their program a few years before them. I decide I'll hold out for the bigger audience. I'm hunting the Lion once again, and this time I intend to shoot to kill, or at least fatally embarrass.

The following evening I'm in Bushwick at Quixotic Books, the one lighted window on a block of boarded-up storefronts. The back wall of the store is covered with a mural of that famous scene from *Don Quixote,* the time-out-of-joint knight and his sidekick tilting at windmills. A large display table features titles recommended by the store's employees. I pick up a book at random, to enjoy the texture of its cover and the heft of it in my hands. When I flip through the pages that new-paper scent whiffs up at me and I briefly reconsider my allegiance to the e-reader.

I timed my arrival to be ten minutes late, but when I get there the event hasn't started and no one seems fussed about it. Writers. The two rows of folding chairs set up in the back of the store are empty, and the author — I ID her, barely, from the publicity shot on her website — is chilling at one side with a few other people. I recognize one of the guys from Lionel's writing group — and Isabel. That *is* a lot of makeup.

Things get under way, finally. Someone from the bookstore introduces the author, Suzanna Cratchett, as an exciting new voice, and recites a list of prizes and fellow-ships that she's been nominated or short-listed for. Suzanna thanks everyone for coming and says, high-pitched and with a lot of hair swishing, that she'll read from the scene where Kirsten, her protagonist — a young woman from Minnesota who relocates to New York to pursue her dream of being a writer, and swishes her hair around when she's nervous — has an epiphany about the novel she's failing to write while smoking pot on her fire escape. There's an accent of astonishment in Suzanna Cratchett's voice, like she can't believe people are actually sitting here listening to her blather on about this thing she made up, and it endears her to me. Unfortunately I can't say the same about her book, which I tried to speed-read last night and gave up on after two chapters of exquisitely written, emotionally astute observations about teenage Kirsten's tormented inner life as she waits for the boy she's crushing on to call her. (Spoiler: he doesn't.)

After the Q&A, the audience gets up from their chairs and resumes chatting. A table clinky with bottles of alcohol is unveiled, and the decibel level of the room exponentially increases shortly thereafter. I skulk about in the graphic novels section, from where I can observe Lionel. He looks relaxed and well scrubbed, like he recently emerged from a bubble bath of confidence. I couldn't tell in the bar's dim lighting, but he's grown out his facial hair into a neatly trimmed stubble situation. I wonder what Coraline thinks. She's always preferred clean-shaven guys.

I wait for him to step over to the drinks

table for a refill and come up behind him. "Hey, Lionel!" I say like I just spotted him.

When he turns he gapes at me for a moment. "Claudia! What are you doing here?"

"The same thing you are," I say. "Attending this reading."

"Really?"

"Yes. I've been known to read a book every now and then."

His face eases into a smile. "You know I didn't mean it that way. I just didn't think this would be your kind of book." He sotto voces: *"Nothing happens."*

Despite myself I smile back: that has been my feedback on every single book he has recommended to me. Goddammit, I forgot how much I like the guy. *"But it's beautifully written,"* I say, which is his standard rejoinder.

"It is." He shakes his head. "Such gorgeous sentences. Here, I'll introduce you to her."

Suzanna Cratchett is in the midst of recounting some anecdote to a small congregation, but Lionel just swings up and says, "Congratulations! You were amazing." Instead of being pissed, she squeals, "I'm so glad you made it!" and hugs him like they're at a ten-year reunion. I guess that's what it's like to move through the world as a tall, blond, good-looking man. Coraline acts the same way, but she's always hyperaware of the effect that her beauty has on others. I don't think Lionel even registers the way he gets treated, and I don't think I've fully understood that until now.

"This is my friend Claudia," he says. "She's a fan."

Suzanna beams at me. "Thank you!" she says. "It's so awesome to hear that people outside my group of three friends have read the book."

"It's beautifully written," I say.

Lionel says, "I heard the *Times* is reviewing it."

"Oh my god," says Suzanna. "I'm so nervous I could barf."

Everyone else talks for a few minutes about how wonderful Suzanna's success is, how much she deserves it, how delighted they are for her. Then Suzanna says to Lionel, "I should congratulate you as well. Landing a story in *Zinc Cabin.*"

He gives her the *aw shucks* smile. "They probably confused me with someone else. Somewhere out there a Tionel Limbers is waiting to hear back from *Zinc Cabin* on his Great American Story."

I say, "Lionel, are you getting a story published?"

"Next month," he says.

"What?" I say. "I can't believe you didn't tell me!"

"It's not a big deal."

"It's a huge deal," someone says. "*Zinc* fucking *Cabin,* dude."

"What's the story about?" I ask.

Lionel shrugs. "A family."

"You can do better than that."

Someone else — Isabel — says, "It's so good. We read several drafts of it in workshop."

"Does anything happen?" I ask.

She frowns at me. Her long face has a mournful cast to it that makes me think of a basset hound. But I might just be biased.

"I was just wondering. Lionel tends to write stories in which nothing happens."

Lionel says, smiling so broadly his cheekbones might fracture, "Claudia calls it like it is." He glances around. "Are we still going to a bar after this?"

"Plenty of things happen," says Isabel. "But that's just plot." She says that like plot is the crutch that weaker writers use to hoist themselves along. "What matters in the story is the emotional worlds of the characters."

"Wait," I say. "Is this the story about the mother who leaves her children behind in

China and then brings them over to the U.S. several years later?"

"You've read it, then," says Isabel. She sounds disappointed that Lionel would share his literary masterpiece with a pleb like me.

I look at Lionel. He's watching me like he's just noticed a stick of dynamite peeping out from the collar of my hoodie.

"No," I say. "My sister . . ."

I expect Lionel to try to head me off, but he remains freeze-framed. There's a subsiding in my chest, the tide pulling out and out. Isn't revenge supposed to be fucking awesome? This can't be how the *wuxia* hero feels as he's preparing to crack open the skull of the man who betrayed his family.

I say, "I heard about it from my sister."

Lionel calls my name as the door of Quixotic Books bangs shut behind me. I keep going for a few steps and then turn around. He stops where he is on the sidewalk, as if there's some invisible blockade preventing him from getting any closer.

"What?" I say.

"Did Coraline really tell you?"

"She doesn't know. Not yet."

"Then how did you . . ."

I say it started with the way he acted at

Smorgasburg, his evasiveness about his writing, and then hearing from Coraline, later, how his attitude toward our family seemed to change after he returned from his writing retreat. "I thought maybe the two were connected," I say. "It was a guess." Albeit pretty much confirmed: after talking to Coraline I checked the masthead page of the *Zinc Cabin* website and saw a Jennifer H. Lane listed as its fiction editor.

He makes a turtle-retracting-into-its-shell-type motion with his head. "I never meant to hurt her."

The way he says that — apologetic, sure, but also like he couldn't help any of it — really pisses me off. I say, "Then you shouldn't have tricked her into telling you all those things about our family so you could write us into your fucking stories."

"I didn't trick her," he says. "I asked because I wanted to understand her. Because I loved her."

That last sentence sinks between us, dragged down by the hard weight of the past tense. I say, "But you don't . . . anymore?"

After a moment he says, "I do. But I'm not sure if we're right together."

I say, "You're not. She should be with someone better."

We watch each other, our breaths

locomotive-puffing white into the haloed night air. Lionel's not wearing his coat, just a flannel shirt with the sleeves rolled up. I think of Sarah Reaves and hypothermia. Sarah goddamn Reaves, still not leaving me alone. Lionel might be a bastard, but I don't want his frozen corpse on my hands. I'm about to tell him to go back inside when he says, "Someone who doesn't mind that everything has to be about her?"

"If you mean that," I say, "you don't really know my sister."

"Of course I know her," he says. "I know that she's completely uninterested in what's important to me. I know that she never hangs out with my friends because she sees the world as a high school cafeteria and they'll never be cool enough for her." His words wisp up and away. "I know the reason she loves me is because I'm nicer to her than anyone else she's dated. And, for a while, all that was okay."

I wish I could tell him he's wrong, that everything he said is a vicious distortion of who Coraline is, but — fuck. I guess you can't always pick your weapons in your duels. "Then you also know what it means to her," I say, "what she told you about Taiwan. Our mother. It's like, it's the secret bedrock of who she is. Everything else is built on it, and she never lets anyone see that."

He doesn't say anything. He does know. That's why it's a good story.

"She told you that. And you took it and used it to get what you wanted. Which wasn't, I don't know, to find a cure for cancer or something potentially excusable like that. So you could be published in a magazine that no one even fucking reads."

He pushes his hair away from his forehead. "Capote —"

"If you try to compare yourself to Truman Capote I will fucking kick you in the balls." I wonder if the past several months of being around Becks is influencing me. "Also, the guy was an unhappy, lonely narcissist." Even if *Breakfast at Tiffany's* breaks my heart in a different place every time I read it.

"It didn't start out that way." He speaks so quietly I can barely hear him. "It really didn't."

"What if you told her?" I say. "About the story. You could ask her if it's okay." There's a chance, I think, that Coraline would forgive him. She's forgiven worse, although those men mattered less. "And also . . . how you feel. About the other stuff."

Lionel is silent. I will him to want Coraline to forgive him, and to want to forgive

333

her as well. That would prove they truly do love each other, wouldn't it? Two people with each other not because all their edges match but simply because they long to be.

"The issue has already gone to press." His expression is soft, unformed, as if until he spoke he wasn't sure of what he would say. As if he still isn't. "It's too late to change anything."

"In that case," I say, "I can't wait to read it."

III.

There's this trope in *wuxia* narratives. A boy — it's always a boy — wants to become the greatest martial artist of all time, so he travels to some godforsaken part of China to beg a legendary master to take him on as a disciple. He's turned away but continues to mope around outside the temple or cave or hole in the ground where the master has resigned himself to spending the rest of his days in atonement for some past tragedy that will continually be alluded to but never satisfactorily explained. In some cases all the boy has to do is survive the inhospitable elements. In others, the master issues him some ridiculous task, like filling a well by carrying water in his cupped hands from a river miles away or finding the one black grain of rice in a granary's mountain of white. He gets frostbite or heatstroke, blisters his feet raw from all the trips to and from the river, nearly goes blind staring at the rice. And finally, right when he's about to lose his mind, or his extremities, the master appears before him and utters some variation of *I give up, you pigheaded fool, come in if you want.*

I picture myself loitering on the sidewalk outside 11 Harrison Street, waiting for Komla to show up in his knit cap and boa constrictor scarf and greatcoat — he still dresses like someone with tropical bones — so I can ask him to let me rejoin Veracity. He would smile at me, detached, benign, and tell me he's sorry but I have the wrong person. And then he would enter the building, and I would be left standing there hoping no one had witnessed that encounter.

No. I'll need to offer up more than my grovelingly penitent self if I'm going to get back into Veracity. Which I am. Because I need to know the truth about Sarah Reaves, and I need to know what Veracity is really after.

Cycling home after my manifestly unfulfilling confrontation with Lionel, my face and my hands numb from the cold, my wrist twanging with pain like an out-of-tune banjo, heartsick for my sister, I couldn't stop thinking about deceptions. Lionel's and Jude's. Sarah's and Iris's. Mister Misfortune's. My own. My brain was churning along, angry and miserable, until a new piece of information got lodged in there and everything screeched to a halt. (Out in the flesh world, I had to jam the brakes to avoid careening into a bike path bollard.) Komla had deceived me as well. I remembered him saying to Sarah first that Veracity wouldn't be able to review third-party chat records and then later, so smoothly it felt like the current of the conversation had been flowing in that direction all along, asking Sarah what specific details we should be looking out for in those same records. I remembered his refusal to tell Iris anything — not why Sarah came to us, not even what Veracity was about — while asking his questions, looking through the documents Iris brought, forming his own conclusions. He was interested, from the beginning, in what Sarah was up to. Why she came to Veracity, what she was hoping to learn. He didn't take her phone from me so he could give it to the police, or return it to Iris Lettriste, or even toss it into the dumpster. He wanted it for his own investigations.

And if so, then there must be more to Veracity than I know, and I want in on that. Komla let me go because he wasn't sure if he could trust me, maybe, or he felt it was unsafe — especially after the bike accident

— or he didn't think I could be of use. Time to prove him wrong.

#1. Get into Dispatch.

The Zen-like simplicity of the Dispatch log-in page feels at once calming and taunting, like one of those koans that promise enlightenment through gobbledygook. Empty white background, two fields for username and password. I tell myself all I need to do is think like Sarah Reaves. Problem being, I barely knew Sarah. Arguably, I didn't know her at all. The person I met was Sarah Reaves's version of Iris Lettriste, with Sarah herself peeping through the chinks.

Wait a sec. I try *irislettriste* for the username and *floraorfauna* for the password. Nope. With caps? Still no. I try swapping them around. Still no.

I mouse over to close the website. What am I thinking? Of course I have no chance in hell of guessing this.

Except my intuition is telling me that, if this were a game of Marco Polo, someone would be yelling "Polo!" right in front of me. I just need to thrash around for a bit longer.

I type in *ReavesLettriste* for the username. I leave the password as *floraorfauna.*

The log-in refreshes: THE PASSWORD YOU HAVE ENTERED DOES NOT MATCH THIS USERNAME.

Whoa. Have I really just guessed Sarah Reaves's username?

I lean back and pop my knuckles one by one like a professional safecracker about to undertake the job of their life. Now for part two. It's possible that Sarah's password consists of a random set of numbers, letters, and symbols, the way all our passwords are supposed to, but I doubt it. She was a writer; she would have gone in for words. A phrase of some significance to her, maybe, or a string of terms related to what she was using this service for.

I find myself thinking of what Iris said about her sister's favorite childhood books. Why not? I google the series and try the title of the first book (*Eloise*), followed by the second (*Eloisein-Paris*). Dispatch informs me that after three more attempts I will be locked out of my account. Way to up the stakes.

I tap my fingers on the keyboard and think of the *wuxia* ingenue. At least his tasks were theoretically doable, given sufficient persistence and time. Here I have an infinite number of choices. Set me up next to a monkey on a typewriter and I'd still be guessing long after it has banged forth the entire works of Shakespeare.

But that's not quite right. I might have an infinite number of choices, but the right choice is, obviously, whatever Sarah decided on, and I can't help feeling like I should know what that is. The Plaza. Why do I keep thinking of the Plaza?

Of course. Not the book, the hotel — not the hotel, the stationery — no, not the stationery. What was written on it. And underlined.

Iris Lettriste saying, *I've started the book. It's called* Dispatches.

I close my eyes and visualize the piece of paper. The four words in a column, the lines dashed off beneath them. What would that give me? *pat — Precis — city — Roman.*

Two more attempts, says Dispatch.

I felt so sure! Unless I mixed up which parts of the words were underlined? I close my eyes again.

Comp<u>at</u>ibility?!
<u>Precis</u>ion
Vera<u>city</u>
<u>Roman</u>tick

I'm not misremembering. Sarah chose the letters within each word that would form

340

their own words. Unless she did that just for kicks, nothing to do with formulating a password to safeguard files about . . . what?

Then I realize what I overlooked. I type it out — *pat?!PreciscityRoman* — and click LOG IN.

Instead of instantly refreshing into another rejection, the screen goes blank. Has the website crashed? And then I see: it's loading a new page.

I let it all out like a fatalistically loyal sports fan whose team has just reversed a hundred-year losing streak. When I'm done jumping up and down on my bed and shouting about how awesome I am, though, I realize that Dispatch has just redirected to another log-in portal. What the fuck?

I peer at the screen. Because I have logged in from a device that Dispatch doesn't recognize, it requires me to enter a verification code before I can proceed. It asks me to select how I want to receive the code, via email or text.

"Come *on!*" I say. After I've cracked Sarah's log-in credentials in an incredible feat of intuition and memory? Even in *Inspector Yuan and the Melancholy Poet* the inspector got to enter the cave behind the waterfall once he correctly guessed the final line of the dead poet's masterpiece, no further work required.

I read through the message on the screen again. Email or text. To think just two weeks ago I had Sarah's phone! Whereas now —

Now Veracity has her phone.

I tell Dispatch to text the code to Sarah's phone. Maybe Komla and Becks will figure it's me, maybe not. Either way, I want them to know someone else is looking.

#2. Get ahold of Mister Misfortune.

Yelp! describes Contadina, between Lexington and Third on Eighty-Third Street, rather casually as an Italian bakery-café. It turns out to be a marbled, mirrored place with globular lights and snotty waitstaff, somewhere an Upper East Side matron would stop in for a post-Bloomingdale's lunch. At least it has pastries. I get a hot chocolate and a croissant and park myself at one end of the high counter that runs along the wall. It feels like overreaching to ask for a table.

When he comes in his face is immediately familiar, thanks to my having spent last night looking online through headshots of all the male faculty members who teach classes at the Columbia School of Journalism. Not one of the guys on my shortlist — which just goes to show what little I know about what straight women find attractive — but I'm still pleased that my theory about Mister Misfortune, and Sarah's reasons for taking a leave of absence, is correct.

He stands by the door and looks around. He's a genteel, rumpled man with an abstracted air to him, like he's someone whose interior world takes precedence over anything going on around him. When he glances in my direction I wave at him. He raises his eyebrows: *Really?* I raise my eyebrows back at him. After a moment he comes over. He pulls out the barstool next to mine and lowers one butt cheek onto it like he needs to be able to take off running at any second.

"I'm Claudia," I say, and look at him expectantly.

He hesitates. "Michael."

I don't expect to remember but I do, this man's face before me and the name below his faculty picture all syncing into clarity: Professor Michael Lindenberg. Damn. All that profile reviewing for Veracity must have helped me develop this skill, quite useless except under the present circumstances.

I say, "Thanks for meeting me."

Michael Lindenberg looks at me. His eyes are the palest blue behind his wire-rimmed glasses and nested with lines. His beard is streaked white, even though his hair remains dark, like age is colonizing him from the bottom up. This close, the force of his sadness almost topples me off my seat. So he did care for Sarah after all.

Which doesn't mean I should rule him out, not yet. To take my own liberties with another Oscar Wilde quote: any number of men kill the thing they love.

"What happened to Sarah?" says Michael.

A few days ago I texted the number that was the source of the messages I read on Sarah's phone. I said that the reason Sarah didn't turn up for their appointment was because she had passed away, suddenly, and I could provide more details in person. Yesterday I received a reply asking if I could meet at this time and location. A take-control kind of guy.

Now I tell him the official story: suicide, apartment, Strobinex. When I'm done he nods. "What was your connection to Sarah?"

I realize: he was testing me. "You already knew," I say. "How she died."

"I have a contact at the Office of Chief Medical Examiner." He takes off his glasses and rubs at his eyes like he's been staring at a screen for too long. "And the NYPD."

"I met her while she was researching her story," I say. "Did she tell you about it?"

Again, no surprise. "A little. That was why she wanted to meet. When she never showed up."

I let that statement settle, feeling a bit like a Puritan waiting to see if the witch will sink or float. I don't get the sense he's lying, but I do get the sense he might be a good liar. If he is telling the truth, then here's my confirmation that Sarah was chasing a story after all. The contents of which, presumably, are locked away on Dispatch.

Michael Lindenberg says, "Got to know her how?"

"Sorry?"

"Did she interview you? Bump into you at the New York Public Library? How well did you know her?"

"Well enough to know about you," I say.

After a moment he says, "You're evading my questions."

"What if we take turns?" I say. "We can answer each other's questions."

He shifts himself fully onto the stool and gestures at me to go first.

"What do you think about the idea that Sarah killed herself?"

"If you told me she had been murdered," he says, "I would find that less unbelievable."

All right, he's either the cockiest murderer

in the world or the dumbest. And if Professor Michael Lindenberg were ever motivated to off someone, I don't see him being either. He's a journalist; he understands the power of a narrative. If he had murdered Sarah Reaves, he would be raising the levees of his suicide story right now — *things weren't going well for her, she seemed depressed, I was worried, I wanted her to get help but she refused* — not digging away at them.

Michael adds, and I can hear how much the thought of it pains him, "But I suppose all that shows is that I didn't know her as well as I believed I did."

I don't say anything.

"What has any of this got to do with you?"

I tell him I work for a company in the matching industry; I can't reveal which one. Sarah came to us as part of her research into her story. She didn't show up for our final meeting, and several days later her sister contacted us trying to find out more about why Sarah had taken her own life.

He places his glasses on the counter in front of us and stares at them like he's prepping for a levitation act. "I'm surprised her sister wanted to know."

"Why?" I ask.

Everything he says only sharpens the picture of Iris and Sarah that I already have:

the sisters didn't get along, Iris disapproved in any number of ways of how Sarah was conducting her life, Sarah resented how Iris would use her own successes to magnify Sarah's failures. "If not for the situation with the apartment, I don't think they would have been in touch at all."

"Iris letting Sarah stay in her apartment?"

"Is that what Iris told you?"

"That was the impression I got," I say. "But I could have been mistaken."

"It was Sarah's apartment as well," he says. "It was supposed to be hers."

I feel like someone has pointed out that, yes, I may be staring at this picture, but have I noticed it's hanging upside down? "The one on East Eighty-Ninth Street?" That must be worth a million dollars, most likely more. "That's *Sarah's* apartment?" The possibility never occurred to me. A central piece of the Sarah Reaves puzzle is that money, like so much else, was something she needed.

"It was," says Michael. The apartment belonged to their father, and when he passed away he left it to Sarah. She didn't want to sell, but she couldn't afford the taxes and maintenance on it, so she reached an arrangement with Iris. They would own it jointly, and Iris would cover the ongoing expenses.

And now that Sarah is dead, Iris is the sole owner — and the first thing she does is put the unit on the market so she'll have the cash for her new place. Maybe it doesn't take a kingdom, just a piece of Manhattan real estate.

Or maybe that *is* the kingdom that's at stake here: their father's legacy, and his love. Playing favorites right up until the end. Could his death, and the apartment bequest to Sarah, have unhinged something in Iris?

I say, "What if Sarah *was* murdered? For that apartment?"

Michael, who's slouched into himself on his stool like a morose jellyfish, straightens slightly. "You mean," he says, "her sister . . ." He stops. I watch him considering this, turning it around, holding it up to the light. What a relief, being able to discuss the M-word with someone without either getting shut down or having them freak out.

Finally he says, "Why would Iris care about the apartment so badly?"

"It was their father's final gift. He always favored Sarah over Iris, and it was hard for Iris. When she found out the apartment was going entirely to Sarah . . . she must have felt that Sarah didn't deserve it." The words sound familiar — and then I realize they're a variation of what Coraline said to me on Thanksgiving: *You don't deserve it. The way she loves you.* I say, louder than necessary so I can muffle the memory of my sister's accusing voice, "Also, Iris is in the process of buying another property. She needs the money from selling this apartment to pay for that."

Michael puts his glasses back on. "Even if that's all correct," he says, "I had some access to the police report, and I don't see how anyone could have set this up." It was Sarah's regular medication. Her dosage for the day she died and the next three days were missing, corresponding to the amount of the drug found in her system. There were no irregularities with her remaining supply of Strobinex, no signs of force, not even any visitors to her apartment in the days preceding her death. "That's why the police were able to rule out foul play so conclusively. It just wasn't possible."

The illusion none of us can see through. My head throbs like I've been clonking it against an invisible wall. I know the truth is right there, but I can't see it and I sure as hell can't reach it. We sit in silence, our gazes skewed past each other. I picture Sarah's apartment. The crooked blinds, the spindle-legged couch, the yellowy mattress with its mounds of clothes, the photo frame facedown on the bedside table. No wonder Iris didn't want to look at that picture.

"You said her dosage for that day and the next three days were missing?" I ask. "How could the police tell?"

From the way the drugs were packaged, he says. Sarah used a service called A Dose a Day that delivered her medication to her. Each dose was sealed separately and labeled with the date it should be taken as well as any instructions. The box itself dispensed only a single dose at a time: you would tear off one packet from the dispenser slot and the next would pop out. "You can also set up their app to ping you reminders in sync with the labeling on the packets. It's all designed to minimize the risk that you'll forget or get mixed up about what you're supposed to be taking."

Except I saw that app notification on Sarah's phone asking Sarah to reconsider unsubscribing from the service. "She wasn't using A Dose a Day."

He blinks at me. "She was. I remember her telling me about this company. She wrote them up in an article, I think."

"But she canceled her subscription."

"She wouldn't have done that. She loved the convenience. And the report describes the packaging in some detail. It's clearly from A Dose a Day."

I hold on to the edges of the counter as a supernova of a revelation burns its way out to the far edges of my mind. This is it: this must be it.

"You've thought of something."

"It's going to sound crazy."

"Sarah being dead is crazy. It also makes it impossible for anything else to be."

I have to say I like the way he thinks. I run through my theory: Sarah's subscription was indeed canceled, but not by her. By Iris. That would have allowed Iris to drop off in Sarah's mailbox, for the month of October, what appeared to be Sarah's usual supply of Strobinex. Everything about it would have been the same, except for two crucial features: one of the pills was a fatal dosage, and the box contained only twenty-eight doses, not thirty-one. Sarah couldn't tell because of the way the medication was packaged, and when the police showed up the number of pills remaining in the box was the number it should have contained had Sarah actually ingested four regular doses of Strobinex.

"God, it's brilliant," I say, despite myself. "A twenty-first-century locked-room mystery."

351

Michael says, "Are you certain that Sarah's subscription was canceled?"

"I'm pretty sure, but we can call A Dose a Day to confirm. And if they do —"

"Then it wasn't suicide."

His voice has wisped away by the end of that statement. He looks down at the counter. After a moment he says, "I had this fantasy for a while after things ended. She would realize what she had given up and it would destroy her. It was something that was safe to imagine, because I knew it wouldn't happen."

I don't say anything. I can tell I'm the barber's hole in the ground right now, the person Michael is talking to because he can't bear to hold on to the weight of his secret any longer.

When he received my text, he says, and again as he was listening to the police report, which he asked his NYPD contact to read out to him over the phone, it began to feel as if this fantasy that had been swelling under his skin had somehow blistered out into the world and was now infecting the edges of everything. It was impossible. Sarah would never have killed herself. Not for him, not for anyone or anything else, and especially not when she had contacted him just days ago wanting his help with her story. Yet the facts admitted no other conclusion: she had died of a self-administered medication overdose.

"What you've just said," he says, "makes more sense than anything I've come up with."

I say, "Did you tell the police about how you were supposed to meet up with her?"

He pauses. "I would have if I thought it would have made a difference."

The squirminess of the conditional tense. "Why did things end?" I ask. "Between you and Sarah."

"She no longer wanted them to continue." He says that with a kind of strained dignity, like an aging general who still hasn't entirely accepted that, after all his sacrifices for his country, no one needs him anymore.

"Because you wouldn't leave your family."

"She told you that?"

Fair point. "Her sister did."

"She didn't want me to leave them. She said the kids . . ." He shrugs. "It was a good excuse for her."

I want to ask what *his* opinion is on what his leaving would have done to his children, but that would probably sound too judgy. "Maybe she was thinking about her own family."

"Her mother leaving? Sarah made her

peace with that long ago."

Mother? I guess abandonment is equal opportunity. That would explain why it's just been Iris packing away her sister's life, tidying up her death. "Sarah's leave of absence from Columbia," I say. "Did that have anything to do with your relationship?"

The glasses come off again and more eye rubbing commences. He tells me someone lodged an anonymous complaint with the university's ethics committee. As an alternative to a formal investigation, Sarah offered to take a leave of absence until the following semester, when he would be on sabbatical at the University of Hong Kong.

"That worked out nicely for you."

"I didn't want her to," he says. "I told her I would resign."

I'm sure his wife and his children would have appreciated that. I say, to get us back on the sleuthing track and also because if we keep talking about this I might let slip that I think he's a selfish prick, "Should we tell the police about this? I think we have enough for them to reopen the case." Once I say that, though, it occurs to me: if I charge off to the cops now, I can forget about ever getting back into Veracity. I need to let Komla and Becks know about this first.

Michael pauses again. "If you do, I would appreciate it if you didn't bring up the fact that I knew Sarah. Beyond how she was my student, I mean." He adds, "My family."

"Really? A minute ago you sounded like you would have tossed them aside."

His face pulls tight. "You wouldn't understand."

"Maybe I don't," I say. I hop off my stool, ready to be done with Michael Lindenberg.

"Wait," he says. "I . . . There's something I would like to do for her."

"What?"

"The story she was working on. She thought it was about something important." He sighs. "Enough to get back in touch with me." He would like to complete it for her and have it published posthumously under her name. "Will you help me with that?"

And now I feel like an ass — a twenty-five-year-old childless, never-married, not-even-dating ass — for getting snarky with this man about how he's choosing to conduct his personal life. (Even if I still absolutely disapprove.) He did love Sarah. This is how he's able to show it. Hardly as useful as saying he will back me up with the cops if needed, but also a step up from co-opting her work for his own.

I say, "I think she was looking into the

dating platforms' algorithms. I don't know in what way, though." It's residually disappointing that Sarah's story doesn't fit into the murder mystery after all, but I guess that would be too artful for real life.

His forehead creases at me. "What algorithms are these?"

Ah, the world of your average longtime married guy in his early fifties. What insights did Sarah think he might be able to provide? "They try to determine romantic compatibility between users of the platform."

"Based on what data?"

I go over the concepts of step one and step two data. Then I tell him about Sarah's list and what I think the items refer to, although I leave out Veracity: the early matchmaker Compatibility, the consulting firm Precision, the fringe group the Romantick. "Also," I say, "she was trying to find out more about someone she met on Soulmate. It seemed like she thought" — what did Sarah say? — "he wanted information. About her, and maybe other women he'd matched with."

"So that's why," says Michael.

"Why what?"

"She wanted to talk to me." He unfolds the temples of his glasses and then folds them up again, a clicky, thoughtful rhythm.

"I wrote a series of articles on China's social-credit experiment a few years back," he says. "I wouldn't say they were ground-breaking, that sounds too grandiose. Although some commentators did describe them as such. Are you familiar with it, the Chinese social-credit system?"

"Familiar enough." Every now and then NPR likes to do a segment on some poor soul who jaywalked one too many times and now can't get a driver's license or a mort-gage.

Of course he goes through it anyway. Each person is assigned a score that rises if they behave like a good citizen in the eyes of the government, such as performing community service, and falls if they don't, which consti-tutes anything from criticizing the Com-munist Party to misappropriating a handi-capped seat on the train. If your score is high, you get treated well, including being eligible for additional government benefits. If your score is low, life becomes pretty crappy. According to Michael, the Western media has been primarily outraged by the extent of ongoing surveillance that the Chinese population is subject to, the sys-tem's lack of transparency, the notion of a government policing its people's lives. But that's just phase one. By collecting all this data on its citizens' prior acts, the Chinese government hopes to eventually build algorithms that can predict their future behavior. Rather than punishing someone for what they have done, the ideal would be for the initial infraction never to occur at all.

I say, "Sounds like someone in the Communist Party read too much Philip K. Dick."

Having spent some time in China, says Michael, he actually has a degree of sympathy for what the government is trying to do. "People there have lost their sense of how to treat one another as fellow human beings. There's a moral void in Chinese society." He stops. "Ah, I didn't . . . I hope nothing I just said came across as offensive."

I wasn't even thinking about it that way, but now I'm not sure. *Is* it offensive to say to me, basically, that Chinese people — in China — have no moral compass? Every time news of another Chinese fake-food scandal breaks my family talks about how you can't trust anyone or anything in the land of piracy, counterfeit goods, and all-encompassing greed, but that feels different because you should be able to badmouth your own people. Not that I consider the one billion plus population of China to be *my people*. "Just keep going."

"And I just realized . . . you *are* Chinese, right?"

"Ethnically, yes. But as American as you are."

"Of course. That wasn't what I meant. I just . . . I didn't want to add insult to injury. Not that being mistaken for being Chinese when you're not is an insult, I —"

"I really think you should just keep going. What's the connection between all that and the matchmakers' compatibility algorithms?"

He puts on his glasses and blinks at me. "We do that here as well. Companies collect incredible amounts of data on consumer behavior so they can predict how people will spend their money. And it sounds like these dating platforms are in a privileged position in that respect, because their users have an incentive to provide as much information about themselves as possible, to increase their chances of an accurate match."

"To a certain extent." I explain about the lying limitation, the threat it poses to the efficacy of the algorithm. I add, thinking of that interview I read with Lucinda Clay, Soulmate bigwig, "There's also the argument that people don't really know themselves anyway and so you can't trust what

359

they tell you."

He smiles at me like I'm Nancy Drew telling him about this puppy-smuggling ring I uncovered. "That's pretty cynical."

"Actually, I think the person who argued it is an idealist," I say. "Not about humanity, but the potential for data to surmount human frailties."

His smile flattens out. "That's how you lose sight of . . ." He pauses. "Wait. If the matchmakers are having problems with the accuracy of their data . . . what if they're now trying to collect the data they need through ways that they're concealing from their users? To get around the lying limitation. A step three data, if you will."

I feel a twinge of unease. It takes me a moment to identify why: Finders Keepers, Match Insights. But that's different. Our targets might not know that we're monitoring them, but they consented. In theory. "It's possible," I say.

According to Michael, this issue of illicit data collection is a trending one; both Apple and Google recently came under criticism for allowing apps in their stores that were secretly tracking consumers' data usage. He asks if I ever saw any of Sarah's notes. I tell him I didn't, but I know she has an account on Dispatch — it turns out he's the one who introduced that service to her — and it seems like she had a source, or a collaborator, who posts under the username St. Elmo.

As Michael is taking all this down on his phone, he says, "In a way, the situation we're facing here is more troubling than what's happening in China."

He seems to be speaking unironically, so I say, "You're forgetting the part about how there's no authoritarian government telling us how to live our lives."

"There's no need for that. Amazon tells us what we should buy and Netflix tells us what we should watch. These matchmakers, telling us who we should date. Except here we aren't even aware of how we're being directed."

"That's different, though. Their recommendations are based on our own preferences."

"But what are those based on?" he says. Our vendors' algorithms preselect our choices and then tell us these are the things we want. Impossible to verify, since we can never know what they failed to show us, and so over time what they do present to us — what they want us to want — does indeed become what we want.

Funny he should use that word, *verify*. "That's starting to sound like something the Romantick might say."

He shrugs. "The power to predict outcomes is inextricably linked to the power to control outcomes . . . and once you've achieved the former, it may be hard to resist trying the latter."

As we get up from our seats, he adds, "Also, the Romantick was on Sarah's list."

True, and that reminds me. "Did you ever bring Sarah to the Plaza hotel?"

He looks up like I jerked a string attached to the top of his head. "Once." He blinks and then lowers his gaze again. For her birthday, he says, a month or so before they stopped seeing each other. It was a surprise. He could tell she wasn't happy about it, not the way he had imagined she would be. They fought about that and a hundred other idiocies. "She said — how did she put it? — that we were *coming to the end of us.*"

I open my mouth to say that at least we've solved her death, we know what happened to her, we can make sure Iris Lettriste is held responsible. Thank god I close it again, because I realize: none of that matters to him. He has still lost her. Perhaps it even makes things worse, knowing.

"Like we were a story," says Michael, "and there were only a few more pages to go. And

she was looking forward to getting there. To
the end."

IV.

#3. Get a confession out of Iris Lettriste.

I leave Contadina and cycle south to Murkstone Banderby LLP. I'm pretty sure I have enough to seek an audience with Komla and Becks. But — now that I'm so close! — I want the ticker-tape parade return. Komla apologizing for firing me. Becks miffed as hell that I've managed to solve this crime. (That will be especially fun.) And for that, I need something damning from the culprit herself.

I lock my bike across the street and then text her. *This is Claudia. I just spoke to Sarah's ex. He told me some surprising things. Do you have a few minutes?*

She texts back right away. *Yes. Now? Can you come to my office?*

As I'd expected. She's anxious to find out what I've learned, if I know the truth of what she's done.

Five minutes later I'm zooming up

through the giant Lego block in which Iris works, staring at the picture of me that building security took and printed out on my guest pass and wondering if I really look that hideous. The elevator goes direct to the forty-fifth floor and then stops at every floor after that for men and women in crisp collared shirts and silk blouses who are all communing intently with their phones. Quite a few of them look like they're around my age, which makes me feel weird. Could I have been one of them? In my junior year Charles tricked me into taking the LSAT by saying he bet I couldn't score within the ninety-eighth percentile. I did so and then, belatedly realizing the ploy, refused to apply to law school. The thing is, I think I might have enjoyed that experience, reading cases and parsing sentences, arguing over what the principles that govern our society are and should be. But it felt too much like I would be joining the lemmings; also, one of my rules in life is to disagree with everything Charles says about my career.

I get out on the fiftieth floor, where a woman is already waiting for me by the reception counter. She introduces herself as Iris's administrative assistant and leads me through a grayscale section of cubicles — ah, Aurum days, how I do not miss them —

to a row of glass-fronted offices. I feel a bit like I'm in a zoo as we walk past, peering in at the different specimens of corporate lawyer on display. One guy is definitely taking a nap. Two offices past him, there's Iris, staring at one of her two computer screens.

When she glances up I catch the flutter of her eyelids, like she's momentarily abashed by my presence. Is she thinking about how she tried to harm me just a few weeks ago? Maybe even experiencing the tiniest niggle of guilt? She looks much as she did the last time I saw her: power-lawyer outfit, matching earrings and necklace, her brown hair ironed straight. I remember us standing on the sidewalk talking about cycling, how she thanked me for my help and insisted I take her money. She must have intended it as a bribe: *Leave things be.* Unfortunately for her I was too obtuse to realize that, which was why she escalated to threats — verbal, then physical. And instead of shrinking away, here I am again, nosy as ever. Walking myself into the cage of the predator.

The administrative assistant closes the door as she leaves, and suddenly I want to hustle out after her before it's too late. I tell myself I figured out the diabolical mechanics of Iris's plot when no one else could; I can best her now. Plus everyone can see us through the glass. I peek around and accidentally make eye contact with the woman sitting in the cubicle that faces into Iris's office. I smile at her, our unsuspecting witness. She blinks back at me, bemused.

"Would you mind hitting the switch next to you that says *Privacy Setting*?" says Iris. "It fogs up the wall so people can't look in on us."

Fuck. What if I refused? There's no way I can. If she senses fear, she'll know she can get away without giving me anything. I think about the way she murdered Sarah, the way she injured me. She's a killer who keeps herself at a distance. I'm safe enough while I'm right in front of her; it's when I walk away that I'll have to watch out.

At least, let me keep telling myself that.

"Sure," I say, and do it. The effect *is* pretty cool.

"Please have a seat," she says. "And thanks for coming over. Unfortunately today is turning out to be one of those days when I'm pretty much chained to my desk."

"I hope that chain is long enough to let you reach the bathroom."

She lip-smiles. "Just barely."

She starts to explain — she has two deals that are supposed to sign today — and then an email chimes in that she has to respond to right away to save the world from imploding. While she blitzes away on her keyboard I sit in one of the two chairs on the other side of her desk and take the opportunity to survey the room. Superlatively neat, which doesn't surprise me in the least. She's hung up her college and law school degrees on one wall and a row of art prints and exhibition posters on another. No family or other personal photographs anywhere that I can see. The poster closest to where I'm sitting is from a few years ago, a group exhibition at the Tate Modern in London titled *Surrounded I Am All Alone: The Profoundness of Isolation in a Hyperconnected World.* The names of the featured artists run across the bottom of the poster. I recognize a couple of them from Sarah Reaves's chat with Charretter.

"Sorry about that."

I turn back to Iris. "No worries," I say. "Have you heard of the artist Norah Simmons?"

She blinks and then says, sounding cautious, "No. Should I have?"

"Just wondering. You might like her work" — I indicate the poster — "if you like Karsten Auer and George Bloom."

Her surprise that I have any idea who those artists are shows for a moment like a woman sneaking a peek at her compact before tucking it away again. "Thanks," she says. "I'll check her out."

I say, "Was Sarah also into contemporary art?"

The invocation of Sarah Reaves sucks us out of one universe and into another. I sit up straighter in my chair. Game on.

"No," says Iris. "She thought it was pretentious."

She glances at her art wall, and I look out of the window behind her. You would think being on the fiftieth floor would afford you a decent view, but all I see are the mirrored facades of other office buildings.

Iris and I speak at the exact same time, as if someone waved a flag and shouted, *Go!*

"A Dose a —" I say.

"I killed her," she says.

I'm so utterly unprepared for this preemptive confession that I say, "Who?"

Her shoulders hitch up. "My sister. Isn't that what you came here to ask me? You spoke to her ex and he told you what Sarah and I were really like."

Indeed, but . . . "I don't understand." Not only that, I forgot to activate the recording function on my phone. World's worst detective.

"I saw her for the last time a week before

she died," says Iris. "She wanted to discuss making some repairs to the apartment." She pauses. "I don't know if he told you that as well, that the apartment she was living in was really hers. I hated thinking of it that way, so I said . . . It was so fucking petty. All these little lies, they just make the truth feel worse."

"He said both of you owned the apartment," I say.

She shrugs. "I just paid for everything to do with it. Really it belonged to her."

Iris tells me that her final conversation with Sarah twisted itself around, as it had any number of times before, to Iris saying that Sarah should just sell the apartment, and Sarah refusing — but then, unlike all those other times, it continued to twist in on itself, suffocating them both. "I told her that I was done propping her up. If she wanted to keep that fucking place she could take care of it herself." Iris sips in a breath. "Same with whatever she wanted to do next now that she had failed at journalism, after she had wasted my money on the Columbia program she never completed. Failed at her entire life, essentially."

Now I can see it, the monster of guilt that's clinging to Iris's back, its arms around her throat. If envy's eyes are green, guilt's must be gray, and insatiable with reproach. "You think Sarah killed herself because she didn't know how she could live without the assistance you were providing?"

"She said it. *Wouldn't it be better for you if I just killed myself.* Screamed it, actually. I still hear her saying it, every now and then. At the time I thought she was being melodramatic and I said, *Please go ahead.* I might as well have fed her those pills."

I sit back. Everything I thought I had fitted together is coming apart. Iris didn't kill Sarah. She had other ways to exert power over her.

But Sarah's A Dose a Day subscription *was* canceled, and Sarah *did* die from an overdose of medication in A Dose a Day packaging. Those two facts are stakes hammered deep into the earth's crust, beneath all the mud I'm squelching about in, thinking each time that I'll get out but sinking deeper. Together they prove *someone* killed her.

"I'm sorry, by the way," says Iris. "About how I reacted when you texted me a few weeks ago. Too much caffeine, too little sleep. I didn't actually mean anything by it. I just wanted it all to go away."

At least I was right about those anonymous threats coming from Iris. Although that also means they had nothing to do with Sarah's murder — and now I'm truly all out of suspects, and clues, and ideas.

I say, "What I was going to tell you . . ." I feel like I need to offer Iris something significant, some truth about her sister, after what she shared with me. "What I was going to tell you was that Sarah didn't give up on journalism." I give Iris the CliffsNotes version of Sarah's relationship with Michael Lindenberg, including how she was the one to end things and how she took a leave of absence from Columbia. "She was working on a new story after all. She was going to meet with the journalism professor to discuss it. Except she never did, because . . . you know."

Iris's gaze is drifting about like she's in a strange city and trying to find some landmark to orient herself. She says, as much to herself as to me, "Why didn't she say something to me?"

I don't say anything. That's a question that has no answer now that Sarah Reaves is dead.

"Since Sarah died," says Iris, like a strange echo of my thought, "I keep thinking about this one incident from our childhood." They had a slide in their backyard, and once Iris dared Sarah to go down on Rollerblades.

"She didn't want to, but I taunted her into it." Sarah lost her balance halfway and crash-landed. She was fine, aside from a few bruises and a sprained finger that they never told their parents about because they didn't want to be scolded. But when Iris saw Sarah fall, and for the several seconds before Sarah sat up, she felt certain that her sister was dead. "There was this tightness in my throat," she says, "like I was being choked. It was fear, such fear. That was the first time I consciously thought, *I love her. This little brat. If she went away there would be a hole in my world.* And then I spent the next thirty years trying my best to forget I ever felt that way."

V.

On my ride back from Midtown East to Gowanus my wrist begins to ache in a steady *pay attention to me* way, which at least serves as a distraction from my latest failure to solve Sarah's murder. I have to carry my bike up the four flights of stairs to my apartment, and by the time I reach my landing I feel ready to amputate the limb. Why is this not getting better? Should I go to a doctor? They'll just order me to stay off a bicycle for some unacceptably long period of time. I unlock the front door and nudge it open with the wheel of my bike. Maybe I can try biking one-handed?

"Jesus Christ!" I say.

Becks, Max, and some guy I've never seen before all turn around like *I've* gate-crashed their party. Becks is dressed in her usual monochromatic chic, blond hair shining like it has its own power source. In my dump of a living room, the cold hard shell of her glamour, intimidating enough in Tribeca, makes her seem like a member of some impossibly advanced alien race looking in to see if this backwater is even worth their while to colonize.

"Not quite," she says.

Max says, "There she is!"

"What are you . . ." I say. "How did you . . ."

Becks says, "Max was telling me about his artistic process for *Brief Encounters.*"

I realize the three of them are standing in front of the painting that hangs on the wall above the couch. It's my favorite of Max's literary portraits, Holly Golightly (a version that owes a debt to Audrey Hepburn, Most Beautiful Woman Ever) with Jay Gatsby. I'm starting to feel like the one character in a Marvel-DC crossover story line who knows the two worlds are supposed to be separate, except in this alternate combined universe everyone just thinks he's crazy.

Max says, "Becks had a brilliant suggestion. Anna Karenina and Ellen Olenska."

That *is* a good one. I wish I'd thought of that.

Becks says to him, "You should be showing at galleries."

"That's what I keep telling him," says Unknown Dude.

375

Max says, like the veteran of an enduring siege, "You need to know the people who run them."

Becks says, "How many galleries have you approached?"

Max mutters something I can't catch. The distance between us widens like our living room rug just experienced an adolescent growth spurt. Why didn't he tell me he'd submitted his work? Or is the question: Why did I assume he'd abandoned his art because he was having too much fun with his own brief encounters?

"You millennials are unbelievable," says Becks. "All laziness and instant gratification. You should expect at least three times that number of rejections before you start to get anywhere. You're talented, but it's not like you're fucking Picasso. Think of a better title for the series first, though."

That galvanizes me out of my soul-searching and also my shock at witnessing the Blonde Assassin play life coach in my apartment to my roommate. "I came up with that!" I say.

"I figured." Becks barely glances over at me. "It has all your hallmarks of sloppiness."

"It's a reference to —"

"I know, and it's wrong. The whole point here is that these are characters who never encounter each other even though we wish they had. You can't just plug in senseless catchphrases because you think they sound good."

"Um, we'll let you guys catch up on your work stuff now," says Max. "Nice meeting you." He grabs his companion's hand — I belatedly comprehend that this must be Greenpoint; I haven't registered anything about him except that his voice is sort of whiny — and they hustle away.

I wait for the door of Max's room to click shut. "Work stuff?"

"Let's speak in your room." Becks pauses. "Assuming you have a room."

"I'm not squatting here," I say as I wheel my bike the rest of the way into the apartment, kicking off my sneakers as I go. It sounds defensive instead of sarcastic like I intended. I lean the bike against the window ledge. When I turn around I see that Becks has removed her knee-high boots as well, lining them up by the door. The display of cultural sensitivity stuns me, as does how quickly and quietly she did it. She would make an ace assassin. Not a comforting thought to have right now.

Becks glances around when she enters my room, and I can tell she's logging each detail as corroboration of her existing opinion of me. The twin bed, chronically unmade, sheets so frayed you can see the mattress underneath in places. The pile of laundry at the foot of the bed. The Ikea desk and chair that look only marginally more solid than cardboard. The inexorably withering plant by the window that Coraline gave me and that, I swear, I've been doing my damnedest to keep alive. The walls empty except for the photos Blu Tack–ed above my desk. Socks everywhere, like a plague has befallen some tiny, crumpled species of wild creature. I feel the need to say, pointing to the heap of clothes, "Those are clean."

Becks drapes her coat over the back of my desk chair. She's surprisingly at ease, like she regularly pays unannounced visits to dinky apartments in Gowanus. "How's the wrist?"

I realize that I'm cradling it with my other hand. I let my arms swing free by my sides. "It could be worse."

"I see you couldn't wait to get into more unnecessary danger."

Is she referring to the cycling or to something else? I say, "I've read that it helps put life in perspective."

"Not very useful if you no longer have the life."

The air thins out around me the way it

did when I was pancaked under Sarah Reaves's bed, thinking about her sister poisoning her. Deep breath. I look straight at Becks, except I can't quite meet the force of her stare so I aim for those fjord-steep cheekbones, and say, "Is that a threat or a warning?"

She appraises me like I'm a monkey who has scrawled out my first word in the sand after years of tutoring. "Neither," she says. "Do you know why I'm here?"

And the thing is, once she says that — maybe even before she says it — I do know, and it confirms my theory. One of them, anyway. "You *are* trying to find out the truth about Sarah!" My relief feels like a long-lost friend coming in for a hug so heartfelt it lifts me off the ground. I'm not doing this alone after all. Veracity hasn't let me down.

"Among other things. What did you learn from Michael Lindenberg and Iris Lettriste?"

I open my mouth — so much! — and then reconsider. "Am I still fired?"

"I suppose. Not my call."

And I land, hard, like I've been drop-kicked. All right then. I say, trying to sound aggrieved, "You've been tracking me on Finders Keepers." As I'd hoped they would, so they could appreciate all this excellent detective work I've been doing.

"To monitor your compliance with our agreement," she says. "Which has been abysmal."

"But I never gave my consent."

"What the hell are you talking about?"

I repeat what Komla told me, that we are legally permitted to follow our targets on Finders Keepers only because they consent to the collection of their location data when they set up a matchmaker account. "I've never signed up with a matchmaker."

She says, sounding almost amused, "How long did it take you to think up that one?"

"I don't see any reason why I should talk to you about Michael Lindenberg or Iris." I pause. "Or Dispatch."

She blinks, once. "What about to the NYPD?"

"You wouldn't go to the cops."

"I would," she says, "to stop you from behaving like a fucking idiot."

"I'm just trying to figure out what happened."

"If someone did murder her, all this running around you're doing is like holding up a big sign saying *Come After Me Next.*"

Again that oxygen-deprivation sensation, like I've been launched into the cold black reaches of space. Then it occurs to me. Is it possible? "You've dealt with this before."

"Of course I have. The world is full of fucking idiots."

"I meant something like Sarah's death."

"Death?" She says it the way Emily Dickinson might, the invocation of a mutual acquaintance. "No. But it's a problem. I've dealt with problems."

I look at her leaning against my door, arms and ankles crossed. "Becks," I hear myself say, "why did you join Veracity?"

"If I tell you I'll have to get rid of you."

I dredge a sound up from my throat. I was going for a chuckle, but its edges emerge a tad whimpery.

"That was a joke."

"I knew that."

"It was a second chance." She presses one black-stockinged foot against the door and cants herself upright, which draws my attention to the narrow, elegant shapes of her feet. She takes two steps toward where I'm standing, which is in front of my bed in a half-assed effort to block the mess of it. I smell her perfume, faint but unmistakable. Something pops in my mind like a balloon has belatedly burst and spattered incredulity everywhere. Becks Rittel is in my bedroom? If I were an entirely different person altogether, I would consider making a move.

"This is bigger than you know," she says. "And it's a fucking mess. If you go any deeper, forget about getting out. You're staying in until it's cleaned up."

I think of the line I drew for myself in Sarah's apartment, and I have a premonition: where I'm going, that line doesn't even count. It's a scary thought. Also an absolutely thrilling one. "Of course I'm in!" I say.

She looks at me; I can't tell if she's glad or disappointed by my response. Then she says, "Is there anywhere to eat in this wasteland of a neighborhood?"

Ten minutes later, we're sitting in a booth at Groucho's. Becks scowls at the laminated sheet of the menu while I replay our earlier conversation in my head. Why do I feel like I've missed something of significance? Becks asking if I knew why she was here, saying she would go to the police if she had to —

"This place looks like it failed a health safety inspection."

"Probably," I say. "That's why only the strong can eat here."

She puts down the menu. "I guess I survived Laos."

Of all the random places in the world to

have visited. I find myself wondering if she went there alone or with someone, and then I realize: "You're here on your own."

"Do you see anyone else?"

"I mean — Komla didn't ask you to come talk to me."

Right then our hitherto MIA server decides to come over and inquire about our well-being. Instead of responding like a regular person, Becks tells him she wants an egg-white omelette. "We're doing great," I say. "Could I have the gingerbread pancakes?"

The server ambles off, and Becks says, "What makes you think that?"

"You used the singular subject in everything you said to me back at my apartment. Why you were here, going to the —" Do I want to remind her about the telling-the-NYPD option? "What I mean is, it was all *I*. Not *we*, the way it should have been if you were speaking on behalf of Veracity."

"Did the English major make you such an annoying pedant, or were you always that way?"

That's probably as much of an admission that I'm right as I'm going to get from Becks. "Does Komla even know?"

Her gaze skews past me. "He might. He seems to know . . . many things."

My intuition twinges: she had been about to say something else. *Too many things,* maybe?

A man appears at our table. For a moment I think it's one of Groucho's servers, and then I register that he's dressed in baggy gym clothes and carrying a folded electric scooter in one hand, suitcase style. An employee might be able to get away with either of those actions, but combining both seems egregious even by Groucho's standards.

"Did you have to bring that filthy thing in here?" says Becks.

"Of course," says the man. "Look at it. It would get stolen in a heartbeat."

He sets the scooter on the floor and sits next to Becks, across from me. Becks pretzels her mouth and shifts away from him. He's a small guy, a couple of inches taller than me, late twenties to early thirties. Most people probably assume he's white, but I'm guessing he's hapa from the shape of his eyes and the beigy tint to his complexion. He also seems passingly familiar, like I clicked across his profile during one of my verifications, maybe.

"Hi?" I say.

He picks up the menu, effectively screening his face from me. I say, utilizing the principles of Occam's razor and my experience with Aurum Financial's IT department, "You must be Squirrel."

The frayed edge of the menu lowers to the bridge of his nose. He glances sideways at Becks. "That's the Miss Marple thing you were talking about?"

A pantheon of fictional detectives to choose from and Becks has been comparing me to *Miss Marple*? I say, "It's not very respectful to talk about someone like they're not in the room when they're right there."

"You see what I'm dealing with," Becks says to him.

Our server arrives with our food. I enjoy the way both Becks and Squirrel boggle at my discus-size pancakes, stacked high in a moat of toffee sauce.

Becks wipes down her cutlery with her napkin. "Before we get any further," she says to me, "there are some things you should know."

#1. There is no arrangement between Veracity and Match Insights. In fact, there is no Match Insights.

"The information on profiles that Veracity gets comes directly from the matchmakers," says Becks. "They just don't know it."

"We're hacking into the matchmakers?" I say.

Squirrel says, measured yet emphatic, deepening his voice and adopting a hybrid British-African accent, "We commissioned an independent contractor" — he points at himself — "to build a search engine that can locate and extract historical data for a particular dating profile across matchmakers, leveraging on known idiosyncrasies in the matchmakers' security protocols."

I say, impressed, "If I closed my eyes I'd think Komla was here."

He inclines his head like an actor graciously acknowledging the audience's adulation.

This would explain the institutional obsession with secrecy. What I'm surprised at, actually, is how unsurprised I am. But I always knew Veracity was different, including in ways I didn't know about. I say, "So, looking at our targets' chat records, following them around on Finders Keepers . . . we don't actually have their consent to do any of that."

"Consent is bullshit," says Becks. "Ninety-nine percent of people have no idea what they're agreeing to. The remaining one percent don't like it but say yes anyway."

"Why does Veracity do this?" I ask.

"Because we go above and beyond for our clients."

"You hate our clients."

"Off base as usual," says Becks. "I just mildly despise them." She draws her knife across the half-moon of her omelette in a manner I would describe as the antithesis of *mild*. "And there's something else."

#2. Veracity was set up to keep the matchmakers honest as much as their users.

"If not more," says Becks. "Users lie all the time, obviously. But the damage they can do is limited, and most of it is to themselves."

I feel a bit like I'm in a game of Snakes and Ladders where I thought I was a few squares away from payoff and instead I'm spiraling down the back of some humongous python, toward the beginning once again, except the board I'm on now is larger and even more exciting than I could have hoped for. I lean forward. So ready! "What nefarious things are the matchmakers doing?" And part two: *How are we going to take them down?*

"I know what you're thinking, and badly written techno-thriller aside, there is no scenario in which a random group of people trying to overthrow the matching industry will end in anything except total fucking failure."

"I'm not sure what you think I'm thinking about."

Becks sighs. "As you should know," she says, "if you kept on top of *Datebook* like you were supposed to, one of the issues that matchmakers increasingly have to deal with is screening for bot profiles."

I lapsed on my *Datebook* reading once work at Veracity picked up, so thank goodness for Charles's industry reports. "Like those accounts on Let's Meet that turned out to be from Russia's Internet Research Agency."

"Yes." She sounds surprised that I have a clue after all. The vast majority of bot profiles, she continues, are created for the purpose of political interference or to execute some sort of financial scam. Their AI is rudimentary and they tend to push their agendas in obvious ways, which makes it relatively easy for the matchmakers to identify and block them. In the past year, however, Veracity has been recording the emergence of a new, distinct type of bot profile on the Big Three's platforms. "And these . . . they're in a different class. Squirrel can show you."

Once I've swiped through a few of the

profiles on Squirrel's phone, I do start to see the indents of the mold. The same turns of phrase, the same format of self-description. The same types of pictures: one close-up, one outdoor, one activity-based. It would never occur to me, though, if I was looking at one of these profiles on its own.

"How did you find these?"

"We built a filter," he says. "It scans profiles for certain traits and flags them."

Becks says, "We call them synths."

I say, "And the matchmakers aren't able to screen out the new bots?" If Squirrel's one-man filter can catch them, surely a Soulmate or a Partnered Up could as well.

"They could," she says. "Except they're the ones generating them."

I blink at her. "The *matchmakers* are coming up with these synths . . . and then putting them on their own platforms? Why?"

"We don't know," says Becks. "It improves their numbers, that's for sure." Somewhat counterintuitively, having a bunch of fake profiles around boosts a matchmaker's business metrics. The company can report a higher number of profiles than there are actual users, and users remain active on the platform longer than they otherwise would, since in addition to all the legit profiles they also have to sift through the bot chaff.

Squirrel says, "But if that was it, the synths would be dumber. They're too smart for that to be the only reason."

Right then it comes to me that I'm in the information-asymmetry scene in every Inspector Yuan novel where one out-of-the-loop character keeps asking questions so everyone else can reveal important information in a vaguely naturalistic way. And, goddammit, that character is me! My curiosity and my pride tussle for a few seconds. Curiosity ends up on top, as it usually does. I say, "How do you know the matchmakers are behind this?"

"Komla." There's a curtness in the way Becks says his name, as if they had a disagreement and it remains unresolved. It reminds me that she and Squirrel are here, talking to me, without his blessing. Could it be that he still doesn't want me back? The thought makes me feel as soggy as the bottom half of a hamburger bun. I tell myself to focus on what Becks is saying, which sounds like —

"Komla used to work at Soulmate?"

"That is what I literally just said. Yes."

"Sorry." So that's what he was up to prior to Veracity. It's hard to imagine him as a cog in the matching industry's McMachine. "For how long?"

390

Seven years, according to Becks. He was the data scientist overseeing the analysis of step one data for the compatibility algorithms. When Soulmate's management set up a so-called AI development unit, he was assigned to it. The group comprised big-data specialists, software engineers, and behavioral scientists, and their directive was to create a bot that could interact with human users in a sustained and sufficiently convincing manner. Komla's role was to feed the information that subscribers gave to Soulmate, in their profiles and chats and background questionnaires, to the bots, in order to train them to recognize and emulate human behaviors and speech patterns.

"He said none of them knew what the company wanted the bots for. They were just ordered to do this thing, and so they were doing it." A tiny, precise crease indents itself between Becks's eyebrows. "And he never tried to find out."

I picture cog-Komla turning in place, not in the least curious about what he was helping to assemble. It seems most unlike him. "Why did he leave Soulmate?"

He had growing misgivings about how subscribers' data was being used, says Becks, and also what Soulmate might want to use the synths for. At the time he left, the first set of synths were being readied for beta testing. "He started Veracity and brought us" — Becks jabs her chin at Squirrel like the thought of them both being encapsulated in the same concept irks her — "in." By then Komla had been musing for a while over the idea of a service that could provide people with some comfort — or not — that their matches were being honest. His stint at Soulmate had highlighted for him the issue of user deception, and after so long spent working with the abstractions of data, he wanted an opportunity to observe how well the matching process was actually serving individual daters.

"But the other purpose of Veracity was as a means of monitoring Soulmate," says Becks, "to see if the synths would actually start showing up. And now they have, and on the other Big Three platforms as well."

I say, "What's the point of Veracity knowing about this if we don't . . . . do something about it?"

"At the moment we don't have enough to do anything." Veracity might be able to show that the profiles are fake, but we still need proof of a link back to the matchmakers. "Without that, all this just sounds like one of those stories the Romantick love to get off on."

"The Romantick!" I say. "They posted something about the matchmakers putting shell profiles on their platforms." Why do I have that piece of trivia knocking around in my mind? "Are they onto something?"

"What? No. They truly are fucking lunatics."

Then I remember: Sarah Reaves's laptop. Sarah read that blog post. Maybe that was why she put the Romantick on her list. Because . . . "Sarah's story."

Becks's gaze is blue like glacial ice. She doesn't say anything.

"That's what she was writing about, wasn't she? These synths?" Now the pieces start falling like someone has hit play on a sped-up game of *Tetris.* "Charretter. He was a synth. I mean, it was." Rotate, slide, click. "And . . . you knew." I think back on our meetings with Sarah. Komla smiling, asking Sarah why it was important to find out about Charretter, and Becks shoving back, trying to shut Sarah down. "You and Komla. You both knew. All along."

After a moment she says, "The filter picked it up. The patterns of engagement fit." Focusing the conversation on Sarah, asking questions and making suggestions to elicit information about her preferences and opinions. The four-day hiatus in Charretter's activity that we noted would have been for software maintenance; the inconsistency in the way it spoke likely represented an instance where the bot reached the limits of its conversational understanding and a human overseer had to intervene to maintain the dialogue. "I looked at its chat records with the other matches, and they're all the same."

Seeking information, as Sarah had said, and Michael as well. "Could the synths be a way for the matchmakers to collect more data about their customers?" I add, since I should give credit where credit is due, "That was Michael Lindenberg's suggestion. I didn't come up with it."

"I didn't think you had," says Becks. "Obvious though it might be."

Squirrel says, "It's always about getting more data. But to set up something like *this*. I mean, these synths, they're so fucking . . . real." He sounds almost swoony with admiration. "The work that must have gone into it."

Becks says, "The question is what's worth all this trouble."

"Maybe Sarah knew," I say, "and it's in her Dispatch account."

"Maybe," says Becks, like she wouldn't count on Sarah Reaves knowing her right hand from her left.

I sit back in my seat. No wonder Sarah told Jude Kalman he would read about her exploits in the news. And no wonder she was antsy, schlepping around a secret like that. I remember how she looked when we told her what Jude was hiding from her: upset, but at the same time relieved. Also, what Jude told me she said to him, the joke that wasn't a joke: *Is that why you met me, because of what I know about the matchmakers?* She must have feared that he was acting on behalf of the matchmakers, trying to find out what she had uncovered. He hadn't been . . . but someone else had.

"It *is* a gun!" I say.

Across the table Becks and Squirrel glance at each other like they've known for a while that I was teetering on the edge but it's really bad timing that I've plummeted over right now. Becks says, "Do not tell me you have a concealed weapon on you."

"I mean the list. Sarah's list. Chekhov — never mind. They killed her!"

Becks and Squirrel exchange another glance. "Who are you talking about?" she says.

"The matchmakers." I mentally issue an apology to all the authors out there with penultimate-chapter evil-corporation conspiracy reveals. "To stop her from looking into the synths."

Becks says, placing each word like she's stepping stone by stone across a fast-flowing river, "There's no evidence that Sarah Reaves was murdered."

"There is!" I say, and explain what I learned about A Dose a Day.

"You can't prove that," says Becks.

I refrain from breaking out one of Inspector Yuan's favorite phrases — *That is where you are wrong, Constable* — which even I have to admit is annoying, and explain the discrepancy between the A Dose a Day app offering Sarah a discount if she restarted her subscription and the police report documenting Sarah's Strobinex packaging. "The murderer must have canceled her subscription for October," I say, "and then dropped off a tampered box."

"I looked at her phone. There was no notification from anything called A Dose a Day."

Is she accusing me of lying? "Then you must have missed it."

"I don't miss things."

The disdain coats her voice like the congealed syrup on my plate. God, she's infuriating. "Really?" I say. "You wouldn't have her phone without me. You wouldn't know her Dispatch password. You wouldn't even know about the list."

We glare at each other across the table. I can hear the ghosts of her Viking ancestors bashing their swords against their shields, howling for blood. I try to summon the smidge of Genghis Khan that must be in my DNA somewhere.

Squirrel coughs. "She's got you there."

She says without looking away from me, "Shut up."

"We don't need the phone notification," I say. "We can call A Dose a Day to find out if the subscription was canceled and when."

She lowers her fork. I was probably two seconds away from getting my eyeball punctured. I look from her to Squirrel. Neither of them strikes me as a particularly joyous person, but surely they should be pleased at the prospect of solving Sarah Reaves's murder. And, hopefully, obtaining some evidence of the matchmakers' shenanigans from Sarah's Dispatch files. We might not be able to take them down, per se, but we could get some version of the truth out.

"So," says Squirrel. "We keep going? Because what's ahead looks and smells like a huge pile of shit."

"We have to." Becks says it like she's a soldier in a war she never signed up for, but now that she's on the front line she'll keep shooting until she can get back home again. "What the fuck was he thinking?"

Squirrel snorts. "I stopped asking that question a few galaxies ago."

"Wait," I say. "You guys, you *know* who killed Sarah Reaves?"

There's a set to Becks's face that I've never seen before. She says, "Unfortunately."

#3. And Sarah Reaves's killer is . . .

Veracity should never have accepted Sarah's case in the first place, says Becks. "Preliminary online contact, zero offline follow-up. There was nothing for us to verify." And once they confirmed that Charretter was a synth, under Veracity's policies, they should have ended the engagement. "Instead Komla continued to entertain her. When I asked him what he thought he was doing, he said he wanted to see how much Sarah knew."

"Charretter was a bit different from the other synths," says Squirrel. "Typically the synths ask users questions, get people to talk about themselves. They pull data out. Charretter pulled, but it also pushed."

"That art show it wanted Sarah to see," I say.

He nods. "More dimensionality."

Then Sarah disappeared and Iris Lettriste turned up. "I talked to Komla right after Iris left," says Becks. "He was a mess. For him. Still more put together than ninety percent of the slobs out there. He said to me, when I was leaving his office, *If she hadn't come to us she might still be alive.*" At the time Becks thought what he meant was that Sarah's suicide might have been related to her obsession with Charretter, and the information we gave her — or didn't give her — might have contributed.

A few things were clear, though, from Iris's visit. Sarah Reaves had been working on a story about the synths. She must have had a source at Soulmate. "I asked Komla at one point," says Becks, "whether he had any sense as to who it might be. He said he didn't, but I could tell he had been thinking about it as well. He just didn't want to talk about it with me."

Squirrel says, "My money is on someone trying to take out his rival at the company. I love that kind of backstabby shit."

Becks says, "And now, we get to you."

I say, "How I helped to solve the mystery?"

That neck-torque hair flick might be the most strenuous I've seen yet. Veracity was aware of what I was doing from the beginning, she says. Talking to Iris Lettriste and Jude Kalman. Tracking them on Finders Keepers.

Squirrel says, "Your location shows up for us on Finders Keepers. And we keep a log of everyone you look at on that app."

So much for privacy. "I just —"

"Of all the risky, ridiculous things to do," says Becks. "Playing *Murder Most Foul* does not qualify you to be a detective. Reading murder mysteries does not give you some special insight into how someone got themselves killed."

Thinking of all the times in this investigation when Inspector Yuan has oriented me in the right direction, I say, "Actually —"

"The only thing you should have taken away from your murder mysteries, which of course is the one thing you didn't, is how easy it is to get hurt. You're not a fucking superhero. You're not a two-hundred-pound guy. You're a hundred-pound girl who the two-hundred-pound guy picks up and throws across the room. You're lucky you didn't seriously fuck yourself up when you fell off your bike."

"Not lucky," says Squirrel, "technically."

My wrist chooses this moment to throb, like a security system going off long after the burglars have fled with the diamonds.

"But I didn't," I say, "and —" I blink at Squirrel. "What do you mean, not lucky?"

Becks says, "Komla did that to your bicycle."

For a moment the seat crumbles away beneath me. I look at her and then at Squirrel. Neither of them meets my gaze. They truly believe . . . ? Under the table my wrist throbs again; I squeeze it with my other hand.

"But . . . he likes me." I feel like I'm scraping each word out from the inside of my throat. "Doesn't he?"

"He does," says Becks. "And that's why what he did . . ." She pauses. "It's all fucked up."

Squirrel says, "If it makes you feel better, he didn't want you to get *too* beat up. Just enough to scare you, get you to stop messing around."

"And give up the phone," says Becks.

"How the fuck would you know that?" I say. "Maybe he was hoping I would smash my head into the asphalt. It would have saved him the trouble of firing me."

"The car that pulled out in front of you, before the light," says Squirrel, "that was me. He told me to do that."

And now I know where I've seen this man before. I close my eyes for a moment, to try to compose myself, and then open them again, because being shut in the dark right now, even just in my head, is pretty scary. Komla Atsina. What he said when he fired me was right. I have never known him.

Becks says, "I didn't see the A Dose a Day notification on Sarah's phone. And I didn't miss it. I went through each of the items and logged them. Komla must have deleted it before he passed me the phone."

"You're saying he did it," I say, and stop, so she can tell me I've missed her point yet again, all this was just the lead-up to introducing our master villain, the diabolical, depraved soul whom we'll have to spend the rest of this story line hunting down.

"Why else," she says. "Why the fuck else has he done every single fucking thing that he did."

"But," I say, "it's *Komla.*"

She glances away. "I know."

"And he's against the synths. From everything the two of you have been telling me, that's why he left Soulmate and started Veracity. So why would he . . . ?"

Squirrel says, "He left Soulmate because they kicked him out."

Becks scowls at him. "He resigned."

"Technically."

She turns back to me. "Komla has never

been one hundred percent straight with us about how well he knows the synths. It's possible . . . he was more involved than he's told us."

"Because he knows the synths very well," says Squirrel. "No way we could have built that filter to catch them otherwise. Even with my ninja programming skills."

"Right at the start," says Becks, "Komla told us that exposing the matchmakers would not be an option. He didn't want them to fail. Too messy, too many unintended consequences. And he believed in the idea they stood for. It's his fucking mantra, how we should be using data and technology to help us make better choices."

"Then what was his plan to stop them?" I ask.

"Get enough evidence that the matchmakers are the ones putting out the synths and cut a deal with them. They remove the synths and stop defrauding their customers, we keep quiet. From here on out they know someone is keeping an eye on them so they'll think twice about doing anything else sketchy. Matching continues to make the world a better place. Everyone wins. The end."

I say, "Do you think that could work?"

"The utopian bullshit, of course not. Cutting a deal . . ." She shrugs. "I figured it was worth a shot." That tiny crease between her eyebrows again, before she says, "But he's also said other things, a couple of times. Like how a lot of good work went into the synths. And the fact that the matchmakers are misusing them now doesn't mean they should be discarded altogether."

Squirrel says, "You know what that sounds like to me? That sounds like someone who had his own ideas for the synths and hasn't given up on getting his way."

"For fuck's sake," says Becks. "It sounds like that because *I* said it to you."

"You did?"

She flicks back her hair and says to me, "Then Sarah Reaves comes along, and she wants to blow this whole thing wide open. Exactly what Komla doesn't want to happen. Villainize the matchmakers. Discredit the concept of matching. Destroy any chance of doing anything else with the synths. And maybe even more than that. Maybe she knows something we don't about Komla's real interest in the synths, or he's afraid she's on her way to finding out." She takes a breath. "He weighed the costs and the benefits. He decided he couldn't let Sarah write her story."

I pick up my fork and draw circles through

the toffee sauce pooled on my plate. Could this really be the answer: Komla? I think of my bicycle. He was ready to endanger me. Yet he also made sure Squirrel would intervene, as a safeguard.

And . . . murder. Komla might be a utilitarian, but the weight of a life. That's fucking heavy.

I look up. "Do you really think that Komla could kill someone?"

"Anyone can," says Becks. "Haven't your murder mysteries taught you that?"

VI.

The next day we're back at Groucho's. It feels as if we never left, or at least I can't recall anything from the intervening twenty-four hours. The effect is heightened by the fact that Squirrel is definitely wearing the same clothes he had on yesterday.

At the end of last night we decided that Becks would go back to Komla with the Dispatch password I had given her, tell him she had convinced me to stop playing detective, get him to log in to Sarah's account, and make copies of the files stored there. Or rather, Becks decreed she would do all that and then we would meet again to review Sarah's Dispatch files.

"Are you sure?" I asked. "What if he suspects . . . ?"

"He won't. He trusts me."

I said, having read more than one Inspector Yuan mystery where Victim Number Two makes a similar fatally assured assertion,

"Maybe you should have Squirrel go with you. Just in case."

"Did you ever see Squirrel in the office?"

"I've never seen him until last night."

"Exactly. Anyway, he wouldn't be of any help with . . . anything, basically."

Squirrel said, "Next time your Wi-Fi router breaks down, you're on your own."

I said, "If he" — I couldn't bring myself to say Komla's name — "killed Sarah Reaves because of a bunch of bots, he's capable of killing again to ensure no one finds out." I thought of all those meetings with our clients, the way she and Komla could hold entire conversations in their silences. Until Sarah Reaves. "Even you."

She looked at me. I wondered if she was thinking about that as well. "I know," she said.

I don't realize how relieved I am until I walk into the diner and see her sitting with Squirrel in the same booth we occupied the night before, her posture as impeccable as ever. As I'm sliding into my seat she says, "Would it destroy you to be on time for once?"

"I'm so glad you're okay," I say.

She blinks. Then she places a USB key on the table in front of me. "Everything's in there," she says. She tells us that after she and Komla downloaded copies of all the files in Sarah's Dispatch account, he deleted the original files from the account itself. "He said this wasn't information that should be out there."

I turn the USB key, its plastic lozenge, around and around with my fingers. After all my theories, my running after shadows, my lists, *this* is why Sarah Reaves was killed.

I hear Becks say, "How did the call go?"

It takes me a moment to realize she's talking to me, and another to remember the one thing I did do today while fretting over when Becks would text to confirm that she had emerged from her encounter with Komla unscathed and was headed for Gowanus. "As expected," I say, and update them.

After a series of miscommunications with A Dose a Day's help bot — *I see you would like to cancel your account* — that left me shouting, "Human being! I want to speak to a human being!" and, incidentally, with a grudging appreciation of the matchmaker bots' superior chat capabilities, I reached a service center representative who told me she would love to help me once I had verified my mother's maiden name. I almost said *Reaves,* automatically, and then remembered: the daughter who would have changed her name to try to escape her father would have been Iris, not Sarah. "Lettriste," I said. She then confirmed for me that someone had logged in to Sarah's account online in mid-September and canceled her subscription starting from the month of October. That person had also changed the phone number and email address that Sarah had on file, thus ensuring that Sarah never received a notice of her subscription cancellation.

"The invisible hand," says Squirrel. "That would be his style."

"Luckily it couldn't reach to the actual app on Sarah's phone," I say.

Becks opens her laptop. "I hope to fucking god Sarah Reaves found something good."

Becks and Squirrel divvy up the Dispatch files for review while, as always, I'm designated the keeper of the spreadsheet. I type out an index of the documents, logging the date each one was uploaded, its author, and a brief description.

From Sarah:

A collection of Romantick blog posts. I scroll through to see if it includes what I read in her apartment about the matchmakers' shell profiles. It does, and she highlighted a sentence in that post: *By bombarding subscribers with fake profiles, the matchmakers aim to wear them down until they will accept, without any questioning or scrutiny or independent thought, whatever match the matchmaker recommends to them.* Which seems slightly less crazy now.

An interview with an anonymous member of the Romantick who told her that *all* the dating profiles in circulation were bots. Sarah pointed out that it was a provable fact that actual human individuals created and maintained dating profiles. The person's response was similarly highlighted: *All those profiles have been hijacked. Once it's uploaded to their system, the matchmakers take it over. Real people never have a chance.* Okay, *that* still sounds crazy.

News articles over the past decade charting the rise of the Big Three and the development of online dating into its current data-intensive, algorithm-reliant incarnation.

Interviews with users of the Big Three platforms about their online dating experiences.

From St. Elmo:

Three separate sets of what look like profile names.

A PowerPoint deck titled "Project Tilt — Presentation to Polaris (October 20xx)."

An email from Internal-Comms to

Precision-Mgmt with the subject line *[Project News — Internal Only] Precision Advises Soulmate in Acquisition of Compatibility.*

Squirrel: "This makes no fucking sense."

I look up. He's turned the screen of his laptop toward Becks and me. It displays one of St. Elmo's lists of profile names. A heading across the top: ORIGINAL 20.

"These names," he says. "None of them are even in our database."

After a moment Becks says, "If these are older synths, they could have been decommissioned."

"Then why send them?"

I say, "We're assuming that these are dating profiles. Maybe they're usernames for . . . something else?"

Becks says, "Let's just keep going." To Squirrel: "Try the names in the other two files." To me: "If you're done with that index, start going through the rest of the St. Elmo docs. I'll join you if I don't drown in the angst of all these user interviews."

I open up the Project Tilt presentation, enticed by the CONFIDENTIAL stamped across the cover slide. Surely this would be the document in which a matchmaker cabal would set out, in incriminating detail, its twelve-step plan for financial domination. But the deck is more of the corporate cliché

I once — so long ago! — spent my time at Aurum copyediting, a razzle-dazzle of graphs and graphics, buzzwords zinging about. The gist seems to be that in our *data-driven world,* the companies that will be successful are those that go beyond simply *anticipating customer needs and wants.* Instead, *tomorrow's winners* must *harness big data, machine learning, and AI* to *help customers identify their goals and achieve them.* All of this requires a *sustained investment of resources* in order to build a *visionary data strategy and infrastructure.* I'm guessing someone needs a more generous department budget. No express references to the matchmakers or the compatibility algorithms, although the applicability is clear. It strikes me that, in a way, this deck is another version of what Michael Lindenberg said to me.

I close that document and go to the Precision email. It's a brief announcement of the Soulmate-Compatibility transaction. Purchase price: $200 million, a portion of which would be contingent on Compatibility's founders achieving certain milestones. So I guessed right about Soulmate acquiring Compatibility, and it looks like part of the deal was for the founders to stay on.

Lucinda Clay, anyone? I wonder what happened to her cofounder, whether he — or she — is still at Soulmate as well, and, also, what happened to *them*. From the way Komla spoke, the happily-ever-after odds didn't seem to be in their favor.

All this must relate to the synths somehow. Compatibility: the first item on Sarah's list. Komla said that Compatibility had an idea for verifying the information provided by its users. Sarah said that Charretter, our new-and-improved synth zero, wanted information. From her, about her. I think of how their chat record began, Charretter asking about the artists Sarah had listed on her profile and Sarah saying, essentially, that she had lied, a minor deception so she could appear to be someone she was not. (The irony.)

What if Compatibility was the one who first developed the synths, as a way to test the truth of what the subscribers on its platform were saying? In which case —

Squirrel says, "Okay, now I'm getting hits. These synths are acting consistent with Charretter." He pauses. "You know, some of these suggestions, they make a lot of sense."

How did Komla put it? *There would be no*

need for Veracity if Compatibility had succeeded.

I say, "Do either of you know what Komla did before Soulmate?"

Becks says, without looking up, "He was at some data analytics company doing work on consumer preference algorithms."

"Have either of you ever heard him mention a Lucinda Clay?"

She frowns like she's trying to place the name. Squirrel's fingers rat-a-tat across his keyboard. He says, "SVP of innovation? That sounds like a made-up thing."

"Did either of you —"

"Just tell us, goddammit," says Becks.

"I think Komla founded a company called Compatibility," I say, "with this Lucinda Clay. Compatibility came up with the synths, and then Soulmate took it over. Komla didn't like what Soulmate was doing with the synths. He left . . . and Lucinda stayed." Where she's now directing the synths, gathering data to help Soulmate's users overcome their own limitations. So she claims.

I run through the parallels between Komla's and Lucinda's careers. Both of them studied at Cambridge, where they could have met. Based on the number of years Lucinda has been at Soulmate and when

414

Komla left, they would have started working there at the same time. Then: the Precision email. After Becks and Squirrel have gone through it I tell them about the Lucinda Clay interview I read and my conversation with Komla about Compatibility.

Becks says, "He could have been lying to you."

I shake my head. "He was very careful about what he said. But I think all of it was the truth." It seems so clear now that Komla was referring to himself. *If I had to guess, the founders of Compatibility underestimated how inconsistent humans can be. Including each other.* "He wanted the chance to talk about it. She must have been on his mind, given Sarah Reaves and the synths and . . . everything."

"That could explain why you didn't find any profiles from that first batch," Becks says to Squirrel. "If *Original 20* referred to the original synth profiles, on the Compatibility platform, they would have been deleted by now."

That's when I realize. "Komla didn't kill Sarah Reaves," I say. "*She* did. Lucinda Clay."

There's an almost identical blankness to Becks's and Squirrel's faces, like they don't understand what I'm saying, somehow. "But then why —" says Becks.

"To protect her. Everything Komla is doing is to protect her."

After a moment she says, "How can we be sure?"

Her voice is winched tight. Of course they understand. They're just trying to tamp down their hope that I might be right.

I say, "Charretter's and Sarah's profiles were both deleted from Soulmate around the time of the murder. Komla couldn't have done that."

"He could have canceled Sarah's membership. The way he did with A Dose a Day."

"Except Sarah was still receiving notifications from Soulmate about new matches. I saw that on her phone."

"I didn't," says Becks. "He fucking got rid of those, too."

"So her account is still open," says Squirrel. "They just masked her profile on the back end."

"And even if Komla was able to delete Sarah's Soulmate profile without touching her account," I say, "he couldn't have done anything with Charretter. That's a synth. Only someone at Soulmate could have done that."

Becks says, "Coincidence," but I can tell she doesn't believe this herself.

"Lucinda has so much more to lose," I say. "Komla might want his original vision of the synths, whatever that is, but he was able to walk away from them. Lucinda is the one who's leaned all the way in. If Sarah's story came out — that Soulmate has been using fake profiles to spy on its users, to secretly collect their information, to make them think they could potentially find happiness with someone who doesn't even exist — all of that would be on Lucinda. Her career, gone. Soulmate would fire her as quickly as they could and probably blame everything about the synths on her. She could never work in the matching industry again. The media would tear her apart. Lawsuits that could bankrupt her. She might even have to go to prison for fraud. I mean, her world would be totally destroyed." For a moment I'm horrified at how easily a well-ordered, successful life could spiral away because of one thing that a stranger does, one secret of yours revealed. This must have been how Jude Kalman felt about the prospect of his wife learning of his infidelity. Except how much worse for Lucinda Clay. Except that, unlike Jude, someone like Lucinda, capable of conceiving and executing this vast deception, would also be capable of doing what was necessary to maintain it.

"Plus . . ." The thought makes me feel like someone has shrieked their fingernails across my personal chalkboard, but I make myself say it anyway. "If the person who killed Sarah had any idea of what I've been doing . . . I'm pretty sure I'd also be dead by now."

The others don't say anything. Then Squirrel begins to laugh. It's an odd, hiccup-y sound — quite adorable, actually.

"Komla Atsina," he says. "I always knew that man was a fucking romantic."

By the time I reach home it's almost midnight. Max isn't in, yet again, but for once I'm relieved. The consolidated weight of all our discoveries — murder! industry-wide fraud! Komla as immensely flawed human being! — is starting to feel like a vest of explosives I've strapped on, and if anyone comes too close right now I might self-detonate into fragments of anxiety and exhaustion.

Becks and I spent the rest of our time at Groucho's arguing over what to do next, while Squirrel donned a pair of industrial headphones and resumed carnaging in the MMORPG in which, he told me with pride, he was a literal evil warlord. Confront

Komla, obviously — about Lucinda, and also what he really knew about the synths' purpose, which Sarah's Dispatch files provided no clarity on — but Becks thought that only she and Squirrel should do so. She assured me I would do something unnecessarily reckless; I said there was no way I was missing out when I was the one who, not to keep going back to it or anything, had solved this mystery. Eventually we compromised: she and Squirrel would tell Komla what they had learned, and then I would join them.

At that point Squirrel pulled off his headphones. "What about *my* safety?" he said.

Becks said, "What the hell are you talking about?"

"You don't want her there in case we're wrong and Komla did kill the journalist and he goes berserk when we ask him about it. I could get injured, too."

She slid her laptop into her bag. "I'll see you in the office tomorrow at nine. Try to grow some balls between now and then."

It's only when I get into my room and take out my phone to charge it that I see the seven missed calls from Charles. Oh shit. Some Jessie-related drama? Or — something has happened. To Coraline, or to our mother.

I check for voice mails and then remember I never got that set up. No messages from him, either on the Three Cs or to me alone. I text him: *Just saw your missed calls! Everything okay?*

Fifteen seconds later: *CALL ME*

He picks up on the second ring. "Claudia Lin Jiayi."

That both perturbs and reassures me. The use of my full name means he's red-alert pissed at me — god knows why, we haven't spoken since Thanksgiving — but at least no one has died. It's an indication of how out of it I am that it takes me several seconds to register the irony of that thought. I shake my head. Whatever this latest Lin sibling drama is about, I'm not up to playing my part tonight. "You don't sound like a Claudia," I say. "So I have about two minutes before I turn into a pumpkin. Can we talk another —"

"I ran into Ethan Park today and he asked me where you went."

No clue who Ethan Park is. "Where *I* went?"

"After you left Aurum."

Oh *shit.*

"When the fuck did you quit your job?"

Usually I wouldn't make it that easy for Charles, but right now it's almost a relief to say, "Recently?"

"Ethan seemed to think it was over the summer."

And now I remember Ethan Park: broad face and broader shoulders, crinkly eyes, excessive hair gel. Charles's MBA classmate who forwarded my résumé to *his* Andover classmate, the VP of the TMT research group at Aurum Financial, thus bypassing the firm's labyrinthine hiring process. He worked at a hedge fund across the street from Aurum, and soon after I started he took me out for coffee to see how I was doing. He was very sweet, if a tad condescending. I guessed he had a younger sister as well but that, unlike Charles's and mine, their relationship never evolved beyond the stage where she thought he was the awesomest human being ever.

"That counts as recent."

"Have you been unemployed for the past six months?"

The way my brother says that, you might as well swap out *unemployed* for *in a Satanic cult.* "I've been doing some stuff here and there."

"Like what?"

"I don't want to get into it."

He pauses. "Does it have to do with matching?"

"Does what?"

We both know I've conceded the point. He says, "That time I drove you home from Mom's and you were talking about looking for a job at the matchmakers or ancillaries. You already had one. I should have guessed. I thought it was weird that you already knew the term *ancillaries.*"

Did I say *ancillaries*? Shit, I did — and I didn't even register it. What a rookie mistake to make.

"Why did you lie to me?"

I wince at that word, *lie,* the wide-ribboned sound of its censure. "I would have told you," I say. "Eventually. I was setting up to." I hope he recalls as well how dismissive he was about my prospects; I need every square inch of morally righteous territory I can annex. "I just knew you would make a big deal out of it."

He is silent. I picture his expression, creased and long suffering. Iris Lettriste talking to Sarah Reaves.

He says, "You don't remember, but after Dad left, things could get pretty rough."

"I remember," I say. All the almost evictions, the single packet of instant ramen shared among the three of us for dinner

422

when our mother was working the night shift at the restaurant or the cleaning agency, the winter I had a bad flu and, since we couldn't afford a doctor, my mother cocooned me in blankets so I could sweat it out. Of course I remember.

"Do you remember when I stopped going to school?"

What? "What are you talking about?"

"Two weeks into tenth grade. I stopped going to school."

What Charles is saying does not exist in my memory. And not because there are patches of fog in it, through which I can see only colors and shapes but not certainties. I remember him tornadoing out of our house at the same godforsaken hour every morning to get down to his specialized high school in Brooklyn. I remember him sitting at the dining table studying every night. He might as well be saying, *Do you remember when we won the lottery and went to Disneyland?* or *Do you remember when Dad came back and we all lived happily ever after?*

"No you didn't," I say.

"Mom was going crazy about money. That was all she could talk about, how we didn't have any of it and we were going to be out on the streets at the end of the month. And I was afraid something might happen."

"She was always talking like that. You left out the part about there being no homeless Asian people in New York and now we would be the first."

"It was different," he says. "I think we were closer than we had ever been. But it wasn't the being homeless." He clears his throat. "What I thought was there was a reasonable chance that Mom would take you and leave . . . me and Coraline."

"She wouldn't." I say that even before I understand what Charles is saying, because I can tell, just from the pained genteel sound of his voice, like he's being coerced into repeating a vulgar joke, that this is about our mother. What she would and wouldn't do. For us, to us.

"And I thought if I could show her that I was an asset, not a liability, she would want to keep me. And if she kept me, then I could make sure she kept Cor as well."

"Charles," I say, "Mom would never have done something like that."

"She already had."

I sit down on my bed. "That was different."

He found an Asian supermarket in Chinatown that would put him to work without asking how old he was. Loading and unloading boxes, taking inventory, sweeping floors, and stacking shelves. Then he told our mother. "She said, *If that's what you've decided.*"

"I saw you studying," I say. "Every day."

"It was the only way I could keep from losing my mind." Several months in, one of the other servers at Hong Kee Restaurant quit and our mother took over her shift. Charles asked her if he could go back to school. She said, according to him, that he could do whatever he wanted.

What he's saying reverberates back at me: *an asset, not a liability.* All the things Charles did for me growing up. The museums, the school applications, hoisting me onto his shoulders so I could have a better view of the Lunar New Year parade floats. The birthday mysteries. What if it was all to prove to our mother, in yet another way, that he was an asset? Like Coraline, he walked into his new American life and saw me, and understood. What he needed to do to survive. Charles isn't proud, not the way Coraline is. He would have no issue bending himself into whatever role has been cast for him. He did that at Harvard. He's doing that at Precision.

I can't. My brother loves me, I'm sure he does. I've felt it any number of times. When we're in his car and he brakes suddenly, he will fling his arm across the passenger seat like seat belts are a scam and I'll crash-dummy out through the windshield otherwise. Every time I've asked for help he's showed up, making sure to nag me halfway to hell. But: what he said to me while we were driving through hushed, late-night Queens, Symposium a melancholy sweetness through the speakers. You become something if you act that way for long enough. Maybe *that's* the truth of why my brother loves me. And it might have made him a better version of the person he would have been otherwise, but the fact that he felt he had no choice but to be that way — it hollows everything out.

All the noise in my head stills.

Max offering to craft a dating profile for me: *It's just about presenting the best possible version of you.*

Lucinda Clay discussing the matchmakers' algorithms: *In fact, it's my hope that, someday, they can help us make better choices about everything.*

Michael Lindenberg comparing the tech companies with the Chinese social surveillance system: *The power to predict outcomes is inextricably linked to the power to control outcomes.*

And Charretter, asking Sarah in their chat:

426

Is that what you want to be?

I think I know what the synths are trying to do to us, and I wish knowing that, finally, could make me feel even slightly less pathetic than I do right now. My brother and my sister were the best things about my childhood. What a fucking joke.

"So it is a big deal," says Charles. "To me. If that had been my job, at Aurum, I would have been grateful. I would have worked my ass off. I would never have dropped it so I could try out some random thing that I was too embarrassed to tell my family about."

I say, "Maybe you should just have let yourself hate me."

"What?" He says that a beat too slow. "What are you talking about?"

"I never asked to be the favorite." It doesn't even have anything to do with *me.* It's solely a function of the fact that when I was born our mother had no one left to foist me off on — our grandparents couldn't have taken on a third kid — and so she sucked it up and raised me herself. She's prouder of Charles's accomplishments and Coraline's beauty; if I asked her what she thought I should change about myself, she'd probably say, *Everything.*

My brother says, very quietly, "You never had to. You just enjoy it."

"I'm sorry," I say, "that I lied." Also that I have to understand this about my brother, and I'll never forget it. "I'm sorry."

"Look," he says, "Claw —"

"I should let you get to bed. Anyway, we'll see each other in a couple of weeks for Christmas." The word is a wish pressed against the back of my teeth: *Dà gē.* "Bye," I say. I wait for him to hang up before I do.

VII.

I'm half expecting nothing to happen when I hit the buzzer for #3 VERACITY LLC, but after a few seconds I hear the insectoid clicking sound that indicates the door has been unlocked. I take the stairs up. The scent in the stairwell wafting in from the spa on the second floor has changed since I was last here, from phantom field of lavender to phantom orange grove. Veracity's outer office has also changed. As I approach across the elevator bank, I can see through the glass that my desk has been replaced by the overgrown potted plant that used to sit in Komla's room. It looks even more monstrous than I remembered.

I'm about to press the bell when the door to Komla's office opens. Becks steps out. "You look like shit," she says when she lets me in.

"I couldn't sleep."

She arches an eyebrow at me, and for a

judgment-impaired instant I consider telling her about my conversation with Charles last night. She says, "Are you up for this?"

"Of course."

She twists on her heel and strides off. I follow.

Komla and Squirrel are standing at Komla's desk, gazing at one of his two monitors and talking in low tones. They look up at us as we enter. Komla's smile is fragile. It seems misplaced on him, like a false mustache. "Claudia," he says. "It's good to see you."

I'm so befuddled by this opening move — I'd spent my ride over prepping for anger, recalcitrance, denial, all the ways *I* might react if someone confronted me about my plan to cover up a murder — that I respond with "You moved your plant."

"I did. Just for the time being, while I decided what to do with it." He walks out from behind his desk. "Did I ever tell you why I have this plant?"

"Is this digression into backstory really necessary?" says Becks.

His plan had always been to return to Ghana after he completed his studies at Cambridge, says Komla. When he decided to move to the United States instead, a Ghanian friend of his, a botanist, gave him

430

the plant. "A reminder, she said, although I'm not sure I ever figured out what of. It was well-intentioned, but it caused me no end of trouble at customs."

I ask, "Did you come here because of Lucinda Clay?"

He expresses no emotion at the mention of Lucinda's name. "And Compatibility. We began developing the concept while we were at Cambridge. We agreed we would give ourselves five years to build it into a business."

"And that concept," I say, "was to build bots that could help to verify whether, and how, people on dating platforms were lying about themselves?"

He nods. "That was the heart of Compatibility," he says. "The synths." To the world Compatibility was a matchmaker, but that was only because he and Lucinda needed an initial platform on which to test out the synths. They always intended to provide the synths as a service to all the matchmakers, as a means of screening for truth.

"Like . . . Veracity," I say.

"Indeed. You could say that the synths were the original verifiers."

"When did that change?" says Becks. "When Soulmate bought you up?"

Not at first, says Komla. It turned out that

Soulmate's management had no interest in using the synths as a verification tool; they were just looking to introduce bot profiles onto the platform to artificially inflate subscriber numbers. "So we generated the types of profiles they wanted, and they let us continue working on the synths."

Becks says, "But that means the matchmakers were putting out fake profiles while you were still at Soulmate." She pauses. "Much earlier than you said they were."

After a moment Komla says, "Those were very different. They were static bots. They didn't engage at all with users. Any deception . . . it was minimal."

"That's a good one. You should put it on a T-shirt. *Any deception was minimal.*"

"At the time," he says, "it really seemed like we might be able to resolve the lying limitation. You know what that would have meant for matching. The possibility of truly predicting compatibility, the assurance of successful matches. We thought the benefits of that would justify what we were doing for Soulmate." Access to Soulmate's platform allowed the synths to interact with and learn from a much higher number of human users than they previously could. They became increasingly skilled at drawing information from users, relating that back to what the users had previously provided in their profiles, identifying contradictions. "And, of course, the significance of this went beyond dating. The technology could potentially be used to ascertain truth in all areas of online life."

I hear myself say, "Provided no one knew you were doing it."

He turns to look at me. "Yes. Deception was also at the heart of Compatibility."

"Can we get to the action?" says Squirrel, who I now notice has taken the liberty of sprawling himself in Komla's desk chair. "What was wrong with the synths? Why didn't they work?"

"The problem wasn't the synths," says Komla. "It was the humans."

"Always the fucking humans," says Becks.

Komla tells us that, as the synths' data collection capabilities improved, they began to break down because they couldn't reconcile all the data points they had about the users they were verifying. It wasn't that humans were too sophisticated for the synths. In a way, they weren't sophisticated enough. They misremembered and miscast events, they changed their minds and believed they had always held those opinions, they acted in ways contrary to their best interests, they had conflicting desires, they

433

didn't know what they wanted at all. "We realized that a good portion of human inconsistency was simply unverifiable."

Jude Kalman cheating on the wife he loves. Iris Lettriste propping up and undermining her sister at the same time. Lionel betraying Coraline with the story he wanted to know because he loved her so much; and Coraline, in love with him yet indifferent to what mattered most to him. No wonder the synths gave up. I say, "So then you thought . . . maybe you could use the synths to change the humans instead?"

Komla's eyebrows lift. "Aha," he says.

Becks says — I'm not sure whether to me or to Komla — "Are you fucking serious."

"I think that's what Soulmate is using the synths to do now," I say. "They're collecting all this data to better understand how their subscribers think, and then they're using it to affect people's choices. The matchmakers' success depends on making their algorithms so accurate that everyone will want to sign up. But if it's too hard for the matchmakers to actually predict compatibility, because people suck in all the ways that Komla just said, then the alternative is to do things the other way around. Change people into what they're supposed to be so that the algorithms work."

434

No one says anything. I say, "It's already going on in other ways. Every time a company recommends something to us based on what it knows we like, it's shaping our preferences going forward." I add, to Becks and Squirrel, "That's also from Michael Lindenberg." Even if he was only half right. The matchmakers do want control, but because they *aren't* able to predict who we are. Yet.

Becks says to Komla, "Please tell me Lucinda Clay came up with this and you told her to go fly her crazy kite."

"We never intended . . ." He pauses. "All along, we wanted to use what we were learning, and building, to improve things. To make them better." From the data, he and Lucinda saw that people frequently expressed what they wished to be like or to do in their profiles and their chats with potential matches, including in ways that indicated they might not be fully cognizant of their own desires and aspirations — or shortcomings. Komla and Lucinda began to program the synths to identify such conscious and subconscious wishes and to engage with users about them. "I think that was when our ideas first began to diverge. What it meant to make things better."

For Komla, the value of the synths lay in

their potential to provide people with insights about themselves in an effective, empathetic way. The synths could access and process vast reserves of information — data points not only about a particular individual but also about similarly situated users across Soulmate's platform — and they could personalize it all for the actual person they were speaking to at any given moment. They would help that person more fully comprehend who they were, what they wanted. More than that, the synths' insights could target areas of weakness in human judgment and opinion for societal benefit. "Raising users' awareness of their unconscious biases, for example. Questioning assumptions, presenting different viewpoints." Komla smiles. "If we haven't tried it, how do we know it won't work?"

After a moment I realize he is talking to Becks, who has what I can now recognize as her *this is such utopian bullshit* face on. I say, "But that wasn't enough for Lucinda."

"No," says Komla. "Not when the synths could do so much more."

Then a private equity firm called Polaris Capital bought a controlling stake in Soulmate. Polaris replaced the existing management and commenced a series of cost-cutting measures, which included dismantling the synth project. "Lucinda scheduled a briefing with them and came out of it with a promotion and a greatly expanded budget. She can be very persuasive."

Becks said, "You weren't in there with her?"

He chuckles. "She made sure to leave me off the invite. But I had a fairly good idea of how she sold Polaris on the synths, because we had discussed this before. Soulmate's purpose is to maximize profit. Therefore, in order to justify the synths, we would have to show that what we were doing would result in profit for the company. The greater the profitability, the more leverage we would have." The limited-functionality bots that Komla and Lucinda had produced for Soulmate's prior management had only a marginal effect on revenue; far more significant would be the synths' ability to nudge users into conforming with the predictions of Soulmate's compatibility algorithm.

"As you said," he says, looking at me. "And doing so would align with Lucinda's own vision of the synths as a way to improve people's decision-making."

"That was what the Project Tilt presentation in Sarah's files was about, then," I say.

"I think so," he says. "Lucinda was always

so sure that she could keep all her balls in the air. What she wanted to accomplish with the synths. What Soulmate, and then Polaris, wanted from her."

I hear it almost as if he spoke aloud: *And me.* He still loves her, I realize.

I say, "And all that is what Sarah Reaves was going to write about."

This is the first time we've said her name, and for an instant I feel like I've called her back into the office with us, Sarah-as-Iris, watching over our shoulders, waiting to see just what we'll do with everything we know.

Komla says, "It's not clear to me how much she found out."

Becks says, "Enough for Lucinda Clay to kill her."

His gaze shutters like his eyelids have suddenly become too heavy to hold up. Then he says, "There's no proof that she was responsible."

I think of Schrödinger's cat, Komla holding the closed box in his hands. For as long as he doesn't open it, there is a reality in which Lucinda Clay did not kill Sarah Reaves.

"You believe she is, though," I say. "That's why you've been trying to get rid of all the evidence that could show Sarah's death was a crime."

He does not say anything.

Becks steps away from the windows. "Sarah Reaves was a pain in the ass. Whatever story she would have come up with, probably unreadable. But now she's dead, K. She's never going to get to write that shitty story. Date her douchebags. Fight with her even-bigger-pain-in-the-ass sister."

The room feels as rigged with laser tripwires as the vault with the crown jewels in a heist movie. I'm afraid to even breathe too deeply, for fear of setting anything off.

Komla says, "I was the one who told Lucinda about Sarah."

I chomp down on my tongue to keep from superfluously saying *What?!* since it's clear he's just getting started.

"Jesus Christ," says Becks, not sounding at all surprised. "Talk about poor decision-making."

He tells us that the name of the profile, Charretter, caught his attention right away. It was a play on the architectural term *charrette,* and Lucinda had often described her idea for the synths by reference to architecture. "She called it *choice architecture,*" he says. "Shaping people's choices for optimal outcomes."

Once he reviewed Charretter's chat records, he saw the differences between Charretter and the other synths that the verifiers had been tracking. Soulmate was beginning to put into place its plan of using the synths as mechanisms to influence users. He sent Lucinda an email to let her know that someone was asking questions about a profile with the handle Charretter.

"I'm not sure what I was hoping for, exactly," he says to the framed picture on the wall, a photograph of an old-timey street in what looks like a European city, sunlit hues of stone and a distant, lonesome cathedral spire. It's the only decoration in Komla's office, plant aside, and every time I've looked at it I've changed my mind about what place it is. This time I think, *Cambridge, of course, Cambridge.* "To make her slow down, or reconsider. She knew very well how bad it would look, for Soulmate and for her, if people found out about the synths." She never replied. Sarah Reaves's A Dose a Day account was closed two weeks later; Sarah died of an overdose another two weeks after that.

"Even if she did this," says Komla, "if Lucinda did do this . . . I can guarantee that there will be no connection between her and Sarah Reaves. No aspect of their lives would have touched. That's the only way she could have." He pauses. "When you

440

put enough layers between yourself and another person, you're able to forget what you're actually doing."

"I call bullshit," says Becks. "If you know that you push a button and someone dies, you don't push that fucking button. No matter how much easier it would make your life."

"When did you become so certain of that?"

Becks goes still like we're in an *wuxia* movie and he's reached out and blocked off her pressure points. Swatches of red bloom in her cheeks; I get the impression she's preventing the color from spreading any farther through force of will. The air feels tingly with foreboding. I stare down at the gray weave of the carpet and wonder both what Komla meant as well as whether I'll ever become close enough to Becks to countenance asking her.

"I shouldn't have said that. I'm —"

Becks, clipped: "You did. Let's leave it at that."

"Um," I say to the carpet. "She did make one mistake. The final A Dose a Day box. Sarah's account was canceled before that box would have been delivered. If we told the police about that . . . wouldn't it be enough to reopen the case?"

After a moment Becks says, "The police will never be able to link anyone to anything based on that. They'll spend the next six months looking up their asses and then shelve everything again."

That sounds enough like normal Becks for me to feel safe looking up. "We also have the materials from Sarah's source."

From the way Komla and Becks both turn toward me, I can tell I've reunited them in dislike of where this is going. What the hell. "We could tell Michael Lindenberg. About the synths, why Sarah was killed. He has contacts in the police, and he's a big-time journalist. People would listen to him."

"Kapow," says Squirrel.

"No," says Komla. "I want to stop what the matchmakers are doing with the synths, but not by destroying them both. Matching and the synths — they are tools that we have for better understanding ourselves, forming better relationships. It would be a mistake to throw them away, and that's what will happen if someone like Michael Lindenberg gets hold of this story. Journalists have their own agenda."

I figure there's no need to mention how Michael is truffling around trying to find out what Sarah intended to write about. "You sound like you think Sarah shouldn't have been chasing her story."

He sighs. "I think she shouldn't have died for it."

Silence again, a heavy cloth billowing down on us. I think of Charles lecturing me on the superior value proposition of the matchmakers, provided we can find a way around the lying limitation, and then decide I don't want to think about my brother at all, not for a while.

"I will talk to her."

I glance over at Komla.

"If it was Lucinda, I think I can persuade her to tell me." There's a calcified set to his features. "Something like that . . . it's too large. And we told each other everything."

The idea of him taking that trust and binding Lucinda with it burrows into the pit of my stomach. I say, "Are you sure you want to know?"

Becks says, "What the fuck is that supposed to mean?"

He smiles at me like he hears what I'm thinking, and he agrees. "Occam's razor," he says. "This is the simplest way."

What would *I* do if someone I loved fucked up like that? Murder, as premeditated as it gets. For a moment I'm weak-kneed glad that this isn't my choice to make.

"But we must agree." Komla's gaze shifts

to Squirrel, slouched behind the desk, and then to the windows, where Becks is. "What happened to Sarah is about what one person did. Nothing more."

Justice for Sarah in exchange for silence about the synths. I think again of Michael Lindenberg. But even if we were to get him the Dispatch files, that wouldn't be enough — nothing in them proves the synths are a creation of the matchmakers or what they're being used for. If he kept investigating he might be able to obtain more evidence, but that would take time. And if Lucinda found out another journalist was asking questions —

"For now," says Becks.

Komla inclines his head as if he expected this response. "Squirrel?"

Squirrel shrugs. "Sure."

His gaze returns to me, a steady, elegiac darkness, and again I feel like he can hear the tumult in my mind. But really there's no choice, is there? If we want to stop Lucinda Clay, we need Komla's help. I nod. For now.

"Lucinda will be in New York next week," he says. According to Soulmate's staff movement calendar, she's currently in San Francisco, leaving for Beijing tonight. From there she will come to New York for a few days and then fly to Singapore.

Squirrel says, staring at the computer monitor, "Tuesday through Friday." Some keyboard action, and then: "After Singapore she's on leave for the rest of the year. Nothing recorded after that."

Komla says, "We'll have to get to her while she's here."

"Can we find her on Finders Keepers?" says Becks.

Squirrel shakes his head. "She's too pro to get herself picked up on that."

"Or your app is too shitty."

Flying to New York from Asia just to turn around four days later? There must be some important meeting or event she's attending in New York, to warrant all the jet lag and carbon emissions. If we could figure out what that is, we could try to catch her there. Then I remember the charity gala that came up back when I searched for Lucinda Clay. Could that be it? I pull up the event website on my phone: the timing fits. *Join the world's leading fashion companies in celebrating the achievements of minority women business leaders.* Fashion companies, huh. I hold my breath and scroll down to the half dozen corporate logos listed as sponsors.

I tune back in to the larger discussion. Squirrel is telling Becks she is in no place

445

to critique his coding skills when he had to show her how to turn off her Find My iPhone function. "She'll be at the Gatsby Hotel in Chelsea next Thursday," I say. "At a charity gala. She's one of the honorees, so she'll definitely attend."

The others look at me like I've flipped myself over and started walking around on my hands: impressive, maybe, but also useless. Becks says, "If your plan is to wait around outside the hotel like celebrity stalkers, that's —"

"That's one option," I say. "Or I could just get us in. To the gala, I mean."

PART FOUR

PART FOUR

I.

I ask Coraline to meet me for dinner. We're halfway through our appetizers, and Coraline is halfway through her second glass of wine, when she says, "Okay, what do you want?"

"That's a very philosophical question," I say. "Like, in life?"

"You only ask to hang out when you want something from me."

"That's not true. We haven't seen each other since Thanksgiving, and that was . . ."

"A total shit show."

"How did things turn out with you and Lionel?"

"That," says my sister, like she just remembered. "We're taking a break."

I make what I hope is an appropriately sympathetic sound. From Finders Keepers, which Squirrel has reinstalled on my phone, I'm aware that Lionel seems to have relocated altogether to Crown Heights. If the app had a zoom-in capability, I'd guess I'd be looking at Writing Group Isabel's couch, or maybe bedroom. I know it's evil of me, but I hope he gets bedbugs.

"I think you were right."

"Can I get that on record?"

"It's better to be single. You don't have to deal with anyone else's bullshit."

"I never said it was *better*. I just said there's nothing wrong with it."

She tells me that every time she logs in to Partnered Up she thinks, *There are so many fucking people out there.* She receives tens of messages from men a day, and the dating app is continually informing her that a new high-compatibility match has shown up in her vicinity. "All this — it's supposed to make things easier, right? Then why is it so fucking impossible to find one guy I actually want to be with?"

"Maybe it depends on what you want?"

"I want someone like Lionel," she says, "who's not Lionel. At least work is crazy right now so it keeps me from thinking too much about him. What a fucking sad thing to say."

"What are you busy with?" I ask.

She lists half a dozen tasks, none of which relate to the planning or marketing of a gala dinner scheduled to take place in seven days.

"What about the . . . Doesn't your company sponsor an annual gala for charity . . . don't you have to do the marketing for that?"

"What are you talking about?"

"There's a charity gala happening next week. Élodie de Montalivet is listed as one of the sponsors."

My sister continues to frown at me. Could I possibly have gotten this wrong? I imagine Komla and Becks opening the door of an incinerator and seeing, in a teeny pile, the ashes of my credibility.

"Oh! You mean my company, Élodie de Montalivet." Her version is an urbane, infinitely distant relative of mine. "The thing at the Gatsby."

Hmm, it's actually pretty annoying to be corrected like that. "That's what I just said. Can you get me and two other people in?"

"In where?"

"Into Congress. That gala."

My sister looks at her now-empty wineglass. "That was only my second glass, right?"

"Cor, focus. This is important." I remember to add: "Please?"

"Do you even know what it will be like? It's a lot of really rich people wearing really formal clothes getting really drunk and talk-

451

ing about really boring things. It's everything you hate."

"Which is unfortunate, but —"

"What the fuck is going on? Are you having a quarter-life crisis?"

I take a breath. "What I'm going to tell you is a secret."

Coraline leans forward. "I love secrets."

"I know." I explain that one of the honorees at the gala, Lucinda Clay, was once engaged to a colleague of mine. They had an epic falling-out years ago and haven't spoken since. My colleague has decided to move back to Ghana, and he would like to meet Lucinda one last time before he leaves. "He's been trying to contact her, but she refuses to even respond. He mentioned this gala to me, and when I saw that Élodie — or however you pronounce it — was involved I said I'd see if you could help."

"God, that is so romantic. It's like something you read in a novel."

I did crib the plot from *Inspector Yuan and the Vengeful Huntsman,* except in that book the lovers wind up strangled by the woman's overpossessive brother. "Any chance you have extra tickets?"

"There are a bunch reserved," she says. "We were going to offer them to some of our business partners, but I could . . ." She pauses. "I get why he has to be there, obviously. But what about you? And who's this third person?"

"Wingwomen," I say. "Thanks, Cor. Undying gratitude, plus you have the moral satisfaction of knowing that you're helping to make the world a better place."

The way she looks at me, I know she knows there's plenty I'm not sharing. I wonder if Charles told her about my quitting Aurum and if she's going to call me out on it. But all she says is "I didn't know you were close with your colleagues like that."

"A few of us have become pretty tight," I say.

When we leave the restaurant I ask Coraline if she'll order a car to get her back to Williamsburg.

"Oh," she says, "the new guy I'm seeing lives right around here. I think I'll stop by."

"Didn't you just say, about how it's better to be single . . . ?"

She adjusts her scarf around her neck and then sighs. "He makes me feel a bit less lonely," she says.

The night before the gala, I come home to find Max doing yoga on the living room rug. "Hello, stranger," I say. The propulsive force of my gladness at seeing him surprises me; I want to tackle him mid-vinyasa flow. I wheel my bike around him. "Did you get a haircut?"

"Two weeks ago."

Oops. "It looks good. Are you staying in tonight? Do you want to get takeout? It's been a while since we've had our taste buds annihilated by Salaam Spicy Number One."

He folds himself from downward dog into a seated position on his mat. "Benny and I are going to an experimental theater show in Bushwick. Do you want to come?"

"Thanks, but I'm pretty tired." Since when did Greenpoint become Benny, without even an intermediate-nickname stopover? I plop onto the couch to illustrate my statement. "Sounds like . . . things are going well?"

"Yeah." He speaks like he's testing out the word for the first time, trying to figure out the swell and stretch of its sound. "I put my matchmaker accounts on hold last week."

That has never happened before. Max is always, *always* searching, even when he's gushing to me about his current match. "All nine hundred and ninety-nine of them?" I say.

"Seventeen," he says reproachfully. "I've probably missed a couple."

"Isn't that what your dating spreadsheet is for?" I have this sudden sense memory of sitting in a car with Max, the two of us rushing forward through space and time and not even noticing because we're yowling our way through one of the Valjean and Javert duets from *Les Misérables.* The AC gusts arctic against our faces and I can smell the yeasty fragrance of the doughnuts we picked up earlier that morning. Through the windshield the sky rises like a blue wall above the highway and the world is syrupy with light. Max's falsetto cracks at *Two-four-six-oh-ooooone!* and for the rest of the day I'll make fun of him for it. The road trip we took the summer after senior year. We started out in Vermont and said we would go south until we ran out of road. How far did we get? Charleston, pastel charming and languid, which was when we realized we were broke. Max got his parents to transfer him some money and bought us plane tickets to New York. He never let me pay him back.

Max is saying that it's not like he and Benny have had the Talk yet, but for some time now — since the night of the Halloween party, in fact — he hasn't felt the urge to go online. "It's like, before then I was always thinking about who else is out there and how amazing they could be. And now I feel like no one could be more amazing than Benny, so why bother?"

"That's great." I mean it — and yet. All those times when Max banged in through the front door, back from another night of gallivanting, and turned to me like a Shakespearean actor ready for the soliloquy in act 3 when everything's going to shit, and I told him that before either of us knew it he would find his true love and I would be left sitting on the couch lost and lonely without him. Maybe I could say that so readily because a part of me didn't believe it would ever happen.

I stand up from said couch. "We should all hang out soon."

"That would be awesome. I've told him so much about you. I guess technically you guys met that one time, when your colleague came over, but that was kind of weird."

"Very weird."

"That woman — is she your Blonde Assassin? She's intense."

"That's one way of putting it."

"She sent me some names of people at art galleries. To submit my work to."

I squint at Max: he's not kidding. "That's . . ."

456

"Yeah! Super nice."

How bizarre to have that word linked to the concept of Becks. It occurs to me: "Are you going to change the name of the series? Just wondering — I won't be upset if you do. Maybe a very tiny bit, but I'll get over it —"

"Hell no!" says Max. "I think it's perfect."

He clambers upright; he has to get ready. As he's rolling up his yoga mat he says, "There *is* one thing. He's gotten the impression I'm vegan."

It takes me a moment to realize we've boomeranged back to the topic of Benny. "How? You're the king of cheese. In more ways than one."

"It could be because I've been eating vegan when I'm with him."

Ah. I guess we'll never be able to stop deceiving each other, not entirely.

"I figure I'll wait for him to fall hopelessly in love with me before I clarify."

Or ourselves. "No matter what, Max," I say, "you'll be okay. I'll make sure of it."

II.

"What did you do?" I say, appalled.

Three hours ago I met Coraline at her apartment. Neither of us commented on the gaps in the shelves where Lionel's books used to be or the obstacle course of cardboard boxes in the living room. Coraline had already unpacked her makeup gear across the coffee table. She poured us each a glass of wine, sat me down, and got to work.

"I made you beautiful," says Coraline. She lets go of my shoulders — I can see her in the mirror behind me — and cocks her head, considering me. "That might have been the hardest makeup job I've ever had."

I lean forward. I'm having a body-snatcher moment. It's as if an alien has usurped my face, sealed up its pores (that part is cool, I guess), remolded its cheekbone structure, and dialed up its coloring in vivid, slightly frightening ways. And what is going on with my eyes? There's enough glitter to bomb the Westboro Baptist Church, and each time I blink my lashes stick together from all the stuff Coraline coated them with.

"Not that you aren't already beautiful. Like, as a person. But now you're outwardly beautiful as well."

"I can't go out like this."

"What? Why not?"

"I look insane."

"Claudia," says my sister, like she's trying to coax a wimpy child into the shallow end of the pool, "women all over the world leave their houses looking like this every day."

"Like their eyelids are tiny disco balls?"

"You're going to a black-tie gala at the trendiest event space in downtown Manhattan. You need an appropriately dramatic look."

Next my sister wrangles me into what she swears is the least showy of her evening dresses. I'd argue it's less a *dress,* as the term is commonly understood, than a tiny piece of cloth that you tie around yourself — or, in my case, that Coraline ties around me like a high priestess trussing up an animal for sacrifice.

"The entire top half is held up by this knot at the back of my neck?" I ask. "That feels precarious."

"This is perfect on you," says Coraline. "Who knew you had such great legs?" She turns me around. "Or this long narrow back?"

"Not to objectify me or anything."

"Imagine what Mom would say if she saw you."

"You're not going to tell her about this, are you?"

"No way. She'd talk about nothing else for the next decade. Okay, shoes."

We try out eight pairs of my sister's shoes before we find one in which I can walk for more than ten steps without tripping. Still hurts like hell, though. "Now I know how those women in China felt, with their bound feet."

"They got used to it. You will too."

Coraline goes into the bedroom to get ready herself. I stretch out on her couch and stream a Symposium album so I can fill my head with something other than the thought that I'm about to sneak into a fashion gala to accost a murderer. While wearing eyeliner! That might be the most surreal bit.

The sky is dark by the time Coraline comes out. Her timing is excellent: "A Thousand Ships," Symposium's song about Helen of Troy, is just hushing into its final lines. I watch her pad barefoot to the jumble of shoes we left in the middle of the living room and pick out a pair. Her loveliness is incandescent. I imagine how Lionel must have seen her, and all the men who preceded him, as this precious thing to be possessed.

My sister stands up and says something to me. I pop out my earphones. "What?"

"Are you ready?"

It occurs to me: I already knew, even before I asked Coraline for her help, that she would do it. She would cannonball right into this scheme, never mind that she could get in trouble at her job and she doesn't know my colleague from some guy on the street, even though she knows she doesn't know what it's truly about. Because she's fearless, in her own way, and because she would do it for me.

"Cor," I say, "you're awesome."

She smiles and steps into her heels. "I know."

III.

The Gatsby would make a fantastic setting for a murder mystery. Chandeliers blazing up the lobby, jazz and the scent of fresh-cut flowers in the air, the grand swoop of a staircase to upper floors of secrets. You could stab someone as they're reclining into the recesses of this wingback chair, stash their body in the case of that grandfather clock, and then Lindy Hop your way to the other end of the chessboard floor.

Next to me Coraline says, "Oh my god, this place is even more Instagrammable than the Museum of Ice Cream."

"There's a Museum of Ice Cream?" I say. "How have I not heard of this?"

We get in line to check our coats. Coraline is taking pictures of the space to post on her company's social media accounts, texting her colleagues about last-minute logistics, air-kissing attractive people around us and emoting her joy that they were able to attend this event. I hide within the swirl of her professional mania and text Komla and Becks to let them know I've arrived.

After we are through with the coat check, my sister and I head for the Gershwin Room, where the cocktail reception is being held. The room is big and bright and congested; the noise feels like an invisible force that I have to push back against to avoid getting knocked down. "She isn't here yet," says Coraline, "Lucinda Clay. Or at least, no one at Élodie has seen her." She glances around the room. "I have to go introduce some lame people to some other lame people. I'll text you when I hear that she's arrived."

I station myself at the back of the room and watch everyone around me gesturing with their champagne flutes and chittering on like this is some latter-day Conference of the Birds. The men would be penguins, of course, looking slightly strangled by their bow ties; the women, flamingos and cranes and golden pheasants. God, my face itches.

A server pauses in front of me with a tray of hors d'oeuvres, and I realize like a trapdoor has swung open in my gut how hungry I am. He describes the selection to me, utilizing terms like *deconstructed version of* and *elevated take on*.

463

"Do you have to go through that with every single guest?" I ask as I take one of everything. "It feels like it would take a lot of time."

He smiles. "Most of the time they just take something and I move on. But you looked like you were appreciating the spiel."

I soon have cause to regret my enthusiasm. Not because I seem like a little glutton — I am one, after all — but because I'm finding it tricky to navigate one of these concoctions into my mouth without dropping something else.

"You look like you could use one of these."

I glance over. Some guy is holding out a napkin embossed with the hotel's name. The tuxedo he has on, and a courtliness to his manner, makes me feel like I've landed in a Jane Austen novel, the scene at a ball where a most dashing gentleman makes the acquaintance of the heroine. In which case, would he be Wickham or Darcy?

"Thank you," I say. I move to take it and then realize all my fingers are otherwise occupied.

Wickham/Darcy spreads the napkin across his palm so I can unload my spoils onto it. How chivalrous! "You look so familiar," he says. "Did you go to Yale?"

Crap: What if this guy was one of my

verification targets? Maybe he saw me lurking around and my face got tangled up in the dragnet of his subconscious.

"I have a very common face," I say. "People are constantly mistaking me for someone else."

"You have a very beautiful face." He speaks with the authority of a connoisseur. "But it's not just that. You have a . . . je ne sais quoi. It's very compelling."

Or he's hitting on me.

I say, "You really leaned into the French pronunciation there." I do enjoy heterosexual flirtation when the odd occasion arises. It feels similar to playing blackjack during Chinese New Year with Monopoly money: easy excitement, low consequence.

Wickham/Darcy is telling me about the year he spent in Paris after graduation, trying to find himself, when a familiar perfume sneak-attacks: Becks.

"Here's your drink."

We both turn. For an instant I'm stunned by the architectural perfection of her shoulders and her neck. She's wearing a silk halter top, and her hair is drawn back in what must be the Platonic ideal of a chignon. Then she arches an eyebrow and tilts the flute at me. "Yes," I say, taking it from her. "Thank you."

"Sorry to steal her," she says to Wickham/ Darcy, who appears similarly debilitated, "but there's someone over there we've arranged to meet." She places a hand on my upper arm and escorts me off.

I'm so focused on the imprint of her palm against my skin — cool and dry, and callused, which makes me wonder: tennis? sailing? archery? — that by the time I remember and look behind me Wickham/Darcy has merged back into whatever waddle of penguins that is his natural habitat, lost to me forever. "My hors d'oeuvres," I say.

"For Christ's sake. We're about to get a three-course meal."

She continues to steer me between the islands of glitzy chatter. "Where are we going?" I ask.

"Getting into position."

"For?"

She sighs like it's obvious. Fine.

We are nearing a set of doors across the room from the ones I came in through when a voice, echoey through the speaker system, asks us all to begin making our way into the adjoining Rivera Room and take our seats. "Please enter through the connecting doors," says the voice. "Dinner will commence shortly." On cue the doors that Becks and I are facing swing open. Everyone standing around us begins to merge toward them.

"That," says Becks. "I fucking hate crowds."

According to the layout Coraline has shown me, table three should be at the far right of the front row facing the stage. Its table number should also be missing, which will hopefully ensure that it remains relatively unoccupied for the next several minutes.

"She's reached the table," says Becks. We're oozing along in a gigantic human amoeba. I can't see anything except elaborate hairdos and dinner jackets, but I guess Becks has the comparative advantage of height. She adds, "And that's your sister?"

A question I've become accustomed to when someone gets the inaugural opportunity to compare Coraline and me. I say, "We share the lesser half of our DNA."

As more people find their seats, my view clears and I can see the woman who must be Lucinda Clay. In person she's indeed small, but striking in her long shimmery aquamarine dress and with her braids piled in a basket on top of her head. A hummingbird, that's the type of avian she would be. She's standing with Coraline and a third woman, a statuesque brunette, and even though she's just nodding at what the others are saying, I can almost see the air around her vibrating with purposive energy.

Becks releases my arm. "Go."

As I get closer I see my sister see me. She says something, the three women share an effusive *so great to chat!* moment, and Coraline and the brunette move away. Lucinda sits at the empty table and immediately takes out her phone. I count to three and approach. "Hi," I say. "Is it okay if I sit here?"

She looks up as if someone has called to her from a great distance, and I see, before her face widens in a smile, the fatigue seamed into the corners of her eyes and her mouth. I'd bet she hasn't slept well in a while. She could just be seriously jet-lagged, or killing Sarah Reaves could be exacting its subtle psychic costs. Maybe we can break this woman after all.

"Of course," she says. She waits until I've settled myself — most ungracefully: as I'm pulling the chair forward one of its legs snags on the carpet and I almost impale myself against the table edge — to introduce herself. "I'm Lucinda."

"Claudia." A panic earthquake judders through me. Shit, this is really happening. "I'm so excited to meet you. It's so heartening to see a woman of color be so successful in tech. What you've accomplished with Soulmate, improving the algorithms, building up platforms, such an inspiration . . ." I can't seem to shut up with the clichés, like a magician who's messed up the pulling-cloth-from-mouth trick and will gag unless he keeps going. Lucinda listens with the same amused expression as in her photos, although in person it's kinder, as if she gets that I'm making an ass of myself because I'm nervous and she's not going to hold it against me.

Eventually she says, "You know, people talk about matching and tech in the same breath all the time. To me, that tends to obscure what matching is really about, which is relationships."

I nod the way the *wuxia* acolyte does in the scene where his master is inducting him into the principles of whatever animal-themed martial art he will be learning.

At a fundamental level, says Lucinda, matching is about understanding what we want from each other and what we can give to each other. "It's a deeply human mystery. That's what drew me to this business to begin with."

I nod again. "Compatibility."

"Excuse me?"

"How to match people who are compatible with each other."

"Yes," she says. "Yes. Exactly."

I'm trying to picture her and Komla together. I imagine small gestures of solicitude and the joy of a grand idea shared, the quiet comfort of routines, constant intellectual debate. A completeness of understanding, at least for a time. My irremediable inner romantic hopes she still misses him.

"But tell me about yourself," says Lucinda. "What are you working on?"

This was Komla's suggestion, that Coraline ask Lucinda if she would mind being seated at a table with up-and-coming entrepreneurs who would love the opportunity to talk with her. "She would prefer that anyway," he said, "to being trapped with the VIPs." Coraline told me that Lucinda replied to the email request within two minutes with *I'd be delighted.*

"Is this table three?" A guy with a Mephistophelian goatee peers at us from across the table.

"That's what we're hoping," says Lucinda. He pulls out the chair one over from Lucinda's right just as two women come up and ask the same question. I already know who the newcomers are, having had the benefit of viewing the seating arrangements for our table: Adam Schultz, Katya Popov, and Helen Sims-Morrow, all from New York–based start-ups that have launched in the past two years.

Adam sits down, leans across the empty chair between him and Lucinda, and starts telling her about his company, Yogi Yourself, which develops AI-enabled yoga clothing that refines the wearer's poses. "Transformed my warrior two," he says. "Do you practice yoga? Your posture, it's so relaxed and also elegant. Can I send you a sample? I'd love to hear your feedback." Lucinda intermittently asks a question. Each time she does she very considerately glances at me to signal that I'm included in this conversation, even if it's obvious that to Adam he's enjoying a solo audience with Lucinda Clay. I don't blame him; he's just accurately assessing the food chain dynamics, which, in the wild, would be a prerequisite for survival.

On my left Katya and Helen, who appear to know each other from prior female entrepreneur networking events, are discussing a mutual acquaintance whose start-up has landed a big investment by SoftBank.

"I'm so glad for her," says Katya. "This company, it's her life."

"Absolutely," says Helen, "although, you know, SoftBank coming in so early . . . it might not be the best thing. It would be awful if she ended up as another We Work."

I'm reminded of the vibe at Suzanna Cratchett's reading.

"Lucinda Clay!"

Everyone at our table looks up: only someone assured of their eminence, or brazenly un-self-aware, would issue forth with such volume and vigor. A large man with a close-shaven head has paused behind the still-empty chair on Lucinda's right. He looks to be in his early fifties and has the padded, square-shouldered build of a former athlete. "How did the woman of the hour end up at this table?" he says. "Come join us over there. There's still space. If there isn't, we'll kick Ostrowski out."

Oh, shit. If we have a contingency plan for this scenario, neither Komla nor Becks informed me of it.

Lucinda smiles up at him. "The people here are much more interesting, though."

He laughs. "No argument there." Then he yanks out the chair next to her and plonks himself down. "Since we're both here," he says. "I've been meaning to touch base with you. About Tilt."

I pick up my fork — some stealthy server

has placed the first course in front of me, six salad leaves and a calligraphic swirl of vinaigrette; I hadn't even noticed — and begin to eat like I'm so entranced by the flavors I couldn't possibly spare the brain space to eavesdrop.

"Three things. One, I've said it before, but it's worth saying again. Great work. Not just the tech itself, which is fucking impressive. The vision. I wish more people could think big like that."

"Thank you," says Lucinda. "Once Tilt is in place, over time we should see a meaningful increase in subscriber satisfaction."

"Sure, sure. But beyond that as well. Which brings me to two. I spoke to our portfolio companies. A select few, I know we're still getting this thing off the ground. They're all very excited about the idea."

"What about the idea, exactly?"

"You know. Helping consumers make better choices. There's nothing that limits Tilt to matching. It would benefit any consumer-facing business."

And once I hear that, I realize how right this man is. The synths' suggestions to users are so powerful not only because they are informed by all the data the synths have collected about those users, but also because the synths appear to have no agenda of their own. Even though, of course, they do — as Sarah Reaves herself said, at her very first meeting with us. They have Lucinda's agenda, and Soulmate's, and Polaris's. And they could potentially have the agenda of any entity or person looking to influence the American public on the merits of a product or a politician or a policy, provided this entity or person could pay the price being asked for by the humans who controlled the synths.

I take my phone out of the clutch that Coraline lent me: I need to tell Komla and Becks about this. A waterfall of messages cascades down my screen, all from Becks.

That's Peter Stromberg. Partner at Polaris.

Why the hell is he at our table? We need to get rid of him.

What are they talking about?

What is the fucking point of having a phone if you never check the fucking thing.

Lucinda is saying that she designed this technology for the purpose of enhancing the compatibility algorithms unique to the matching industry. "In terms of extending it to other contexts . . ."

"Improving the algorithm is great. Don't get me wrong." Peter Stromberg clears his throat and says, several decibels lower, "But a goal like that, it can get kind of hazy. Lots of variables. We should also be looking at more discrete applications."

Lucinda's voice is clear and mild: "I suppose I was aiming to think big."

"Nothing wrong with that. And I hear you on making sure we get things right if we decide to expand Tilt." Another decibel drop: "That's why I asked Frank McMann to start looking into how we would adapt your work for other monetization strategies."

I peek over and see that he's shifted his bulk closer to Lucinda. "That's the third thing." The softer his voice is, the more amiable its tone, as if he's exchanging pleasantries while waiting for his turn on the golf course. "When I checked in with him yesterday, he said he still hadn't received access to the project drive."

McMann, that tattletale. I google *peter stromberg polaris capital* while I consider fiction's favorite methods of temporarily removing a character from a scene. Wine spill: too messy. Food poisoning: setup required. Urgent phone call or message: too bad we're out of the landline-in-the-hallway era; we'd need the guy's cell number or email.

Which I think I might be able to find.

I pull a picture of him from Google Images and run a search on Match Insights. The guy shows up on Curated, one of the more obnoxious selective-admission boutiques; you need a minimum financial or aesthetic net worth to join. He's been on for only the past five months, no other matching history. I skim through his most recent chat records and find his phone number and personal email in a message to a Sestina007 in preparation for a meetup. Peter Stromberg's efforts at flirtatious banter read like business emails with the odd winking emoji appended; he signs off with *Rgds, PVS.* I'd hazard recent divorcé with preteen kids. His romantic ineptitude makes me feel for him, although as a fabulously wealthy and conventionally successful white man, I'm sure he's doing just fine.

As I text Becks my plan, I hear him say, "I'm sending you and McMann an email to connect on this asap. You can walk him through what you've done so far. If you're too busy I can ask your VP to do it. What's his name, Camden something —"

"Cameron Keller. No need. I'll talk to Frank this week."

I glance up. Peter Stromberg is leaning back in his chair, scrolling on his phone. Next to him Lucinda sits with her back straight and her hands in her lap, studying the bread basket on the table. I realize, a cattle prod of shock: Lucinda Clay is under siege at Soulmate.

"Good." He says that absently. "Did you see that latest *New York Times* op-ed fumigating against preference algorithms? Herrera just sent it to me. The self-righteousness was off the charts."

I say under my breath, "Fulminating." I can already tell that when I get older I'll turn into that insufferable type of New Yorker who interrupts the conversations of strangers to tell them what they're getting wrong.

Lucinda says, "Yes. Basically, beware evil tech company learning more about you so it can better provide you with what you want."

"And the solution is regulation. Of course. Because the government has proven so many times that it can be trusted with our liberties."

"How do you draw the line between these algorithms giving us what we want and telling us what we want?"

They both hush like a mosquito has whined past them and they're waiting for it to circle back around so they can squish it. Then Lucinda turns to me. She's smiling. "Aha," she says. It's such an echo of the way Komla would speak that I feel, for a moment, nostalgic for the couple I never got to meet. "That's a great question. What's your view?"

Why the hell did I say that? Or rather, I know *why* I said that. This is as close as I'm going to get to a face-off with the matchmakers over what they're doing. (For now.) But why did I *say* that?

"Who are you?" says Peter Stromberg.

I open my mouth without having decided who I will respond to first, and like a musical ventriloquism act the man's phone bursts forth into what sounds suspiciously like the helium-infused chorus of a K-pop song.

An amused murmuring rises up from the neighboring tables. Lucinda says, "That's a catchy ringtone."

"Goddammit," says Peter Stromberg. "My daughter must have switched it. She's pissed at me for restricting her screen time." He glares down at the screen and, thank god, answers the call. He listens for all of ten seconds before he says, "Is this a . . ." He stands up. "Hold on." He says to Lucinda, "Let's catch up more later. Get your assistant to set something up with mine. I'm in town until Tuesday."

"I can't," she says. "I'm fully booked

tomorrow, and I'm flying to Singapore the day after."

He's already walking away, phone to his ear. Lucinda shrugs and says to me, with the air of someone looking forward to an adult conversation now that the child has left the room, "Do you need to draw the line? If the end outcome is positive for the user, what does it matter?"

My role for this evening is primarily to act as seat-warmer for Komla, both literally and figuratively, and secondarily to draw the idea of Compatibility, ever so gently, toward the surface of Lucinda's thoughts. *Less is very much more,* said Komla. *We can't have her begin to suspect that we know.* So this is starting to drift off script, but I can't resist. I say, "From the perspective of the user making a choice —"

"Is this seat taken?"

Figures she would interrupt me midsentence. Lucinda and I look up. Becks is standing behind the chair that Peter Stromberg left askew when he made his peremptory exit. Adam Schultz, on the other side, says, "Peter Stromberg was sitting here." He sounds wistful, like he knows he will never again get this close to financier royalty. "He might come back."

"So you should sit down before he does,"

Lucinda says to Becks. "He's not even supposed to be at this table."

Becks glides into the seat in one impossibly smooth motion and introduces herself, as Rebecca, to Adam. Lucinda looks back at me. "Go on."

"Um," I say. I can hear Adam hitting replay on Yogi Yourself's sales pitch, this time at 1.5× speed and enthusiasm. Good luck to Becks. I feel like a radio operator trying to tune in to two overlapping frequencies at the same time, and the result is a staticky mess. "Sorry, what was I saying?"

"You were just getting started, but it seemed like you were about to argue that the algorithms remove a certain degree of choice from the user and that is innately problematic."

I say, "I appreciate you making me sound so comprehensible."

Lucinda smiles. "I spend a lot of time thinking about these issues. Matchmakers are in a unique position because of the service we provide. Our subscribers rely on us to find love, which, personally, I think is one of the most essential things in life. We have a responsibility to ensure that we act in their best interests."

Becks, on our right: "Do you track the metrics around customer retention? We've been focusing more on that at A Dose a Day, and it's yielding some very interesting insights."

There it is, the tiniest shift in Lucinda Clay's attention, a syncopated beat of the hummingbird's wings.

I say, "I'm going to run to the bathroom, but I'd love to continue this when I get back."

As I walk off I hear Adam Schultz, sounding consternated, "Customer retention? Well, like I said, we're beta testing the product right now, so we don't really have customers, in the formal sense of the word."

I find a spot against the wall several feet away, clip on the Bluetooth earpiece Squirrel gave me, and dial in to the conference line. There are two other participants in the meeting, the automated voice informs me. "Hello?" I whisper.

"You have Squirrel. Komla is on as well. Once he takes your seat he'll put his phone on speaker and I'll start the recording."

"Okay," I say. "By the way . . . this earpiece. Was there nothing a bit less dorky?"

I'm about to repeat myself — he might not have heard me given how noisy the room is — when he says, "I think the design of this model is very stylish. I bought one myself, for personal use."

Oops. "I really appreciate you getting it for me."

"I'm going on mute now."

I watch the servers orbit table three, dealing out the next round of oversize plates. Once they leave Komla walks up and sits in my chair like that's been his seat all along. Lucinda doesn't notice him; Becks has engaged her in conversation. I see him take out his phone, and then suddenly the background noise of the gala is fuzzing right into my ear. He replaces the phone in the inside pocket of his jacket.

The woman on Komla's left, Katya Popov, says, "I'm sorry, someone is already sitting there."

He beams at her. "I'll only be a few minutes."

Lucinda turns. Even from where I am I feel the shock vibrating out from her like a long-dormant fault line beneath her has just zagged open. When she speaks, though, it's in the exact same tone, warm and polite, that she has maintained all evening. "This doesn't seem like your kind of scene."

"It was a cost-benefit analysis," he says. "The disutility of attending this event versus the utility of seeing you."

"Really? You thought seeing me would more than make up for the discomfort of a tuxedo and the unpleasantness of making small talk with people you don't know or care for?"

Komla chuckles. "It was close."

After a moment she says, "I'm sorry I haven't responded to your emails. I've been . . . things have been busy."

"Still trying to save the world?"

She sighs. "Is that what you came here to talk to me about? Because —"

"No, no," he says. "All that . . . it's done."

She says, her voice still sharp, "Then why are you here?"

"I'm going back to Ghana. I wanted to let you know."

She picks up her cutlery and takes one bite of her dish and then another. "Hmm," she says. "Do you think it's a restaurant conspiracy to only serve overcooked salmon? Every time."

"But you keep ordering it."

"I do. Maybe subconsciously I keep hoping it will be different. I think you're making a mistake."

A server pauses between them to offer more wine. Lucinda asks for the white. The server moves on to Becks — who, now that Adam Schultz is no longer of use, has shut down the guy like he's an especially toxic Superfund site — and Komla says, "What does it matter to you now?"

"Of course it matters. I want the best for you. I always have."

"I know," he says. "Unfortunately that meant more to you than what I wanted."

Lucinda sighs again and turns her attention back to her unsatisfactory salmon. Komla leans back in his chair and gazes about like one of those tourists on a New York City sightseeing bus. Servers are beginning to clear plates from tables, which makes me anxious. Coraline has told me that the awards ceremony will take place before the dessert course is served, and Lucinda could decide to head out once that's done, especially to avoid being harangued by an aggrieved ex.

She says, abruptly, "You're right that I never intended to move to Ghana with you. But I would have, if I believed you really wanted to return."

"Really? You would have given up Compatibility?"

"I would. You're the one who would never have."

After a moment he says, "I don't see how you could have known that."

"I knew *you,*" she says. "What you wanted, more than anything else, was for Compatibility to succeed. Its ideas to succeed. You

484

couldn't afford to return to Ghana. But you couldn't bear to feel guilty, either, after what happened with your parents. So you pushed your choice to me. You set up a fiction, and I played my part. I became the reason you couldn't go back until it was too late to do so. That's the way you work, Kom. Clean hands, always."

"I think you might overestimate my capacity for deviousness."

"Wasn't that why you told me about the journalist? So I could take care of that as well?"

I swipe up the volume on my phone.

"I told you," says Komla, "so you would be careful. Simply that."

I notice, to my horror: a woman angling toward them from a few feet away, matronly, assured, wearing enough jewelry to light up a Christmas tree. I will her to change her mind, to possess poor depth perception and really be targeting Adam Schultz or Katya Popov, to register that here are two people having a Very Private Moment who should under no circumstances be disturbed.

"Luci," says this woman, sidling into Lucinda's side view on the right, "congratulations!"

Lucinda looks up. It's evident she has no idea who this person is. "Thank you."

"Just wanted to say hi! It was so great having you at the NVCA's spring conference. Did you know —"

"You're with the NVCA?"

Becks has risen from her seat. The woman turns, all puckery at being interrupted. "I'm the executive director, yes, and —"

(At this point I google *NVCA* — the National Venture Capital Association.)

"I had an encounter with one of your employees recently. Are you the person I should be speaking to about his inappropriate conduct?"

A squeaky-toy noise from the woman. "I'm so sorry to hear that. Believe me, we have a zero tolerance policy with respect to such behavior. If we could go over there, it's quieter, you know . . . I will personally make sure it never happens again . . ."

I watch them walk toward the corner of the room by the steps that lead up to the stage. Damn Becks is ruthless. And effective.

Komla's voice: "So you found out who the person was."

Lucinda says, "What makes you think that?"

"You said it was a journalist."

"A freelancer." She places her fork and knife on her plate, aligning them with the care of an installation artist prepping her masterpiece. "And I already knew. She'd come to see me a few months before."

"No way," I whisper, and then am convulsed by panic about whether I'm truly on mute. I check and, thank god, Lucinda did not just hear my disembodied voice float forth from Komla's jacket.

"Really." In the quiet stretch and recoil of that word I can hear Komla thinking about what he said to us, that Lucinda could only have killed Sarah because she didn't know her, had never met her, thought of her only as a problem to be solved. "Why?"

"Why else." Lucinda's voice is so low I can barely hear her through the clink-and-chatter symphony around her. "She told me about some interesting things she had learned and then said she couldn't afford some miracle drug she needed to get her life together. I said, well, now she could."

So that's how Lucinda knew about Sarah's use of Strobinex. Also, why Iris Lettriste had no idea what Sarah's medication was called. She hadn't been the one paying for it after all. As with Jude Kalman, so with Lucinda Clay, except here Sarah had no intention of keeping her blackmailer's promise of silence. How did she justify that one to herself? Lucinda was part of the evil corporate empire, she could so easily afford it, the money was for something essential. Maybe I still don't know Sarah Reaves at all.

Komla says, "Did you talk to her again after my email?"

"No. I didn't see the point the second time." She sounds faintly wistful. "I just . . . I took care of it."

"Ladies and gentlemen, I trust you're having a wonderful time so far." The woman on the stage at the front of the ballroom is the same person who was standing with Coraline and Lucinda earlier. Also, it appears, British, or at least she speaks in the crisp, hoity syllables of a BBC newscaster. As the lights dim, the steady roaring of conversation in the room washes out into an expectant quiet. "Thank you for joining us this evening."

Komla's voice, so gentle in my ear: "How?"

I see Lucinda turn to look at him, and I can feel how much she wants to tell him. Atlas handing off the burden of the world to Hercules, if only for a breath. I imagine the hummingbird's wings beating so hard it tears itself apart.

She says, "The irony is, it might be for nothing."

"What do you mean?"

British Brunette is listing out the names of the gala sponsors, navigating French pronunciation with aplomb. I hear everything twice, her voice echoing again through my earpiece right after she has spoken, and that gives the sounds an incantatory quality, as if they hold some hidden meaning that's transforming us all without us even knowing.

Lucinda turns back to face the stage. "Polaris," she says. "Turns out they have their own ideas about architecture."

"Ah," says Komla.

"And . . . Kom, I made a mistake." She says that like it's a foreign phrase in a guidebook she's trying out for the first time. "I showed them the blueprints."

"The proceeds from this event will help make possible opportunities for the next generation of women and minority entrepreneurs, so they can build the great American companies of tomorrow."

"That's a mistake that can be fixed," says Komla. "It will take them time to understand what we've done. There are steps we could take. Adjust the structures so they no longer sync with the blueprints, maybe, or revert to prior versions."

"Yes," she says. "Yes. I thought of those

things as well. But all in a way that preserves the architectural intent." She glances at him. "Will you help me? Fix it?"

"Always."

I can see Lucinda settle into the comfort of that assurance, and a part of me wishes I could tell her not to, to remain vigilant, that she can't trust the one person she still believes she can.

"But, Lucinda. You have to tell me the rest of it."

"The rest of what?"

"I found out who she was as well. The journalist you spoke with. She had an appointment with me that she never kept."

Lucinda makes a sound, soft, something between a laugh and a sigh.

"Before we get to tomorrow, though, let us celebrate the achievements of today. Our guests of honor this evening are all extraordinary business leaders who have combined trailblazing success with a deep commitment to their community and to making the world a better place."

And, sheltering beneath the polished, long-voweled ceiling of the announcer's voice, Komla says, "All you have to say is that you didn't. Please say that you didn't kill Sarah Reaves."

Lucinda is silent, her face tilted up to the stage.

"Our first honoree is Lucinda Clay, senior vice president of innovation at Soulmate Inc."

So that's it then. We've failed. She must have sensed after all that she would be betrayed.

"You don't know," says Lucinda, still staring straight ahead of her, "how sorry I am that I can't say that to you."

The applause sounds to me like the somber drumming that signals the commencement of a ritual, something we have long forgotten the reasons for yet continue to carry out anyway because we would be lost otherwise. Komla turns his face to Lucinda, and I'm almost certain that he says something to her, but I can't hear it through the noise.

British Brunette runs through Lucinda's résumé, emphasizing how despite her all-consuming corporate responsibilities she's involved as a mentor and an organizer with multiple young-entrepreneur initiatives, to make the rest of us schlubs feel even worse about how we can't finish reading a library book before it's due. At the end, more applause — and I see Komla again tilting his head, speaking to Lucinda.

Lucinda stands and makes her way around the table and onto the stage. She accepts a hunk of metal and glass from an elderly gentleman who looks like the Disney-movie version of Merlin, they both do the freeze-and-grin thing while they're being strobed by camera flashes, and then she takes the podium. "I'll be brief," she says. "I know I'm one of the three obstacles between us and dessert." A polite ripple of laughter. "This isn't for your sake but mine. I love dessert." Another ripple. "So much so I put that in the first dating profile I created, to make sure I didn't end up with someone who couldn't appreciate a chocolate soufflé."

Not that unexpectedly, Lucinda Clay is an engaging speaker. She tells us how she included her dessert-lover-and-proud-of-it status in her second profile, and third, and fourth; and how at some point she started to think about what she and everyone she was meeting on these platforms were telling each other about who they were and who they were looking for. How to best use data to evaluate whether two people were likely to be romantically compatible, which in turn required determining both the accuracy and the relevance of such data.

"We still have a long way to go, but I'm

hopeful that we'll get there. Today marriage rates are higher, and divorce rates lower, than they have been at any point in the past decade; and dating platforms have become the most common way through which Americans meet their spouses. Last year, in fact, my sister got married to someone she met online." She smiles. "And even though it wasn't on Soulmate, I'm still happy for her."

She pauses. "I'd be disingenuous if I didn't acknowledge the concerns that have been expressed around the collection and use of data to improve our lives. How much the matchmakers and other tech companies know about us, and what they might do with that information. The dangers of online manipulation for hidden agendas."

I'm so focused on what Lucinda is saying, and the humming glow of her presence — knowing what I know, there's something wrenching about seeing her alone up on-stage like that, dissembling to us all; I half expect her to burst into flames like a figure out of a Greek tragedy — that it startles me to hear Komla's baritone, a dark bruising over her alto: "I think we've gotten what we need here."

I look back to our table. Komla is leaning across Lucinda's now-empty chair toward

Becks, who seated herself again at some point during Lucinda's speech, but I can tell he's really addressing us all. Becks doesn't say anything.

"That's one narrative, and it's the easier one to buy into, because it just tells us to stop right where we are. To go backward, even. Stop collecting data, stop developing more accurate algorithms, stop thinking about new ways to give people what they want. But there's another narrative, the one I subscribe to, the reason I've spent my career in this industry. Own this technology. Use the tools we have to make things better. To make ourselves better."

Komla gets up. He walks between the tables, down the middle of the room, to the doors at the back, where a pair of servers are standing. I see Lucinda see him leave. One of the servers pulls open a door for him, and as he steps through and it swings shut again, she says, "To find the loves of our lives."

IV.

When I get the call from Iris Lettriste I'm at the MoMA following a target around an Alexander Calder retrospective. The target is alone, but she's wandering about and texting on her phone in a way that makes me think she's waiting to meet up with someone. I tuck myself next to a large black starburst of a sculpture and answer.

Iris tells me that the police have contacted her about Sarah. "They said they were reopening the investigation." Her voice is hushed as if she's embarrassed. "They're now treating this as a potential homicide."

"That's crazy," I say. We've had a Google Alert on Lucinda Clay set up since the night of the gala, but so far there's been nothing except a Soulmate press release a few days ago announcing that she was no longer with the company.

The police asked if she knew anything about Sarah looking into a case of corporate embezzlement, says Iris. A senior individual in a well-known company. "I told them — I remembered what you said — I didn't know the details, but it seemed like she had been working on something."

So that's what the story has become. What one person did, and nothing more.

Iris says, "Maybe that's why she told me she was done with journalism. She didn't want to put me in danger."

"That makes sense," I say.

"Sarah," she says. "Murdered." In the way she says that word I hear how the world has been realigned around her. "Well. I just thought you should know." She takes a breath. I wait for her to sign off; she could probably have billed a client a thousand dollars for the time she's spent talking to me. Instead a silence presses against my ear.

I say, "Is there something else?"

After a moment she says, "Someone else contacted me recently. A Jude Kalman."

Hearing the name *Jude Kalman* issued by the real Iris Lettriste's voice startles me. I clear my throat. "Go on."

He found her number on her law firm's website, says Iris. "He said someone told him I was dead."

"Fake news, obviously," I say.

He told her about his interactions with

the woman he had thought was Iris Lettriste, and she told him the truth about Sarah Reaves, that she had borrowed Iris's persona on Soulmate.

"Did you, um, mention anything about Veracity?" I say, like it's no big deal if Iris has outed me and flatlined my verifier career after I've finally nursed it off life support.

"Of course not." She sounds slightly reproachful that I might have considered she would. "That was what we agreed."

Oh, thank god. "Right. Thanks."

They've stayed in touch, says Iris. "We're meeting for lunch next week. Since we both work in the same area."

Jude Kalman and Iris Lettriste hanging out? It occurs to me that the two of them were matched, indirectly, by Sarah. The profile that Sarah put up on Soulmate, and that the algorithm deemed compatible with Jude, was really Iris's. They would never have met, though, if not for me. For a moment I'm distracted by the thought of my role in this potential romance, and then I realize that Becks might chainsaw-massacre me for it.

Iris says, her tone light, "Anything I should know about him?"

"Did he mention he was married? And has

a daughter?"

"Separated now. But yes."

"That sounds like a good start."

"Miss." The security guard is glaring at me from across the room, which of course makes everyone else in the gallery turn to look. She has the mien and heft of an Easter Island idol. "No talking on your cell phone." Public shaming: very effective.

"I'm sorry," I whisper. "I have to go. But, um, good luck with Jude."

The morning after the gala, Komla told us — Becks, Squirrel, and me — that he was transferring ownership of Veracity LLC to the three of us, in equal shares. "Assuming you'll accept it," he said. The company's lawyer was finishing up the paperwork and would bring in the revised LLC agreement, a single hard copy, for us to review and sign.

We were sitting around the table in the conference room; I realized later that it was because Komla had already moved all the furniture out of his office. I waited for Becks or Squirrel to ask any of the dozen questions pinwheeling about in my head. Becks continued to engage in a staring contest with the far wall. Squirrel's attention did not shift away from his phone. I suspected he was playing some kind of game and, from his facial expressions, that he was getting crushed.

When I got tired of waiting I said, "Why? And what about you?"

Komla shook his head. "I can't be associated with Veracity anymore." He would bring the recording of his conversation with Lucinda to the police after this meeting, he said, and tell them that he had evidence of Sarah Reaves's murder. The police would ask questions about his acquaintance with Sarah, his occupation, his activities. He didn't want to risk them finding out about Veracity. "The less is known about what you do, the more you can accomplish." He paused. "And, in any case, I've lost the heart for this."

"What are you going to tell the police, then?" I asked.

He had prepared a story, he said. "It should work, if we're all careful. People tend to hear what they want to hear."

Now Becks spoke: "So you're just giving up on the synths. Letting Polaris do whatever the hell it wants with them."

After we had left the Gatsby that night, I told the others about the conversation I overheard between Lucinda and Peter Stromberg. Komla hadn't been surprised; he had gleaned as much from what Lucinda said to him, that Polaris Capital was interested in how the synths could be used to deliver outcomes through the secret manipulation of consumers' opinions.

"I'm not giving up on anything," said Komla. "And neither should any of you."

Once he walked out of the office, he said, there was to be no more contact between us and him. He would give us a phone number and an email address, to be used only if absolutely necessary.

I said, "But what are you going to do, then?"

He chuckled, a dusty sound. "I'm exploring some options." Komla-speak for *I'm not going to tell you so stop asking.*

As we got up from our seats Becks said, "What do you want us to do with it? Veracity?"

He spread his hands. "Whatever you would like. It's yours now."

Squirrel said, still without looking up from his phone, "Does this mean I have to be on-site from now on? Because that's going to seriously cramp my style."

"God no," said Becks. "Stay away as much as possible."

Komla turned to me. "Claudia, would you mind staying for a few more minutes?"

He waited for Becks to close the door of

the conference room behind her before he said, "I don't expect you to forgive me. I just wanted to tell you how sorry I am. And how glad that you came back to us."

I fumbled around for a response that could encompass how I felt about all that he had done for Lucinda, and to her, and also my manifest awkwardness at my boss apologizing to me for an intentional infliction of bodily harm. "I understand why you did it," I said.

He regarded me. "Yes," he said. "I truly think you do."

Toward the end of Julia's annual *Christmas Carol* reading party, which is really an excuse to drink hot toddies and eat sticky toffee pudding and try out atrocious English accents, I ask Maddie and Julia what they would do if they found out that the person they were dating had committed murder. Most people have left; it's just the three of us and one of Julia's friends from work. I'm tucked on the couch next to Maddie, who has managed to coax Julia's famously aloof cat, Earl Grey, onto her lap. Julia's studio apartment, as always, is soporifically warm.

Julia's work friend Kyle asks, "Are there, like, extenuating circumstances?" He puts me in mind of a teddy bear, short and stocky, clumpy dark hair and bright eyes, an earnest manner. I have the feeling he's still here because he's hoping to time his departure with Maddie's. He's not her type at all, but who knows. The longer I'm at Veracity, the more I think I agree with Komla that most people have no idea what they're after.

"None whatsoever," I say. "Cold-blooded, premeditated murder. And you love this person. He — or she — is The One. You'll never love anyone else like that again."

"You can't know that," says Maddie.

"I'm the master of this hypothetical." I reach out to stroke Earl Grey and he springs away and onto the floor.

Julia, sprawled out on the rug in front of us, pushes her curls out of her face and says, "I'd turn him in. But I think true love is a hoax anyway."

Maddie says, "I don't think I could do that. Although if the police came to me, I don't think I could lie to them, either."

"You couldn't," agrees Julia. "You couldn't even lie to your mom about smoking pot in tenth grade."

From the overstuffed chair Kyle says, "I'd lie to the cops. To protect her."

"What about you, Master of the Hypothetical?" says Julia.

I hug my knees to my chest. "I think," I

say, "I'd do everything I could to help her get away."

V.

Things at Veracity go back to the way they used to be, less or more. Clients fret about whether inconsistencies in what their matches are saying reflect forgetfulness, early-onset Alzheimer's, or nefarious intent. Becks gripes about how annoying everyone is. Squirrel manifests as a surly electronic presence. I analyze chat records and populate spreadsheets and track our targets' movements on Finders Keepers and on bike. December is one of my favorite months for cycling in New York because all the fair-weather cyclists have gone into hibernation, we aren't in nor'easter season yet, and the cold is bracing without being debilitating. I bike up to the Botanical Garden in the Bronx one day, down to Coney Island the next.

At the same time, everything is different. Komla's absence, for one. The office feels too large now, the air too thin. Every now and then I walk into the pantry still expecting to see him there, scrolling on his phone while waiting for his tea to steep. The tea itself continues to be delivered, in refill bags, every month. I like to think it's because he remembers me and not because he hasn't gotten around to canceling the contract.

From her steadfast refusal to ever discuss him, I can tell Becks misses him as well. We moved his *Little Shop of Horrors* plant back into the room that used to be his office, but otherwise we've left it empty.

Also, we're going after the synths.

Okay, that's how I would put it. How Becks would put it is that we're monitoring the situation to see how Soulmate's deployment of the synths might change now that Lucinda Clay is gone. Of the profiles flagged by St. Elmo, around half of them remain active. So far we haven't spotted any indications that Polaris is using the synths to push any particular product or service or even viewpoint; any suggestions the synths make appear to be motivated by thoughts, opinions, and preferences that the user has already expressed.

What's worrisome, though, is that our filter is tagging fewer and fewer of St. Elmo's profiles as synths, even though we know they are — which implies that, if newer synths emerge, we won't even be able to tell. Squirrel has been tweaking his code, with no change in results, leading to inimical exchanges between him and Becks whenever he comes into the office. During the most recent one, he came right out and said it: the synths were evolving beyond his ability to recognize them. When he and Komla had built the filter, they had done so based on traits that Komla knew the synths to exhibit from his work at Soulmate. This latest set of synths, several generations later, lacked a critical mass of those characteristics, and Squirrel's efforts had failed to identify any new, unique characteristics that could be applied to the filter. "Other than those generally also shown by humans, I mean."

That silenced even Becks — for a breath. Then she said, "Sounds like all you're saying is you're shitty at your job."

I said quickly, before things could deteriorate further, "These profile names came from St. Elmo. If we could get him — or her — to feed them to us for now, we'd have an up-to-date list of the synths, and if we have more examples to analyze, Squirrel may be able to improve the filter . . ."

She flicked her hair back. "That's a lot of ifs around someone we don't know the identity of or how to reach."

"Dispatch," I said. "We could post a message on it asking St. Elmo to contact us." In *Inspector Yuan and the Storm of Swords*, that was how the inspector drew the fugitive out of hiding, by carving cryptic messages into the trunks of the trees in the forest where the guy had hunkered down.

"Hmm," said Becks, like she was trying to pinpoint why that plan was fatally flawed. Then she said, "If you want to waste your time doing that, be my guest."

I've uploaded a file from ReavesLettriste, Sarah's username, saying that we are a group who was in touch with Sarah Reaves, learned of what Sarah and St. Elmo were trying to do, and would like to help. All of which is true enough. I included an email address that Squirrel provided me with. I've been checking that email account, and Dispatch as well, every day. Nothing yet, but the document status on Dispatch is marked as read, so I know at least that St. Elmo's seen it.

Actually, Becks did bring up Komla once. It was after our first client intake meeting without him, with a man who suspected he might be dating a pair of identical twins. As I was leaving the conference room, Becks said, "Why do you think Komla wanted us to be there with him that night? When he talked to Lucinda?"

I turned back. "To help."

"He could have handled it himself. Everything that Lucinda said that's relevant was in his conversation with her."

"For moral support?"

Becks leaned back in her chair. "I think it was a precommitment strategy."

I looked at her. "Like . . . Odysseus and the Sirens?"

"Sure."

I thought through that analogy. "That if we hadn't been there, if it had been just him and Lucinda, he might not have been able to follow through with the plan."

"Potentially."

That was when I remembered Komla bending toward Lucinda, the applause rising up around them like a vast, invisible flock of birds taking flight. "Right at the end," I said, "before Lucinda went onstage, I think he said something to her. Twice. It wasn't picked up by the speaker."

Becks nodded. I realized she had noticed that as well, and, unlike me, she never forgot about it.

"Do you think . . ." I said.

"I don't know," she said. "I don't fucking know."

"Why didn't you ask him at our last meeting?"

She stood and picked up her laptop. "I decided I would trust him."

VI.

On Christmas Eve I get to my mother's place a whole thirty minutes before the time my family has arranged to meet, which would be impressive if not for the fact that really I had intended to arrive an hour early but took an impulse detour along the way. I press the doorbell. When my mother opens the door she says, "What are you doing here?"

"What? I'm supposed to be here."

"Yes, but later," she says as she walks back into the living room.

I follow her in. I'm not getting the pleased vibe from her that I usually do when I visit; she must still be upset from Thanksgiving. "I thought I'd try to be early for once," I say. "Were you in the middle of something?"

"I was thinking."

"About?"

"Things."

Interesting, and potentially ominous. "I

brought egg tarts!" I say, lofting the plastic bag. "From your favorite place. I thought we could eat them and . . . chat."

"Funan Bakery?"

"Yes? It's that stall in the Flushing Mall food court that has no food safety rating and never closes except during Chinese New Year."

"I don't buy egg tarts from there anymore," she says.

"Since when?"

Since, it turns out, someone from her Chinese folk singing class bit into a brass tack that was embedded in one of the tarts. Although that wasn't the deal-breaker; rather, the stall owner's refusal to apologize or to refund the victim the cost of the egg tart. "It was a premium flavor, too, which is more expensive. Kiwi, I think. After that I texted all three of you to tell you to stop giving them any business."

"I guess I never received that text." Or, more likely, never read it. "That's terrible. Also, the idea of a kiwi-flavored egg tart. Should we throw this away?"

"Of course not. You've already paid for them. We'll just cut them open before we eat them."

"That might make a good method of murder," I say. "Hiding something small

511

and sharp in a dish and then serving it to the person you want to kill."

My mother says, more thoughtfully than the comment would seem to warrant, "It would."

I set down the bag of suspect egg tarts on the coffee table. "Mom," I say, "I'm sorry."

"For what?" she says, as if she needs me to get more specific when there are so many outstanding misdemeanors on my part.

"For being a lousy Chinese daughter," I say. "Probably also a lousy American one."

"No," she says. "By American standards, you are average. American children are very focused on themselves."

"I'll try harder. I've started reading *The Analects.*" By this I mean I've downloaded a Project Gutenberg version. I *have* read the Wikipedia entry, though, which must count for something.

"What's that?"

When I google the title in Chinese and show it to her, she informs me that while Westerners believe *The Analects* (which real Chinese people know as *Lunyu*) to be the how-to guide on Confucianism, in fact it is only one of seven key texts and was not even considered part of the original canon. "You should read *Xiaojing,*" she says.

More googling and some false positives

before I establish that *Xiaojing* refers to the *Classic of Filial Piety,* a text that is an extended conversation between Confucius and a disciple of his. "I'll see if I can find a decent translation," I say. Fingers crossed that none exists.

After a moment my mother says, "Thank you for trying. Well, for saying you will try." She turns toward the kitchen. "I can make some tea."

"There's something else."

From the way she turns back to me, I can tell she knew we weren't done. "The thing is," I say, "I'm not who you want me to be."

She says, "Who do you think I want you to be?"

"Someone who cares about their appearance. Which I do, by the way. It's not like I leave the house without brushing my hair or washing my face or anything socially unacceptable like that." I take a breath: must pace self. "Someone who has a well-paying, high-achieving job. Someone who's dating a nice Chinese boy she'll marry within the next five years and start having kids with. Someone . . . like that."

"What's wrong with those things?"

"Nothing! They're awesome. They're just not things I particularly want."

"What do you want, Claudia?" says my

mother, like she's inquiring about the upkeep of a troublesomely exotic animal.

"I want to wear T-shirts and jeans and sneakers," I say, "and not bother about makeup, and have Max cut my hair whenever it gets too long. You know, he's actually become pretty good."

"Your bangs are crooked."

"Good for someone with no formal training who cuts one person's hair every six months," I say. "I want a job that's fun and interesting and lets me get out there on my bike and meet new people." And find out things about them that no one else knows, and try to solve the unsolvable mysteries of love, and every now and then uncover a conspiracy.

"You're not going to become a bicycle messenger," she says.

"I won't if you're really set against it," I say, that being an easy give. I take a breath. "And I want you to stop talking to me about finding a nice Chinese boy. Because I" — and I really do mean to gun the accelerator but, being a chicken, I swerve — "might not."

My mother does not say anything.

"Find a nice Chinese boy, I mean."

"I know what you mean," she says.

"Okay," I say.

"Okay."

We gaze at each other, and I find myself thinking, as I do now and then when I'm watching my mother and trying to anticipate what's in that fiendish mind of hers, about how we look so alike, me and her, on either side of thirty-seven years and a lifetime of compromise. My smile is toothier, but that might just be because I've had a happier go of things so far.

Then she sighs, in the way she does when she wants to show that the fruit cart guy is being petty by not giving her that discount on the cantaloupe, and says, "Two out of three."

"What?" I say.

"Nice — Chinese — boy," she says like she's speaking to someone for whom English is a second language. (The irony.) "Two out of three is okay."

"What is happening here?" I say. "Are we . . . bargaining?"

"Of course," she says.

A nice boy, a Chinese boy, or a nice Chinese . . . non-boy. Is this my mother's way of saying that she knows and she's okay with it? My mind and my body feel slightly out of sync, like if this were a multiverse situation we might just have warped out of our preexisting reality and into a neighboring one.

My mother says, "Maybe this will make it easier for you to find someone who will have you."

If this were a multiverse situation, there must be at least one reality in which my mother isn't mean.

The doorbell rings. Five minutes to the hour — that must be Charles. "I'll get it," I say.

I'm half right. It's Charles, and also Jessie. The fuzzy earmuffs clamped around her head make her look like a fox spirit caught midway through assuming her human guise. "I didn't know you were joining us!" I say to her.

She smiles at me. "I couldn't pass up an opportunity to spend time with Charles that didn't involve him being on conference calls or answering work emails."

"She regrets agreeing," says Charles. "The whole time in the car —"

She looks at him. He clears his throat. "Ah," he says. "Hey, Claw." And then, to my surprise, he hugs me, one-armed, clumsy. His coat is scratchy against my cheek and, for a moment, he feels like a shelter.

When he lets me go I say, "Hey yourself. You smell like barbecue."

He holds up the plastic bag in his hand. "Your detective instinct strikes again."

When they enter Jessie goes into the kitchen to offer to help my mother with whatever she's doing. Charles and I stand in the living room like coworkers at the office Christmas party with no one else to talk to. After a moment he says, low, "I haven't told Mom or Cor about Aurum. You can tell them when you're ready. Also, whatever you're doing now. All . . . when you're ready."

That sounds like an olive branch being rustled limply in my direction. "Which means you've told Jessie?"

He pushes up his glasses. "Damn. You're good." He tells me that he had dinner with Jessie the night after we spoke, and she asked why he seemed so upset. He pauses. "She said maybe the reason you didn't want to tell me about switching jobs was because you thought I might feel bad. Because I'd gotten you the position. She also pointed out that you hadn't asked me to find you that job in the first place."

"What? How did she know that?"

"She said, *Your sister seems like the type who would want to do things her own way.*"

Huh. "I think you should hold on to her."

"I'm trying," he says. "I'm trying."

Coraline whirls in at a quarter past six, which stuns us all. "You're almost on time," I say. "What happened?"

"Pre–New Year's resolution." She dumps two bags of wrapped presents on the couch. "I don't think I can keep this up. Punctuality is really tiring."

From the kitchen my mother issues an order for everyone to bring their dishes over, which is when I find out that this Christmas we're trying something new, a potluck dinner instead of going out to Golden Phoenix. "What?" I say. "Who suggested that?"

"You did," says Charles. "Last Christmas."

Crap. "I brought egg tarts," I say. "Although they might have tacks in them."

Over dinner, an eclectic but tasty miscellany of fried noodles (my mother), rotisserie chicken (Charles), Cobb salad (Jessie), lemongrass pork (Coraline), and chili prawns (also Coraline), Charles tells us he just found out that someone he knew, an ex-colleague, passed away. The official story is cardiac arrest brought on by overwork, but there are rumors that he killed himself. He was only in his midthirties, and he was under a lot of pressure at his new job.

"It's so crazy," says Charles. "I mean, I was at his farewell party in March. He was all psyched. He was moving to San Francisco, he'd landed this great job at Soulmate — I guess, at the time, it seemed like a great job . . ."

My mother: "Claudia, stop poking around in the noodles like that."

I retract my chopsticks; I hadn't even realized what I was doing. "Sorry." I'm feeling suddenly shivery, like I've gulped down a glass of ice water and the cold is now soaking through my insides. Someone previously from Precision, now working at Soulmate, who dies unexpectedly. What if this is why St. Elmo hasn't responded?

I say, "You know, I think I might have heard about this person's death. On . . . NPR."

Charles says, "NPR did a story on this?"

"Something about young corporate professionals and stress. What was his name?"

"Cam Keller." My brother grimaces. "The guy who was running my project. Now I wish I hadn't griped so much about the way he left things."

Coraline says, "Can we talk about something else? This is a major bummer on Christmas Eve."

It takes me a moment to remember where I heard the name. The gala, Peter Stromberg asking Lucinda to brief her colleague about her project. *If you're too busy I can ask your VP to do it. What's his name, Camden something* — And Lucinda, that imperceptible strain in her voice: *Cameron Keller.* He worked for Lucinda. He would have known what Project Tilt was all about.

I take out my phone and text Becks some incoherence about Cameron Keller and Soulmate and St. Elmo and heart attacks. This poor guy's death could be a morbid coincidence. That's the default answer in real life, if not in mystery novels: one thing happening, and then another, and none of it meaning anything at all. Distantly I hear Coraline talking about a friend of hers who went to Seoul for plastic surgery. "This is what she used to look like . . . and what she looks like now. Isn't it amazing?"

I'm about to ask to see the before-and-after pictures, to distract myself if nothing else, when Becks's reply slides onto my screen. *So much for my trying to be nice and not spoil your holiday.* Three seconds later: *Since you've heard, let's talk tomorrow.*

"How do you know it's the same person?" says my mother. "I think she's playing a trick on you."

I'm still staring at my phone when the next text appears.

And this time if you do anything stupid, god

help me, I am going to kiss you.

*   *KILL YOU. Fucking predictive text. I mean: I am going to kill you.*

One thing happens and then another. Maybe all of it means nothing, or maybe everything has already changed and the question is what happens next. I type my reply and hit SEND. Suddenly I can't wait to find out.

ACKNOWLEDGMENTS

My parents, for a lifetime of love: my mother, Cheo Hock Kuan, the strongest, wisest, most inspiring person I know; and my father, Pek Beng Choon, whose constancy anchors us all.

Pek Lijun, caring and creative and generous, who has provided so much support and feedback (writing-related and otherwise) over the years; and Pek Wenjie, who will always be my adorable little brother. Growing up with you both was one of the best parts of my childhood, and your companionship remains one of the best parts of adulthood. (Also, now we fight less.)

My writing teachers: John Crowley and Marian Thurm at Yale and Josh Henkin, Ernesto Mestre, and Julie Orringer at Brooklyn College. Also Helen Phillips — both Yale *and* Brooklyn College — for being so gracious with her time throughout this entire process.

The BC Fiction MFA crew, especially Nate Bethea, Emma Bushnell, Chris Cappelluti, Eve Gleichman, Casey Gonzalez, Bo Lewis, and Lisa Metrikin.

Cathy Sweetser, for being a dear friend and my one-person fan club.

Chad Sell, for all the encouragement and commiseration as we progressed on our respective creative paths, and also for being an excellent email correspondent and forgiving me (repeatedly) for being a terrible one.

Other early readers of what eventually became *The Verifiers:* Paa Kwesi Imbeah, Bee-Seon Keum, Sebastian Krujatz, Rob Larimore, Sheila Lin, Aseem Sood. Your time and your thoughts are very much appreciated.

Elizabeth Sobel and the *Brooklyn Review* for my very first story publication, about a clone with identity issues.

Heidi Pitlor and *The Best American Short Stories* — I remain in residual disbelief that students are now forced to read my stories in their English classes.

I really lucked out with Julie Barer, my insightful, indomitable agent, and with Anna Kaufman, my brilliant, indefatigable editor. Both of you understood and loved and believed in *The Verifiers* from the very beginning and never gave up on it. Immense gratitude. Nicole Cunningham at The Book Group is always so helpful and efficient. Michelle Weiner at CAA provided some early and entirely unexpected good news at a time when it was much needed.

Everyone at Vintage who helped turn this book into A Book: Lisa Davis, Julie Ertl, Annie Locke, Vi-An Nguyen, Kayla Overbey, Nancy B. Tan, Alexa Thompson, Rima Weinberg, and Christopher Zucker.

Angela "Inspector" Yuan, smart and funny and astute and steadfast, without whom everything (the taxes, the refrigerator, my bicycle, my emotional equilibrium) would be in shambles. Thank you for sharing this journey with me.

ABOUT THE AUTHOR

Jane Pek was born and grew up in Singapore. She holds a BA from Yale University, a JD from the New York University School of Law, and an MFA in fiction from Brooklyn College. Her short fiction has been anthologized in *The Best American Short Stories.* She currently lives in New York, where she works as a lawyer at a global investment company.

The employees of Thorndike Press hope you have enjoyed this Large Print book. All our Thorndike, Wheeler, and Kennebec Large Print titles are designed for easy reading, and all our books are made to last. Other Thorndike Press Large Print books are available at your library, through selected bookstores, or directly from us.

For information about titles, please call:
(800) 223-1244

or visit our website at:
gale.com/thorndike

To share your comments, please write:
Publisher
Thorndike Press
10 Water St., Suite 310
Waterville, ME 04901

WITHDRAWN
UPPER MERION TOWNSHIP LIBRARY

8.3.2022